Readers love the Little Goddess series by AMY LANE

Rampant, Vol. 2

"With the intensity (and the stakes) jacked to eleven, *Rampant, Vol. 2* is a white-knuckled thrill ride of a resolution, leaving the reader with a tantalizing peek into what's in store in the next book in the series."

—The Novel Approach

Rampant, Vol. 1

"I think *Rampant, Vol. 1* is my favourite book in the series."

—Prism Book Alliance

Bound, Vol. 2

"As usual, Amy Lane blew my socks off with this story and left me in a huge book hangover because there simply isn't other books out there written like hers."

—Inked Rainbow Reads

By AMY LANE

GREEN'S HILL
The Green's Hill Novellas
Green's Hill Werewolves, Vol. 1
Green's Hill Werewolves, Vol. 2

ALL THAT HEAVEN WILL ALLOW
All the Rules of Heaven

LITTLE GODDESS
Vulnerable
Wounded, Vol. 1
Wounded, Vol. 2
Bound, Vol. 1
Bound, Vol. 2
Rampant, Vol. 1
Rampant, Vol. 2
Quickening, Vol. 1
Quickening, Vol. 2

Published by DSP PUBLICATIONS
www.dsppublications.com

ALL THE
RULES OF
HEAVEN

AMY LANE

DSP PUBLICATIONS

Published by
DSP PUBLICATIONS

5032 Capital Circle SW, Suite 2, PMB# 279,
Tallahassee, FL 32305-7886 USA
www.dsppublications.com

This is a work of fiction. Names, characters, places, and incidents either are the product of author imagination or are used fictitiously, and any resemblance to actual persons, living or dead, business establishments, events, or locales is entirely coincidental.

All the Rules of Heaven
© 2021 Amy Lane

Cover Art
© 2021 Reese Dante
http://www.reesedante.com
Cover content is for illustrative purposes only and any person depicted on the cover is a model.

Mass Market ISBN: 978-1-64108-224-2
Trade Paperback ISBN: 978-1-64405-661-5
Digital ISBN: 978-1-64405-654-7
Library of Congress Control Number: 2020938601
Mass Market Paperback Published February 2021
v. 1.0

Printed in the United States of America
∞
This paper meets the requirements of
ANSI/NISO Z39.48-1992 (Permanence of Paper).

Mate and the kids—check. And Mary, for being there—but this book wasn't her favorite. So this book is sort of dedicated to me—it was written to please me, and while nobody else may love it, I know I do.

AUTHOR'S NOTE

FOR THOSE of you interested in the fairy hill Tucker mentions, by all means check out my Little Goddess stories. In real life, Foresthill is a teeny community. In Amy's land, there are more things in heaven and earth….

FOR THE SAKE OF MOMENTUM

THE BED that dominated the center of the room was hand-carved, imported ebony, black as night, and the newel posts had been studded with an ivory in-lay, random designs supposedly, dancing around and around in a way that made the unwary stop, lost in the intricacy of runes nobody living could read.

The wallpaper had once been an English garden jungle—cabbage roses, lilacs, mums—riotous around the walls, and the grand window was positioned stra-tegically to catch the early-morning sun overlooking what might once have been a tiny corner of England, transplanted by the cubic foot of earth into the red-clay dirt of the Sierra Foothills.

That same dirt was now the dust that stained the windows, layering every nuance of the old room in hints of bloody deeds.

The tattered curtains no longer blocked out the harsh sun of morning, and the wallpaper curled from the walls in crackled strips. The carpet threads lay bare to the hard soles of the doctor who tended to the dying old woman, but she had no eyes for the living person taking her pulse, giving her surcease from pain, making her last hours bearable.

Her eyes were all for Angel—but nobody else could see him, so he rather regretfully assumed that she appeared crazy to the other people in the room.

"No," she snapped contentiously. "I won't tell you. I won't. It's not fair."

Angel gave a frustrated groan and ran fingers through imaginary hair. This was getting tiresome.

"Old woman—"

"Ruth," she snarled. "You used me up, sucked away my youth, drained me fucking dry. At *least* get my name right!"

Angel winced. The old wom—Ruth—had a point.

"I'm sorry the task was so difficult," Angel said gently, containing supreme frustration. She was right. What Angel had asked Ruth Henderson to do with her life had been horrible. Painful. An assault on her senses every day she lived. But Angel needed the name of her successor—he needed to find the person and introduce himself. Angel really couldn't leave Daisy Place unless he was in company of someone connected to it by blood or spirit.

"You are not sorry," Ruth sneered. "You could give a shit." She looked so sweet—like Granny from a *Sylvester the Cat* cartoon, complete with snowy white braids pinned up to circle her head. She'd asked her nurse to do that for her yesterday, and Angel, as sad and desperate as the situation was, had backed off while the nurse worked and Ruth hummed an Elvis Presley song under her breath. The music had been popular when

Ruth was a teenager, and it was almost a smack in Angel's face.

Yes, Angel *had* taken up most of her life with a quest nobody else could understand, and now Ruth's life was ending and Angel was taking the peace that should have held sway.

Her breath was congested and her voice clogged. Her heart was stuttering, and her lungs were filling with fluid, her body failing with every curse she lifted. She'd been a good woman, performing her duty without question at the expense of family, lovers, children of her own.

It was a shock, really, how bitter she'd become as the end neared. A pang of remorse pierced Angel's heart; the poor woman had been driven beyond endurance, and it was Angel's fault. It was just that there were so many here, so many voices, and Angel would never be released, would be trapped here in this portal of souls until the very last one was freed. Angel was incorporeal. Ruth was the human needed to give voice to the souls trapped in this house, on these grounds. If she didn't give a very human catharsis to the dead, they would never rise beyond the soul trap this place had become.

And now that she was dying, she needed to name a successor, or everybody trapped at Daisy Place would be doomed—Angel included.

"I'm sorry," Angel said, regret weighting every word. "It probably seems as though I didn't care—I handled everything all wrong. We could have been friends. I could have been your companion and not your tormenter. You deserved a friend, Ruth. I was not that friend. I'm so sorry."

Ruth blew out a breath. Her words were mumbles now—Angel understood, even if the doctor and nurse at her bedside assumed she was out of her mind.

"You weren't so bad," she wheezed. "You were in pain." A slight smile flickered over the canvas of wrinkles that made up her face. "You made my garden bloom. You couldn't prune for shit, but you did try."

"It gave me great joy," Angel confessed humbly. No more than the truth. Angel had loved that garden, loved the optimism that had laid the fine Kentucky bluegrass sod and ordered the specialty rose grafts from Portland and Vancouver. No, Angel couldn't prune it—couldn't hold the shears, couldn't hold back the tide of entropy that the garden had become—but that hadn't stopped the place from being Angel's greatest source of peace, even stuck here in this way station for the damned and the enlightened.

"I know it did." There was defeat in Ruth's voice. "Promise me," she mumbled.

"What?" Angel would take care of the garden until freed from this prison—there was no question.

"Promise me you'll be kind to him."

Oh! Oh sweet divinity. She was going to name an heir.

"To him?" Angel asked, all respect.

"I left him the house, but the boy hasn't had it easy, Angel. He'll be here soon enough. Be kind."

"I need his name," Angel confessed. "If I don't know his name, I'll never find his soul."

"Tucker," she whispered, her last breaths rattling in her chest. "My brother's boy. Tucker Henderson. Be kind," she begged. "He's a sweet boy…. Be kind."

Triumph soared in Angel's chest. Yes! Ruth Henderson's successor, the empath who could hear the ghosts and help exorcise Daisy Place! Angel wanted to cheer, but now was not the time. With invisible hands but tenderness nonetheless, Ruth Henderson's ghostly companion stroked her forehead and whispered truths about a glorious garden in the afterlife as the good woman breathed her last.

BLIND FAITH

TUCKER DIDN'T know how it happened—he *never* knew how it happened. One minute he'd be walking into a restaurant for dinner, and the next a stranger would stop by his table and strike up a conversation. Twelve hours later, Tucker would have a new friend— and a few used condoms.

It had cost him girlfriends—and boyfriends. He never planned to be unfaithful. He rarely planned to go into the restaurant or bar at all. He'd be strolling down the street, a bag of groceries in his hand and a plan for dinner with—once upon a time—friends, and he'd feel a draw, an irresistible pull, a rope under his breastbone tugging him painfully into another person's bed.

He'd tried to resist on occasion, back when he'd had plans for a normal life.

When he'd been younger—a green kid freshly grieving the loss of his parents—it had worked out okay of course. *Any* touch had been okay. He'd been alone in the world, and the empathic powers his aunt Ruth had warned him about had arrived, and suddenly he was seeing a host of people who shouldn't exist, wandering around in the world like everyday folk.

Sex had been comforting then.

He'd lost his virginity when he'd gone into a Mc-Donald's for a soda after school and ended up trading blowjobs with the cashier—who happened to be his high school's quarterback—in the bathroom.

They had both been surprised (to say the least), but then Trace Appleby had broken down into tears and wept on Tucker's shoulder because he'd never been able to admit he was gay until just that moment. He said he'd been thinking about taking drastic measures, and although he'd never been more explicit than that, Tucker had gotten his first inkling of what was to come.

Given how lost he'd been, how heartsore, it had seemed like a karmic mission of sorts. He was kind of excited to see what came next.

Next had been right after high school graduation, when he'd been *working* at McDonald's—he and a friend had ended up doing it in her car in the upper parking lot. Afterward, *she* had broken down on a bemused Tucker and told him that her boyfriend had been cheating on her but she didn't have the courage to leave him.

Until right then.

Tucker started to harbor suspicions that *next* might not be as wonderful as he'd hoped.

Less than a month later, when he stood up a girl *he* liked because he'd wandered into a bar and slept with a guy who'd been thinking about going to a party so he could get high and woke up thinking about college instead, Tucker began to understand.

And the only comfort sex had offered him then had been the comfort he apparently gave others in bed.

He'd explained it to his friend Damien the next day. First, Damien had needed to get over the "Oh my God, you're *bi*?" But after that he'd been pretty copacetic.

"So you're saying God wants you to get laid," he'd concluded.

Tucker sort of frowned. "That does *not* sound like the Sunday school lessons I got growing up," he said. Of course, his parents had been gone for about two years at this point, and he hadn't attended a church service in a very long time.

Then he remembered something his father had said.

He'd been born late in his parents' life—they'd been in their fifties when their car had skidded off the road during their date night—but his father had been a kind man, active, with salt-and-pepper hair that hadn't even started to thin. He'd had laugh lines and kind brown eyes, and he'd told Tucker to go to church and soak up the feeling—the feeling of being protected.

"Ignore the words, son. Some people need them, but you're just there to know what it's like to find shelter from the storm."

Oh. Apparently Tucker *was* shelter from the storm. Maybe God really *did* want him to get laid. Or the gods, really. Tucker had already identified vampires and elves and ghosts and werecreatures among the hosts of not-humans who walked the city streets with him. In an effort to broaden his knowledge, he'd begun taking classes in comparative religion, ancient language, arcane lore, and anything he could find even remotely connected. School was fun at that point—but the broader lessons hadn't started to set in.

He looked at Damien, wishing that Damie was bi too, because he had a rich red mouth and dark blond hair and green eyes and freckled cheeks, and Tucker had wanted to kiss him for a long time.

But Damien was the kind of guy who always landed on his feet. If he got detention in school, he'd meet a pretty girl who'd want to be taken out Saturday night. Once when he'd been out of work, his car had broken down, and the Starbucks he'd gone into while he waited for the tow truck had been looking for a cashier.

Damien always found a sheltered path through life's difficulties, simply on instinct. He never needed shelter from the storm.

He'd never need Tucker.

Tucker had always been the guy with pencils when the teacher gave a surprise test, the guy with the extra sandwich when someone forgot their lunch, or the guy with the spare jacket or the shoulder to cry on. Even before the McDonald's blowjob and the sobbing quarterback, Tucker had a reputation as the guy people could talk to when life threw them a curve ball. He was a sympathetic ear.

Or an empathetic ear.

Talking to Damien, remembering his father's definition of religion in contrast to his college professors', it occurred to him that being the sympathetic ear might have become his cosmic mission in life—with the added twist of sex. Suddenly both the sympathy and the sex felt like a chore.

"Never mind," Tucker had said, his heart breaking for the things he was starting to see he'd never have. "I get it now. I'm an umbrella."

"And I'm an ice cream cone," Damien replied, because he thought that was the game.

Tucker hadn't been able to play, though. He was too busy thinking about how many ways being an umbrella could go wrong.

He'd found them. One night when he was in his twenties, he'd resisted the pull, sobbing from the wrongness in his chest, the displaced time, the pull in his blood and corpuscles to wander into a restaurant and come home with God or Goddess knows who. But he wanted to be faithful—his *heart* was faithful, dammit, why couldn't his body be?

He'd gotten home to a message on his phone—the father of the girl he'd fallen in love with had died, and she'd needed to leave town.

Tucker could have written it down to coincidence, but by then he didn't believe in coincidence. He'd given up on relationships for a while.

Not long enough, but a while.

And that had been many years and one eon of heartbreak ago.

So by the time he arrived at Daisy Place, he was tired, old at thirty-five, exhausted by his karmic mission, and so, so lonely.

But by then his gift, the empathic pull that led him to other people's beds and their cosmic epiphanies and karmic catharses, had been honed to a science. It had used him often enough that he knew what to expect.

The night the Greyhound dropped him off in the middle of what kind of passed for a town, suitcases in hand like a kid in an old musical, he didn't set about trying to find a ride to Daisy Place immediately. Sure, the press under his breastbone had started almost directly after he'd gotten the call from his aunt Ruth's lawyer, and it had been subtly building ever since, but he knew this game well enough to know that Daisy Place wasn't at critical mass yet. First, he needed a room to sleep in—and he'd felt the other pull, the older, more painful pull, for a mile before the bus had slowed at the depot.

Someone here would give him a place to sleep, and he could see to Aunt Ruth's inheritance in the cold light of day.

Sure enough, he was in the middle of a g*inormous* hamburger that had been cooked in an actual ore cart from the gold-rush days, when a tired-looking woman in nice comfy jeans, a skinny-strapped tank top, and flip-flops strode into the converted post office/restaurant and threw herself into a chair at the table next to him.

The restless, painful ache in his chest that had guided him there gave a little *pop*, and he could breathe again.

"Hey there, pretty lady," he said, shoving a plate of fries toward her. "Is there anything I can do to help?"

She had blond hair—artfully streaked and ironed straight—adorable chipmunk cheeks, and a full and smiling mouth. The girl took a fry gratefully and tried to put that mouth to happy use. She failed dismally, but Tucker appreciated the attempt. Putting a good face on things for other people was an unnecessary courtesy, but it was still kind. Thin as a rail, with a few subtle curves, she was in her late twenties at the most and seemed to have the weight of the world on her shoulders.

"It's been sort of a day," she said fretfully. "You know—a day?"

Tucker thought back to when he and Damien used to have this discussion, and his stomach twisted hard with regret. "I've had a few," he said softly. "What happened with yours?"

"It's just so stupid." She sighed and looked yearningly at the untouched half of his two-pound hamburger.

Tucker cut off a quarter of it and put it on the fry plate for her, and her smile grew misty.

"Thank you," she said softly. "I mean, I was going to order my own, but eating alone…."

"Sucks," he said, nodding. "So, I'm Tucker Henderson—"

"Old Ruth's nephew?" she said with interest.

"Yes, ma'am." He hadn't seen Aunt Ruth in several years. She'd helped administer his parents' estate, sending him personal checks every month—ostensibly to help him through college, but the estate was more than enough to live on. He'd appreciated the gesture, though, and had called or written with every check, but she'd never asked him up to see her at Daisy Place, and Tucker….

Well, Tucker's entire life had become the inescapable knowledge, the pull under his breastbone, the pressing weight of being some sort of karmic tool. Quite literally. Leaving downtown Sacramento—where he didn't even have a car because he never knew when he'd get the call and stopping when walking or riding his bike was so much easier than driving—had been beyond him for a couple of years. Aunt Ruth didn't ask, and he didn't insist.

They'd barely spoken about the reasons—but she knew. He was very aware that she knew.

"I'd come to visit, Auntie, but I've got… uhm, things. Things I can't explain."

A sudden electric silence on the telephone. "Oh, honey. I'm so sorry. I know those… things. I have them living in my house. You be careful. Those things can be difficult on the soul."

"Folks are going to miss her," the pretty woman said in the here and now, her smile going melancholy. "Most of us played in her garden at one time or another."

Tucker remembered his own time there, stalking imaginary lions in the jungle of domesticated flowers that ran riot over what must have been ten acres of property. All of the people wearing strange clothes, walking through the benches and over the lawn. He was pretty sure he was the only one who had *those* memories, though. He'd eventually figured that seeing ghosts was part and parcel of the whole empathic gig. It had taken having a lot of "imaginary friends" until he'd been about thirteen and figured it out, but whatever. His parents had only visited Ruth a handful of times when he was a kid, but she'd always had cookies—the good kind, with chocolate. None of that persimmon crap either.

Ruth had been sweet—if eccentric. He'd always had the feeling that she had a particular ghost of her own to keep her company, but if so she hadn't mentioned his name.

"I didn't know the garden was a whole-town thing," he said. A town the size of Foresthill probably had a lot of close-knit traditions.

"Well, my grade school class anyway," the girl said with a shrug.

The skinny high school kid with spots and an outsized nose who was waiting the few tables in the place came up to them. "Hiya, Miz Fisher. Can I get you anything?"

She smiled again, but it didn't reach her eyes this time. "A diet soda, Jordan." She gave one of those courtesy smiles to Tucker. "Ruth Henderson's nephew seems to have taken care of my meal."

Jordan nodded, gazing at "Miz Fisher" with nothing short of adoration. "I'll get you the soda for free," he said, like he was desperate for her approval. "It's not every day your English teacher just strolls in on your watch in the middle of July."

Poor Miz Fisher. Her courtesy smile crumbled, and what was left made Tucker's heart wobble. There *was* a reason he hadn't quit on life after his second attempt to ignore his empathic gift had backfired so horribly. This woman was part of it.

"Former English teacher," she reminded Jordan gently. "Remember? They had to cut the staff this year."

Jordan's smile disappeared. "Yeah," he mumbled. "Sorry, Miz Fisher. I'll go get your soda." He wandered away, the dispirited droop of his shoulders telling Tucker everything he needed to know about how much this woman—homegrown by the sound of things—had been appreciated by her community.

"Lost your job?" Tucker prompted. "Miz Fisher?"

"Dakota," she said, taking another fry. "Dakota Fisher. And yeah."

Tucker knew that wasn't all there was to the story. He cut her hamburger into bites and handed her a fork. He might not have known squat about this town, but he was on his own turf now.

BY THE time they left the restaurant, he knew how much Dakota loved teaching. By the time they got to her tiny cottage and got their clothes off, he knew how much she loved her hometown and her parents and the kids she'd grown up with. And helping people.

By the time they fell asleep, sated and naked, she knew what she had to do. It wasn't what *Tucker* would have predicted, not at all, but it was right for her.

That's what Tucker did—what was right for other people. Because the results of doing what was right for him were too awful to face again.

WHEN THE simple white-walled room was still gray with predawn chill, he opened his eyes and blinked.

Damie?

No. It couldn't be.

But the young man sitting cross-legged on the foot of Dakota Fisher's bed *looked* like Damien Columbus. Dark blond hair, freckles, full lips, green eyes—so many superficial details were there that Tucker could be forgiven for the quick gasp of breath.

He blinked hard, then got hold of himself and took in the nuances.

No—this person had a slightly more delicate jaw, a pointier chin, and his eyes were... well, Tucker had never seen eyes the actual shade of bottle glass outside of contacts and anime cartoons.

And whereas Damie had worn skinny jeans and tank tops—looking as twinky as possible for a guy who'd professed to be straight until... *don't go there, Tucker*—this guy was wearing basic 501s and a white T-shirt. He looked like a greaser or a Jet, right down to the slicked-back hair.

Although—and this had been the thing that had first terrified Tucker to his marrow—this guy was also dead. Or astral projecting. Or something. Because his body wasn't depressing the frilly yellow-and-pink coverlet on Dakota's bed even a little. He just sat/hovered there, tapping the bottom of his red Converse sneakers with his thumbs, scowling at Tucker as if Tucker had somehow disappointed him.

"Can I help you?" Tucker mumbled, squinting at him some more. Oh yeah. The more Tucker looked, the less this guy resembled Damien. Which was good.

Because he wasn't sure how to deal with… Damien. Watching him sleep naked.

Not after all this time.

But then the penetrating gaze of this stranger, this not-Damien, wasn't doing him any good either.

Tucker hadn't been with anybody of his choosing in a long time, and he'd assumed the part of him that *did* choose had been killed off by grief. Imagine his surprise when he felt his stomach flutter.

"You were supposed to be at the house last night," the young man said. "I waited up."

"I found something better to do," Tucker replied, rolling his eyes and keeping the flutter to himself. "I'm sorry. Nobody told me there would be a ghost at the house waiting for me."

The ghost did *not* look appeased. "You need to come with me as soon as—"

"Mm… Tucker?" Dakota stretched, her tank top coming up under her breasts and her frilly white drawers dropping right below her neatly trimmed pubic hair. Tucker had been with women—big, small, short, tall, sophisticated, and plain country girls—and he never seemed to get over how the slightest changes in grooming or shopping or a perfume or a hair product could make such a difference from one woman to the next. He didn't actually have a preference—not anymore—but he sure did have an appreciation for what Dakota did, personally and to herself.

"Hey, hon," he said softly. "You go ahead and sleep. I've got some stuff to take care of at the house this morning." He bent over and kissed her cheek. "I'm so glad you got that whole career thing sorted out," he said, stroking her lower lip with his thumb. "You know where I'll be if you ever want to talk again."

He saw the familiar emotions pass over her heart-shaped, animated face. Disappointment at first, because he wasn't going to stay, and for whatever reason, he'd helped this person feel better the night before. Then there was the "Oh my God, what have I done?" recognition—very often, the person he was with was as much a stranger to one-night stands as they were to Tucker himself.

And finally—oh, there it was—relief.

Yes, definitely relief.

She realized that she didn't know Tucker, didn't know him at all, and he was leaving her, but he was doing it respectfully, and he was letting her know any future contact would be fine.

But he wasn't going to be in her bed anymore.

Then Dakota did him one better. "Thank you," she said, her eyes growing a little sad again. "You really did help me figure some stuff out."

Tucker smiled slightly. "That's what I'm here for, darlin'. Can I use your shower?"

NOT-DAMIEN FOLLOWED Tucker into the shower, and Tucker shook his head. It was like this ghost or whatever hadn't learned the rules of being a ghost yet.

"Hey, do you mind?" he muttered, shedding his boxer shorts quickly and jumping into the water before it had completely heated. California had been in a drought for years—every drop counted.

"I don't mind at all," the ghost said, appearing right in front of him as the cold water pounded his neck.

Tucker choked back a yelp. "Man, get out of the goddamned shower or I'm calling the state and donating the house!"

The ghost gave Tucker's body what was supposed to be a contemptuous look, but somewhere between Tucker's face and his knees, it paused and grew a little heated. With an effort, not-Damien met Tucker's eyes. "I am above lust," he said with the dignity of a desperate lie.

"I don't care if you lust after me," Tucker lied back. His attraction to this not-Damien creature was super irritating when he was naked in the shower. He grabbed some flowered body wash from the shelf and sniffed. Not bad—women did know how to smell. He dumped some on a sponge and continued, "I'm not afraid of finding a man in my shower. I'm pissed off. My entire life is a supernatural sexual violation. But I'd rather not have one looking me in the face while I rinse my cracks!"

Not-Damien's mouth opened slowly while Tucker sponged his pits. "I am *not* a violation! I am a *guide*!"

Tucker soaped up his member, which—probably befitting his karmic mission or whatever—was of a gratifying size. "Guide this," he said crudely. "If you're not out of here by the time I soap my hair, whatever you want to use me for, I'm not doing it."

Not-Damien scowled. "I'll be waiting outside the bathroom," he muttered.

"I'm not going to try to escape my fate," Tucker promised bitterly. "Believe me, I've learned the hard way. Whoever is in charge doesn't *like* us to have too goddamned much free will."

The ghost's scowl softened. "What happened to you?" he asked, looking like a wounded choirboy. "Your aunt said you were such a sweet boy."

"None of your business. And quite frankly, she never mentioned you." Dammit. He looked so much like Damie, the wound opened again, fresh and bloody and bright. "Just go."

There was a faint breeze, carrying with it the odor of new sneakers and indigo dye—and the faintest scent of citrus and lavender—and Tucker was alone.

But not for long.

Not-Damien was not actually waiting for him outside the bathroom, as Tucker feared. Tucker had a chance to wash, dry, and even shave using the kit from the suitcase he'd left in the kitchen.

Dakota slept on through it—probably pretending, but Tucker didn't mind. Sometimes when you woke up with a stranger, faking sleep was just courtesy.

Or that's what he thought until he walked back to the kitchen to grab his luggage and make his exit out the front door.

She was awake, barely, yawning through coffee and blinking through the morning-after mess of her hair. She'd kept the tank top on and put on cutoffs this time, and she still looked sort of delicious and sexy. Tucker had a moment to regret that he wasn't a real person to her, because if he'd had a life of his own, he really would have chosen someone exactly like Dakota Fisher.

"Heya, darlin'," he said, kissing her cheek. "I thought you'd sleep in."

"I really could have," she mumbled. "Then I remembered—I live down three miles of dirt road, Tucker, and it's already eighty-five degrees outside. It would be really frickin' rude of me to let you walk that hauling your two suitcases."

Tucker hadn't thought of that, and the kindness made him blush.

"Thank you," he said in a small voice. "That's really nice of you."

He had a cup of coffee with her, and then she grabbed her keys and the smaller suitcase. She went first, bumping her way across the porch and down the steps of her little house, and he followed. Not-Damien was standing outside the door.

He frowned at Dakota and then turned his glare to Tucker as Tucker maneuvered his big old suitcase over the threshold.

"I thought you said—"

Oh my God. "It's over ten miles away, asshole," Tucker hissed. "I'll meet you there!"

The self-recriminatory look on not-Damien's face was almost worth the aggravation of knowing the dickweed would be waiting for Tucker once he reached his destination.

"Sorry," the ghost said and disappeared, leaving Tucker feeling the faintest bit sorry for being such an ass. But not enough to worry about it.

"OH MY God, Tucker, are you sure?"

Tucker looked at Daisy Place and swallowed. "Yeah," he said weakly. "I'm hunky dory."

Peeling mint-green paint adorned the window and door frames, but the rest of the house was a collection of rotting shingled siding and rusty tin roofs. Was it Tucker's imagination or did the entire house *slant* at odd angles so that the west wing dipped down and the east wing tilted up, and the middle seemed to loom bigger and smaller with each of Tucker's deep, steadying breaths?

"It looks like a cult of Satanists lives in the basement," Dakota said frankly. "You could always room with me for a few weeks. I'm going into the sheriff's department today—my uncle said he could get me a job as a deputy. You know, in a month I might even be able to use a gun."

Tucker tried not to stare at her. Of all the unexpected outcomes of his magic sexual karma, he had *not* expected the former English teacher to scream "I'm gonna be a *cop!*" in the middle of orgasm.

And yet she had. And apparently she also had follow-through.

Tucker thought seriously about her offer and then about what a live-in girlfriend with a gun would do if he asked her to drop him off in town so he could sleep another random stranger into a life epiphany.

"I'm pretty sure the only Satanists in there are the rats," he said with a toothy grin. "I think a gun would be overkill."

"Okay," she said doubtfully. "If you're sure."

He kissed her cheek. "Darlin', I'm good. And I can't thank you enough."

With that, he swung out of her little green Ford Ranger and hauled his bags from the back. He took a few steps away and waved so she could leave and then peered through the red dust up the walkway.

Sure enough, the ghost of not-Damie was waiting at the door, arms crossed and a sort of resentful apology on his pouty-mouthed face.

Tucker sighed. Maybe the Satanic rats would eat him alive tonight and he wouldn't have to live with whatever fresh hell the karma gods had planned.

NOT-DAMIE. ALSO, NOT-A-GOD

As ANGEL watched Tucker haul his suitcases up the broken cement pathway, he tried not to bang his head through the support post for the porch.

So much for his resolutions not to push the resident empath again.

He'd promised—he'd *promised*—Ruth Henderson that he would try to be a friend, a companion, to her nephew, but dammit! He'd been so excited about meeting Tucker Henderson, so prepared to be kind, to welcome him with open arms and gratitude, that finding out the jackass had spent last night catting around had really ticked him off.

Although Tucker hadn't seen it that way. What had he said? His entire life was a sexual violation?

That hadn't sounded like a man who'd been happy to wake up in the bed of a beautiful woman. Not at all.

And seeing Tucker sex-sated, sleepy, looking warm and human and mussed.... Angel pushed that thought away. He didn't feel things like this. He didn't have human reactions or feel warmth or attraction. He just… he *didn't*.

But that didn't change the fact that Angel had kept pushing Tucker's buttons.

Damn. When would he ever learn?

"I'm sorry, I'm sorry," Tucker muttered. "Am I late? Did all the dead people suddenly come alive? Did my shower hasten the zombie apocalypse? Did taking time to shave put all mankind at risk?"

"Did you at least have time to eat before you got laid again?" Angel snapped, and then he really did try to thunk his head on the support post, only it went through it instead.

"Augh!" Tucker dropped both suitcases. "Oh my God. Do you have any idea how weird that looks? Stop that!"

"I'm sorry," Angel said, a contrite, sincere echo of Tucker's sarcastic apology. "I'm sorry. I didn't mean to be an ass. I didn't mean to frighten you. I'm sorry. I really was asking if you'd eaten."

Tucker stood on the porch, holding his hands to his eyes. "Is your head out of the post now?"

Angel double-checked. "Yes. Yes—all body parts accounted for."

Tucker sighed with relief and took his hands away from his eyes. "Better. Did you say food?"

At that moment, a grocery van pulled up the long, slanted driveway and swung around to the front of the house. A low three-layer brick wall marked the edges of a concrete parking lot that faced what appeared to be overgrown gardens. A decrepit toolshed marked the corner. The space was huge—it had made Dakota's job easy when she'd backed her truck out—and this guy had no problem, even in the oversized van.

Angel smiled hopefully. "Supplies and sandwiches," he said, hoping that as offerings of contrition went, this was a good one.

Tucker swallowed and then smiled.

Angel had noticed this when Tucker was naked in bed, but somehow seeing that smile in the sunshine made it so much more apparent—Tucker was really a very handsome man. In his early thirties, with careless dark hair and blue eyes, he had a strong chin in a rectangular face that highlighted some stellar cheekbones. His mouth was full, with a good-humored curve, but Angel hadn't noticed that until he smiled. Some of the bitter care fell from his face then, on his forehead, in the lines of his mouth. For a moment he looked innocent and, as his aunt had maintained, sweet.

"You?" he mouthed, and Angel nodded, not sure if it was possible to feel heat prickling up and down his skin. He may have had a certain way with electronics and phone messages, but he really *didn't* have a corporeal body.

Still, Tucker kept that sweet smile, and Angel fought the temptation to hold his incorporeal hand to his incorporeal face to check.

"Thank you," Tucker said. The naked gratitude on his face did something fierce and unprecedented to the center of Angel's being, where humans maintained the heart sat, regulating emotion. The twisting, swelling sensation where Angel's chest would have been, had he had a corporeal form, was both unpleasant and exhilarating, and it shook him to the marrow of his invisible bones. As he watched Tucker walk down to take the crate of groceries and sandwiches from the delivery boy, he felt the slightest flicker in the projection he'd chosen to show Tucker for their acquaintance, and he thought frantically, trying to figure out what he'd changed.

Tucker was smiling to himself as he walked back up the porch steps, and he looked at Angel to share the smile and stopped abruptly.

"Man, that is *some* shirt!"

Angel looked down, and in place of the plain white T-shirt—which, it had seemed, every human had been comfortable in for at least the last fifty years—he was wearing a button-front Hawaiian shirt that looked like the victim of a tie-dye grenade.

"Oh my God," he said, heedless of the blasphemy. "What in the—"

"You got puked on by a rainbow!" Tucker chortled, his good will apparently easy to earn with food and bright colors. "Dang, ghost guy, I don't know what made that happen, but if you keep doing stuff like that, you might be useful to have around after all."

"Useful?" Angel sputtered, embarrassed. "Useful? Do you have any idea who I am?"

"No," Tucker said. He set the groceries down on the porch and reached into his pocket. "Yes! I knew I had the key." He put his hand on the doorknob to unlock Daisy Place and let out a low moan.

"Oh hells!" Angel muttered. "Tucker, let go—"

"Stop." Tucker fell to his knees, his hand still locked around the handle. "Oh God, make it stop."

Dammit! All those spirits, all of that cold energy locked in the house for weeks. Of course the cold iron of the doorknob would be where that energy was stored. Oh Jesus. Poor Tucker. He convulsed, moaning, his hand locked on the doorknob like it contained an electric current.

He couldn't let go, and his deathlock on the doorknob was *hurting him*.

Angel needed to make it stop. Oh, Angel hated to do this. Ruth hadn't talked to him for a week the first time he'd done it to *her*.

"I'm sorry, Tucker," he murmured, hoping Tucker would forgive him, and then placed his hands over Tucker's and pushed until the cold iron of the doorknob burned against his palms. Tucker groaned and crumpled to the porch, sobbing.

"What in the hell?"

Angel sighed and sat cross-legged, running phantom fingers through Tucker's hair, watching as the strands were disturbed by the breeze of his movements.

"That's what I was going to tell you," he said in the silence that followed. "You need me. I'm your contact for the things in this place—sort of a psychic filter, really. There are too many souls here in Daisy Place, their stories locked inside by silence. Once they tell you their stories, they're free to move on. It's… well, your aunt called it a catharsis exorcism. You're an empath, right?"

Tucker grunted, still shaking in pain. "Yes, I've been cursed by the fucking karma gods. What do they want now?"

Angel didn't know how to answer that. "Ghosts speak to you, right?"

"Sometimes. Usually, it's… something else," Tucker muttered. "But yeah, I see ghosts all the time. They're not usually that talkative." He gave Angel a sour look before closing his eyes again. "With one exception."

Angel sighed because, while he didn't remember the details, he *assumed* this was how he'd come to be trapped here himself. "This entire house is the exception," he said. "The ghosts here are trapped—they *need* to talk. This house was built on a foundation of iron." How did one explain supernatural metallurgical alchemy to a man who was barely conscious? "And there's an iron track that circles the entire property, with just enough gold, silver, platinum, and lead mixed in. It attracts souls—some who died here, some who just stayed here, and some who…." He thought about all the things he couldn't remember about himself. "Some who wander in. They get stuck here in the silence of all the metals. They can't go up or down by themselves. It's like, all the metal here, it freezes them in place. So they need an empath, someone with abilities, to see their stories, give them just enough humanity to set them free."

Tucker groaned, rubbing his face. "You need someone to make them human by telling their stories?" he asked, his voice clogging.

"Otherwise they're trapped," Angel tried to explain. This was a terrible burden—he knew it. He'd known it when he'd presented it to a teenage Ruth. Explaining it to Tucker, a grown man, should have been easier, but he was assailed by the vulnerability he'd sensed underneath Tucker's prickly exterior.

The bitterness was apparently hard-earned.

"Isn't it enough?" Tucker snarled. "Isn't what I do enough? Do the gods really have to fuck with me this badly?"

"Why?" Angel asked, confused. "What else you do?"

Tucker struggled to sit up and wiped his face with his palm. "Nothing. Not a damned thing. Don't mind me. I get tired of fucking my way through life. What's your job in all of this?"

"I'm a witness, mostly," Angel said. "It's like the spirits need someone to live their catharsis moments, and someone to see what hurt them and give them absolution." Angel's one clear memory after his arrival at Daisy Place was of Ruth touching an old coin she'd found in an empty room. He'd been there to see her live through the guilt of a businessman not giving the quarter to someone who'd been desperately hungry. She'd been shaken, sobbing with the intensity of the sadness, and Angel had felt the freedom of the soul released. But in the years that followed, they'd realized that wasn't Angel's only function.

"I'm also a… filter," Angel simplified. "I keep… well, if you'd have let me touch the doorknob first, I would have bled some of the worst of that away." He grimaced. "Ruth actually kept gloves nearby at all times, and I'd sort of give her a priority list of what to look at that wouldn't hurt her, or when she'd have to use the gloves."

Tucker nodded, looking numb, like he had nowhere to go with that information. "There's milk in that box," he said after a moment. "We should put it in the fridge."

And Angel really had to admire him then, because the man hauled himself onto unsteady feet and used his T-shirt to grab the doorknob while he unlocked the door. He propped the solid slab of oak open for a moment, and Angel sensed it first.

"Get back!" he ordered, and Tucker must have been far more sensitive than his great aunt because he was already in motion, sidestepping so he was out of the doorway before the massive rush of psychic energy left him a sobbing, quivering mass of pain on the porch again.

"And that was?" he asked through gritted teeth once the last of the energy trickled out.

Angel shrugged, feeling sheepish and defensive. "Well, the entire property is usually their playground. The real estate agent locked up the house, and they were sort of confined inside."

Tucker rolled his eyes as though bored, then stuck his head in the door. "It is thirty degrees colder in here than it is outside," he announced as he returned for the crate of groceries. "Please, *please* tell me that's a perk."

Angel brightened. "Actually, yes. It's hellish in the winter, though, but most of the time, the house is just naturally cold."

"I shall learn to knit," Tucker said grandly, and then he swept into his inheritance like it hadn't just tried to kill him.

Twice.

TUCKER SEEMED to be in a better mood after the sandwiches—both of which he'd eaten in quick succession.

"Have you been lumberjacking?" Angel asked in amazement. "Running? Doing push-ups all morning?"

"Nope, nope, and nope," Tucker replied, wiping his mouth delicately with a paper napkin and getting rid of the mayo on his upper lip. Then yawning. "It's been a high-energy day, though. And I metabolize everything faster when I'm working."

"Working?"

"That little thing I did where I passed out and almost wet my pants—do you think that just *happens*?"

Angel gaped at him. He seemed to remember Ruth having a healthy appetite, but nothing like this.

Tucker rolled his eyes and kept on eating. "So," he said at last, delicately licking his fingers and then wiping them on a napkin. "This is the catch, right?"

"The catch?"

"Free room, free board, Aunt Ruth's inheritance—I just have to live here for the rest of my life and touch shit and faint?"

"You have to tell their stories," Angel said firmly. "Even if it's just to me." He shrugged. "And since you're an empath, I see them when you touch objects or intercept ghosts, so 'telling me' is more a matter of living them yourself."

Tucker looked at him skeptically. "So given that, it's always 'just to you'?"

And this was the awkward part. "Uh, no. Some of the more recent ones, if there's a living participant or a descendant or—"

"So one touch, one ghost?" Tucker's glance took in the entirety of the house and grounds. "Because that seems easy enough. I know this place was a hotel for quite some time, but Ruth should have taken care of them all."

Angel blew out a breath. "Well, it's more complicated than that. You have to… to read their *entire* story. Sometimes the thing that got them stuck here wasn't in just one coin or one brush up against a doorknob, or even one visit. Ruth once had to tell the story of secret lovers who met here at least ten times in the course of their life. It's detective work, really."

Tucker groaned for a moment and buried his face in his hands. "You know, there's a fairy hill about fifteen minutes away. Even the humans have to know it's there. Wouldn't *they* have an empath you could use?"

Angel took a deep breath in spite of his incorporeal form. "We don't talk about that," he said with dignity. "Ever."

Tucker peeked through his fingers. "That's... uh, absolute."

But Angel dug in his heels. "Please, don't mention them. They're not even supposed to exist." Angel had no idea where this knowledge came from, but it seemed certain, like something he'd known from the beginning of his existence.

Whenever that had been.

Tucker's bitter laugh rattled through the kitchen. "Look—from what I've seen, those folks don't give a shit if they're supposed to exist or not. They're sort of here. I mean, *right here.*"

Oh no—Angel was not about to let himself be distracted. "Even if they did exist," he said, throwing arrogance around his shoulders like a cape, "they can't come *here.* This place has cold iron, pure silver, and soft gold in its foundation. That pretty much repels any of the, uh... well, the people we don't talk about and pretend don't exist."

"Oh." Tucker's shoulders slumped. "That's too bad. I saw a lot of them in Sacramento. They were like ghosts—they were everywhere. They were nice people. I liked the werecreatures especially."

"I *told* you," Angel snapped, "they don't exist!"

"Fine! Fine! They don't exist." Tucker huffed and stood up to put the groceries away. "And thank you, by the way, for the groceries, and for keeping the electricity on. Was that you?"

Angel nodded, relieved. Apparently Tucker's temper didn't last long. "I'm afraid I couldn't keep the dust out," he said apologetically. "But I'm rather good with electronics." Angel gave his best, most winning smile, because Tucker still seemed irritated about the fairy hill, which absolutely did not exist. "I did have a cleaning service come in and clean up the old—Ruth's bedroom, and the guest room next to it."

"And whatever the hell that was didn't knock *them* on their asses?" he asked. It was true—he did have a right to be frustrated.

"They came in through the side door. That one there." Angel gestured. "It was added when Ruth updated the kitchen, so most of the ghosts don't use it. They prefer the french doors to the back porch or the front door." Angel shrugged. "That's one of the rules of ghosts, I guess—"

"They respect thresholds," Tucker said. "Yes, I know. I got my college education in folklore, religions, and old languages."

"There's a degree for that?" Angel asked, eyes wide because that could mean his next hunt for an empath might not be nearly so desperate.

"There is now that I've graduated," Tucker said grimly. "So where do I stay?"

"Well, like I said, I had two rooms cleared out— your aunt Ruth's and her live-in nurse's. Do you have a preference?"

Tucker stared at him blankly, closing the refrigerator behind him. "Preferably a place where nobody I know has died."

An odd sort of shame swept him, and Angel had to fight to keep his expression calm. He was asking this man to sacrifice his future for this house, and he could offer him no suitable place to live. "I'm sorry, Tucker. Like you said, this place started as a hotel—one of the few in this relatively uninhabited place for over one hundred years. It only closed down when your aunt was a very young girl. There's a lot of history here. Someone has died in pretty much every room of the house." He gave a sheepish smile. "Usually more than one someone. And sometimes it's not just dying that keeps spirits here. If something life-changing happened here—heartbreak or falling in love or losing a loved one—that soul will stick around too. But your aunt was the *only* person who died in her room for a good seventy-five years."

"Ooookay? So I can face the psychic residue of total strangers or the psychic residue of a poor woman who was lonely and bitter and pissed off that she was locked up in this mausoleum with no company and no help. Which one ever shall I choose?"

Ouch. "How do you know she was lonely and bitter and pissed off?" Angel asked plaintively. He liked to think they'd achieved a certain rapport in the later years, a certain job satisfaction, as it were. He'd certainly missed her when she'd passed. He'd even mourned her passing, although he seemed to exist with the certainty that she was much happier now.

"Because I'm lonely, bitter, and pissed off already," Tucker snapped. "And I just got here."

"Well, not *too* lonely," Angel sneered, wishing he could get that vision of Tucker, sleepy and sex-sated, out of his mind, but it kept playing back on a loop. There was a certain... touchability to Tucker's body, although Angel had no memories of ever being able to touch.

Tucker leveled a flat gaze at him. "You go ahead and think that's what you saw," he said, no inflection in his voice whatsoever. "In the meantime, show me to my room. I'll take the one without Aunt Ruth, thank you very much."

"Of course," Angel mumbled, feeling shamed for no good reason at all.

Tucker grunted. "Do you have a name?" he asked after a moment.

"Angel," he said, brightening. "That… that is my name." Because that's what Ruth had called him, right?

"You don't sound too sure," Tucker said suspiciously, and Angel fought the urge to just disappear.

"Your aunt called me Angel for fifty years," he said with dignity. "You may call me Angel too."

Tucker grunted. "Of course," he muttered, and Angel had to fight the impulse to thunk his head against a wall. For one thing, his head would probably go *through* the wall again, and Tucker had made it clear he'd had enough of that.

Don't Touch That, Dammit!

Tucker was exhausted.

Sex for epiphanies usually did that to him—it was one of the reasons he'd been so dependent on his aunt Ruth's generosity and his parents' inheritance. Besides never knowing when he'd have to duck out on work, there was the fact that his sex life would literally kill him if he didn't take a day to rest.

Between that and the damned doorknob, he felt like he'd dragged his ass after his annoyingly obtuse guide through at least three miles of dark, psychically burdened tunnels in a tour of the old hotel. *Finally* they ended up back near the kitchen in order to find the *one* room that was not filigreed, curlicued, paisleyed, or cabbage-rosed to goddamned death.

"What?" Tucker asked grumpily, taking in the plain twin bed with a wooden frame, a single blanket, and hospital-white bedsheets. "Are these the maid's quarters or something?"

"The live-in nurse's," Angel said, apparently not getting the irony. "Ruth had cleansed the entire room the year before, so she stripped it down and ordered the furniture. The nurse cleaned out everything before she left, and she seemed like a happy girl...."

Tucker set his suitcases down, ran his fingers over the top of the clothes bureau, and closed his eyes. "She's off to get married," he said, smiling because weddings still made him happy. "And she loved Aunt Ruth, even if she thought the old bat was looney tunes." He grimaced. "Abi the nurse's words, not mine. But yeah. She was innocuous enough. I'll be fine here." Being an empath had its uses sometimes—getting a reading like that was one of them.

The room really *was* stripped down—the wallpaper had been removed and wood paneling installed, and the floor had been sanded to boards and then stained. Plain wood, spartan and unfettered with tragedy.

"It's like she made it for me," Tucker muttered. He toed off his shoes and placed them neatly at the foot of the bed, then pulled off his shirt and his jeans and folded them loosely to put on top of the dresser.

"What are you doing?" Angel sounded scandalized. "You're not going to... to...." He made vague motions that got really specific just as he—ghostly apparition that he was—blushed.

Tucker squinted at him. He was looking less and less like Damie by the minute, and something about his slightly pointier features was getting more and more appealing.

"No, there is not going to be any sex for one here today," he said, yawning. "I'm tired, Angel. It's been a longassed day and it's barely noon. I'm going to bed for an hour or three, and we can resume this stimulating discussion about how much of a life I won't have just as soon as I wake up."

"You're tired?" Those wide eyes were going to kill him. They were becoming almost waifish, and when Tucker had had a type—male or female—that had been one of his types.

"Yes, my ghostly companion, because that is what happens when you have sex for hours instead of sleeping. Now, you can sit on the dresser or the end of the bed or go do your bills or watch yourself some TV— I'm uninterested in what you do without me as long as I get some shut-eye. So are we good?"

"Yes, that's fine," Angel said, looking down like it wasn't. "I'd assumed you'd want to start seeing the ghosts immediately, but anybody would be tired after the grand tide almost washed them away."

"Grand tide?" Tucker asked, crawling into the blessedly clean sheets. The blanket was barely enough, and Tucker made a mental note to bring his own stuff— including blankets and camping gear—up to Foresthill.

"It's the wash of souls that was pent up in the house. There's an ebb and flow, you see—it's why you can *usually* walk in the house and not be assaulted. The cleaning person was last here a couple of weeks ago, and they came in and out from the side entrance, so the ghosts got really backed up. Usually it's different. They go out, and they go in, and when it's their time to have their stories told, that's when fate intervenes with an object for you to read."

Tucker narrowed his eyes, feeling punchy and coquettish. "Are *you* fate? Come on… you can tell me. I won't tell."

Angel snorted. "You *are* tired. Go to sleep. Call when you need me. And Tucker!"

"Wha—" Tucker sat up, awake suddenly. "What? What's wrong?"

"Sorry." Angel looked almost comically chagrined. "Look. Don't touch anything without me. This room is safe. Anything beyond this threshold could be dangerous."

Angel regarded him with those sober green eyes—pretty green eyes—and Tucker groaned. God, no being attracted to the ghosts. "Just be here when I wake up, okay?" Because attractive or not, the ghost he knew was actually more comforting than nothing at all.

"Sure," Angel said, and then he floated up to the top of the dresser, folded his legs, and rested his chin on his hands.

Tucker rolled up tight in the one blanket and closed his eyes. He was cold, the pillow was flat, and the mattress was as hard as a rock.

"The nurse slept here?" he asked, his eyes closed against the spartan room.

"Yes. She said it was restful."

"She lied. I hope Aunt Ruth left her a buttload of money."

Angel grunted. "She did, in fact. How did you know?"

Tucker could hear her thoughts, seeping through the flatiron of the pillow like acid through a table. She'd tried—but even the kindest people could be driven out of patience by someone who demanded the unreasonable. *Damned old lady, does she think I trim her toenails for the hell of it? I'd better get some fucking money.*

"She was not happy here," Tucker muttered, even though Abi had tried hard to be kind. The contradiction between Abi's happiness about getting married and her resentment of her employer was part and parcel of most contradictory humans—he was not surprised. "You know what would be nice? A puppy. Puppies are always kind. They want to lick your face. If I had any control of my own life, I'd want a puppy."

"Do you think a dog would stay here?" Angel asked, surprised. "Dogs are very susceptible to psychic influences. I'd be afraid the grand tide would drive a dog insane."

"God, you suck."

"I beg your pardon?"

"It was my one good thought, asshole. I'm trying to make the best of a bad situation, and you give me 'Oh, I'm sorry, your one ray of hope would be driven insane.' It would have been awesome if you'd just bought into my little delusion for the span of a nap, you know?" Because little delusions had gotten him through since his parents had died and he'd realized that no part of his life would ever be his own again.

"I'm sorry," Angel whispered. "You're right. I'm not very… empathetic. It's why places like this need people like you and your aunt."

"Awesome. Well, I need a puppy." Tucker had never wanted a dog before in his life, but suddenly, in this new place with the cold of the iron and the chill of the unhappy souls surrounding him, he wanted something. Something warm. Something that gave simply and expected only affection in return.

Tucker fell asleep dreaming of loyal, trusting eyes staring at him as he slept.

The eyes were green.

TUCKER AWOKE in the late afternoon.

The room had a window that faced north, into the riotous entropic garden, and the sun was enough to

Tucker's right that the west wing of the house cast a long shadow over the greenery. For a moment, as he lay staring into the world beyond the soul-trapping antique he slept in, he could see them. Women in Edwardian dresses walking, arms linked, along the garden path. A man wearing the uniform of a WWII aviator, gazing off into the sunset with melancholy in his eyes. Children sporting various periods of dress, darting around in what appeared to be a free-for-all game of hide-and-seek.

Those were the happy ones. Tucker concentrated on them, ignoring the sinister man in gambler's garb with a knife in his fist. The beaten young woman, covered in blood, dragging the scalp of her attacker behind her. The two young men, running hand in hand from a mob that would catch them if Tucker didn't look away.

There was too much tragedy in the world. And Tucker could only do so much. He closed his eyes against the worst of it and tried to find his center.

He found it in the thought of a puppy and wanted to cry.

Angel was right. A puppy wouldn't be able to take all of this; dogs were already too attuned to ghosts as it was. Maybe a cat? Not that cats didn't see psychic forces—cats just didn't give a shit. If something freaked a cat out, they hissed and let it alone. A cat wouldn't offer unconditional love like a puppy could—but if a cat *did* love you, it could return affection.

Okay, then. The purring of a cat would have to be enough. Tucker was finally living in a place that didn't expect half his rent in a cleaning deposit, and where he could let the cat go outside without the fear that it might become a victim of traffic. Ten acres spread outside his window, and there may be ghosts, but there were also birds, mice, and voles. A cat could weather the psychic storms of this place—and maybe give Tucker some stability as well.

But a cat would want to roam the house. Tucker couldn't blame it. He felt trapped in this room by its very existence. The one "clean" room here, and it was vaguely corrupted with the memories of an irritated nurse. Tucker wondered if he could bring his next "mission" here, and perhaps they could refresh the room with a sexual epiphany, giving the place the sort of joy it didn't have now.

But it would still be just one room. Tucker closed his eyes and pushed out with his imagination, remembering the oppressive Victorian décor he'd seen on all sides as he'd walked from the kitchen and down the corridor. Fifteen rooms, Angel had said, not including Aunt Ruth's and this one here. Well, sort of. He'd said, "There should be fifteen bedrooms," which didn't bode well since he'd existed at Daisy Place for at least seventy-five years and should know *exactly*. And he hadn't been counting the bathrooms either.

This had probably started off as a large family residence before it became a hotel, possibly a B and B–style place, which is what it had been before it had become a burden on the back of a frail old woman.

Tucker wasn't ready to populate the place with a family again, but he *could* make it into a B and B. One room at a time.

He opened his eyes, and the macabre pageantry of souls on the lawn didn't bother him quite so much.

"Angel?" he said, swinging his feet over the side of the bed. "Angel, are you awake?"

"I don't often sleep, but I do rest," Angel said from his pose on top of the dresser. "What do you need?"

"For starters, I need a cat."

"But—"

"And for finishers, I need some books on home decorating, some home improvement tools, and a fuck-ton of paint."

"Tonight? I thought we'd start with an object or two. I have a pretty paperweight picked out—"

God, this guy had an agenda. "Sure. Whatever. We'll do the paperweight. You show me the room, we'll start with the paperweight—but make it a good room, Angel, 'cause I'm spending the next month touching shit and clearing the place out. If I can't change being stuck here, I'm going to change where I'm stuck. You understand?"

Angel hopped from the dresser like he was a real boy and nodded. Standing, he was short—five eight or nine to Tucker's six two. He regarded Tucker soberly, as though giving real weight to his words, and Tucker tried not to let his chest get too achy at the sight of those vulnerable freckles. *Aw dammit, Damien! You would have hated this place. We could have wreaked beautiful havoc here and made it lovely.*

All he got back from Angel was a brooding silence.

"What?"

"What do you think will happen to this place, once all of the psychic energy is gone? It's an energy trap, Tucker. Do you really mean to let people stay here again?"

Tucker shrugged, standing up and wandering to the window. The ghosts were starting to wander in, fading as they got closer to the house. He wondered if…. "Why not? I mean, we could even bill the place as haunted. It'll be great!"

"But... but...." Angel actually sputtered, flailing his hands in untold directions as he tried to find words. "It will self-perpetuate. Don't you understand?"

"What were *you* going to do with it?" Tucker demanded. "Raze it to the ground? What good will that serve?"

"What good?" Angel asked blankly.

"Yes! It was obviously built as a place to trap souls—"

"Not trap," Angel said primly.

"Of course trap," Tucker argued. "If it wasn't a trap, why won't they leave on their own?"

Angel blinked. "You know, in almost seventy-five years, I don't remember your aunt ever asking that."

"Well, we'll put a pin in it," Tucker said. "You're the one who told me it was surrounded by fairy-repelling metal. I'm pretty sure that's not great for the souls who get stuck here."

Angel was mouthing the words "put a pin in it," and Tucker took a deep breath.

"It means 'save it for later,'" he said patiently. "Can you tell me why we shouldn't let people stay here now?"

Angel shrugged. "A hunch? Empirical evidence? Just... history? It attracts the living too—people coming to this house or this hostel were troubled, in transition in their lives. So if they visited here and never found peace—"

"They didn't know to stop wandering," Tucker acknowledged. "I get it. But that doesn't mean it has to die! I mean, it was obviously built for a purpose. I looked out there at the garden—not all those people were bad. Maybe it does have a purpose, but not a sinister one. Maybe we should keep the old place from crumbling around our ears and find out, you think?"

"No," Angel muttered. "I do not think."

"Lucky you, I am here to do the thinking for you," Tucker said grandly. He looked outside and watched the shadows stretch longer. Well hell—it was July. If they were stretching that long, odds were good it was near nine o'clock anyway. "But the home improvement will wait until tomorrow. So will the cat. In the meantime, let's get a snack and get busy."

He slid into his loafers, yawned, scratched his head, and grinned. Angel stared back at him, still probably trying to find a reason the plan to renovate the place wouldn't work.

Screw him. Tucker had long ago learned to accept that his life was not under his control. God knew when he was going to be forced to wander down the street and into some stranger's bed. But he'd learned that the things he *could* control—what to eat, how he decorated his apartment, how he chose to keep his body in shape—these were the things that made his existence as sweet as it could be.

He had found the equivalent of roast beef au jus, Henri Matisse paintings, and tai chi in this situation, and he wasn't going to let a snarky, opinionated ghost talk him out of it!

BUT OH Lord, did Angel try.

"I don't understand!" he complained as Tucker began pan-toasting the bread for a roast beef sandwich. "You hated this place on sight. Why would you want to fix it up?"

"I don't understand!" Tucker whined. "You're supposed to be helping me do shit here, and all you can do is complain that I'm doing it wrong. Jesus, I've been here less than eight hours. Give the rookie a chance."

With a practiced flip, he turned the bread and let it brown in the remaining butter.

"It's just that we don't know what will happen if you start replacing objects and taking down walls." Angel wrung his hands—actually *wrung his hands*—like an aggrieved '50s movie heroine.

"What will happen?" Tucker rolled his eyes. "What will happen is that I'll be less inclined to hang myself from the ceiling fan and create a new cursed object!"

"You'd do that?" Angel asked. And now that the echoes of their bickering had died down, Tucker heard shock and concern.

He sighed and threw the roast beef on the bread and then added the onions he'd browned earlier. Unbidden, he remembered those days after Damien... after the funeral. He'd crawled into bed for days, barely surfacing to go to the bathroom. The only thing that had pulled him out of bed was the same thing that always pulled him—the painful punch to the gut that said it was time to go change somebody's life. He'd managed a shower, and clean clothes that had hung on him like rags, and he'd even made it into the restaurant. He had no clear memory of the young man or the sex in a cheap hotel that had followed. What he *did* remember was the guy on the phone the next morning, whispering to his best friend, "Lor, you've got to come and get me. I think I slept with a homeless man last night. You're right. I'll go to rehab. This is it—I've totally hit rock bottom, and I need to change my life."

Tucker had feigned sleep and waited until the guy left, and then he'd cried. He'd wept for hours, until the maid had kicked him out and he'd dragged his sorry ass home.

He'd spent the rest of the day cleaning and vacu-uming—and shaving—and when he'd gone to bed that night, he'd made a resolution.

This was a calling, and it had been since that first blowjob in McDonald's. His job was to help people through the most painful decisions of their lives. And whether he liked it or not, his natural sex positivity and pansexuality was the catalyst. So it was like the priesthood, except sort of the opposite. He could either drink and mope his way through it, or he could enjoy the things he had.

"Once," he said now in response to Angel's question. "Once it was that bad. As to whether or not it gets that bad again, I'll leave that to you to sort out."

Angel was quiet for a while, and Tucker sort of forgot he was there. He sat down with his sandwich and a glass of milk, grateful for the coolness of the milk and the way the grilled onions burst butter on his tongue. He was savoring another bite of his sandwich when Angel spoke, startling him.

"Will you miss your home?"

"That depends," Tucker said after he swallowed.

"On what?"

"If I'm allowed to make this freakshow into a new one."

"Your aunt didn't want anything changed," Angel said humbly.

Tucker sighed. "She was probably like me," he said after chewing for a moment.

"How?"

"This thing you want me to do—give up the things I want to channel ghosts or help people make epipha-nies or, hell, generally transition whether it's in life or death—this thing is not easy. Or fun. In fact, it's sort of ruined my life. So when I sit down to eat, I want my goddamned sandwich just the way I want it. 'Cause it's the thing that gets me through the day."

"She wanted the house the way she remembered because it comforted her." Angel's voice was full of dawning realization, and Tucker couldn't blame him for his obtuseness if he was willing to consider someone else's thoughts.

"Yup."

"You want to change it because you want something that's yours." And now Angel's voice was full of understanding—another epiphany—and Tucker's resentment faded a little.

"Bingo!"

Angel gazed off past Tucker's left ear, and for a moment, the shape of the person Tucker had seen all day faded a little, like a picture in the sun. It returned, and Angel's hair was darker, his face a little longer. Not a dead ringer for Damien now, but more like his older brother.

Tucker blinked at him, and he blinked back, apparently not even registering that he'd changed.

"Who in the fuck are you?" Tucker asked, his voice surprisingly level.

"I'm Angel." He offered a complacent smile, and Tucker rolled his eyes. That was probably all the answer he'd get for now.

He took a breath and finished his sandwich.

AFTERWARD HE washed up and stepped out onto the porch, looking to see if the ghosts had returned. Someone—Angel?—had left the side door to the kitchen open. They would have to come back into the house right through where Tucker was standing.

But they had been doing just that. For one thing, the kitchen was not that big—just a long, narrow strip attached to the back of the house as though tacked on as an afterthought. The floor was brick and the walls bare sheetrock. The table Tucker had eaten at was made of giant slabs of barrel-sanded, barely seasoned wood, with four-by-fours in the same condition screwed securely to the top and crossbars of two-by-fours for support.

The stove was a masterpiece—relatively modern, gas, clean as a pin—and the basic array of pots and pans was simple and high quality. The modest stainless-steel refrigerator was big enough for a family of six, but at present only stocked for one.

In a normal house, on a July afternoon, this kitchen would be about ninety degrees without air conditioning, but even as Tucker had stood over the stove, he'd felt no more than a faint warmth. As he leaned against the doorframe and watched some of the lingering spirits run toward the threshold in the fading light, he wondered when he would be able to go back to his apartment and pack all his stuff. He would need a lot more sweatshirts if he was moving in.

He watched as two women, dressed in the slim skirts, puffy-sleeved blouses, and straw hats of the turn of the century, walked toward him, holding hands. One had bright blond hair and a sort of faded, worried smile, while the other—fierce, freckled, redheaded—scowled at a phantom somewhere behind and beyond where Tucker was standing.

He watched them, fascinated, as they wandered in, their mouths moving in animated conversation, and he wondered what they were saying.

Closer, closer, the chill of their touch no more than a breeze off a mountaintop….

"*BRIDGET, DO you think he'll come?*" the blond one asked timidly. She loved Bridget's practicality, but Sophie lived her life in worry, and sometimes it was nice to have someone worry with her.

"*Aye, I think 'e'll come.*" Bridget's Irish brogue slapped Sophie raw.

"*But... but we assumed he wouldn't. You said he'd stay back east. That he didn't care enough to—*"

Bridget took a great breath and turned to her, cupping her cheek in the lamplight. "*I was a fool, Sophie girl.*" Her thumb, rough from laundry and sewing and the thousand tasks a day she did because Sophie had been forbidden from working for so long, scraped under Sophie's cheek, and Sophie shuddered. "*'E'll come because 'e owns us, that one. I didn't believe it, aye? And then....*"

Sophie nodded, biting her lip, and both of their eyes fell upon a letter on the richly varnished desk. Sophie liked the desk—maple wood, the comforting red of it like Bridget's hair—and it complemented the wallpaper, which was a confluence of giant fluffy chrysanthemums in blazing autumn colors. The bed was soft and the quilts warm upon it—autumn colors again, because whoever had decorated the place had possessed something of a gift. This room had been their haven, their sanctuary, their place to hide, and their home for the past three months, and Sophie dreamed of a home of her own where she could build such a room for her and Bridget.

The letter from Sophie's brother sat unopened, like a grim granite reminder of reality in the middle of their happy golden dream.

"But maybe James will want us," she said. "Don't you think he'll want us? He's always loved me."

Bridget's pity was hard to stand. Sophie had so little to offer this relationship.

"He does *love me!" Sophie declared. Breaking away from Bridget, she strode to the desk and opened the letter, ripping the paper in spite of the unused letter opener right next to the ungainly paperweight.*

Her breath came more quickly as she read, her lungs straining against the stays of her skirt.

"Oh Bridget—Bridget, you'll never believe—"

There was a sudden clatter, and a voice from downstairs called out, "Mrs. Conklin? Mrs. Conklin? You have a guest!"

Sophie let out a little moan, and her palms started to sweat. Oh no. She was going to—

"You will not *be sick, Sophie girl!" Bridget snarled. "You let me handle this. I'm the dumb servant, and that's all they know, you hear?"*

At that moment there was a pounding up the stairs, and Sophie took a deep breath against her corset.

Her vision went black, and she fell limply to the clean wood floor.

TUCKER PULLED in a great gasp of air, his lungs burning as though he'd held his breath for hours. And again. And once more as he sagged against the doorframe, eyes gazing sightlessly into the darkness of the yard beyond.

"Tucker?" Angel sounded worried, as though he'd said the name more than once. "Tucker? Are you okay?"

Tucker took a few more breaths, the vision imparted by the two ghosts keeping him in a stranglehold until he could focus on at least one clear detail.

"Chrysanthemums," Tucker muttered weakly. "On the wallpaper. Where are they?"

"Up the west wing stairs, third door to the left."

Tucker looked at him, eyebrows raised.

"I've been here a while. I know lots of things about the house." Angel gathered his dignity about him, and Tucker blew out a breath as the last of the spots cleared from his eyes.

"It couldn't have been the door next to mine," he muttered, hauling through the kitchen and leaving his plate on the table and the pan in the sink. The vision was so fresh it didn't matter that the women had probably been dead for nearly a century. He felt compelled to solve their mystery *now*. "It's never 'Oh Tucker, it's on the ground floor, just past the stairs so it's close to the kitchen,' because that's too fucking easy, isn't it? It's got to be a thousand light-years the fuck away!"

"Tucker, I wasn't going to start with them. I don't know much, but I know their story isn't easy...."

He came out of the kitchen and turned right toward the entryway. There were two sets of stairs—the stairs from the east wing immediately to the right of the entryway and the stairs to the west wing, slightly behind the entrance to the kitchen. All Tucker really had to do was venture out the kitchen door and pull a U-turn before the dining room. Later it would occur to him that this could possibly be the least convenient layout for a kitchen and a dining room, but right now, he just had one goal in mind.

He wanted to see the Chrysanthemum Room.

"Top of the stairs, three doors down to the left," he panted, while Angel whined behind him.

"No! No, you can't! You don't know what you're doing yet. Let me research their objects first. C'mon,

Tucker, I've only scratched the surface of the mysteries here, and there are some objects that are dangerous!"

But Tucker had seen it, had seen *them*, and they'd been vibrant and young and real. He'd felt Sophie's fear and the roughness of Bridget's hands on her cheeks and the crispness of starched linen against her skin. And the damned corset, of course, but all of it had made those women so desperately real to him. He wanted in their world, to know who they were to each other, to know what happened to them.

What had the letter contained? Who was the "he" they'd been so interested in? Who was their mysterious guest, and why would Sophie be so frightened that she'd actually swoon—with a little help from a skirt bound up to her ribs.

Tucker felt the same drive, the same pull he usually felt when he needed to go downtown and find someone to seduce into changing their life. The curiosity— *Who will I meet now? What will they look like? What will they need from me?*—and the thrill of discovery were some of the pleasures he allowed himself, some of the balms to soothe the ache of having no family, no friends, no job. The people he was destined to help made him less resentful of being karma's bitch.

This thrill—and the promise of helping the long-deceased residents of this house—was even greater.

He had time to notice the threadbare carpet, the hardwood splintering under his feet, the peeling veneer of the doors and tarnished gold plating of the doorknobs before he spotted the door with a small plaque showing a painted chrysanthemum on the front.

He remembered to slow down and use his shirt to turn the doorknob, and then he stepped on in.

Soul Voyeur

Angel hadn't mentioned it. When he'd told Ruth, it had sort of freaked the poor old girl out.

He'd known her several years by then—she'd started to ask him how he knew when the spirits had passed on, how he knew their stories before she even told him, and he'd figured that since they'd worked as a team successfully for so long, she deserved to know.

She didn't speak to him for a year.

He never talked about it again, and he tried to minimize the times it crept into their interactions from that moment on.

But he wasn't sure if he'd be able to hide it from Tucker for very long at all.

For one thing, Tucker didn't do what was asked of him—or even expected. Angel couldn't coach him through his first ghost encounter; it had already happened.

Angel had seen it unfold clearly in his mind, like humans saw a movie projected against a wall.

Much like he'd seen the image he'd based his form on. Not *too* close—just close enough to inspire trust. Angel needed to inspire trust. He needed Tucker to talk to him. Not so much in order to accomplish the mission but to… to satisfy that *thing*, that thing inside him that had gotten him into this position in the first place.

The closest Angel could put voice to it was an itch. Fifty-five years ago, when Ruth Henderson had been young and carefree, the great-granddaughter of Seth and Gretchen Henderson, who had built Daisy Place, Angel had gotten an *itch*, and he'd been trapped here ever since.

Ruth had helped him—her natural talent had let her see the ghosts even before Angel had gotten caught in the trap that *was* Daisy Place. It wasn't until Angel had become trapped there and had spoken to her that they'd developed the rapport that allowed them, as a team, to free the spirits. She'd been talkative once, and excited about her invisible friend, Angel. When he'd been there to hear the stories of the other spirits, they'd both felt the catharsis, the joy, of giving another being freedom.

Angel had been so confused—he really couldn't remember *how* he'd become trapped, beyond the itch thing. And his own memories had been dark and filled with pain with no remembered source. But that joy, after Ruth had told the first story, that had been important. He'd seized on that. *That* was his purpose here; he'd been sure of it.

And he'd convinced Ruth that it was her purpose too.

Only then Angel had watched, helplessly, as Ruth's youth, her spirit and joie de vivre, had shrunk in upon itself, had shriveled, leaving bitterness and loneliness in its place. He'd had no idea what to say to her, what to do for her. The work they were doing was vitally important. He could let her leave for brief sojourns, let her brothers and their families visit, but he could never say the words that would allow her to be free.

Three little words.

Let it be.

And the worst part, the most frustrating part, was in spite of his enforced stay here, in spite of working so hard to escape, to resume his full duties as he should wish to (what were those again?), that itch, that abominable itch, the thing that had so ensnared him in Daisy Place to begin with, was a constant irritation in the pit of what should have been his groin.

And the only time it went away, was even close to assuaged, was when he was watching the lives of the departed scroll across the memories of Ruth Henderson, and now, hopefully, her nephew Tucker.

Angel had watched, half-yearningly, half-despairingly, as Tucker had experienced his first vision. He loved this part. He did. He never understood the motivations—not the way Ruth had—but seeing the lives of the departed had been his movie, his novel, his long-running TV series, the one that broke his heart.

And then he'd seen what Tucker had seen, and if he'd known how, had possessed the mechanism in his heart or soul or form, he would have wept. There was a quality to Tucker's visions that had been missing from Ruth's. He'd witnessed human innovations in the last fifty-five years, had seen televisions go from black-and-white to color, from tubes to pixels, from standard definition to high definition.

This was the difference between a black-and-white, fifteen-inch screen and high-definition color in 3D with surround sound on a screen the size of the house.

Immersed as he had been inside Tucker's mind as it lived through the simple conversation between a woman of privilege and her maid, he'd felt closer to those people than he ever had before. They'd *lived* for him, and for those breathless moments, that itch in his core had been soothed, and he'd been able to breathe as though he had a real chest, sucking real oxygen into pink and healthy lungs.

He wanted to enjoy this feeling, to revel in it. He wanted the time to savor what this could mean for his duties, but apparently Tucker wanted leave to tear into the walls and change the world before Angel could even understand it.

It was infuriating. And Tucker? Tucker was two steps ahead of him, with or without his pleas to just please, for the love of all that was holy, slow down.

"Wow," Tucker breathed, doing a slow pivot of the room. "Angel, look at this place. It's like they *just* packed and left. I swear, there's hardly any dust."

Angel blinked. "That usually means the ghosts are busy," he said, hoping Tucker would listen. "Agitated ghosts are unhappy ones. This could be a not-great sort of place to deal with your first—"

"Look!" Tucker interrupted without even slowing down. "The desk. Did you see the desk?"

"Yes, I see the desk where the letter was," Angel said, disconcerted enough to blurt out the truth—the one that had so frightened Ruth.

"Really? You can read the visions in my head?"

Oh no! Tucker had only just gotten there. "Yes! But how did you—"

"Well it only makes sense," Tucker said, and Angel wanted to cry with the simplicity of that acceptance. Oh God—how much easier it would have been between Angel and Ruth if the older woman had been able to see that he wasn't *trying* to intrude on her mind. The ghosts were *projected* into his consciousness, like movies on a screen.

"If we're working together," Tucker continued, "you've got to see too, and you need me for *something*. But the desk—do you see it?"

Delicate scroll-footed maple wood, almost sensual with the curved facades and the narrow little "ankles" that attached the feet.

"It's beautiful," Angel said softly, skating an incorporeal finger over the surface. He frowned. It should have been humming with voices, this desk. It had sat there during the most intimate revelations of more than a hundred years of visitors to Daisy Place. It should have been a quieter, softer version of the doorknobs.

"It's silent," he whispered, not feeling a single hum. "Tucker, open the drawers. Is there something in here? Coating the wood? Embedded in it?"

Tucker frowned and turned away from wondering at the wallpaper and reverently finger-petting the antique quilts.

"The desk?" He held his hand over the wood just as Angel was doing. "That's odd. It's giving off the same vibe as the quilts. Sort of like it's absorbed more energy than it's emanating." He pulled out the lower drawer and then closed it, shrugging when it proved empty. The one in the middle had antique stationery in it, as did the one on the top right. The bottom left had a hole punch that revealed nothing more to Tucker than a bored child and a ruined bus ticket. And so on, right up to the top middle.

Tucker reached out to pull on it and then snatched his hand back, as though from a stove. "It's burning," he hissed. "Freakishly hot. Angel, can you feel that?"

Angel held out his own ghostly hand and let out a gasp. "There's… oh dear. Tucker, there is *power* in this drawer. In this one in particular. You must take great pains to not touch the metal without my—"

Tucker was ripping off his shirt, and Angel paused in all the things.

Tucker Henderson had a beautiful mortal body. Long-muscled, lean. His ribs were maybe a little too prominent, but Tucker probably expended energy at an amazing rate. He had a small spot of dark curly hair on his chest, vibrant against his pale skin, which was now flushed with pink, probably from his frantic journey through the house and up the stairs.

Angel had seen him naked—that morning, in that woman's bed—but he hadn't appreciated him, hadn't been able to imagine the heat coming off his body, the faint smell of sweat and fabric softener, the tang of salt.

Hadn't imagined the taste of Tucker's skin.

Angel's body—his incorporeal, imaginary construct of psychic energy—began to do uncomfortable and potentially embarrassing things. For a moment, the place where his chest should have been began to burn, and he reminded himself to breathe.

Then remembered that breathing was an illusion, and constructs of psychic energy shouldn't need to process oxygen. He did it anyway, because there was something soothing about the repetition, and concentrated on watching as Tucker rattled the metal-fastened drawer until the lock gave.

The burst of psychic energy that crashed into them both knocked Tucker on his ass and sent Angel into a vertigo spin around the room. When he finally managed to pull himself together, so to speak, Tucker was struggling to his feet, panting.

"That was—" He caught his breath. "—really fucking unpleasant. Is the whole house like this?"

"I gave Ruth the easy ones," Angel confessed, too rattled to dodge the question. "She... I felt bad for her."

Tucker regarded him with unfriendly resignation. "Wonderful."

"You've had a chance to live somewhere else besides Daisy Place," Angel responded defensively. "She started doing this as a child!"

Tucker straightened from his half crouch over the drawer and ran his hands through his wild hair. "Poor Aunt Ruth," he said grudgingly, and Angel sensed that beautiful empathy in him. The emotion was almost as compelling as Tucker's bare chest.

"I was trying to start you off with something easy," Angel said, thinking of a flowered paperweight in a room three doors down.

Tucker grimaced. "Well, I actually appreciate the thought," he said on a sigh. "Now can you make yourself useful and get over here? Tell me if there's anything nasty in the damned drawer."

Angel waited until Tucker used his shirt to open the drawer wide and then hovered over the contents.

"Letter opener is clear," he murmured.

"Surprise!" Tucker pulled it out and ran his thumb over what seemed to be a still-sharp edge of a long, tarnished stiletto of silver.

"The fountain pen is clear—but still messy." Damn.

"There goes my shirt." The blotch was surprisingly large.

"Maybe wait until I clear the whole drawer?" Angel suggested testily. "Besides, you're intruding on my space!" This last was absolutely true—if Tucker was any closer, he'd be wearing Angel like skin, and that would be unpleasant for them both. The human fear of ghostly possession was based on an uncomfortable amount of truth.

"Fine." Tucker huffed and folded his arms. "Keep going."

"Okay, the scissors are... uh, no. Don't go there." Bad things. "The, uh, glass bottle—" Angel's entire body was washed with heat. "Not relevant."

"Bad?" Tucker asked curiously.

"No, just, uh, not relevant."

"Here, let me be the judge of that."

Oh dear.

Tucker's long-fingered hand darted into Angel's vision and wrapped around the bottle. Angel made a little sound of wanting in his throat, and he found he was helpless to resist watching the story as it unfolded in Tucker's head.

BRIDGET WAS helpless—when she was never helpless. She lay sprawled on her back, naked in the daylight, at her mistress's mercy.

"Oh Lord, Sophie girl...."

Sophie, who was so lost, so fragile in their lives outside this room, was smiling at her wickedly, the sort of carnality in her eyes that had repulsed Bridget in the men who had taken her, reeking of entitlement, using her body because it was convenient and disposable.

With Sophie it filled her, warm and syrupy, with the kind of desire that women dreamed about when yearning for their prince. Bridget had found it in her princess.

Slowly Sophie dripped raspberry syrup from a slender green glass bottle over Bridget's bare breast. Bridget gasped as it cooled her nipple and fought a moan and a laugh both as it drizzled down the underside of the pale, freckled swell.

"Oh, my darling," Bridget breathed. "You have made a mess!"

"Then I'd best clean it up, hadn't I?" Sophie asked, mischief dancing in her eyes.

"Oh aye...."

Sophie's tongue, neat and pink as a cat's, darted out and licked, and Sophie's shoulders, bare like the rest of her, covered Bridget's body as she knelt by the side of the bed and followed the trail of the sweet red syrup.

"Oh dear," Sophie whispered, her voice a guttural purr. "We seem to have run out of syrup." She was licking the mouth of the bottle, sucking the thick, smooth glass into her mouth and hollowing her cheeks as she cleaned it of everything but her spit.

Bridget's mouth went dry. "Whatever will we do?" she asked, half serious. Sophie's laugh, filthy as a dockworker's, sent a warm gush of fluid from Bridget's sex, and she writhed, her core swollen and aching with anticipation.

"We'll find something," she promised, pushing at Bridget's thighs until she lay, bent at the knees, legs spread wantonly.

"Oh dear Lord. Ah, Sophie!" Her voice broke as Sophie's lips, tongue, and fingers began to move in concert within Bridget's plump folds. Sophie was skilled at this, finding the tiny knob of sensitive flesh with her

tongue and tormenting Bridget until her hips arched off the bed.

Sophie stilled Bridget's flailing body with the flat of her palm right under Bridget's navel.

And then, with the cool pressure of the smooth glass bottle easing into her sex....

THE THUNK of the bottle hitting the top of the desk broke their trance.

"Oh my," Angel whispered, looking wildly around the room for the two lovers, expecting to see their plump, pale curves spread across the bed in joyous abandon.

"That was personal," Tucker said, half laughing. Angel locked eyes with him desperately, hoping to be grounded.

He was sorely disappointed.

Tucker's cheeks were unevenly pink, his skin blotchy with arousal, and his eyes were fever bright. Angel's gaze raked the flushed skin of his throat and chest, then down his rippled stomach to his....

Angel heard a faint moan, and realized he'd made it.

Tucker looked at the swell in his cargo shorts, lying fat and unapologetic along the side. "Uh, yeah," he said, grinning cockily through what looked to be a combination of embarrassment and desire. "That was pretty damned hot."

"It was private," Angel squeaked. "I didn't know—"

Tucker shuddered and adjusted himself, hips undulating in excitement. "Well, now we do!" He looked around the room and sighed. "You know what? I'll get back to this place tomorrow. Right now, uh...." He smiled at Angel sheepishly. "If you could maybe give me fifteen minutes alone in my room." His hips moved again, and he let out a breathy moan. "Maybe half an hour."

And then he disappeared out the door and down the stairs, leaving Angel staring at that green glass bottle.

He closed his "eyes" and tried to find his center, but instead he heard Tucker's noises reverberating through the boards of the house. Tucker was joyous and unashamed, and instead of locking himself away from the uncomfortable surges of human emotions that rocked his energy matrix, Angel found himself going adrift.

Tucker moaned, and Angel was lost in the sound, lost in the vision of Tucker's body, naked and exposed, while Tucker stroked his own erect cock in a long-fingered fist.

Would one hand be on his chest? Angel was fascinated by his chest, by the dark hair against the pale skin, by the nipples that were such a delicate pink. Would he be pinching his nipples? Would he tease himself?

His moans escalated, and so did Angel's imagination. Would he cup his testicles? Angel had been a voyeur more than once in this place, and even Ruth had stumbled upon some sexually charged artifacts. Angel had seen men do this, had seen them roll the tender balls delicately under the skin of the scrotum. Would Tucker touch himself underneath? Would he—

Another moan, this one deep and soul-ripping, and Angel let out a little moan of his own, closing his eyes and appearing on Tucker's dresser. He kept his head, stayed invisible, but he saw, and it was just as he'd imagined, except he hadn't thought of the sweat shining from Tucker's flushed skin or the scent of semen and perspiration that saturated the air.

Or what it would do to Angel to see Tucker's legs spread lewdly while he tried to penetrate himself with a spit-slickened finger.

"Oh *yes!*" Tucker cried out, and Angel took another breath, disappearing again and reappearing on the kitchen floor, close enough to hear Tucker scream, "Oh *hells* yeah!" but not in the room, not seeing him spurt seed all over his hand and his abdomen and chest.

But he imagined it. And he wrapped his imaginary arms around his imaginary knees, rocking back and forth and wishing, wishing, oh, wishing…

For that part of being human he'd assumed he could never have.

HE WAITED another half an hour and then went back to sitting on top of the dresser.

Tucker had turned out the lights in the kitchen and the bedroom by the time Angel got there, and had visited the tiny adjoining washroom as well. But he hadn't bothered to put on pajamas, and in spite of the blanket wrapped securely around his shoulders, Angel had no doubt that he slept naked. Angel watched him for a while, picturing every sweep of skin, every mole, every imperfection under the bedclothes, until he realized that he'd started timing the breaths of his imaginary body to the breaths of Tucker's real one.

He finally conceded to exhaustion and closed his mental eyes to sleep.

When he awoke, Tucker was already up and dressed. He'd left the sheets in a predictable tumble on the bed, but he'd cleaned up in the bathroom after he shaved. He'd shoved his clothes in the drawers, but the suitcases were still standing open in the middle of the floor.

Angel narrowed his eyes and sighed. He'd rather suspected Tucker wasn't the kind to clean up after himself—but then, if he was waking up with someone new a lot, why would he get into the habit?

"Angel!" Tucker called from the kitchen. Angel appeared before the echoes of his name stopped ringing through the house.

"Yes?"

The pan Tucker had been holding clattered into the sink. Breakfast had been french toast this morning— Angel thought of Tucker eating french toast with that sort of decadent enjoyment he poured into everything and regretted not waking up sooner.

"You startled me!" Tucker laughed. "Look—someone is going to come pick me up so I can buy his truck—"

"I beg your pardon?" Fast! So fast! Ruth's time had been so much slower, but Tucker, born to this time, in a city not that far away, seemed to move so quickly.

"I looked him up this morning, told him I'd just moved in, and he said that was fine. Computers, Angel—they really do make the world go faster."

Angel clearly remembered Ruth getting internet. At first Angel had worried that the strange metallurgy of Daisy Place would render the entire operation moot, but apparently Daisy Place had the best internet in the hills. Go figure. And he had to admit, he'd made frequent use of it, even before she'd passed away.

"You should say a prayer of thanks to your aunt," Angel muttered, remembering an entire day spent trying to convince the old woman that it would be a pointless expense. No, Angel's grasp of the future had always been a little weak for a supernatural being. Ruth had accused him of being an old man in a beautiful ghost's clothing, an insult that had provoked Angel to dress in neon clothes and sequins for the next month.

He and Ruth had really enjoyed irritating the crap out of each other. He missed her so.

"I will, just as soon as I get my hands on a truck and get to the nearest home improvement store."

"There's an Ace in town for the basics," Angel supplied, hoping that's all they would need.

"Excellent. If I need anything bigger, I'll go to Auburn." Tucker frowned. "After that, an animal shelter. I need a kitten."

Angel felt his eyes go wide and his eyebrows go up, and Tucker suddenly noticed him.

"Your eyes are still green," he muttered. "And still the same shape. But your hair is sort of reddish—your entire face has changed." Tucker pulled in a big breath. "And Angel, your chest is broad as a *barn*!"

Angel looked down at himself in shock. "I, uh…."

"You have stubble! Oh my God, do you have stubble on purpose?"

Angel tried desperately to remember what he'd been thinking when he'd pulled power from the aether around the house and surged. Tucker had been deep into his own pleasure, and Angel had….

Oh Lord.

Angel had wanted to inflict that pleasure upon him.

And this form he was wearing—apparently, he'd thought that would be the perfect form to pleasure Tucker in.

"Do you find this form pleasing?" Angel asked, his mortification complete.

"I usually like my guys a little skinnier," Tucker said, shrugging. "But it's the person inside the body first, okay?"

Angel nodded helplessly. "I shall await your return," he said, dispirited. He'd wanted to spend more time with Tucker this morning.

You wanted to see if he'd touch himself again.

Yeah, that, but Angel wouldn't admit it!

"You could come with me," Tucker said with a wink; then he frowned. "Right? I mean, you met me at Dakota's house—"

"I'm bound to the house and to you. Yes, I could definitely accompany you." For a moment, Angel perked up, but then Tucker sort of deflated.

"Yeah, but I wouldn't be able to talk to you in public, and that would be rude."

Angel swallowed—even though it was something he didn't have to do, his mouth and throat worked in concert like that. *Living people do these things. What is happening to me?*

"Maybe after you get the truck. Why a truck, though?"

Tucker ran his hands through his messy hair. "Usually I walk. It's why I took the train to Colfax and then a bus here. I get… well, sometimes I need to stop and eat or have a drink on my way home. It's hard to explain." He scowled and then took a deep breath and seemed to let something go. "Anyway it's easier when I'm walking. But up here, it's all so spread out. I figure if I'm going to be renovating the place, I'll need to haul stuff. So yeah. Truck, supplies, kitten. If I'm stuck here like Aunt Ruth, I might as well enjoy it." He grinned and then turned his head, responding to a honk from the front of the house. "Gotta go, Angel. See you in the evening!"

He went running out the door, leaving Angel trying to remember why he'd felt the urge to swallow and imagining sitting in the front of the truck while Tucker drove, windows down and breeze ruffling his imaginary hair.

THE SHAPE OF THE THING

"TUCKER HENDERSON?" The guy in the truck was a burly forty-fiveish, with graying brown hair, weathered lines at his eyes, and battered knuckles. He was dressed in faded jeans and a clean T-shirt that read Straight but not Narrow.

"Josh Greenaway?"

"Yessir, pleastameetya. I understand you're looking for a truck." He grinned, revealing a slightly crowded if pleasing smile, and Tucker found himself liking the guy on sight.

Tucker backed up and walked around the truck, taking in the buffed-out dents under the primer and Bondo and listening to the purr of the thing in idle. A Chevy half-ton, the online ad had boasted power steering, power brakes, AC, and a newly refurbished transmission, and Tucker didn't see a rust spot or untreated flaw in the body, which had originally been painted electric blue.

Yeah, it had been battered and even bruised, but it wasn't broken.

Tucker grinned back at Josh. "Looks great! How's it drive?"

Josh winked, unhooked his suicide-closure lap belt, and scooted to his right. "Hop in and see. Anywhere you need to go?"

"The hardware store," Tucker said. "But I was going to wait until I bought the truck."

"Forgetaboutit. Sit down, let's take her for a ride, run your errand, and you can see how you like it. I told the missus I'd be gone until lunch. As long as I bring sandwiches home at one, I am doing no harm to anybody, right?"

"Not a soul," Tucker said, nodding. This guy elicited no tug in his gut, no karmic pull, and Tucker breathed a small sigh of relief. For a morning, anyway, he could have a friend.

A friend who didn't float in midair and try to tell him how this supernatural gig worked.

He shoved away his irritation at Angel—and his curiosity too, for that matter. He was getting out of that spirit mausoleum and spending some of his inheritance, a thing he didn't do often, actually.

He slid behind the wheel, remembering the power of driving a car, soft and comfy like a handknit pair of socks. His father had taught him before he and Tucker's mother passed away, back before Tucker had figured out that life really wasn't fucking fair.

But he'd learned to drive in his dad's modest Toyota sedan, and this? This was a *truck*! Tucker was higher off the road and in charge of a metal behemoth, and backing the thing out of the driveway proved that the steering wheel was as sensitive as a baby's tickle spot.

He swung the thing around and stomped on the gas, and the V-6 roared into action. He let a low, evil chuckle of joy escape.

"Oh man. This thing is like driving a jetliner! I'm getting *chills*. Why, oh why are you letting this baby out of your sight?"

Josh laughed in delight. "Well, we're selling her because our oldest son needs something that gets better gas mileage so he can drive down the hill to go to college. It's a helluva commute—this thing sucks gas like water. I've got a smaller truck for everyday stuff, and my wife has the minivan for the other three kids, so Brutus here is the one to go. And it's a good thing you like driving it because you just turned toward the forest and away from town. There's a turnout in about half a mile—it does a loop around your property, actually, if you want to take that way. You'll end up about a mile from town."

Tucker giggled. "Well, I wanted to know more about the place." He enjoyed driving for a moment, keeping the window rolled down and smelling the pine and red-dirt dust and enjoying being someplace besides the city. Josh kept up a steady stream of commentary on the truck and his kid and how Josh needed his kid to get out of Foresthill so the boy could find a boyfriend and leave his mom and dad alone. Tucker nodded in understanding and studied the road ahead—and the property to his left. He'd just noticed that the tree line was drastically different in the property around Daisy Place than it was for the whole rest of the area when he spotted the turnout, right before Sugar Pine National Forest.

"Why is Daisy Place all willow and oak instead of pine?" he asked, thinking it was significant.

"I don't know. But then, if you haven't noticed, your entire inheritance is sort of wonk-fuckit, right?"

Josh had a way with words.

Tucker slowed down, turned into the side road, and about caught his breath.

"Now *that*," he said, remembering Angel's discussion of the strange metals buried below the property of Daisy Place, "is just fucking creepy."

Josh let out a low whistle. "Yeah, well, it's gotten worse since I was a kid. You don't really see it until someone points it out."

On the left side was darkness; on the right side was light.

Sugar Pine Lake rested in a valley, and the forest from Highway 49 was almost a spacious one. The underbrush was sparse, the trees far enough apart for sunshine to get through. Off-road dirt bikers and mountain bikers liked the spot because it offered challenge *and* visibility. That was the forest on the right of the dirt track that connected the two main roads.

The forest on the left, Daisy Place, sat dark and dank. Friendly, independent trees like willow and oak had no business in this area, but they grew anyway, overgrown with mistletoe, ivy, and thick weeds. Tucker, who knew nothing about topography or botany, thought the grounds of Daisy Place would be more in keeping with a Southern mansion or the forests of the Northeast before the pilgrims landed.

A veil on that portion of the land quite simply darkened the sun, leaving the vegetation primeval and the shadows threatening.

"That is not good," Tucker mumbled, remembering Angel's duties. Apparently, the ghost hadn't been talking out of his ass about the massing of souls over the property.

"Yeah, well, it's always looked like that over the cemetery. Like I said, it just now got bad over the whole stretch of property."

Tucker was busy negotiating the mostly washed-out dirt road. "I'm not breaking this thing, am I? Because I really fucking like it."

"Nossir, it does this about every day. I really need to put gravel on our driveway. It's not county property, and it stretches about a half mile."

"Good. And ceme... ter... y...?"

Because that must have been it.

"Yessir," Josh breathed, his voice hushed and respectful. "That's the one."

Tucker risked a glance at Josh, wondering if he saw what Tucker did. Because what Tucker was seeing was *not* an ordinary cemetery.

Most cemeteries are laid out very orderly—little rectangular earthen repositories for horizontal storage while the human bodies fought embalming fluid to decompose.

The graves Tucker was passing were randomly set out and randomly marked: angel headstones, giant sheets of granite, tiny sunken plaques—all of them vied for space in a haphazard arrangement over uneven, unkempt ground...

That stretched into infinity.

Real infinity, mile upon mile of erratically spaced graves stretching into the blackness of a dimensional horizon.

Tucker kept his foot steady on the gas and said, "That's a little bigger than I expected."

"Naw, bout an acre at the most. It's full of the folks who passed away at the house. Daisy Place was founded around the Gold Rush. You knew that, right?"

"I assumed." Which he had, even before Angel had told him, because much of California had been. Coming up the I-80 corridor, the giant statue of the prospector in Auburn was one of the most prominent reminders of the state's history of exploration, entrepreneurship, and raw tragedy and greed. Daisy Place, with all of its Gothic sprawl, had probably been built to accommodate the newly rich and the young men out to find their fortunes, expecting it to take a week or two at the most. Much of the town was like that—including the place where Tucker had been eating his first night in Foresthill, the Ore Cart.

In fact, Tucker could see more than a few miners and pioneer women among the masses of spirits wandering the *road to dimensional hell* that apparently existed in his backyard even as he drove by. A bearded prospector with no teeth and maggots in his beard waved at Tucker from the side of the road, his appearance made no less grotesque by the fact that most of his body was poisonous green vapor.

Tucker thought that the poisonous green actually highlighted the maggots.

He swallowed back his nausea and kept his eye on the bend in the road, praying that the dimensional pathway to wherever the fuck it went disappeared when he turned left. It had to, right? Because that thing was big enough to suck up a semi, and this town was too damned small for semis to just disappear.

"It is a little creepy, isn't it?" Josh pondered, and Tucker managed a weak grin.

"You should try living next to it," he said.

And finally they came to the bend in the road. Tucker slowed the truck down so that he didn't rip the transmission out of it, and the road became paved and leveled out considerably.

The dimensional porthole visible from the east side of the road had vanished.

Even though the psychic darkness remained, casting a patina of despair over the entire property, the graveyard appeared much as Josh had probably seen it—disorganized, haphazard, but entirely human and earthbound.

Tucker fought an audible swallow and resisted the temptation to wipe his clammy hands on his jeans.

"Okay, so about a mile down this road, then?" he asked, hoping his voice didn't crack with the excess brightness.

"Yeah, then we'll see the southbound road and we can get back on the highway. How'd she drive on the dirt road, though? Like a dream, right?"

"She was an angel," Tucker said fervently. Because if this truck could deal with that amount of supernatural interference and not self-destruct, it was a *keeper*.

"Yeah, anything newer, with all of that electronic shit that goes into it, usually sort of shorts and dies on that road. I didn't want to tell you about it, because I figured you'd think I was just a crazy yokel, but you gotta know, folks think your place is haunted."

Tucker didn't consider himself a brave man, nor one particularly invested in self-control, but he managed to keep himself from laughing hysterically for the rest of the trip, and he would always be proud of that.

THEY WENT to Auburn for a bigger selection, and by the end of the trip to the hardware store, Tucker had managed to relegate the dimensional porthole to where-the-fuck-ever into the mental column of "home improvement." He was renting a sander, buying floor stain, gloves, chemicals to strip the walls, some paint so he could make the trim in the Chrysanthemum Room gold and orange, to keep the room's original tone, and all of the tools he thought he'd need. By the time he'd finished, he was looking forward to fixing the house up, one room—and one set of ghosts—at a time.

He also threw in a spade and a post-hole digger from sheer instinct, because the graveyard had to be a part of that, right?

Angel had said the property was a portal to the afterlife. His job with Ruth had been to clear the ghosts, and after seeing that graveyard, Tucker could appreciate his urgency in the matter. The graveyard was clogged, like a highway or an artery—or a toilet. Obviously, it was so clogged that even ghosts like Angel, who were self-aware, couldn't find the way home.

Tucker's brain didn't even trip over the concept of a self-aware ghost—but it should have. Because that was what Angel had to be, right? A ghost who knew he was a ghost?

Or was he something else?

It didn't matter. Angel was his helper now, and one of the things he had to help Tucker do was to get the entire back forty of Daisy Place's occupants able to *find their goddamned way home*. He figured that each ghost he cleared would make that portal a little easier to tackle, right?

And if not, well, he was here for the duration. He'd figure something out.

Catharsis was his gift—and maybe in his old life, it had meant getting close to people and helping them find a new way through their life. Apparently here, where there were more ghosts than live people, catharsis was still his gift. But his karmic mission had changed to helping the spirits on their way.

Whatever. As long as he didn't have to sleep with the ghosts of old prospectors, he was going to call it a win.

JOSH WAS good company through the store, telling him what he'd need for the projects and how much of something to buy. He even offered to lend Tucker a floor sander, which Tucker took him up on just so he'd have a reason to reconnect. By the time they were done, it was twelve o'clock, and Tucker stopped by a sandwich place so Josh could bring food home for his wife.

"She's a local artist," Josh said proudly. "Three stores on the boardwalk sell her jewelry, and four in Auburn—she's real popular. And it sounds like she could create her own hours, right? But she really can't. She's got orders to fill, so she needs to get shit done." Josh worked at a car dealership in Auburn, fixing up the old ones that the new guys with their electronics couldn't handle, and he was just as happy to find someone to chat with on his day off.

"Well, it's nice of you to help her with lunch," Tucker said, because that was the sort of thing you were supposed to say to married people.

Josh shrugged. "Well, she promised me that if I could get out of her hair and feed her, we could have afternoon sex, since the kids are all off with their friends. Not only that, but if you're writing me a check for the truck, we can go out tomorrow night. You know, the things you do to keep the marriage happy!"

Tucker had to laugh because, as far as he knew, no-body had ever been that frank about it. "I really didn't know," he said honestly. "But I'm always open for tips and information."

Josh cocked his head as they were standing in line, the big dolly behind them loaded up with everything from a stepladder to paint rollers. "Why is it that you haven't found someone?" he asked curiously. "I mean, I know not everybody gets married when they're twen-ty, but you're not a bad-looking guy. You're bound to get lucky sometime, right?"

Tucker grunted, appreciating his equal-opportunity approach to matching Tucker up with a companion and then wondered how much of a chance to take with him.

"Josh, you know how you didn't want to tell me about how car electronics short out and die on the east road to my property?"

Josh looked around the hardware store casually, as though wondering who was going to hear. When it appeared *nobody* was listening, because the clerk was bored shitless ringing up lightbulbs for the person in front of them and everybody else was just too damned hot to give a shit about anything but getting home and doing home improvement—or leaving it until sunset—to actually listen, he nodded.

"Yeah, I know."

"Well, the reason I don't have a boyfriend or a girl-friend is something like that."

Josh laughed. "Does this have anything to do with living in a haunted house?"

"You actually think it is?" Apparently he hadn't been kidding before—Tucker was a little surprised.

"My oldest boy, Andy, he used to deliver groceries there and take care of the lawns. He kept going on about

Ruth's friend Angel that he never got to see. Gave me the creeps, I'm telling you."

Tucker blew out a breath. Okay, so you couldn't *really* hide a giant haunted mansion in a town with less than two thousand people. That was somewhat reassuring. But he had to answer Josh's question. "It's hard to explain. But it's like that graveyard—whatever's going on, it doesn't happen often in nature."

Josh looked perplexed for a moment; then he grinned. "So you got the magic clap, right? You have sex and your wang shoots green lightning, and the person you're with turns into a frog."

Tucker could barely stop laughing to have the clerk ring up his purchases. By the time they emerged from the hardware store, he had a peculiar sense of lightness in his chest.

It wasn't until after he'd followed Josh's instructions down past Todd Valley to a decently sized, sprawling, *non*suburban house that he started to get a clue as to why he could breathe.

Josh's wife stepped out to meet them.

Between the ride through the graveyard and getting the sandwiches, Tucker had heard enough about the Greenaways to feel like he'd known them all his life, and Rae was almost exactly what Tucker expected. She had a broad face and curly hair that escaped rubber band and scrunchy. Her brown eyes looked out at the world with a sort of wry and gentle skepticism that was possibly what happened when you were raising four children.

Josh had told Tucker that their oldest, Andy, was twenty-two, trying to find a way to go to college in Sac, where the rent was appalling and he could only work part-time, and his younger three—Tilda, Murphy, and

Coral—seemed to be growing in complementary and completely different directions. To Tucker, it sounded like the couple put a lot of effort into being good parents for a diverse group of kids, and this woman, with her wide hips and her capable hands and a face without makeup, looked like she was strong and whimsical enough to do that.

Rae welcomed them into a house that looked like a hurricane had hit it and sat them down at a cluttered kitchen table without shame. To the left of the table, up against a big bay window that faced the front yard, a work desk dominated most of the kitchen. Tucker studied it for a second, seeing three-dimensional sketches of curious shapes, embellished by the occasional jewel, twining sinuously into what could easily be a pendant or an earring.

"Pretty," he said, captured by the lines of the drawings, the glittering display of finished products lining the back wall.

"Yeah, pagan, Viking, Enochian—you name the symbol, I've researched it and put a jewel on it." Rae gave him a grand gesture. "Take a look while I clear the table."

Tucker moved closer to the desk, and unbidden, his hand raised to about six inches from the pendants suspended from a corkboard on the wall next to the window.

He could feel the energy radiating from them—fertile energy, energy for strength, energy for…. "Oh…."

The pendant was a simple silver pentagram, locked inside a circle, with a blood-red garnet cut for the center.

He held his hand out a little closer, and the pendant gravitated toward him, tugging against the chain until it was about six inches from the wall.

"You can have that one," Rae said, not sounding put out at all.

Tucker glanced over his shoulder. From where she stood, Rae could see very well that her jewelry was arching off the pegboard toward him. "How much?" he asked, respectful of her livelihood. The thing hummed as it reached for his flesh, and he felt the pull in his chest. Oh... oh, something inside him needed this. Needed it so much.

"Take it," she ordered.

Tucker jumped, and the pendant did too, right off the corkboard and into his hand... where it burned. Tucker shoved it in his pocket and scowled at the red scorch mark across his palm.

"Took you long enough," Rae said mildly, putting milk and glasses on the table.

"Thank you?" Tucker offered.

She shrugged. "You don't work with symbols and not have some odd things happen from time to time. It's a symbol of protection, and it's yours, that's all. Josh, could you have taken any longer with these sandwiches?"

"Well, we went to the hardware store," Josh replied, having apparently missed out on all the floating jewelry. "Tucker here needed to be introduced to the town."

"The town is so small, you sneeze and you miss it." Rae laughed. "You had to take him to Auburn, didn't you?"

Josh shrugged. "Well, yeah. He's trying to clean the old place up and restore some of it. He needs more than a couple of screws and a wrench."

Rae eyed her husband with exasperation. "Well, so do I, but sometimes that's all a girl gets when she's gotten rid of her kids for the day."

Tucker laughed. "I really can go—"

Rae shook her head. "Sit down. We need to eat and digest. My jewelry likes you, and I have to admit, I'm really curious. But since you know what we're going to do afterward, you know…." She looked at him meaningfully, and Tucker fell a little in love.

"Don't linger," he said.

"Don't linger," she agreed. "So, are you gay?"

Tucker almost choked on his sandwich. "Bi." He looked at Josh, with his openly friendly shirt. "Do you know someone who is gay that you're trying to set up?" he speculated—although he was pretty sure he knew who it was.

"Andy," Rae confirmed through a mouthful of sandwich. "Our oldest. He keeps thinking he's going to find someone in this one-horse burgh, and we keep telling him he really needs to go to school in Sac, because it's just not happening here. But you seem okay with Josh and his shirt of loud politics—"

"I'm being supportive," Josh said with dignity.

"You're being an asshole. You hope people will get in your face so you can argue with them," Rae replied.

Josh shrugged and nodded. "That's fair. But still—"

"Still, the point is, I was just asking him so we could see if Andy had a chance."

Tucker had to laugh. "Uhm, no. I'm thirty-four. Twenty-two is officially too young for me." It wasn't really, but it made a convenient excuse. The idea of being set up with these nice people's kid made Tucker feel decidedly odd. And of course, Tucker wasn't into dating.

"Damn," Josh muttered. "That kid is going to be a virgin forever."

"Well, my virginity is going to grow back," Rae muttered sourly. "Me and my boy can be spinsters together."

"You guys are, uh, really involved with your children," Tucker said, not even *trying* not to laugh.

"We thought I couldn't have any," Rae said after a moment. "It took us… three years? Something. Before I got pregnant with Andy. But we don't take them for granted."

Oh. Emotional honesty. Tucker needed to reciprocate.

"My folks died when I was seventeen," he said baldly, keeping the part about how confused he'd been, since it had been then that truly glitchy part of his gift had manifested. God, he wished his mother could have guided him. She'd been so supportive of everything he'd ever done. "You just keep interfering with their lives. They need to appreciate you."

"Aw, hon." Rae put her hand on Tucker's. "You're a sweetheart. Josh didn't tell me—what do you do for a living?"

And here was the part where he lost them. Damn.

"Well, my degree is in history, literature, old languages, folklore, and comparative religions," Tucker said brightly. "So mostly I live on my inheritance and read."

Josh chortled, but Rae tilted her head, chewing the last of her lunch as she did so. "That's not the whole truth," she muttered. "You have an angel on your shoulder, telling you what to do."

While Tucker gaped and floundered for words, he saw Josh looking at the clock for the third time in five minutes and decided that was his cue.

Somebody wanted to get laid, and Tucker was a third wheel.

"That's my signal to leave, isn't it?" he asked, finishing his sandwich off with an easy smile.

"Sure, hon," Rae said, standing and taking their trash to the can under the sink. "That's considerate of you—but don't think we don't want you back someday when we *don't* have a date." She winked at her husband as she washed her hands and then moved to let Tucker do the same. "In fact, I think you should make it a point to call us up before the week is out."

"Hey!" Josh said quickly. "We need to give him directions to Margie's. He wants a cat!"

Tucker dried his hands on the offered towel and thanked Josh gratefully. Suddenly, the idea of a pet and neighbors who knew and liked him sounded like the ultimate in luxury.

"I do indeed."

Rae tilted her head again, regarding him steadily. "You're here in time for one of Margie's kittens. That is interesting."

"Rae Anne!" Josh growled, and his wife actually waved him off.

"They're spooky-assed kittens, Josh. He's going to notice."

Whatever. How spooky could a kitten be? "I promise, it won't put me off," Tucker vowed. "But I need directions first."

A few minutes later, Tucker bid the couple a cheerful goodbye as he started his newly purchased truck. He paused before he backed out and pulled the pentagram out of his pocket, where it was starting to burn uncomfortably. With care, and a wink in Rae's direction, he laced it over the rearview mirror, hoping the spell of protection would work on the truck instead of making Tucker's skin burn through his 501s.

Rae nodded, and Tucker backed out, wondering about the symbol and its sudden decision to jump ship off its happy little corkboard. Protection—wasn't that what pentagrams did? Well, Tucker always needed more, right?

"You look happy," Angel said, taking a seat next to him as soon as he cleared the driveway.

"Augh!" Tucker had to work really hard not to wreck the truck. "God, Angel, could you at least warn a guy? How do you do that, anyway?"

"I don't know," Angel said vaguely. "It's fuzzy. I didn't used to be able to go off the property when Ruth was there, but I can with you—but only you. That is so weird."

Tucker waited to turn right on 49, always a challenge because there seemed to be more cars on it than someone would expect for a town of less than two thousand.

"Yeah, everything about this situation is weird. But yes, I look happy."

"Why?" Angel asked, sounding a little tentative and half afraid.

"Well, if you want to know the truth, I might have a chance to have friends." It was perfect, actually. Life was informal around here. If Tucker got invited to dinner and felt the pull instead, he could politely decline and ask them over the next day.

"Why couldn't you have friends before?" Angel asked. "You're not like Ruth. She saw ghosts *all the time*, not just at Daisy Place. If she tried to leave for a long period of time, she'd come home more exhausted than when she left."

Tucker frowned. "I see them sometimes—enough that it's common, not enough that I can't take a crap." His first playmate had been a ghost, a little girl who had died in his parents' house nearly fifty years before Tucker had come along. He remembered that about the time he hit puberty, playing with her had become a chore, like playing with a little brother or sister. "I wonder if it's an effect of living at the mansion."

"What were you thinking?" Angel asked, sounding puzzled. His new form didn't look like the sensitive type—Tucker wondered at the contrast.

"I was thinking about my first ghost," Tucker said. "I... I was stupid. I got too old to play."

"What does that mean?"

Tucker grunted. "It's like when you have a little brother or sister, you know? You think you're too old or too cool to play with them and make a big deal about how they owe you. But she was trapped there, and I was her only company, and one day she just...." He rubbed his cheek, and he could almost feel the cool touch of her gentle, understanding kiss. "She said it was okay, I could grow up, and that it was time for her to go see her parents anyway." He'd watched, helpless and miserable, as she'd faded into thin air for the final time. He'd missed her acutely after that, not quite as grown up as he'd thought he was.

"This memory makes you sad," Angel said, sounding puzzled.

"I hurt her feelings," Tucker muttered. *Jeez, ya baby. Do you think all I have to do with my day is stay here and play dolls?* God, were all thirteen-year-old boys assholes? "It wasn't very nice of me." It was maybe his first real lesson in how careful you had to be with human feelings and the supernatural world. Too bad he hadn't learned.

"I've done that," Angel said, and now *he* sounded sad. "It's a hard lesson to learn."

Tucker eyed him sourly. "What are you doing here, Angel? I actually had sort of a good day."

"Are you going to get a cat?" Angel asked curiously.

"It's on the list." Tucker had been planning on visiting a shelter before Josh told them about their friend.

"May I help?"

Tucker had to remember to close his mouth. "That's unexpected."

"It's just," Angel said with dignity, "that I don't know what my presence will do to an animal. You need to find one that…." He floundered, and his broad hands gestured as he tried to find words.

"Likes you?" Tucker supplied, semiamused.

"For lack of a better word." Angel let out a breath—which should have been impossible, but Tucker could almost feel the breeze of it when he turned his head. "We need to find an animal that the presence of the supernatural does not torture."

Oh hell—he had a point. "Cats are pretty savvy to you guys in between worlds, aren't they? I mean, that might be a problem."

Angel turned a winning smile toward him, and Tucker couldn't help but notice that the redhead he was wearing today was handsome and capable, and his smile looked like sexy sin.

Again, it was unexpected.

"We will hope," Angel said, like he was speaking to a child.

Well, Tucker suddenly really hoped he was right, so there was no argument coming from that direction.

But there *was* another subject at hand.

"So we hope. Sort of like we hope the dimensional void over the graveyard doesn't swallow up the house?"

"You saw that," Angel said in the same tone someone *living* might have said, "You saw the stain on the carpet," or "You saw I ate the last of the cake from your birthday party."

"Yes, I saw that! What in the hell is it doing there?" And more importantly, "Did Aunt Ruth know?"

"No," Angel said with a sigh. "It didn't start getting bad until she was bedridden and couldn't release souls anymore—"

"That's bullshit," Tucker said. "The locals have been watching it get worse for more than thirty years."

Angel gasped. "Really?"

Tucker risked a look at him and saw real alarm. "You don't go look?"

"I've been busy," Angel said defensively. Then he sighed. "And it scares me. So many souls, and I can't do a thing for them. It's unpleasant."

"Will bad things happen if *I* go there?" Not that Tucker wanted to go there—not really. The lurid green-lit prospector wasn't going to leave his inner eye alone anytime soon.

"I don't know." Cold seeped through Tucker's T-shirt, and when he looked, he saw Angel resting his hand on Tucker's bicep, as unselfconsciously and as naturally as any human. Any good-looking, fascinating human. "Please don't, Tucker. Let's just do our job for a while and see if it gets better."

Tucker sighed. "Yeah, sure. Wait—is that Tornado Alley?" He stopped for a second and laughed. "That's really sick."

"What's sick?"

They'd come to a small trailer park—the kind with the really big, fancy, well-appointed trailers that had more square footage than most permanent homes.

"Naming this place Tornado Alley when it's in the middle of the woods. Not even flatland woods, but mountain woods."

"Tornadoes don't hit the mountains?"

Tucker brought the truck to a stop in the driveway of 1313 Tornado Alley and turned around to study Angel before killing the ignition. "There's too much disruption to the air flow up here. When were you born, Angel? Most kids get that sort of thing in school. Or on TV. Or on computers?"

"I was in Daisy Place when your aunt was around fifteen years old," Angel answered, returning Tucker's look levelly. "She only recently got the internet and cable."

His image flickered, and when he came back, his lower lip was fuller and his chin just a little more square.

Between that and the limpid green eyes, Tucker was remembering what it was like to have a choice in who he crushed on, something he hadn't believed in since he was seventeen.

He turned toward the trailer with an effort, wondering if Angel had chosen that form deliberately to dick with him.

"Wow. This woman never met a wind chime she didn't like," he said, the awe completely legitimate.

"They're pretty," Angel defended, sounding dignified.

"They're chaos," Tucker contradicted grimly. He shivered, remembering the sound in his head as he'd held... as he'd held.... "Bad memories."

Angel frowned at him. "How could you have bad memories of wind chimes?"

The side door of the trailer opened, and Tucker hushed him. He didn't want to talk about that.

The woman who came out was in her early fifties, slender, vital, with recently dyed hair pulled back into a ponytail. She wore sporty little capri jeans and a tank top, the sort of outfit that would have done Laura Petrie proud.

"Hi. Are you here about the kittens?" She smiled, and Tucker had a sudden yearning for his own mother. She'd been like this—cute, hip, friendly—the kind of woman who didn't seem to age because she didn't let herself get old.

"Yeah, did Rae Greenaway call?" Tucker could easily see the two women being friends.

"She did indeed. But she didn't tell me there'd be two of you. I'm Margie Miller, so pleased to meet you."

Tucker barely managed to shake her hand.

He and Angel gaped at each other for a moment, and then Margie turned back toward the stairs. "Come along. They're all in the playpen right now. You can see which one you want."

SEEN

"UH, SURE," Angel said after a quick glance at Tucker, who shrugged. "How many kittens are there?"

"Seven—a lucky number. You two are the first to come by, but they're more than weaned and ready to go home." She looked over her shoulder at Tucker. "Mr. Henderson?"

"Yes, ma'am," Tucker said, that hint of infatuation Angel had seen in his eyes when he looked at the woman present in his voice. Tucker seemed to have an affinity for this woman. For a moment Angel's temper flared—dammit, Tucker seemed to have affinity for everybody *except* Angel, but as Angel took a breath (a *breath*), he reminded himself that sometimes affinity wasn't sexual. This woman could see Angel. Maybe they were simply resonating as people who could see the supernatural.

"Rae told me you bought some pet supplies at the hardware store. You *did* remember food, didn't you?"

"Yes, ma'am," Tucker confirmed, darting a glance at Angel. "Kitten food."

"Good. Kittens need food, comfort, and a bed, hopefully near their human. And they need to be fixed." She scowled, and it was not Angel's imagination—the woman's sharp brown eyes took them both in. "This mama just wandered in, but usually I get all my cats fixed immediately, you understand?"

"Yes, ma'am," Angel said in reflex, and she seemed to be fine with that.

Still, Tucker took the lead up the small flight of stairs to the landing, and he made sure to hold the door open so Angel could walk over the threshold without walking through the door itself.

And straight into heaven.

"Oh dear," he said, his heart sort of exploding. Seven of them? Had she really said seven? They were adorable, frolicking, sleeping, purring little puffballs, all of them as excited about being alive as Angel had ever seen another being.

He was not aware of sitting down in front of the pen and staring longingly at the little creatures, but when Tucker sank down with a little thump beside him, he could not guard his heart.

"Oh, Tucker," he whispered in awe. "They're *beautiful*. What a marvelous idea. Are we really going to bring one home?"

Tucker's lips curved up wryly. "Yeah," he said, and the word was gentle.

"Go ahead," Margie told them. "I'll go get you two some iced tea—it's hot out there! You stay here and pet kittens."

Margie practically danced into a kitchen that, all told, was as large as the one in Daisy Place, which was saying something. Tucker and Angel were left to pet kittens and try to figure out how to not give away the fact that she was looking at a ghost.

"Here," Tucker said after a couple of awkward moments where the two of them looked at her over their shoulders and then looked at each other. "Let me get one. Any preferences?"

Angel shook his head. They were all equally lovely. Except the particularly squishy little gray one, lying on its side, trying to eat its own feet. Well, he did seem to be just a tiny bit… more special than the others.

"This one," Tucker said promptly, picking up the foot-eating wonder. "I can see you gazing at him longingly." Tucker picked the cat up with an unanticipated gentleness, and Angel was caught between looking at the cat as it melted into Tucker's capable hands and looking at Tucker's capable hands.

"Hello," Tucker mumbled, burying his face in the kitten's ruff. The kitten played with his fingers and then gave it up and tried to eat its feet again.

"Look at its paws," Angel mumbled, scooting into Tucker's space and running a finger along the smooth pink of the kitten's paw pads. "They look like squishy little beans."

The kitten lifted a paw and batted at Angel's finger, and Angel batted back, fascinated. Its fur was soft—so soft—and Angel could *feel it* against the backs of his knuckles. He gave a little yelp when the kitten sank its teeth into the pad of his thumb.

And then he rocked back on his heels, locked eyes with Tucker, and gasped.

"Angel…," Tucker breathed, "what was that?"

"He bit me," Angel said, half laughing. "It hurt."

"But you are a"—his voice dropped—"*ghost*. How did that happen?"

Angel thought carefully to make sure he told the truth. "I have no idea. I am not supposed to be corporeal."

The kitten, unimpressed with their great and existential matters, started kicking at Tucker's wrist, catching it with his back paws.

"Easy there, Squishbeans," he said, holding the kitten up to his face. Tentatively, Squishbeans patted his nose, and Tucker smiled. Then he looked at Angel with consideration and held the kitten up to *Angel's* face. The kitten's cool little paw hit his nose with a tiny barefoot sound.

Angel gasped and then blew a cool stream of air across the kitten's nose.

Squishbeans closed his eyes and let the breath fan its whiskers.

"This," said Angel, "is very interesting."

"It's not interesting, son—it's a kitten!" Margie laughed as she came back in, a tray of iced tea in her hands.

Angel risked looking up into her eyes. He saw nothing but a warm smile and a somewhat motherly woman fussing with iced tea.

"It's a lovely kitten," he said formally. "Tucker, is this the one you want?"

"Possibly," Tucker said, pulling Squishbeans into his lap. "But I think I shall have to pet every one." He looked meaningfully at Angel, and for the first time, Angel got the hint. Angel needed to pet *every* kitten to see if they all reacted to his presence like that.

"I'll do the honors," Angel said, reaching into the pen.

He didn't try to pick them up—mostly he just chased them around, because no, the kittens did *not* like his presence. He could feel them batting at his hand, but when they didn't connect, they'd hiss and go pounce on the next kitten down the line.

"You're stirring them up," Tucker said, his voice quiet. Squishbeans was still in the crook of his arm, purring.

"We know the one we want anyway," Angel agreed, something swelling in his chest, sweet and piercing.

And then he saw it, the slight quirk of disappointment in the corner of Tucker's mobile mouth.

"I'm sorry," Angel said, suddenly not mindful of Margie in the least. "This was supposed to be a thing for you, and it turned into a thing for me. That wasn't supposed to—"

Tucker winked and hugged the kitten even closer. Squishbeans started to purr so loudly Angel could hear him from four feet away. "It's a thing for both of us. We're roommates. It's okay."

"That's roommates in the code way, right?" Margie said, breaking the intimacy that had fallen over them.

Angel blinked at her. "What does that mean?"

"She's asking if we're lovers," Tucker said dryly. "And sorry, Margie, but we just coexist together in Daisy Place. Angel is there to sort of clean the place out, and I'm going to fix it up when he's done."

"Oh." Margie's mouth drooped. "Well, that's too bad. You're perfect for each other. But I suppose you could be good for Josh's son, Andover."

"*Andy*!" Tucker sputtered. He reached above to the coffee table for one of the glasses of iced tea so he could take a hasty sip and compose himself.

"This surprises you?" she asked. "Don't tell me you're one of those horrible bigots who thinks that's awful."

"No, I'm just not used to being set up with my friend's kids. Besides, his parents already mentioned the possibility, but he's too young for me. And I didn't know his name was Andover—that was definitely a surprise."

"So you *are* gay?" she asked—not as though she were prying but simply clarifying.

"I swing a lot of ways," Tucker replied playfully, and Angel could tell he was back on his stride again. It was interesting, the way he recoiled from the idea of being matched with someone, but he didn't mind talking about his sexuality.

"What's your favorite way?" Margie asked, bantering more than invading.

"Hm...." Tucker gazed thoughtfully into space while letting Squishbeans abuse his fingertips again. "I think it's slow. Slow is my favorite way. But I have nothing against fast and hard either. So, you know, lots of ways to swing."

Margie burst into a peal of delighted laughter. "That's marvelous. How about you... I'm sorry, I didn't catch your name?"

"Angel," he replied promptly, trying to think of a way to answer the question honestly. "And I swing the right way with whoever might be there at the time. That's how I swing."

Margie laughed at that one too, and urged iced tea on him.

"I'm sorry," he said regretfully, trying to decide how to deal with this one. "I'm just not a fan of tea." As far as he knew.

"Well, you've made me laugh, and I think you're taking one of my babies off my hands. I think I can forgive you."

"That's kind," he said, meaning it. "And we're really grateful for the kitten." He looked around the pen, frowning. "Where's the mother cat?"

"Well," Margie said, leaning forward. "It was the oddest thing. The mama cat showed up on my doorstep all skin and bones. She looked all the way dead, not half-dead. If she hadn't been walking in on her own power, I would have buried her. But she came in the house, found a towel on the floor in the washroom, and curled up there, hissing, at about eleven o'clock at night. I just figured she'd either die during the night or leave in the morning."

"She didn't?" Angel asked, fascinated.

"Well, she died—but first she had a litter of kittens. I got up that morning and there were seven kittens trying to nurse from a cat that was damned near decomposing." Margie shuddered. "Creepiest thing I ever saw. I buried the cat under a bush in my backyard, and you know, I think the bush is dying. But the kittens were just as happy and as lively as anything I've ever seen. I think I'm going to keep the last two, because they *are* such good company. And I hand-fed them, you know? I hate to see them go."

"I bet," Tucker said. Angel glanced over and saw he was holding Squishbeans up and examining him thoroughly, as though looking for something most kittens wouldn't have. "So, uh, Margie, do you have any idea where this cat came from? I mean, did anybody in town remember seeing her?"

Margie shrugged. "Well, I told old Bill up at the grocery store about her—I had to, he was the only one who carried kitten formula, and I was desperate. He said he'd seen a clowder up right by your house, Tucker. You know, by the turnout where the old graveyard is?"

Tucker caught his breath and looked at Squishbeans again. Squishbeans responded by trying to eat his (her?) tail, and Angel shrugged. Well, maybe it *was* a graveyard cat, but like the other kittens, it saw him, responded to him, although only this one seemed to think he was a decent fellow.

It was like Angel's dream request for a cat—except Tucker had been the one to wake up with the sudden need.

Angel cocked his head at Tucker, who ignored him and continued to banter with Margie.

Roommates. But she'd asked them if they were lovers.

Angel didn't know what this feeling was in his stomach, but he *did* know that being Tucker Henderson's lover would have more benefits than just a fluffy gray kitten named Squishbeans.

They spent a pleasant hour there. Margie was warm and funny, and she talked occasionally about her children—a daughter in San Diego, a son in Portland—but she also talked about the townspeople in Foresthill. She owned one of the boutiques where Rae sold her jewelry, and Tucker seemed to enjoy letting her ramble and gossip. He kept his head cocked and a slight smile on his face while Squishbeans maintained a perma-cuddle in his arms, and Angel got the feeling he was soaking up the human contact—and the discussion of other humans—like a flower in a drought soaked up water.

Finally, though, Tucker finished both their iced teas and then stood gracefully. He stretched, careful not to disturb the kitten in his arms, and offered his hand to Margie.

"Thank you for a lovely afternoon, milady."

"Anytime, young sir. If you and your 'room-mate' ever wish to come by just to visit, you are very welcome."

Angel frowned to himself as he followed Tucker out. "Why doesn't she believe we're just roommates?" he asked, thinking they were out of earshot.

"It's in your eyes, Angel!" Margie called out. "Stop looking at him like that."

Tucker startled and looked at him, and Angel studiously looked away. Behind them, Margie burst into a delighted cackle of laughter, and then Tucker got in the truck, saying loudly, "Let me get the door—it sticks."

Angel stood obediently and then made a show of climbing into the cab while Tucker reached across him and slammed it shut.

Then Tucker put Squishbeans on the seat between them and looked at him apprehensively. "Is he going to stay there, you think? Because I *didn't* bring a crate, and you *can't*…. Seriously?"

Oh…. Angel could *touch* him. The cat curled into his cupped hands with the ultimate of trust, and Angel gathered it to his chest and let that purr vibrate through his incorporeal body.

"Damn," Tucker said, blinking hard. "That's… that's really fucking weird."

A peace Angel had never known emanated from his soul. "Tucker, this cat… this cat was the *best* idea. I've *never* felt about *anything* the way I feel about this cat."

Then Angel remembered that bittersweet look on Tucker's face when he'd been holding the cat while sitting on Margie's carpet. "Is that bad?" he asked, hoping not, because that might ruin it. "Do you want to go in and get a cat that's just for Tucker?"

Tucker reached across the seat and ran a finger down the cat's nose. "Naw, Angel. We might as well share this one. I do not know the deal with these grave-yard zombie baby cats, but this one here seems to have been tailor-made for you."

Angel's feeling of well-being remained, but he was able to disengage his mind from it for a little. "That was a *very* strange story," he said, searching his memory and intuition. "Do you think the cats are evil?"

Squishbeans purred some more, and Angel hunched his shoulders around it—wait. Her. Angel wasn't sure how he knew, but he knew. Her.

"I doubt it," Tucker said, rubbing his chest. "At least *that's* explained."

"What's explained?"

"The sudden urge I had to get a cat. It really *wasn't* for me." He sighed a little. "But that's not a bad thing either. I saw some curry and coconut milk in the grocer-ies you bought. Thai chicken, here I come!"

Angel managed to fully pull himself away from Squishbeans. "You'll find something," he said quietly. "Something yours."

Tucker's mouth twisted a little. "Are you kidding? I've got my own pet ghost and a cat who can move through dimensional space. And Thai food. I'm good."

But Angel heard the bitter covered up by the bright. *He's not, Squishbeans. There's something in him so hurt he's trying to forget it by keeping busy with food or projects or cats.*

"Will you be missed back in Sacramento?" Angel asked.

"Well, it's only an hour down the road," Tucker said, shrugging. "And no. Most of my college friends drifted away after school. I don't work, so, you know.

No work friends. The folks at the gym might, but they're used to people dropping out all the time. The bookstore maybe?"

Angel frowned. "Why didn't you work?"

"For the same reason Aunt Ruth didn't work," Tucker said shortly. "And the same reason graveyard cats are born just in time for you to get one. The same reason I just *had* to get up this morning and get a truck and supplies and a cat."

Oh. "None of these things are coincidental," Angel hazarded. "And your aunt Ruth didn't work because the things she did with her talent were necessary."

Tucker touched his nose, and then, before Angel could ask the obvious question, said, "Hey—there's the turnout for Daisy Place. Do you think I should pull all the way up to the side of the house?"

Angel shook his head—he knew this one. "See how the driveway slopes up and then levels off? And then turns into the garage, with the paved space in front of the house?"

"I do. I thought I'd—"

"The property line—the one that's marked with all that metal—starts at the line of the slope. If you park on that level place, you're good, but if you turn right to sit next to the house or, heaven forbid, try to park in the garage—"

"The car starts having problems," Tucker deduced. "I see. Well, good point. Thank you. So why do the internet and cable—"

"I have no idea," Angel said shortly. "I think it was to make me look bad in front of your aunt, but that's just supposition."

Tucker's gurgle of laughter startled him. "You were against it."

Angel scowled. "It should have been a disaster. It wasn't. I was glad for her, and *very* glad for you, but nothing about Daisy Place points to something so obviously technology-based surviving."

"Hm." It was a pondering sound, and Angel waited. "So we need to add the graveyard, the ghost cats, and Margie, who can see you, to our list of... quirks. And we still have ghosts that need clearing out. I say we stay focused on the ghosts." He waggled his eyebrows lasciviously. "Because finding that bottle led to one of the best moments I've had in a *while*."

Angel's jaw tightened, and he had to make a conscious effort not to transfer some of the pressure to the kitten. *I doubt that, Squishbeans.* "You could always date your friend's son, Andover."

And like that, Tucker's forced ebullience fell flat and leaden in the front seat of the truck.

"I don't date," he said, voice cold and still. "It's bad for everybody."

"But that young lady—" Angel was so confused.

"Let's just say that's how my talent works, okay?"

It had been such a good day—with the kittens, with the friend who could see Angel, with the conversation that hadn't seemed to hurt—Angel didn't push it.

"Okay," Angel said. He was still confused, but Tucker's anger seemed to lighten a little. Squishbeans went back to being the center of the universe once more.

GHOSTBUSTING A NUT

DINNER WAS *great*, and Tucker made extra so he could have some the next day. He decided that home improvement should probably wait until the morning, but he was determined to have another crack at the room.

"You could always take a rest," Angel said. He was still carrying the cat, and Tucker was still wondering how that was possible.

He hadn't wanted to make too big a deal out of it, but the timing seemed very suspicious. So did the zombie ghost cat giving birth. He loved the kitten—not even Tucker was that hard-hearted—but he could still remember that urge to go get a cat.

It was the same urge that had propelled him to get a truck, to meet Josh and Rae, to meet Margie, who could see Angel, and to go get a cat that was, apparently, the best thing to happen to Angel since he'd gotten trapped here at Daisy Place—something he still wouldn't talk about.

Tucker had picked up Squishbeans, and he'd felt the little *pop* in his chest, the one he usually felt when he was sitting across from a girl or a boy he was about to do the wild thing with.

Making conversation with Margie had been one of the hardest things he'd ever done after that. A part of him was trying to get over feeling used—the karmic forces had actually driven him into the world at large to find a cat for Angel.

A cat.

But a part of him was *relieved*. It was a *relief* to know that those forces he'd served all these years, the forces that had pretty much ruined his life—*those* karmic forces—were actually capable of compassion in a wholly nonsexual way.

For the cost of some cat litter, Tucker'd had his faith renewed.

But that did *not* mean he was ready to rest on his laurels. It was time to empty some drawers, to strip some wallpaper, and to see what was under the bed.

Except he might want to wait until Angel was ready to set down the kitten, because it was important they both be on task.

"Do I have to?" Angel asked plaintively. "It's a big house. She could get lost." This form, with the narrow green eyes and the reddish hair, looked way too tough for the vulnerable curve of his lips. For whatever reason, Angel could *touch* this animal—and after fifty-five years of being a disembodied ghost or whatever, Tucker would probably not want to give that up either. Okay, fine. Tucker sighed and tried not to be a driven asshole now that Angel had given up the role.

"Tell you what. You hang out on the bed with the kitten, and when I need you, you put her down and come do your thing."

"Why put her down?" Angel asked suspiciously.

"Angel, do you really want her to feel what we do when we hit something bad?"

The dismay on his face was sort of heartening. So Angel *could* be human, and not just in a charming, "Oh, this is new and wonderful!" way. Compassion was something Tucker believed in very much.

"No," Angel whispered, stroking the cat's whiskers. Squishbeans purred, and Tucker secretly plotted how to get the kitten away from Angel so he could have her in his bed. For one thing, she was warm. For another, that purr was pure comfort.

"Okay. Now set her down, and let's clean out that drawer."

Angel did as he asked, looking thoughtful. "Do you want all the stuff in the drawer, or do you just want the things that pertain to the women and their adventure?"

Tucker had read enough mystery suspense novels to know this one. "Everything," he said grimly. "You never know what's going to come in handy later."

Oh, he'd learn to regret those words.

For one thing, the stuff in the drawer, put there for whatever reason, was sometimes the most boring stuff in the world.

"The hole punch almost stopped my heart with mundanity," Tucker said with a yawn. "I want you to know that. If I die in my sleep, it's because I had a dream where I had to use that thing again and again and again and again and again and again, and I bored myself to death *while I was asleep*."

"Yes," Angel agreed, "but it was better than the snuff box."

They both shuddered. The silver snuff box seemed so innocent, sitting there in the corner of the protected drawer. But Angel had reached in to touch it and gasped, saying, "No, Tucker, don't—" just as Tucker had reached in to bring it to light.

Tucker had forgotten to cover his hand with his T-shirt, and they were both touching the object when wave upon wave of violence, hostility, and a pathological hatred poured into their souls. Tucker could only identify the source as male, and every use of the box had been tainted with addiction.

"Not snuff," Tucker gasped when they'd managed to let go. "That was *not* snuff he was snorting!"

"No, it wasn't." Angel let out a little whimper and drifted back to the bed, and Tucker let him.

"Well, now we know what it's like to be addicted to cocaine when you're crazy as a shithouse rat *and a* horrible person."

"That was a *bad man*!" Angel burst out. "How could such evil… oh, Tucker. I don't want to touch that man again!"

Tucker eyed him with compassion. "You didn't get a lot of those?" he asked quietly.

Angel shook his head. "We got some people who were unpleasant," he admitted. "But… but I liked Ruth. And she was so sweet, so fragile at the beginning. And then she got stronger, and I realized how she was imprisoned here, and—"

"You saved her," Tucker said, sinking onto the bed next to him and running his hand through his sopping nest of hair. His whole body was still shaking in reaction. "You tried to keep her from the worst of it."

Angel grimaced and held his hand out for the kitten in an obvious bid for comfort. "I didn't realize I'd be saving it for someone else. It just all seemed so unfair."

Tucker's mouth twisted, and he hated that this was the expression he was giving Angel, but it was all he had. "That's the truth. Are we going to have to tell that guy's story too?"

Angel regarded the kitten sadly, holding his fingers up to get her to play. "Yes," he said. "But he seems to be connected with this room too. Maybe if we tell the story of the women—"

"Well yeah—that's why I said check everything, remember?"

Some of Angel's dispiritedness faded. "You're very smart," he said, and the sincere admiration in his voice made Tucker's stomach turn over.

"I'm not," he said stiffly, putting on the cotton gardening gloves he'd bought that day. "Here—I'm going to put *everything* out on top of the desk, even stuff I find under the bed and in the closets. What we need is a *rating* system. You're going to hover over the thing and give me a scale of one to five. Ones are the hole punch or the letter opener—so boring it almost stops my heart. Fives are the snuff box—so awful it makes me want to stick an ice pick up my nose for a DIY lobotomy. Everything else—"

"Wait!" Angel said, surprising him. "What about the good things?"

"What?"

"You know… the…." Angel blushed. Color actually washed across his face, and a faint sheen of sweat appeared on a forehead that was, for all intents and purposes, a psychic oil painting.

Tucker was so fascinated watching something that shouldn't happen that it took him a moment to realize what Angel was talking about.

And he blushed himself.

"The glass bottle?" he asked, fastening his eyes on the acres of repeating chrysanthemums on the wallpaper.

"Yes. That. That wasn't bad. That was... good."

"Oh yes. Yes, it was." The chrysanthemums were gold and orange and brown and white, with glimpses of green stem and lined in black. The black lines took on a life of their own, writhing sensuously, becoming a buxom woman with blazing red hair, a slender woman with shining gold. They rolled across the wall, laughing, making love, or became flowers with long skirts as their stalks, great hats as their flowers, walking the halls of Daisy Place primly, arm in arm.

Tucker stared at them, fascinated, a sexual flush heating his body in the preternatural cold of the mansion, and tried grimly not to think about the form-shifting ghost playing with a kitten on the bed.

Because he was starting to emanate sex vibes in the worst of ways.

"So do you want those separate?" Angel's voice sounded constricted, and Tucker tore his gaze away from what seemed to be haunted wallpaper and met his eyes.

And gasped.

"Again?" he asked, none of his arousal dissipating.

Angel was a chrysanthemum—a woman—with glossy blond hair and limpid green eyes, wearing a slim green dress that showed generous cleavage at the V of the neck.

"Oh damn!" She sounded both plaintive and surprised. "I was *not* supposed to do that."

Tucker held his hand to his mouth, trying hard not to laugh. "But you've been doing it since I got here. This is my second day, and you've been three people already."

"I'm still the same person," she muttered, white teeth sinking into a tender pink lip. "I just... I was the same form for your aunt for fifty-five years. A teenage boy, sandy hair, green eyes. I have no idea why I can't hold it together around you!" Impatiently she pushed imaginary hair from her eyes and frowned.

"Whatsamatter, Angel? Do you need a cosmic scrunchy?"

Angel glowered at him, her green eyes sparking with irritation. Tucker stared into them, mesmerized. They were the same eyes she'd worn in her last form— bright bottle green that seemed perfect until he saw the little flecks of rust brown in the iris—and Tucker realized that even if they hadn't been the same color, there was something in there, a clear green sort of light that had been in his eyes when he'd been not-Damien and when he'd been the hot young roughneck and here, now, the blowsy blond in the green dress.

"Your eyes," he said softly. "Your eyes are the same."

This Angel had a soft jaw and the beguiling round face of a woman in her early thirties. Her sweet little mouth made a delicate moue. "Yes?"

"Yes," Tucker said, lost in those eyes. He suddenly wanted the hot young roughneck back so he could see if they were as beguiling in a man's form. He remembered Angel's delight at the kitten, his earnestness then, replacing the driven workaholic, and thought that maybe they would be.

"Ouch!" Angel's sharp word broke the spell, and she grimaced at the kitten, who continued to chew on her red-tipped, manicured fingers. "So." She shifted uncomfortably and shook that amazing hair back again. "Do you want a different pile?"

Tucker had to shake himself back into what they'd been talking about, and he squinted at the objects on the desk. Yes, she was right. It didn't matter what shape or gender she wore—they had a job to do.

"Yeah," he said after a moment of sorting objects. A diamond hairpin, a shell from a beach, a cameo brooch, a tortoiseshell comb. He'd hit the jackpot in the delicate dresser near the bed. The dresser itself stood on tall, thin, spiderlike legs, and it held almost entirely women's toiletries. "I'd say these would all be good." He picked up a glass paperweight with dreamlike strands of green winding through the glass and a single bright orange fish. It was large and heavy—bigger than a softball—and it would have been exquisitely beautiful, but a sizable chunk of glass was missing from the bottom. There was also some unpolished glass roughing up the bottom, as though something had been glued or affixed to that part of the weight to make it flat. It had a surprising heft to it—a ten-pound paperweight?—and Tucker couldn't figure out if it was physical or psychic, but he had trouble looking at the weight for more than a moment. His gaze kept shifting off of it, glancing to other things.

"This is bad," he murmured thoughtfully, holding it in two hands. The skin under the gloves got hotter, and the object seemed to get heavier, almost bowling ball heavy, as he stood.

With great deliberation, he put the weight on the far end of the desk, with the snuffbox. Then he put the women's toiletries on the other end, pending Angel's examination. He put the green, uhm, bottle on that end, figuring that would mark the good side, and then put the hole puncher and the pen and the "Oh my God fifty people going potty can you imagine the boredom!" polished wooden dowel from the toilet paper holder in the middle.

"Okay, so how's this?" he said. Angel stood up after one final pass to make sure the kitten would stay and sashayed over to stand next to Tucker. Tucker closed his eyes and inhaled, smelling nothing but imagining flowered body spray in the place of lime and musk.

Either smell turned his key.

"So we've got good, bad, and boring," Angel observed. "I like it. Did you get a glimpse of the man who used the snuff box?"

Tucker shuddered. "Yes. I'd recognize him again if he wandered into someone else's vision."

Angel *hmm*d. "Okay, yes." He began to point so Tucker could sort. "These objects are neutral—I see so many people doing so many things with them that they're useless. This one"—Angel pointed to a mother-of-pearl-handled brush—"is strong both ways. It has conflict, good moments, and bad moments. This one has a story."

Tucker took hold of the brush and then sat on the bed, closing his eyes and getting ready. The kitten licked his thigh through his jeans briefly and then trotted toward the pillow to curl up on the cushion like she belonged there.

Angel came to sit by him, apprehension clear in those wide green eyes.

"Ready?"

"Sure." Very carefully, Tucker pulled off one cotton glove and took the brush in his hand.

BRIDGET STOOD behind Sophie in a richly decorated room in Baltimore, this one with cream-colored wallpaper and mauve brocaded curtains. With clean, methodical strokes, she mastered the thick blond mass of Sophie's hair, and Sophie gazed at her in the mirror with worship.

"You're so good with it, Bridget," she said breathlessly. "I've grown so tired of my head being jerked on, and you're just so tender."

And still the brush slid through the coarse and silken strands with a lulling precision.

Bridget's hands were shaking. Her sex was swollen and aching with desire, but she must not, must not reveal these things to the innocent Sophie, who trusted Bridget as the only human being to talk to her in this strange and vast mansion that Sophie had recently arrived at.

"Ye must not've had much of a ladies' maid if they tugged on yer hair so," Bridget reprimanded. She'd seen how the people of this house treated Sophie—the master was cold to her, his wife worse. Their son, Sophie's husband, paid attention in obsessive, uncomfortable flurries and then left for extravagant amounts of time, playing with his mates. Bridget would resent him for that neglect if she hadn't seen the relief in Sophie's eyes whenever the man left.

"Oh, Bridget, I've never had a maid. My father's a pastor in Wilmington. He's a good man, but poor. Pastors are. Thomas's horseless lost a wheel as he was driving by my father's place one day. He made a

hideous row about it—terrorized my father something awful, saying that only a fool would keep his road so poorly it could do that much damage. I brought him some lemonade to take some of his anger from Father, and he thought I was pretty."

She smiled then, tentatively, as though embarrassed, and Bridget readjusted her thinking.

"Ye are pretty, Sophie girl," she said, her voice gentle. Ah, a pastor's child. Ripe for the taking by a rich bastard like Thomas Conklin. Wonderful. Well, Bridget had been her ally since she'd been dragged into the Conklin mansion, practically a child bride. She would continue to be her friend—

Sophie stopped Bridget's ministrations with the brush by bringing her hand up to capture Bridget's. "Do you really think so?" she asked, hope shining in her eyes like tears. "I've heard it from my father and brother, and Thomas and his father—" She shuddered. Master Conklin was a frigid, foreboding figure of a man. "—say it all the time. But...." She bit her lip and glanced shyly in the mirror. "I never really wanted to be pretty until you brushed my hair, looking at me like that."

Bridget tried to shift her hand away. Sophie's touch sent shock waves through her body, but Sophie turned around and clasped the hand—and the brush—to her lips.

Bridget gave up and rubbed her rough, hard-worked thumb along the angel softness of Sophie's cheek.

"Aye," she whispered, her voice rough and low. "I think yer beautiful."

She lowered her head then, thinking to lay a quick kiss on Sophie's brow, but Sophie tipped her head back, her lips soft, ripe, rich red with promise, and Bridget dipped her head just a bit lower....

TUCKER MADE a soft noise, hoping he could see their lips touch, their mouths open, the kiss land, but as he reacted to the vision, it changed.

SOPHIE'S HAND shook, but she continued to brush her hair as she regarded the sinister dark-suited figure in the mirror.

"No," she said, proud of how strong her voice was. "I don't know where Thomas has gone."

"Well, aren't you his wife? Shouldn't you keep better track of him?"

Her heart—fueled by anger—began to beat more steadily and stopped its fearful stuttering. "I am a stranger in a strange house," she said shortly. "I have no resources to find him, and if I wandered around calling his name, I wouldn't be a grown woman, I'd be a terrified child."

She was *a terrified child. The elder Mr. Conklin produced that fear in everybody. Sophie had seen him strike out at servants carrying full trays of food, shattering china and splashing tea all over the ceramic-tiled floors—and the person in question. Mrs. Conklin came down the stairs at least once a week with her face heavily powdered—a mark, a bruise, a split lip buried deep beneath. She rarely went out into the world, and when her face was that heavily powdered, her friends were not allowed to call.*

Bridget told her that the lady had fewer and fewer friends each year.

"Don't be impertinent," Conklin sneered. "You're a country whore, and why my son didn't tup you and leave you is one of the great mysteries of life."

It was a mystery to Sophie too, given that Thomas's first sexual attention to her had been in their marriage bed. He'd done his duty—she was no longer officially a virgin—and had then rolled off her and gone to the study for a glass of port.

Sophie rather suspected Thomas didn't like tupping.

At least not tupping her, *at any rate.*

"I was a virgin when I married," *she said quietly, her jaw locked and grim. It wasn't that her virginity had defined her, but she respected her father, respected his kindness, and would not want him shamed by this man's low-spirited insults.*

"The hell you were." *A cruel smile flirted with his thin lips, and he pulled a filigreed silver box from his waistcoat and took a pinch of whatever he kept inside with a superior sniff.*

And then whatever bond of propriety had held Thomas Conklin Senior in the doorway broke, and he stormed into Sophie's bedroom, the grimness of his black suit dominating the pleasant white room. Sophie turned partway, holding her hands out in defense and fear, but Conklin was a big man, brutally strong, and he thrust his fingers up through her long silky hair and jerked her head back.

"You're a whore," *he whispered into Sophie's ear, his breath foul. From this close, Sophie could see the furry tunnels of his nose and the hole burned in the membrane between nostrils.*

"No," *she denied, not sure what he wanted from her.*

His hand cracked across her face, hard, and she yelped in pain.

"A whore!" *he cried, but she wouldn't let herself agree.*

"No."

With a roar he dragged her by the hair and threw her across the room onto the bed, and she lay there, helpless, as he lifted her dressing gown and dropped his trousers.

"No," she whispered. "No. No. No."

TUCKER GASPED, sobbing, and tried to let go of the hairbrush, but the image shifted again, and he was stuck there, stuck in time, while....

SOPHIE COULDN'T look at her swollen face in the mirror as Bridget pinned her hair that night.

"I'll kill 'im," Bridget muttered.

Sophie shook her head, unable to stop the tears. "He'll kill us both," she said, voice leaden. "And his son will help him bury our bodies."

She'd never fooled herself into believing that her husband loved her. But when he'd started to show her attention, there in her father's yard, she'd seen her parents' poverty and how hard they had to work to feed the children they had, and she had hoped. Hoped that this handsome, rich man could take the burden of her care off her parents' hands.

Bridget crouched at her knees then, leaving her hair in tumbles down her back. "Sophie girl," she begged, taking her hands. "Do ye have family? Someone you could hide with? Someone the old man wouldn't think of facing down?"

"My brother," she said, thinking. "James." James had fought all his life, fighting through high school, boxing through his violent youth. He was a railroad worker now, a foreman, with broad shoulders and arms like steel cannon-shot. "He'd defend me. But he's

working in the railyards of Sacramento, Bridget. I don't know how we're supposed to—"

"Write him a letter," Bridget said, her green eyes dancing deviously. "Write him a letter, and I'll have the valet write a reply like 'e's yer brother."

"But won't they—"

"They don't think none of us can read. The valet has good writing, though—writes 'is daughter twice a week. If we make that bastard think ye've been summoned, we can get money to travel across the country, and maybe your brother'll take you in—"

"Not directly to him, though," Sophie said, worried for James. "He's a good man, Bridget, but we don't need to drag trouble to his door."

"Someplace nearby. We can ask the telegraph office where's a good place. We can stay there a while—"

"Money!" Sophie said, the exhilaration of escaping this vast tomb of whispers and lies suddenly so close to her heart that she could feel it beat faster. "Bridget, we need money to get away from—"

"Aye. It's why we'll have the fake letter from yer brother—they won't listen to yerself, we both know that. But if a man bids you come, ye can ask yer husband, the useless sot. Tell him ye want to visit family, that ye need cash to travel. He throws money about like sand, Sophie. Make him throw some yer way."

"We can write James for real when we arrive," Sophie said, seeing the plan. "Tell him why we ran." Oh, they could do it. Sophie may have been a virgin when Thomas had come to her father's door, but she knew what her husband wanted in bed now. He would come and use her and go—but if she made a game of it, laughed like a wanton, he'd give her money so he mightn't feel guilty about how long he stayed away.

Bridget looked up at her, face shining with tears. "Ye do that. But let us flee this place. What he did to ye today...."

She burst into tears, and Sophie stroked her curly hair back from her face. She took the brush Bridget had placed on the dresser, and while Bridget lay sobbing on her lap, Sophie pulled the pins from her hair, one by one.

The last one had a jewel on the end of it, a sparkly fake diamond, and Sophie touched it briefly. Bridget's sobs had stilled, and Sophie set the pin down and began to coax that riotous mane from her face. "It's the only frivolous thing about you," she commented. She didn't want to talk about that afternoon, or how Bridget had found her, half-naked, bruised, and bleeding, on the floor next to the bed. Her whole body ached, and would for days, but Sophie longed for her soul to fly free of pain.

"All ladies' maids dream of being grand ladies sometime," Bridget said, taking the pin from Sophie.

"That's not what they should dream of," Sophie said, continuing with the brushing. It soothed her as much doing it as it had when Bridget had done it to her.

"What, then? More tea trays? More laundry?"

"No," Sophie murmured, remembering her parents, poor but happy. "A small house of their own. Dishes they chose themselves. Nobody's laundry but theirs. Those are dreams fit for queens."

"Or peasants," Bridget said dryly.

"I'm not afraid of laundry," Sophie told her, turning her so that Sophie could continue with her hair. "I'm afraid of the king in the castle, the one who terrorizes the maids and the princesses and destroys his prince."

"His prince isn't much of a man." Bridget sniffed disdainfully.

But Sophie wasn't sure. There had been moments of kindness there, of joy—at least of interest. But the gallant suitor who had brought home a blushing bride had shriveled under his father's scorn.

Maybe he wasn't strong—but then, he'd been grown in rocky soil, soaked in acid, and watered in wrath.

"Some place with good earth," she murmured. "So I can grow a garden, like my mother. Chickens, maybe."

"Aye," Bridget murmured, lulled by the gentle strokes. "Some place like that."

FINALLY TUCKER was able to put down the brush. It fell from his limp grasp, and he flopped back on the bed, the sweat soaking clean through his T-shirt and into the quilt beneath him.

"Oh, Angel," he panted. "This is awful. It's *exhausting*. Please tell me that somewhere in all these rooms are the ghosts of miners who just came up broke and wanted to get laid!"

"I'm sure there are some of those," Angel said, her new, feminine voice soothing as Tucker lay there and let the sweat dry from his body. "That… that was not easy."

Tucker closed his eyes against the terror, the violation, and the fucking *resignation* they'd felt at their lot in life. "I want to think of them somewhere peaceful," he said. The kitten wandered up and started licking the salt from Tucker's hairline. Tucker let her, still lost in the poignancy of two lovers, running from the world that had booted them so rudely in the kidneys.

"Where would they be?"

"The ocean," he said automatically, although the ocean might terrify Sophie. "No, a riverbank. One that doesn't flood. They'd have a cottage. They'd have a garden and chickens and do their own laundry, and nobody would bother them." Or peer into their personal moments like a voyeur, but he didn't say that.

He just waited for the fine trembling to stop while he put together the things he knew and the things he had.

"The snuff box," he said, his eyes still closed.

"It's here," Angel said, as if she recognized the significance.

"The rat fucker—"

"Her father-in-law?" Angel clarified, since Tucker had obviously lost her with the swear word.

"Yes." Tucker opened his eyes and was overwhelmed by Angel's bright green eyes within inches of his face. "Augh! Ohmigod, you're close."

Angel scooted back on the bed, swinging her hair over her shoulder as if she'd always had long hair and it was no big deal. "Sorry," she said stiffly. "I didn't mean to startle you. But you were referring to her father-in-law?"

"I can't even call him by a name," Tucker snarled, loathing ripping from deep inside him. "I mean... poor Sophie!"

"Yes." Angel dropped her eyes and petted the kitten disconsolately. "That was horrible. I've.... Your aunt Ruth and I have seen that. Not often. But enough." She shivered. "I don't understand how people can be so awful."

"Well, this guy was obviously... okay, crazy. And drug addicted. And sort of a dick anyway. But worse than all of that, he was *here*."

He and Angel met gazes, and for once they were on completely the same page—that snuff box had belonged to Thomas Conklin Senior. "He was here. And somebody needs their story told."

"God," Tucker muttered. "I really hope they got away."

Angel dropped her eyes, concentrating on the orange stitching of the quilt. "Tucker, people here…. If their ghosts are here, on the grounds, that usually means…."

She couldn't say it, but Tucker knew. It was very possible that Sophie and Bridget had died here—but perhaps not. There was always the other possibility: that the ghosts he saw here were just what remained of two women whose time here had been pivotal in their lives.

Tucker shook his head and tried to rid himself of the bitter disappointment filling his heart. "It was a nice dream," he muttered, pushing himself off the bed. He staggered over to the dresser and looked at the objects there with dead eyes and leaden limbs.

"I can't finish this tonight." When he had sex with someone, he would feel a drain, a pull, something bigger than the normal energy expenditure during coitus. It was one of the reasons he couldn't hold down a job—it wasn't just that he didn't know when he'd be subject to someone else's body, but he had to sleep off the hangover the next day.

This was worse.

"I'll start work on the room tomorrow," he promised, not that Angel had a vested interest in the remodeling. Tucker looked around at the old-fashioned wallpaper, which was starting to give him the creeps, and the dusty splinters of hardwood. "I'll see if I can move the furniture out while I'm fixing stuff up. It'll be a pain in the ass in the hallway, but then, you and me are the only ones who'll be coming in."

Angel nodded, looking as tired as Tucker, and then reached for Squishbeans.

The animal slipped right through her incorporeal hands.

"Oh dammit!"

Tucker found he had enough strength to laugh. "Don't stress yourself, sweetheart. I can carry her."

Tucker reached for the kitten, but instead of looking grateful, Angel glared.

"Are you being condescending because I'm a woman?"

Tucker was tired enough that he actually had to think about that one. "I'm not sure. I'm pretty sure it's because you're a ghost. And you're being sort of cute." He held out his hand and thought some more—it was a valid question. "I think if you were being cute as a man, I'd be just as condescending. Except, you know, I'd be thinking I was being playful."

"Well, it *sounded* like you were being sort of a condescending prick," Angel muttered, eyes narrowed. "This is a problem with incorporeality, not a problem with internal genitalia."

Tucker did a slow blink, and then his head did a slow throb.

"Okay. Fine. I'll examine my chauvinistic tendencies tomorrow, okay?"

"What are you going to do for the rest of the evening?" Angel asked plaintively, following him out the door.

"Oh God—is it only eight o'clock? This has been the *longest* day! Well, I've got my computer, and I've got a Netflix account. Do you have any preferences?"

"Netflix?" Angel said curiously. "What's Netflix?"

Tucker laughed softly. "Wow. I think it's time you learned about *Buffy the Vampire Slayer*. And another guy named Angel. And a guy named Spike. I think this will make our evenings very pleasant together, you think?"

"Sure, Tucker," Angel said, trusting as a child. "If you want to spend pleasant time together, I would love to be your companion."

"That's a little formal," Tucker muttered, but still he led the way down the corridor with rooms (more rooms—oh my God, *more rooms*) flanking either side, then down the stairs. A companion. That was actually sort of nice. Margie, with her assumption that they were lovers, had missed the best part of that, really. Having Angel here meant he at least wasn't alone.

True to his word, Tucker set up the computer on top of the dresser and turned them both so they could watch from the bed. He left Angel and the kitten watching the first episode and visited the shower, grateful for the modern, if basic, amenities of hot water and shampoo.

It would have sucked going to sleep wearing that fear sweat on his skin, especially if Angel was going to be sitting on the edge of the bed while he slept.

He paused for a moment to figure out why that should bother him. Was it, like Angel said, because she was a girl now?

But when he thought of Angel, he wasn't really thinking about gender. He was thinking about his/her prissy little speech pattern and the gentleness that her weird agenda seemed to hide. He was thinking of green eyes, almost like a cat's, watching a kitten with a sort of desperate affection.

He could, simultaneously, think about the sweep of blond hair across a pink cheek and the gruffness of stubble across the edge of a square chin.

Huh.

He'd been cheerfully bisexual since his first and second sexual encounters—but he'd never thought about this before. Was there a difference between bisexual and gender-transcendent?

He groaned as the water pounded his chest. No. He was not going to ponder this now—but he *was* going to mind whether he actually condescended to pretty, plump blonds, because Angel was right. If he only called her "sweetheart" when she looked like a Barbie doll, that should stop right now.

And he had so many things to think about—things that *weren't* gender-transcendent, shapeshifting ghosts.

"Hey, Angel," Tucker said as he came out of the bathroom, one towel wrapped around his hips and the other drying his hair. "What do you say we take a look at the graveyard tomorrow. Maybe if we're together, it won't look like a soul-sucking vortex of...."

Angel was sitting cross-legged at the end of Tucker's bed, her attention focused on his computer screen, green eyes wide, mouth pink and wet and surprised into an O.

"Do we like?" he asked, laughing a little to himself. If she liked *Buffy*, wait until she got hold of *Supernatural* and *The Flash* and *Smallville* and *iZombie*.

"This is so exciting," Angel said, completely without irony. "The blond cheerleader is really a slayer!" She wrinkled her forehead. "Is this real?"

Tucker shrugged. "Probably not. How's this—everybody else thinks nothing like *Buffy* can possibly happen, and just because *we* know better, that's no reason for *us* to assume this is anything more than entertainment." It was like crime shows with serial kill-ers. If you did the math, there were more serial killers in all the crime shows combined than real people. So yes, serial killers existed, but no, ninety-nine out of a hundred times when they showed up on television, they weren't real.

Angel frowned at him for a moment, and then allowed herself to be pulled back into the action. "I would rather believe it's real," she said, with a sort of touching ingenuousness. "At least in *Buffy*, they don't condescend to the cute blond girl."

"Oh God."

Tucker reached into his dresser and grabbed a pair of boxer shorts and a T-shirt, and just as he was about to drop the towel....

He remembered he was naked.

In front of a woman.

Being nude in front of a man didn't bother him—bisexual or not, he'd been undressing in locker rooms since junior high. But Angel was a *girl* now, and unless he was making love to a woman, being naked was just not... not acceptable! He turned his back to her and hoped his bare bottom got minimal exposure while he dressed.

Angel noticed, though.

Tucker came back and sat on the bed, pushed him-self into the far corner and picked up Squishbeans. The kitten apparently didn't have a partial bone in her body. She plopped on Tucker's chest and began purring, and the exhaustion that had so sapped Tucker after his vi-sion settled onto his shoulders like an old sweater.

"I've seen you naked before," Angel said while Netflix geared up for the next episode.

Tucker sighed. "So sue me. Women *are* different somehow. I don't know what to do about that."

"I have seen human behavior, past and present, up close and personal," Angel mused. "I don't know if I've ever been quite so aware of how different they are treated." She cocked her head, limpid green eyes regarding him soberly. "Do you think it's a biological thing? Is that why women are expected to be submissive?"

Oh God! "No!" Tucker said shortly. "I've known some very strong women in my time. It's not biology—at least, not most of it. It's… it's *sociology*. I think, you know, women need to be protected sometimes. They get pregnant, that's hard, they need help. And men… just confused that shit and made it about who's better and stronger and who's weaker, and things got toxic somehow. And now we've got all these set-in-stone social rules, and some of them are just politeness, and women have been sort of shit on for so long that it comes across as condescension, and—augh!" He thunked his head back against the wall. "Look," he said at last, "I'm sorry I called you sweetheart, but no, unless we are sleeping together, I will not change clothes in front of you while you're a girl."

"Huh." Angel shifted position on the bed, lying on her stomach and swinging her feet over her bottom, exposing curvy calves and plump thighs.

"Huh, what?"

"I wonder what Buffy would think of that?"

After two episodes? Buffy probably didn't want to see anybody's naked body yet either. She hadn't gotten busy with Angel until season two, right?

"I think she'd think I'm too old and not hot enough for her and then shut down whatever is happening in the graveyard immediately."

Angel rolled her eyes. "It's not killing anybody right now. Hush!" That last was probably because Netflix was done buffering and the next episode had started.

Tucker grunted and settled back to watch comfort television, but the part of him that always worried was not going to be appeased.

That graveyard needed to be looked at. There was something very wrong there.

Squishbeans purred on his chest, and Buffy did her thing on his computer, and for a moment he could forget about graveyards stretching into alternative dimensions, two people he was starting to care about who had probably been dead for over a century, and gender-bending ghosts with perceptive, vulnerable green eyes.

GATEWAY

"DO WE have to?" Angel asked, not sure why this made her so uncertain.

"Take apart the bed? Yes."

Tucker stalked around the thing, taking a look at the way the frame was put together. In the last two days, he had moved the desk into the corner, stripped the windows, removed the light fixtures, and—in his words—"felt up the creepy-assed wallpaper." But it was now time to move the bed.

Angel wasn't so sure it would *ever* be time to move the bed.

"What if something awful happened there!" Angel asked, feeling a little desperate.

Tucker grunted. "Yeah, well, I've been there, done that. It was horrible. I don't look forward to doing it again. But right now, it's either feel up the rest of the stuff on the desk—"

"You slept for twelve hours," Angel said humbly. She was beginning to think that Tucker was a much more powerful empath than his aunt Ruth. Angel's involvement in his visions was far more immersive—both in the pleasure and the pain.

The fact that Angel hadn't noticed that, had simply been swept away by them, had felt more connected to Tucker than she ever had to Ruth—that was part of the power.

It hadn't felt like a vision. It had been *real*.

And what it had done to Tucker had been real too. He'd been exhausted, sleeping for twelve hours and wandering the house like a zombie for eight hours after that before going back to sleep. Angel had ordered groceries for the next morning, wanting there to be fresh eggs and cheese—lots of protein for Tucker, to sustain his work as an empath. But that had only been the surface reason.

The truth was, Angel saw Tucker as needing her, far more than Ruth had ever needed her. Ruth had treated her as a friend, a nemesis, an irritant, and Angel had responded that way. Of course, it hadn't been until the old woman had passed away that Angel had realized humans don't always ask for what they need.

Tucker was an object lesson in this idea.

He didn't ask for anything, but when Angel gave him something unexpected, the gratitude, the relief on his face, told Angel far more about what he had grown to think life would give him than any plea for help.

So now that Tucker was ready to move on with the cleansing of the house—literally—Angel found she was unwilling to let him. Not when they both knew the cost.

"Tucker, you don't have to do this," Angel begged. "Please."

"Aw, Angel," Tucker teased, "are you worried about me?"

"Yes," Angel said, and then backtracked, because that had sounded far too enthusiastic. "If you were to be unable to carry out your duty, the house would fall to ruin. The spiritual excess—"

"Is already forging a psychic void to a hell dimension," Tucker said dryly, obviously referring to the graveyard. "When are we going to check that out again?"

Angel whimpered. Honest to heaven, whimpered. "Do we have to?" she asked, sitting down on the old mattress and picking reluctantly at the blue-and-white striping. Tucker had stripped the bed completely and taken the bedclothes to a laundry service, asking them to treat the linens as delicates to help preserve them as long as possible and to simply steam the quilts and spot-wash them.

"Angel, it's terrifying over there. You have to see."

"But…." Angel choked, a little abashed. "We're working as fast as we can. This is the only way I know to do this task. How do we—"

"Well, for starters, you let me take apart the bed." Tucker winked at her, and Angel bit her lip, afraid and frustrated—and tingly.

He was so damned irrepressible.

"Fine," she said, running her hand over the bedrails. She felt the waves of it, thundering through her energy field. "Are you wearing clean underwear?"

Tucker wrinkled his nose and thought about it for a moment, tunneling his fingers through his hair. "No," he said after a moment. "I mean, they were clean this morning, but we've been mucking around a lot in the heat and the dust, so yeah, in an hour or two, I'll be grateful to shuck them and jump in the shower."

Angel rolled her eyes. "More grateful than you can ever imagine," she muttered, then stood. Four old pillows graced the bed, and she gestured toward them. "You may just want to get naked and lie down, because we both know what's going to happen after you lock your hand around the metal." Because what he'd felt from the bottle that had sent him down to his bed to masturbate in all his glory had been only a fraction of what Angel was getting from the bedframe.

Tucker's eyebrows went up. "*Really*?" he asked.

"Yes, really," Angel retorted.

"Well, if that's all that happened here, do I really have to—"

"Yes." And this was what was pissing her off. "Because it wasn't all Bridget and Sophie. There were a lot of different energies there, and you never know if those people are going to pop up somewhere else."

Tucker started to laugh uncomfortably. "So I'm going to have an orgy in my head?"

Angel wondered—was she blushing? She wasn't supposed to feel anything physical, but her "body" was hot, the heat pulsing under her energy shell in a peculiar, supple way.

"Something like that," she conceded. "I don't feel any violence here. Just lots and lots of…." She wrinkled her nose. "Fluids. Fluids and lust."

"Oh God," Tucker muttered. He looked around the room with purpose, his gaze landing on the giant pile of cleaning rags he'd brought upstairs. He'd used maybe three of them on the room, getting rid of the grime and dust that had settled everywhere, and what was left was a mostly clean bucket of water, mild hand cleaner, and a still-giant pile of clean cotton cloths.

"Okay, I think we have the necessities," he said, grabbing one of the rags and the bucket of water. "Lotion would be nice. Lube would be better, but…." He shrugged and studied the moldings on the ceiling. Angel understood, sort of. Going downstairs and fetching the lubricant would be like admitting he was going to have a supernatural sexual experience.

Angel could see how admitting it was going to happen would be far more disconcerting than the actual event. Or so she thought.

"Okay," Tucker said, shucking off his gloves and trying obviously not to make eye contact. "You promise—nothing violent?"

There was need in his voice, and Angel scanned again, just to make sure.

"Some of the participants were a little… enthusiastic," she said delicately, and Tucker groaned.

Tucker took another breath. "And nobody's going to try to jump into my ship, right?"

Angel stared at him blankly. "What do you mean?"

"Well, you can read my thoughts and be there when I see these stories. That's only a… a hop, skip, and a jump away from full possession, right?"

Angel's mouth dropped in horror. "A ghost taking over your body?" Ruth had never mentioned it—but then, Ruth hadn't had *Buffy* as a primer either.

"Well, yeah. I mean, mostly what I've experienced is like being in a movie with surround sound, but I'm a little worried here. Sex can be pretty overwhelming to the senses. Nobody's going to try to take me over, are they?"

Angel thought about it. "Well, no. I mean, I don't *think* so. Tucker, that sort of thing takes sentience, right? When I opened the front door for you, I had to direct my… my*self* into your body. What's going to happen here is just memories. Like you've been doing. Except there'll be a lot more people. And everybody's naked. And some of them are…." Her eyes widened. "Tucker, sometimes this bed had more than two or three people in it. And some of them used paddles!"

"You're killing me, Angel. Killing. Me. Enthusiastic. Great. Not just an orgy, a big rough sex orgy fucking around in my brain. Dear *Penthouse Forum*."

"You're writing a letter *now*?"

He let out a strangled laugh. "Note to self: Angel has spent over fifty years locked in an old house with my maiden aunt—the legitimization of porn is not a thing."

"I know what pornography is," Angel said stiffly. "It is a terrible, demeaning, objectifying thing."

"Yeah, Angel, unless you're horny and you don't want to go out and hurt anybody's feelings getting laid."

Angel gasped. "But… but you have no problem at all with promiscuous sex! The first morning I saw you, you were with some poor young woman who—"

"Who was grateful for my presence," Tucker said bitterly. "Angel, has it occurred to you that this whole ghost-hunting gig isn't my first barbecue? That I'm *used* to being used by the powers that be?"

"I don't understand what that has to do with—"

"Fuck it," he snarled. "Let the hatesex orgy begin!"

He put both bare hands on the edge of the bed as he stood and let out a gunshot of a gasp.

"Holy mother of God."

Angel was forced to stand and watch as Tucker, both hands clenched tightly around the brass rail, began to shake, sweat soaking through his shirt—and his jeans—as he stood.

An erection pushed hard against the placket of denim, and as Angel watched, Tucker yelped, the sound startling in the tense room. Before the sound faded away, a dark stain began to seep through his jeans, but it wasn't over.

Tucker moaned, and his erection remained, straining, probably uncomfortable, as Tucker shook, lost in the tumbling of body after body, the satiation of lust after lust assailing the mortal conduit who had voluntarily channeled them all.

Angel pulled back from his consciousness, afraid of getting lost.

Tucker moaned loudly in the throes of his second climax and fell to his knees, his hands never leaving the bed. He fell forward, his head making contact with the metal, and he screamed, the extra touch probably charging through his body like sexual electricity.

This time, when he came, he whimpered.

Angel had had enough. "Tucker, let go," she said clearly, and his only response was a moan. "Let go! Dammit, Tucker, let go!"

"No, no, no, no, no…," he chanted, but much like with ordinarily powerful coitus, Angel couldn't tell if this was "No, it feels too good!" or "No, I'm being violated or harmed!" In this case, it was probably both, and Tucker's face was both blotchy and pale, swimming in sweat, and the veins in his forehead were popping with strain.

"*Tucker*, *let go*!" Angel roared, and this time he did, slumping to the ground in a puddle. The first thing he did as he slid to the floor was fumble with his fly and thrust his hand in.

Angel didn't even have time to leave.

Or that's what she told herself.

Because the truth was, if she'd had a body, it would have been in the same shape as Tucker's. Swollen, sweating, aching, deep in her bones. Her sex felt swollen—*but I don't have genitals*—and her breasts felt tender—*but I don't have breasts*—and a place deep within her, in the core of her body, screamed for possession, for hard, sure, absolute touch.

I am neither male nor female, and this is impossible!

It was a scream in her head, a psychic cry for help, but nobody heard. Tucker let out a breathy prayer as climax hit him again, and Angel collapsed on the bed, trembling and locked in her imaginary body as she experienced a painful surge of arousal that should not have been possible, should not have affected her at all.

By the time she could concentrate, could relegate her body construct to the back of her mind, Tucker was sobbing, one last painful orgasm being squeezed out of his body by his overwrought brain.

For a moment there was silence, punctuated by Tucker's dying sobs, his harsh breathing echoing off the walls, counterpoint to Angel's own.

She should not have been breathing at all.

"Tucker?" she asked after a minute—or an hour.

"Nunh."

"Can you move?"

"No." Unequivocal.

"I'll get you a pillow," she said. And then, before she could ask herself if this was possible, she gathered Squishbeans in one hand and then….

It worked.

She picked up the pillow in her other hand and walked it to Tucker, bending to tuck it next to his ear before sitting, cross-legged, by his head.

Tucker groaned and grabbed the pillow with what looked like the last of his strength—and his one clean hand.

"Do you think we'll have to do that with every bed?" he asked wearily, the sound of tears still in his voice.

"Not all of the beds are still in the rooms," Angel told him kindly. "And as for the rest...." She blew out a breath. "I'll... I'll screen them carefully. We can plan for that next time."

"Yeah, how about with Quaaludes?" Tucker asked dreamily. "Something to make it all slower. Less. Not as intense."

Angel brushed fingers through his hair and wondered, since Squishbeans was in her lap, if he could feel it. "If you can get a prescription, that would be good."

"Easier just to get someone to make me pot brownies." He giggled, and the sound wasn't quite sane. "God. Would that be better or worse on pot brownies?" With a choked sound in his throat, he rolled to his side and pulled his hand out of his pants. He wiped it on his T-shirt before tucking it under his cheek.

"Angel?"

"Tucker?"

"Don't take this the wrong way, but I wish you couldn't see me like this."

Oh. Oh no. He was embarrassed. "You did something really brave tonight, Tucker. I'm only sorry I couldn't protect you better."

Tucker nodded, tears sliding from the corners of his eyes to his pillow.

"That's nice of you. You didn't seem this nice when I first got here. I like you nice. It must be the kitten."

"No," Angel whispered, almost sure he'd fallen asleep. "It was that you wanted a kitten for yourself, and you picked one out for me." She kept up the stroke through his hair, and he smiled and tilted his face into her touch.

"Feels nice," he murmured. "Real human touch. Not sexual. God, I miss it."

Angel gasped—but she didn't pause. She kept up the motion, figuring it was soothing him as he slept. She was exhausted too, and she lost track of time. One moment she was running her fingers through Tucker's hair, and the next, she was asleep as she sat, kitten on her lap, chin tucked against her chest.

"BUT YOU took apart the bed! It's in the hallway! Why would you do that if you're not going to finish?"

Tucker grunted and threw a knapsack with sandwiches and water bottles into the truck. "I wanted to get the bed out of the way so we didn't have to... feel it anymore."

No other pieces of the puzzle of Sophie, Bridget, the monstrous father-in-law, and the mysterious brother had been found on the bed.

But the aftermath of that touch had put Tucker out of commission for another day. Twelve hours after the brush, twelve hours after the bed. It was slowly dawning on Angel that having a more powerful empath was not always to their benefit. When Angel had been dealing with Ruth, they'd been able to get to the catharsis of the soul after a week or less—but not at this rate. Not with Tucker. Of course, Angel had openly admitted that she'd given Ruth the easiest of the jobs, but this one?

This one wasn't easy. There were too many pieces in motion with these objects and these ghosts, and some of them were too painful to touch more than once.

"But why not finish with the room?" Angel asked almost desperately. Tucker looked so tired! His body moved slowly as he swung himself up into the cab, and as Angel materialized next to him, she felt a twinge of bitterness. Couldn't he just do something human? Something physical and not empathic? Ruth used to garden, clean house, even, when she was younger, have friends over for cards. "Why can't you spend a couple of days doing something normal?"

Tucker grunted. "You're the one with an agenda, Angel. Don't get all upset with me now that I've jumped on the 'let's clear the ghosts the fuck out of here' bandwagon!"

"This is not good for you," Angel said crossly, and was rewarded with one of Tucker's manic little-boy smiles.

"You sound like my mother!"

Angel caught her breath. She knew Tucker's mother and father had died fifteen years earlier in a car crash. Ruth had been devastated, and Angel had been... unaware. Unaware of human grieving and how hard it must have been for Ruth to exorcise other people's ghosts when her heart was laden with the memory of her own people, whom she loved. Angel hadn't wondered, then, why Ruth wouldn't ask Tucker to come live with her. Now that she saw the extent of Tucker's abilities, she thought she knew.

If Tucker had come to Daisy Place when he was a young man, it would have destroyed him. He would have been trapped here, wretched and bitter, before his time.

Ruth had kept him away, living on a stipend, to give him a chance to live, and whatever had happened to Tucker to make him so angry now, there were still deep pockets of kindness, like gold ore, and enthusiasm, buried like silver, in the mysterious caves of Tucker's heart.

"What did your mother sound like?" Angel asked softly. Suddenly it became imperative to know.

"She was always telling me not to study so hard, to eat well, to remember my sweater. Don't pet that strange dog. Don't walk barefoot where there were stickers and bees. Don't stand next to a draft. It was like my whole life she was giving me advice to protect myself, and then nothing could…." He swallowed.

"Protect you from losing her," Angel filled in. And then, because she couldn't help herself, "What about your father?"

Tucker let out a nostalgic laugh. "He… he was in awe of her, I think. She had me when she was forty, you know? By the time they passed away, they were in their fifties, and she just kept him running laps and eating kale, telling him, 'Dammit, we waited long enough for him. I want to see my grandchildren!'" Angel could hear his grunt of pain across the cab of the truck. "That didn't pan out for them, really, and they weren't hip and young. But Dad followed her into anything. He told me again and again that when you found someone who made you your best person, you had to be grateful for them." His face—pale from the two psychic encounters—lapsed into sorrow.

Angel could not remember feeling crappier in fifty-five years of being an awful friend and a worse person.

"I'm sorry," she said, wishing she had left it alone. "They sound like lovely people. I just… I didn't mean to pull up the sad things in your heart."

Tucker cast her a watery grin and started the truck.

"They're good things too," he admitted. "I think I needed to think about them right now. Taking apart that bed was—"

"Not the greatest part of being human," Angel said delicately.

Tucker darted a glance at her, and his face colored charmingly. "No. Not that way. I mean, sex can be great, you know?" He didn't wait for Angel to respond, which was good, because Angel had no frame of reference. "But not like that. It was all just so—" He shuddered, and his flush washed away. "—soulless. Children could have been conceived on that bed, but the onslaught of it all…. I did not need to be there." He sighed, and she wondered if an actual woman could have smelled the embarrassment sweat rolling off of him. "*You* did not need to be there."

Angel couldn't look at him when she said this. "You have nothing to be ashamed of." He did not. He'd been caught in the throes of a supernatural vision. She'd stayed there—why? Because watching him orgasm was fascinating? Because he'd needed her?

"You won't look at me," Tucker mumbled. "I mean, I know we're only working partners, and you're not even alive, but at least we were talking."

Oh.

Oh hell.

"I made you do it," Angel said. "I made you mad and forced my… agenda on you, and you grabbed it, even though you knew it was going to be difficult. I am feeling the shame here, Tucker. I am not shaming you."

Tucker's mouth quirked at the corners. "How about no shame for either of us, okay? If you can't look at me, Angel, I've got no one…. Never mind. Just no shame."

"Now we sound like vampires," Angel grumbled. And oh yes, she'd seen them around town.

"There're vampires here? I've seen a few in the city, but I didn't know they'd be out here too!"

"They come with the fairy hill," she said sharply. "Which we do not—"

"Yeah, yeah, we do not talk about. I understand." Tucker's humor seemed to be restored, and Angel took a deep breath.

"Well, we shall check out the cemetery," she conceded, "and see if there is anything to be done. And then you can go back home and rest—"

"And you can catch up on *Buffy*," he said with grim humor.

"There must be a way for her and Angel to get back together," Angel said tearfully. "There must!"

"Well, sometimes it's not your first love who's your best love," Tucker said thoughtfully, like this would mean something. "Sometimes it's an unlikely person you meet later and have trouble being with in the beginning."

Angel narrowed her eyes. "If you're giving me spoilers, I'll hog Squishbeans for a week."

Tucker laughed. "No spoilers, I promise."

The atmosphere in the cab lightened for the five minutes it took to get to the cemetery, but Angel couldn't help but wonder—who was Tucker's first love who wasn't his best love? It sounded like he knew.

More importantly, who was the unlikely person he would meet later?

HOW DREADFUL it was to be wrong.

"Oh, Tucker. This is bad!"

The ghost of an indigent miner swiped an angry hand against the windshield, leaving a swish of green like the mashed corpse of a big bug.

"Right? Let's get out, though, and see—"

"What if they're hostile?" Angel asked, because the cluster of ghosts whirling around the graveyard seemed to be truly massive.

"Not right now. Watch. See? As we drive by, they're fading away. They're afraid of you."

"How do you know they're not afraid of *you*?" Angel demanded, because it did seem he was right.

"Because they didn't do this when I drove by with Josh."

Oh Lord, there'd been mortals here. People passed this section of the property every day! "Did your friend see the ghosts?"

"No," Tucker said, and it wasn't Angel's imagination—he sounded a little sad. "He said it looked dark, so he's not immune to it. But he didn't see the random graveyard stretching into the hell dimension. He didn't see what I see."

It must have been lonely to be so singular. Was this why Tucker knew so much about seeking out no-strings companions?

"I see it too," Angel told him and looked out the window stoically. She wished she didn't. The swarms of the undead were parting before the truck, but Angel could make out plain farm women in cotton dresses, miners in overalls and thermal shirts, children in knee pants or dirty tunics. "These people couldn't all have died here. Not even in the town, Tucker. There's far too many of them!"

"I know. It's like the place—the graveyard in particular—just sort of sucked them in."

"Why would somebody lay a foundation like this?" Angel muttered. "I wondered that when I came, and I wonder that now. *Why* would someone create a property that is essentially a giant ghost trap?"

"Don't ask me," Tucker muttered. "I'm just the hired muscle. Now I need you to get out first and come over to my side. They hate you, but they're looking at me like they want to jump in my body and use it for a meat puppet, so, uh, yeah." He shuddered, and Angel remembered their conversation before he grabbed hold of the bed frame. "Not doing that."

Angel glanced around to Tucker's side of the truck and gasped. He wasn't kidding. The ghosts were gathered around the driver's side as Tucker slowed down, staring at him with hunger in their eyes.

That fear Tucker'd had, that fear of being possessed—*this* was what he'd been talking about. These ghosts weren't the tame ones, the mere visions that populated the house. These ghosts were *angry*, and they wanted *life*.

Angel, who trafficked in the world after life, was suddenly afraid.

"Tucker, how long do we have before they figure out they can get into the car?"

Tucker shook his head. "They can't. The glass, the metal, something about the space of it is different. They're treating it like a house or a property boundary."

Angel frowned. "Are you sure it's not this symbol of protection hanging from the mirror?"

"Oh!" Tucker gave a bark of laughter. "I'd forgotten about that." He touched it and frowned. "It's still… hot. Still hot in my hands. I don't think I could wear it comfortably, but you're right. It's probably what's protecting the truck."

Tucker stepped on the gas and drove the car to the far side of the road, the one obviously marked by the change in metallurgy, by the absence of anything in a bilious color scheme or smoky shades of gray.

"But I've got an idea." He stopped the car and looked at Angel. "We still have to get out, but…." He grimaced. "Remember when you touched the doorknob through my hand?"

"You want me to do that?"

"Here. My backpack. I'll put it on; you touch my back through it. Hopefully it will give me enough of whatever you're wearing to keep them out of my skin."

Angel felt an imaginary pulse fluttering in her throat. "Are you sure?" she asked. "Tucker, this could… uh, take a bad turn."

"Yeah, and then it could veer left off of 'bad' right onto 'wrong,' and then go south straight to hell. I am aware, Angel. But…." He rubbed under his breastbone. "I wish I could explain it to you. Why I have to go look. There's a thing here I need to see. I just…." The expression he turned toward Angel was pleading. "Angel, this radar in my stomach, it's sort of imperative. And it's been tingling since I woke up after the bed thing. I wish I could explain it better than that, but—"

"You didn't tell me?" Angel asked, surprised. "Oh, Tucker, you never ignore an empath's feelings. That's very important. It's good that we came. Bad things happen when that's not addressed."

The bleakness on Tucker's face touched Angel in a broken place she didn't know she had. "I know. Oh, believe me, I totally know. So I know it's scary. I've passed graveyards in the city that haven't been this populated. This is bad shit right here. But I've got to, man… sweetheart… hell, whatever. I've *got* to. You understand?"

"I understand," Angel said. "Tucker, who taught you how to use your powers?"

"Now? You want my life history now?" Tucker unhooked his seat belt, then grabbed the knapsack and put it on his back.

"I'm just wondering. You did have a mentor, didn't you?"

"Not anyone in particular. Now grab my shoulder and let's get out of the car and see if anybody tries to possess me."

"They can't have you," Angel muttered, feeling indignant. "You're *mine*!"

For an electric moment, they stared at each other, Tucker's brown eyes wide with surprise. Angel bit her lip, not exactly sure how she'd meant that, but the words were out and couldn't be taken back. That same imperative Tucker—and Ruth—had felt when addressing ghosts seemed to have hold of Angel in this matter.

Tucker was hers.

"Careful, sweetheart, someone might take that the wrong way," Tucker muttered, breaking the spell and sliding out of the car. He gave Angel time to slide too, carefully, so they were still touching.

They landed on the hard-packed dirt of the road, and Angel grunted. "Tucker, this is hard. Can I—you won't feel my weight, but can I ride on your back?"

"What about the pack?"

"I'm not solid. It'll pass right through me."

Tucker scrubbed his face with his hands. "Just make sure *you* don't go right through me, okay?"

"I'll do my best."

"You know, maybe I was wrong," Tucker muttered, holding his hands behind his back so she could get up. It wasn't necessary. She was already straddling him like a little kid looking for a ride, her dress—green—riding up her thighs in what would have been a wanton way for a human, and she was as secure there as Tucker was on the ground.

It was almost like she could feel his lean, rangy body between her thighs, almost like the heat of him was seeping through her entire being.

She was, perhaps, a trifle *more* secure than Tucker was on the ground.

The ghosts were backing up, a sickly DayGlo rainbow of spiritual energy parting as Tucker trekked from the untainted property where the truck was parked, across the rutted dirt road, and over the dry irrigation ditch at the shoulder. He clambered up the side to the property line and found the small gate—mostly a frame for the barbed wire and a rusty latch—that would let him onto Daisy Place proper.

Into the morass of the undead.

"God, it smells like swamp ass," he muttered. "Can you smell that? Whole damned county is bone dry, and look!" He shook his wafflestomper as he lifted his foot, and clots of damp earth and vegetation flew off. "Can you believe that shit?"

Angel sniffed delicately and realized that her scope of human sensation was limited to Tucker. Tucker smelled very nice, actually—he used some sort of musky body wash, and of course his clothes were starting to smell like cedar from the closet, as well as pine-scented dust, because they were in Foresthill.

"I cannot smell the swamp," she said, and even to her ears, her voice was a little dreamy.

"Lucky you," Tucker grumbled sourly. "So, Angel, what does the graveyard look like to civilians? Can you see that?"

"Yes," she said, squinting a little. Tucker grunted, as if she'd just become heavier on his back. "It's… plain dead grass on hard dirt, random headstones. Not inviting but not…."

"Apocalyptic either. Here—let's go check out the headstones. I want to see the difference between the ones mortals see and the ones we see."

"Tucker, there aren't any ghosts around the graveyard. Either version. Do you think I could jump off your back and help you look?"

The sound that came from Tucker's throat was as close to fear as Angel had heard him make. "Can we not?" he asked reluctantly. "They are…. Angel, look how they're looking at me."

Angel looked over her shoulder and wished she hadn't. The ghosts had closed in, standing in a loose semicircle behind Tucker, glaring at him as though he was to blame for all their ills.

Angel wrapped her arms around Tucker's shoulders and held on tight. "You can't have him," she shouted. "He's mine!"

The glow thinned just a tad, but Angel couldn't stop the shudder that pulsed through her—and then through Tucker.

"I'm flattered," he muttered, pulling his foot from the sucking swamp that kept trying to eat his boots. "But you're actually *under my skin*, sweetheart—I mean, Angel—and it's making it hard to concentrate."

Angel pulled back a little. "Sorry, Tucker."

"No worries. You know, I call men sweetheart too. You know that, right?"

"Out of bed?"

Tucker grunted. "Fine. Point made. Anyway, here we are. Okay, how many graves do we have here, in real time?"

Angel counted. "Seventeen. Do you want me to read the names?"

"Yeah. Damn. There's a notebook with a pen inside the back…. Thank you?"

The otherworldly energy was strong here. Angel had just reached into the backpack without using the zipper, seized the items he'd asked for, and pulled them out.

"I'm not sure how exactly that works," Angel mumbled. "The energy here—it's the same sort of thing Squishbeans does for me, but Squishbeans makes me solid when I hold her. Not completely, but enough to pick up a kitten—"

"Or a pillow," Tucker said, voice gentle.

"Small objects," she returned humbly. "But here it's…. Can't you feel it? It's like I can grasp the raw electricity from the air and drink it!"

"Yes, Angel, that's what I meant by 'This place is as creepy as hell.'"

Angel shuddered. "Oh no. Hell would be far creepier."

Tucker made a sound of frustration. "Well, I'm not going to walk down that alternative-universe graveyard road and into the interdimensional rift to find out! Can you *write* on that tablet, since you're sucking electricity through a stovepipe?"

"Sure," Angel said, trying to help. "What would you like me to write?"

"Well, I'm going to point to a headstone, and I want you to tell me if it's real or… dimensional, okay? And then I want you to write the names down, separate columns.

The stuff that's on the earthly plane and the stuff that's in whatever this other plane is. Can we do that?"

"I can, but I don't know why," Angel muttered. But Tucker was already pointing, and it was her job to cling to him with her legs and write.

She used the back of his head to balance the pad on—he didn't seem to mind—and one headstone at a time they made a list. Helena Catherine Grayson, b. 1865 d. 1912. She was "real." The headstone next to hers, which looked no less weathered, proclaimed Sarah Lynn McArdle, b. 1956 d. 2001 was in the other dimension. Together they mapped both sides of the graveyard—the solid, earthly side and the ghostly otherwhere—and Angel had to admit, some of the things they discovered were odd.

"Wait," Tucker muttered. "What was that last one? That last dimensional one?"

"George Ezra Alvarez?"

Tucker stumbled. "Yeah. That one. God—could that be? No. There's got to be…. Angel, what was his death date?"

She read it off, and Tucker started doing that mental math. "Oh. Oh hell. That's got to be him. Okay. That's a clue. It sucks, but it's a clue. Okay, we're done with the earthbound ones. Who's our next dimensional trespasser?"

"Damien Alexander Columbus, born September third, 1984, died—"

"I know when he died," Tucker croaked. Throughout the graveyard, the ghosts who'd refused to follow them in rustled, and Angel looked around at them, worried.

"Tucker, we should—"

"I can't be here anymore," Tucker mumbled.

"Good, because we should—"

"How could that be him? Angel, do you have any idea?"

"Tucker, we need to go!" Angel's voice cracked in panic, and Tucker pulled his mind from whatever personal hell he'd been visiting to see his actual, er, virtual surroundings.

"Oh hells," he muttered. "Angel, are you holding on tight?"

"I'm actually under your skin," Angel confessed, waiting for his rebuff.

"Stay there," Tucker said grimly. "And don't let anyone else in. You hear me, Angel? You said it. You claimed me first. None of these other assholes get to ride me, right?"

Tucker had turned already and was trotting toward the edge of the graveyard. The spirits waiting when he got there parted, but nobody was giving as much ground as they'd done earlier.

A ghost reached for him. Angel could feel the burn, like humans described acid, and she screamed, hugging Tucker tighter, sending energy through their skins until the ghost shrieked and disappeared. Tucker moaned in pain, and then another one tried, and another. And still Tucker kept trotting, keeping the property line as a goal in front of them as Angel sank deeper and deeper into his skin.

Another ghost screamed, and this time Angel felt it, the burn, not just in Angel's consciousness but on Tucker's body, and Angel let out a sob.

Don't stop! Tucker begged inside their shared space. *I don't care how much it hurts. Dammit, Angel, have my back!*

This ghost tackled them, full body contact, and Angel shrieked as she threw it off, electrifying both of them, repelling the ghost with psychic energy the same way she'd picked up a pillow.

I'm sorry, I'm sorry, I'm sorry! Angel gibbered, and Tucker just kept running, although the ghostly bodies seemed to stack themselves in front of them like bricks.

Again, another one jumped on Tucker's back, and Angel started swearing, using all the words Tucker was so fond of. The agony faded, and Angel heard Tucker— of all things—laughing.

Picking up bad habits, there, sweetheart.

Don't stop running.

Wasn't planning on—

Oh no! Angel was looking through Tucker's eyes now, so completely merged that she could probably speak through his mouth, if that hadn't been a violation. And Tucker was stumbling to a halt, just before the dividing line. Just before freedom.

Damien?

Oh Lord. She heard it in the tone of his voice, felt it in the ache in his chest. Tucker had *loved* this person. Tucker still grieved him.

It's not him! Angel begged, wishing she'd given Tucker a more thorough education on what a ghost was. *It's his energy, but not his soul. His soul wants what's best for you, Tucker. But this thing—*

Damien. Oh God. Damien. I'm sorry.

Damien the ghost had been handsome in real life— dark blond hair, green eyes, a thin nose, narrow chin, and playfully full mouth. Angel recognized him then, from his first day with Tucker. Angel had skated the surface of Tucker's mind, trying to find someone he'd trust, trying to find a form he'd care about so Angel wouldn't have to work so hard at being human.

His attempt at deception might have just saved Tucker's soul.

Don't trust him! Remember, you didn't trust me? You were right! He's not real, Tucker. Now run!

And Tucker lifted a foot, and another. Ghost-Damien lunged toward them from the side, but Tucker was almost at the edge of the property line, and as the spirit wrapped his arms around Tucker in a blistering embrace, Tucker screamed and took the final step.

Ghost-Damien wailed and faded, captured by the graveyard energy and held there, as Tucker and Angel broke free.

Tucker kept running until he got to the truck. He slid into the cab, and Angel scooted out of his body gratefully and then took a good look at him.

"Oh God, Tucker."

Tucker's face was blistered, down his cheek, down his neck, and probably all over his torso and arms too. He took a breath and coughed, blood spattering his hand.

"Oh fuck, Angel," he muttered. "I am fucked up."

"Can you drive?" Angel asked. She didn't like the look of the blisters—his skin had a sort of noxious cast to it, and whatever a doctor might put on it, it wouldn't fight the psychic sickness sinking into his flesh.

"Yeah," Tucker coughed.

"I'm going to merge with you again. Do you mind?"

"Just let me stay me, okay?" His voice hit a plaintive note, forlorn and sad, and Angel had a sudden thought that one not-quite-real companion wasn't enough here.

"I promise," she said gently. "I'm going to see if I can push the... the deadness out. The blisters will need to heal, but I'm going to try to get the supernatural stink out."

"Fine," Tucker muttered. "You do that. I'm going to drive to the hospital and—"

"Don't go," Angel begged, wondering if she was wrong about this like she'd been wrong about the internet. But there were good reasons too. "It's so far, Tucker. Drive to Margie's or to Ms. Fisher's. Josh and Rae's. A friend. You need a friend, Tucker, someone real."

"Great," Tucker muttered. "Here, let me find the phone so I can—" He coughed some more, and Angel jumped into his body while he was trying to drive, cough, and get on the cell phone all at the same time.

Angel could feel it, the green sickness, pulsing just under Tucker's skin, and she aligned her energy as closely as she could with his. But there was something else there, something painful and bitter and horrible, making Angel's hold on Tucker weak and her fight against the sickness even weaker.

She waited, screaming in his head with the effort, as Tucker spoke in halting sentences to Josh, and Josh told him to just get back to the house; he'd meet Tucker there and get him inside.

Tucker clicked the phone off and Angel spoke low and urgently inside his head.

Tucker, you have something in you, a bitterness, an anger. It's hurting you. It's making your aura weak. You need to let it go.

Tucker's response was verbal, a scream of pain and frustration that echoed through the frame of the small cab.

I know it's comfortable, but dammit, Tucker, can't you tell me a little bit of it? Just a bit? It's pushing me out, and I need some room to work!

"I don't know what to tell you!"

Tell me about Damien.

"Oh God," Tucker muttered brokenly. "We were friends in high school. And I loved him." His voice broke. "I was so in love with him."

Were you lovers? Angel tried to suppress her jealousy. She was not the first person in Tucker's life—she'd known that since she'd seen him asleep in Dakota Fisher's bed.

"No," Tucker whispered. "No. Because I was bi, and he was fine with that, but all he talked about was girls."

Oh, Tucker. I'm so sorry.

"It wasn't your fault!" Tucker wept—and yes, he was weeping, finally, from pain in his body and pain in his heart. Angel could feel the puke-yellow of bitterness fading a little, into the gold of nostalgia.

Please, Tucker, heal. Heal just a little, and I can help you heal the rest.

"What do you want me to say?" he begged, his voice nothing more than a harsh whisper, his lungs still crackling with the pain of Angel's electricity burning away hostile spirits.

Did he ever know you loved him? Angel wanted to weep. It was the wrong question. She should have been asking something practical, like why the memory haunted Tucker worse than the terrible energies reaching into his body, but so help her, she needed to know.

"Yes," Tucker said. The truck swerved, and Angel risked his wrath and took over, jerking the wheel with stiff hands. "Sorry. Sorry. I'll try not to kill us. Yes. Yes, he knew. I told him, and he was… he was kind, Angel. I know he looked horrible, as a ghost—"

They all do. It's because their energies are here but not their souls. But still, Angel hated to think of that snarling face, that bitter, screaming anger, housed in the diaphanous form of what had once been a friend, a lover never touched.

"But he was such a kind boy," Tucker sobbed, blood and spittle running from his lips down his chin. "He was so kind, and he didn't want to hurt me. And then, one night, he called me up. He said he'd been dreaming about me. About us kissing. He said he wanted to kiss me. And I'd loved him for so long. I'm sorry. I didn't want to follow the pull that night, Angel. I'm sorry. I didn't want to. I was selfish. I'm sorry. I'm sorry. Oh Damien, I'm sorry."

Angel gave a mighty psychic scream inside his body and clenched all the muscles not used to steer the car. Oh yes! There! The layer of putrid guilt, it was diminishing, leaving healthy grief in its place. Not all of it. Some of it still lingered, but Tucker's voice was broken, his lungs too damaged to talk anymore, and Angel needed to help him steer home.

Together they yanked into a skidding right-hand turn and then a quick left, the truck rambling to a stop almost past the rise. Angel/Tucker stomped on the brake, and Tucker moved his hand to kill the engine. Finally, both of them slumped, exhausted and frightened, in the front seat, while Tucker dragged in lungfuls of sweet, sweet air.

Hold on, Angel warned. *I'm going to drive out more of the toxin now. It's going to hurt.*

"Bring it," Tucker said, so obviously in pain that Angel couldn't stand it anymore.

Augh! she screamed, long and loud, so long and loud that the truck's front window cracked, the crack spreading with her squat-thrust-shove of poison out of Tucker's body.

For a moment, nothing gave, and then she heard Tucker, in his head, thinking, *Don't hurt yourself, Angel. You're trying so hard.*

And that was it. That little bit of kindness and his aura firmed up just enough. Angel screamed again, and together they watched the yellow biliousness of spiritual poison evaporate into the air.

Tucker slumped sideways, his breathing much less tortured, and Angel sank a little deeper into his consciousness to take stock of his pain.

His lungs were no longer blistered, and neither was his skin. The parts of his chest that had been sweating, the skin broken and bleeding, were no longer stuck to his shirt, and his face showed a little bit of heat exposure, as if he'd fallen asleep in the sun with a T-shirt on his head.

But he was exhausted—too tired to move. Angel pulled out of him, hearing his sigh of relief as the uncomfortable fullness of two souls in one body diminished. Diaphanous again, she slid out of the cab of the truck and waited for Tucker's friend to come help.

LET THE HEALING
BEGIN

"No," TUCKER mumbled as Josh and his son, Andy, helped him out of the front of the truck.

"No, what?" Josh asked good-naturedly. "No, you can't explain what happened, or no you're not going to the hospital?"

"No hospitals," Tucker said firmly. He'd always seen ghosts, but until today, he'd never been afraid of them. Seeing ghosts in a hospital was a terrifying thought. "Just take me inside. I need to rest. I'll be fine."

"Want to tell me what in the hell happened?

"I visited the graveyard," Tucker muttered. "There was… waste. Someone had dumped antifreeze on the ground—I tripped and fell in it."

"Then you'd be dead," Josh said. "Here, Andy, link hands with me under his ass."

"Sure, Dad." Andover was a good-looking kid—a muscular chest like a barn, his mother's plainly pretty looks with haphazard dirty blond hair and big brown eyes, and his father's guileless smile and square jaw. He could probably hoist Tucker over his shoulder and keep walking, but that wouldn't do much for Tucker's self-esteem, would it?

"Okay, I'd be dead," Tucker muttered, leaning on Josh more than he wanted to. "But I'm not. I just need to rest. To eat. To—"

"Stay away from ghost-infested graveyards," Andy said baldly. "Jesus, what did you think? All that toxic yellow smoke was swamp gas?"

"What toxic yellow smoke?" Josh asked suspiciously.

"I saw actual individual spirits," Tucker said with dignity. "How is it you saw yellow smoke and your father only saw a small broken graveyard?"

"Mom's got witchy blood," Andy said. "And if this is a witchy thing, you're going to need your own house, even if it's haunted as fuck."

"Andy!" Josh complained. "Language?"

"Dad, even you can see it's creepy. Tucker here should have stayed away unless he had a medium. Or some help."

Together the two men walked up the long driveway and the porch steps, taking Tucker through the grand ruin of the front entrance. "There's a small bedroom past the kitchen to the left," Tucker said. "It's got a bathroom and a bed and my computer, but not much else. Sorry, guys. No butler serving cookies."

But Andy was as smart as his father and as intuitive as his mother. "*Did* you have help, Mr. Henderson?"

Tucker grunted, everything in his body aching, including his heart and head. "Kid, I *am* the help."

Andy and his father deposited Tucker gently on the bed, and Tucker leaned over, fully clothed, and put his head on the pillow. Every wrinkle of his clothing chafed, but he was not yet so depraved that he'd undress totally in front of this pinup model of a kid.

Andy crossed his arms. "Huh. Are you really?"

"What are you talking about?" Josh said, sounding confused.

"Dad, didn't you ever wonder why Ruth stayed here alone, all these years? I delivered her groceries from the time I was twelve until I got out of high school. She talked to me sometimes."

"Maybe tell me about that later," Josh muttered, obviously not comfortable. "First, Tucker, is there anything you need?"

"Advil and a swimming pool full of water," Tucker muttered. And a shower—but again, not in front of Andy and his father. "Ice water. I'm parched." The burns had faded, but the aftereffects of having healed from something that had sapped him of all moisture remained.

"Dad'll get it," Andy said promptly. "I'll go get a chair—"

"From the kitchen," Tucker said weakly. "Don't bring anything in from the house."

"'Kay," Josh said. "Andy, keep an eye on him, okay?"

"What does he expect you to do?" Angel asked acerbically. "Jump up and dance?"

Tucker smiled tiredly. "Don't worry, Angel. I'll be fine."

"That was *very*, *very* dangerous, Tucker."

"Aw—she's worried about me," Tucker replied. "Did you hear that, Andy? She's worried about me."

"Tucker!" Angel gasped.

It took him a couple of breaths to figure out why.

He opened his eyes and looked to see Andy squatting next to the bed and looking around.

"I know he's here," Andy said, his voice deep. Oh, he really *was* adorable. Nice chiseled chin and eyes of this amazing deep brown.

How long had it been since Tucker had taken a lover *he'd* wanted?

Unfortunately, it couldn't be this kid.

"*He* is awfully cozy for someone who didn't just save your life," Angel sniffed.

Tucker laughed and turned his head toward the wall. "Andy, what good will it do if you know? I appreciate your help," he said, suddenly sore and exhausted in ways he didn't know he could be. "But your dad doesn't need to know what's going on here. He doesn't need to know there are ghosts, or that Ruth spent her life helping them out of Daisy Place and on to wherever. And you don't need to be involved in it either." Tucker's voice broke a little. He thought of the amount of work he had to do, of being trapped in this house for his entire life. Of being caught under a hard and never-ending rain of spirits that would one day drown him.

Angel was suddenly there, between Tucker and the wall, facing him with grave eyes.

"You're not alone," she said, pulling her hair behind her, where it would fall in a gentle golden puddle, Tucker was sure.

Tucker reached over to stroke her cheek, wondering if it would be soft, and his heart broke a little when his fingertips passed through her skin. There was a sudden meowing and a scrabble up the side of the bed, and Squishbeans curled up to make a nest in Tucker's hair, kneading with comforting claws and purring.

"Thanks, Angel," he murmured, and then he fell asleep.

Josh woke him up with water, and then Andy was there with juice, both of them careful not to dislodge Squishbeans, who had taken up residence on his chest. Angel was conspicuously absent when they were there—he wondered if it was so they wouldn't talk to each other and freak Andy or his father out, but that was all he could wonder about before he fell asleep again.

A few hours later, Rae Greenaway was there with soup, and Tucker tried to stay awake long enough to thank her and to tell the family they didn't need to worry about their crazy neighbor with his freaky, nonspecific, exhausting ailments.

But he managed to drink a little bit of cooling soup, mumble something about how his shoes were still on, and then fall asleep once more.

He woke up in the morning wearing nothing but his boxers, with a little tray of juice and water by the bed. Angel was sitting on the chair that the Greenaway family had been using, peering at him worriedly through anxious green eyes.

"What's up, Angel?" he slurred. Then he squinted. "And hello, leather daddy of my dreams."

"Goddammit," Angel muttered, and then the big, bald, burly motorcycle guy in leathers disappeared, leaving the male Angel with the reddish hair and freckles in his place. "How are you feeling?"

"Horny," Tucker muttered, just to mess with her—him. "What was with the getup?"

Angel grunted, the sound particularly suited to this version of him. "I wanted someone you would find less vulnerable. I wasn't sure you trusted me as a woman."

"I trusted you to save my life," Tucker said honestly. "I trusted you to watch over me. Why would you think I didn't trust you?"

Angel shook his head and looked abashed. "You seemed to need the Greenaway family an awful lot."

Oh. Tucker tried to struggle to a sitting position, but he realized that whatever had been left over from the hideous, excruciating dermal burns had pretty much knocked him on his ass.

Well, there was no reason to let Angel see that.

"I didn't mean to need them this much," he said, feeling foolish. "*You* told me to call them, remember?"

Angel narrowed his eyes, and Tucker had to admit he looked scarier when he did that in *this* form than he had as a buxom blond. But that didn't mean he'd taken this version of Angel more or less seriously than the other version.

"Don't look at me that way," Tucker responded obstinately. "You know it's true."

"I didn't mean you should make eyes at Andover and try to wiggle into their family like a tick!" Angel argued.

"Well, that was unexpected for me too." Tucker tried not to pout, because it had been wonderful as well. "Please, I promise I won't tell them the family secrets, but…." He thought of all those college friends who had wandered away. All of the dates he'd broken because he was going to sleep somewhere else that night, all of the people who had gotten married and moved on, moved out of downtown, gotten too busy to write.

Who kept tabs on a grown man who couldn't seem to keep his fly zipped even if it meant letting down his friends?

"But what?" Angel prompted.

He felt so weak. "Don't make me give them back." God, he missed family. He missed talking to his mom as she made cookies, and awkward games of catch with his dad. They'd been older, but they'd been kind, and they'd been there for Tucker his entire childhood. He guessed he was spoiled that way, but he was so grateful for that part of his life.

And he yearned to have just a little bit of it back.

"I won't," Angel said. And then, on a deep exhalation of ghost breath that actually fanned Tucker's face, he confessed, "It's my fault too." Tucker might have used this as fodder for the argument if he hadn't felt so out of it. "I was… used to being Ruth's only real contact," Angel continued, shamefaced. "I thought that it would be you and me. I didn't realize that I wasn't enough for a young, vital person—"

"It's not that you're not enough," Tucker groaned. "And stop trying to fade away in embarrassment—it's creepy. It's just, you know, family." Was this what relationship arguments sounded like? It *seemed* like a relationship discussion, but Tucker's last relationship discussion had been with Damien, and he couldn't seem to remember past the moment when…. Never mind.

Angel grimaced. "I must tell you, Tucker, I haven't seen the best of family in the stories here."

"Well, yeah. No wonder you're skewed." Tucker yawned. He hadn't even gotten his orange juice or water, and he was going under again. "Just be nice to these people. Try not to make me any weirder in front of them than I already am."

"You're not weird," Andy said, venturing into the room. Tucker startled, but Andy kept on talking. "You're just haunted. Apparently by the same guy who used to bother Ruth. You know, Mom knows a medium. Are you sure you don't want a cleansing?"

"No," Tucker said shortly, heart still beating a little fast, "and if I did, I could probably do my own." Crap. He had to remember to heed his own advice. He rolled over and sat up, careful of Squishbeans, who was tucked into the small of his back. "I like Angel," he said, trying for a smile.

Andy rolled his eyes. Well, he was young.

"Yeah—you and Ruth both liked Angel. I think the guy's whole job is to make people throw away their lives on this hunk of junk." He had a smoothie in his hand, and he swung the chair around and sat before handing it to Tucker.

Tucker took it, shuddered with the cold, and pulled the blankets up around his bare chest. He was tempted to try the frightened-virgin act and ask who had undressed him but decided if it had been this superperceptive kid, that would fall under "I'd rather not know."

"Angel could care less about the house," Tucker said, sipping. Oh wow. He could taste the protein powder, but it was secondary to the fruit and the—was that Sprite? Oh *baby*, the non-health-food health-food smoothie. "This is magical. Did your mother make this?"

Andy grinned. "It's my mother's recipe, but she and Dad are, you know, working, taking care of the little kids. Grown-up stuff." Andy whistled and looked around the house guilelessly. "Just two guys, alone in this mansion. Nothing to do...."

Tucker rolled his eyes. "We're not hooking up," he said dryly. "You're cute, but young. And I'm...." He let out a breath and then slurped up some more magical smoothie. "Damaged, Andover. You know that, right?"

Andy's grin faded. "What *is* your damage? I mean, I've got to be honest—when we heard Ruth's nephew was inheriting the place, we sort of expected it to be contracted out and either razed to the ground or completely refurbished. And you haven't really moved in, but Dad says you're doing renovations?"

Oh Lord. "I should go get my shit," Tucker muttered. "Now that I have a truck, I should go down and give up the lease on my apartment and come back."

"No job?" Andy asked. "No people? You just... picked up and left?"

Oh Jesus. Well, Tucker wasn't going to tell him shit that he hadn't even told Angel. This whole "karma's bitch" thing was so personal. It was one thing when your friends thought you were a slutty dick, but when it wasn't even your choice? When you were a slave to the forces in the universe that wanted to use you for your magic wang?

"Did you ever watch *Ghost Whisperer*?" he asked.

"No, Tucker. Is it as good as *Buffy*?" Angel replied. He'd left the seat and was now sitting cross-legged at Tucker's side, and Tucker smiled fondly at him.

"No—but it's not bad watching, though. But remember?" he asked Andy. "She kept having to do stuff, even if it was dangerous? Because that's just what you do?"

Andy thought about it. "That's all those shows," he said slowly. "You have a gift, and you can either use it to help the world or you're a twatwaffle."

"Exactly," Tucker agreed. "Well, twice... twice I tried to back out of whatever my gift asked me to do." He remembered his broken confession to Angel in the cab of the truck and wished he felt even near strong enough to go bolting out of the damned bed. "The results were way worse than being a twatwaffle," he finished. "You learn.

You learn to use your gift to help people. It's the reason the gods gave you a gift, you know?"

Andy nodded sagely. "Is that what you were doing out in the graveyard?" he asked.

Tucker nodded. "Trying to figure out what my gift needs me to do," he said. It was, for once, completely the truth.

"Well, finish up the smoothie. What your gift wants you to do right now is get some sleep. Then tomorrow me and Dad'll help you move out of your apartment in Sac."

"You don't have to," Tucker said helplessly. "Why would you even—"

"Because it sounds like the only way to get you out of here," Andy said bleakly, "even for a day. And if you could see how pale you are, you'd know what I'm talking about. Now hurry up and drink so you can go to sleep."

Tucker took a giant swallow and then tried one last bid for sanity. "Andy, don't get attached to me—"

"I know, Tucker. You're the kind of guy who goes wandering into graveyards when the ghosts really *are* out to get you, because you think it's what your gift needs you to do. And whatever the reason you were all alone, you're not now. My dad seems to love you. Margie says you and Angel are the sweetest boys, and she's sure roommate is code."

Tucker groaned. "Does she even know Angel's a—"

"Ghost? No. She has no idea. My folks didn't tell her. I guess they heard me talk about him enough that they're sort of resigned to Angel being real. The whole town can't have the same imaginary friend, right?"

Tucker took another healthy swallow of smoothie and looked at Angel, who looked guilelessly back.

"Angel, you little slut. How many psyches have you been sleeping with?"

"My appearance to everybody else is all your doing, Tucker," Angel said solemnly. "I promise you, I've only ever voluntarily appeared to you and your aunt."

Tucker laughed a little. "Well, you're apparently not a secret. Are you going to be okay here while I go back to Sacramento tomorrow?" He yawned. Oh hells—he was done.

"Yes, Tucker. Squishbeans and I will be fine."

Tucker looked at the kitten, who appeared to roll her eyes at him too. He picked the little fuzzgoober up and plopped her on his chest.

"You could always freak him the hell out and pick up the cat," Tucker mused.

"I am *not* a parlor trick," Angel said with dignity.

"Can he do that?" Andy asked, eyes alight with interest.

"He can," Tucker said, "but he's not excited about it. Thinks it's beneath his dignity."

"One more question." Andy took the empty smoothie glass away from Tucker, and Tucker belched, politely covering his mouth with his hand.

"Thanks." Tucker yawned. "Shoot."

"When Dad and I pulled you in here, you were babbling about Angel as a girl. Why?"

Tucker moaned. "Because at the time she was one."

Andy grunted and started collecting empties. "Ruth never said anything about Angel doing that. Think he did it special for you?"

Tucker thought of the big bald leather-wearing biker Angel had tried to be that morning. "I'm sure of it, but Angel doesn't talk about it. One minute, he's a perfectly ordinary-looking guy—"

"Good-looking, right?"

Tucker looked away from Angel's amused smirk.

"Yes. What makes you say that?"

"Because the guy's got to have something if you and Ruth are willing to dedicate your life to him." With that, Andy stalked away, cups in hand, muttering to himself, and Tucker put the kitten down so he could get up and go to the bathroom.

"You should ask him for help," Angel said reluctantly.

"I thought you didn't want me dependent on family," Tucker chided as he pushed himself heavily to his feet using the bedrail. "God—stiff, sore, everywhere. I feel like my bones are brittle." His muscles were taut, like aging rubber bands.

"I have suddenly changed my mind," Angel said with dignity. "Family sounds like a wonderful idea."

Tucker stared at him for a moment and then turned away. He hobbled to the bathroom and did his business carefully, then came back, still feeling the grit of exhaustion behind his eyes.

He slid under the covers, conscious of the house's ever-present cold, and turned toward Angel, cuddling the kitten.

"What?" Angel asked, as Tucker fought to keep his eyes open.

"I've got nothing," Tucker mumbled. "I mean, no reply to that. Just… don't go anywhere when I sleep, okay? With the Greenaways in the house, stay here. It would suck if Andy decided to perform an exorcism or something because he wanted to get in my pants."

"You two could perpetrate coitus right here, and I wouldn't be able to stop you," Angel said, his stiff voice indicating he didn't think this was a wonderful idea.

"You totally just did," Tucker said, laughing at the picture in his head. "It'll never happen. Night, Angel."

"Day, Tucker."

Tucker's lips twitched, but he was too tired for the comeback.

RAE WAS there with soup that evening, and a cribbage board. Her younger children—aged ten, fourteen, and seventeen—played three-fouls-out softball as the sun went down, and Tucker lay on his side and watched them moving in and among the spirits as they embarked upon their stately waltz on his lawn.

"What do you see?" Rae asked, pushing her perpetually fuzzy hair out of her eyes.

"Tilda should go into pro softball," Tucker responded. The teenaged girl was sturdy, muscular, and determined. She could pop a fly ball gently up so her younger sister, Coral, could catch it, or level a haymaker at Murphy, her brother, to get him back for being a snot.

"That's not what your face says," Rae observed, shuffling the cards. "You look more concerned than that."

Tucker closed his eyes as a gentleman ghost with a mustache and a leer walked through the oldest girl. Tilda shivered, looked around, and popped up another ball—but Tucker had seen it. She'd responded.

"This house is no place for children," Tucker said bleakly.

"Bullshit," Rae said, dealing. "Children are needed here to drive out the ghosts."

Tucker shot a surprised look at her. "Andy thinks you don't believe in the ghosts."

"And that is absolutely stupid, since Andover got his witchiness from my side of the family," Rae said calmly. "His father told him there was no such thing as ghosts and that Angel was a product of the old woman's imagination. Ghosts scare Josh, you know." Of course he knew.

"Ghosts scare me," Tucker said, shuddering. On the lawn, Coral gave up on softball and went to play that game with the stick and the hoop. Except she was playing the game with little girls who had died over a century before. Tucker whimpered, and Rae looked over her shoulder.

"Coral's the witchiest one of the four," Rae told him sagely. "Andy is so damned jealous it's not even funny. He kept trying to bring her over here when Ruth was alive so she could tell him what Angel looked like."

Tucker grunted.

Rae gestured for him to make his play, one eyebrow cocked in amusement. "What?"

Tucker lay down his card and moved his peg and finally relented under her no-bullshit mom-gaze. "He probably thought Angel was hot and was trying to get supernaturally laid."

Rae tilted back her head and laughed. "Well, I did try to pawn him off on you the first day we met."

"He's pretty persistent," Tucker told her.

"He comes by it honestly." Rae winked, and Tucker remembered her insistence that he leave so she and her husband could have their no-kids-in-the-house date. Well, the family wasn't one for hiding, that was for sure. Rae sobered. "He really needs to get out of here," she said softly. "He's gotten accepted into Sac State, and I'm pretty sure he could get a job down there to feed himself, but it's housing that's killing us. I

mean, if he was coming on to you when you could barely move, you know the boy needs to go have himself
some adventures, right?"

Tucker nodded, thinking about his apartment.

And in spite of not having the gonna-get-laid
"pull," he felt a little *pop* in his chest.

"He could always take my apartment down in
Sac," Tucker said without thinking. "I was going to
give up the lease, but it's rent-controlled and sort of a
steal. There's no reason for me to give it up now."

Rae frowned and then played her card. "Hon,
you're awfully tired. I'm not even sure we should let
you up tomorrow—"

"You have to," Tucker said weakly. "Tomorrow I
get up and we go move me out and Andy in. The next
day, I can start stripping the floors and the wallpaper,
and the next day...."

Crap. He couldn't tell her his plan about moving
Sophie and Bridget on.

"What? And it's your turn."

Tucker played his card. "I just have some stuff to
finish. I need to get that room upstairs all cleaned out
and beautiful. Then I can start on the next one."

"Hon, what are you doing?" Rae asked in
exasperation.

"Beating you at cribbage and watching your
youngest daughter play hoops with ghosts."

"Well, besides that. What are you doing with that
damned room? At the damned graveyard? What is the
reason you came to this rotting piece of crap and decided to make our lives better?"

Tucker looked away from the window, where Tilda
was standing in the middle of several admiring female

ghosts who clapped their hands every time she popped the ball, and looked back at Rae.

"There's something very wrong at Daisy Place," he said at last. "Angel is here to clean it out. It's the reason he's been here from the very beginning. Ruth wasn't moving fast enough, and the cemetery...." He needed to look at Angel's notes. He had an idea about the cemetery, but he wasn't going to share it with Rae. "I think that's why the cemetery is so bad," he said, even though it wasn't the *only* reason the cemetery was bad.

Rae grunted and turned around to look out the window. Murphy was sitting in a shady spot, reading a book, and a wizened old woman was reading over his shoulder. Every so often, he would dart a glance up toward her, frown, and turn his face back down.

"I know they're out there," she said softly. "I can sense them. I know Angel has been sitting behind you on the bed and was there before you woke up. I know there are some sweet ones, just sort of trapped, and some evil sons of bitches I don't really want near my children, no matter how much they're 'not real.' But I don't know what to do about them." Then she turned back to Tucker and their game of cribbage. "Fifteen for two. Go, hon."

Tucker went, advancing his peg. He was clearly winning, which surprised the hell out of him because he'd never been that great at card games.

When he was done with his play, he looked back up at Rae Greenaway.

"That's my job." He shrugged. "My family, this place—I'm sure I'll do some research eventually. But each stage knocks me on my ass. Tomorrow, moving Andy in and me out? That's practically a rest day for me. I may actually come back here and sleep like a normal person."

Rae smiled slowly. "Can you really sleep in a haunted house?"

Tucker laughed. "Well, let's put it this way. When I got here, I could hear the person who used to sleep on this bed muttering to herself—and she was stuck here with my aunt Ruth, so I didn't see her best side. That was not fun. But in the last three days, shit has gotten so dire, her aura is completely gone. This whole room—"

"Wait. Let me." Rae closed her eyes and breathed in deeply. "You smell like cedar." Her smile was completely at peace. "Josh smells like Joshua pines, Andover smells like wool—everybody's got a smell. You smell like cedar wood." She laughed and opened her eyes. "You're like mothballs for ghosts," she said whimsically.

Behind him, Tucker heard Angel snort in approval.

"I am indeed." Tucker patted the bed he was sitting on. "And right now, I am one of three auras in the room."

Rae rolled her eyes. "I am barely a spit in the wind compared to you two. Okay, then, this room, it's all yours. I've been in your kitchen—it's got you and Angel all over it. But the rest of the house…." She shuddered. "Can you really do this on your own?"

Tucker added up his crib for six points, again vaguely surprised. "You know why I'm redecorating the room upstairs?" he asked.

"You'll tell me. And you are kicking my ass." She counted her crib for two.

"I never win at games—it's like this room is blessed or something. But when I'm done with a job, I want a record of it. So I figure this place has, what? Angel said fifteen-plus rooms to clear out?"

Rae *hmm*d noncommittally as she dealt, and Tucker looked up from another superlative hand.

"What does that mean?"

She shrugged. "Look, I don't know how many rooms your lawyer put on your paperwork—"

"Twenty-one," Tucker said, because it had stuck in his head. Three sevens—a graveyard number.

"Yeah, well, Andy used to come over and put away groceries—"

"I know that. It's why he thinks he knows everything."

Rae snorted *and* rolled her eyes. "Well, that's a twenty-two-year-old for you. I'm sure you knew everything at twenty-two as well."

Fuck. Involuntarily Tucker recalled Damien stealing him out of class so they could go swimming. They'd rented an inner tube and laid down on it, stomach first, their sides touching as they stared into the water and paddled the lazy parts of the American River. Tucker had turned his head, and Damien laughed, so close to Tucker they could have kissed. His hair had been streaked by the sun, and gold flecks had glinted in his brown eyes. *I know he could love me. I know he could. If I just lean forward, he'll kiss me, and he knows about the curse. He'd understand. If I just lean forward and our lips meet....*

Tucker had been sure of it. He'd known.

But he'd never tried.

"I did and I didn't." He coughed, trying to clear the sadness out of his throat. "Some shit you have to learn the hard way."

"Yeah," Rae said, looking at him like she could see what he wasn't saying. Well, she'd just said she was "witchy." Perhaps she could. "But Andy used to run down the halls and count the rooms. And the first day he came home all excited—he'd counted eighteen rooms altogether. We were impressed. But he told Ruth the next time he delivered groceries, and she was upset. Seems there were only supposed to be fifteen. So he counted again. Four times."

Tucker closed his eyes and groaned. "Let me guess."

"Different answer each time."

"Oh hell. Angel—how many rooms are in Daisy Place?"

Angel made a clearing-the-throat sound, and Tucker looked behind him. Angel's sheepish grin and apologetic shrug were *not* reassuring. "Fifteen the last time I counted?" he qualified.

"Are you shitting me?"

"I didn't know it was a requirement of relieving the ghosts," Angel said with dignity.

"Can you go count?" For some reason, not knowing was almost more unsettling than the graveyard.

Angel sighed and sat back so hard he actually thumped against the wall. Rae gasped and dropped her cards and then glared at them both.

"Tell him to stop that!"

"He didn't do it on purpose," Tucker muttered. "Angel?"

"No," Angel said regretfully. "I get… lost."

"Lost," Tucker echoed dumbly.

"Yes. I…. You know those movies where the hallway stretches out forever?"

"Oh God."

"I'm in that hallway, and I can't find my way to the end."

"Oh God."

"The last time I tried, Ruth said I was missing for a month." Angel looked sorrowful, and Tucker reached out a helpless hand to comfort him.

"That's awful," he said, voice husky.

Angel smiled beatifically. "I was nowhere near as brave as you were."

Tucker's chest expanded and gave a giant throb, and then Rae interrupted, sounding concerned. "What's wrong?"

"I'm living in the house from *The Shining*." Tucker swallowed and tried to keep it together. "I mean, I could do it when it was finite, you know? But the graveyard, and now this? It's every horror movie ever made! It's every haunted house, it's every carnival ride, it's—"

"It's going to be fine," Angel said, and Tucker, who could have sworn his heart was going to start beating through his ears, heaved a big sigh and leaned back in bed.

He was suddenly exhausted.

"There is no finite room count," he said, gulping this truth down dry like every other pill at Daisy Place. Then he remembered his restoration job and brightened. "But I have money—my plan still stands. When I get rid of a ghost, I'll fix the room. Maybe when the rooms are bright and shiny clean, they will stand still enough to count."

He threw his cards down, knowing he could have won with that hand. "But I can't do it today."

Rae cleaned up the cards and smoothed his hair back from his head, acting like a regular mom. "No, you can't," she said softly. "But look. My kids are comfy here, and you're giving Andy a way to get out. You don't have to do it alone."

Tucker smiled gratefully but still pulled away from her comfort in favor of healing sleep.

THE NEXT day, Tucker hopped out of bed bright and early and then fought not to fall back down.

"Are you going to make it?" Angel asked from the bed, and Tucker actually jumped in surprise.

"Oh my God, we slept together!" He'd asked for that—he had. But he was still surprised it had happened.

"Well, not in the biblical, coital way," Angel said, sounding almost sad about that. "But you were afraid, and I stayed."

Tucker scrambled for balance, both walking to the bathroom and inside himself. All of the things he'd avoided thinking about the day before, when playing cribbage had been a stretch for his abilities, came flooding back now.

Angel—inside him. A pure, glowing soul, both masculine and feminine, filling him with power and pushing the pain, the guilt, out of his pores, and the poison with it.

"I've got to—"

"I know," Angel said mildly. "You have to go relieve yourself and figure out what's going on in your head. I'll be here when you finish."

Well, since Angel understood, Tucker was going to take his time.

He came back drying his hands and smelling his pits. "I am *rank*," he muttered. "I'm so gross, I think I made the bedclothes gross too. I'm going to shower and then start the laundry." He looked up at Angel, the calm, auburn-haired, green-eyed, broad-shouldered version of him that he'd settled on the day before, and started to sweat a little.

"Do me a favor and let me shower alone this time, okay?"

"Of course," Angel said, those very specific green eyes guileless and accepting.

But Tucker was midway through the shower, pondering which one of Angel's forms he was *least* attracted to—because they all seemed disconcertingly appealing—when a hand materialized through the shower cubicle and knocked on the wall adjacent.

"Augh!" God, that was weird.

"Sorry." Angel sounded very disgruntled. "I forget when I'm solid and when I'm not. The rules for that keep changing. But the Greenaways are here, and Rae is about to start—"

"Augh!" Tucker cried again. The water had just turned ball-shrinkingly cold.

"Laundry," Angel finished.

"Okay, fine, Angel. Move!"

Tucker came out of the shower and toweled off, noticing that Angel still hadn't left the bathroom. Well, he hadn't had a lot of respect for personal boundaries when they first met either, and the last few days that distance had been dissolving disconcertingly fast. Tucker wouldn't mind so much, except Angel's regard—which had seemed fairly sexless at the beginning—was growing more and more... not sexless.

In fact, those little looks from under Angel's auburn lashes were increasingly *sexual*.

"Why's she doing laundry?" Tucker asked suspiciously. He'd brought clothes with him into the bathroom, and he slid his boxers on first and adjusted himself. "And what are you looking at?"

"You have burn scars," Angel said quietly. "They weren't there when we met."

"Oh." Tucker looked across his stomach, the insides of his arms, his inner thighs—all of the places his body had begun to boil with the fury of the unhappily dead—and saw that his body showed ravages of old, painful burns. He touched the pale part of his bicep in wonder. "It's smooth," he murmured. "Just a little mottling—like it happened a long, long time ago."

"I'm sorry," Angel said. Tucker didn't even startle as Angel's finger skated the diaphanous line between sensation and space. "Your beautiful skin...."

Tucker sighed and tried not to let his vanity show. "It's old now. People will hardly notice." He smiled and tried to crack a joke. "People don't sleep with me for my looks anyway."

Angel's finger slipped, and Tucker could actually *feel* the point of contact.

"Why wouldn't they?" he asked, and Tucker became aware that, by human standards, he was standing very close to a man... woman... entity he had begged to share his bed.

No, not in *that* way, but in an intimate way. Angel had perched on the corner of the bed while Tucker had been flirted with by Andy Greenaway and then cozened by Rae. Angel had been there when the kids had come in and watched a movie on his computer, and then, when the voices of the Greenaway family had faded down the hall of his haunted mansion, Angel had been there, quiet and staunch, to help keep him from freaking out when he closed his eyes and saw himself—saw *them*—surrounded by dozens of hostile spirits who all wanted to jump into Tucker's body and take the helm.

Tucker vaguely remembered waking up crying in the wee hours of the morning. Angel's voice had soothed him, and a feeling of well-being had enveloped him, allowing him to go back to sleep.

And Angel was standing—so damned real Tucker could almost feel his breath—close enough for Tucker to see the remains of freckles on his nose.

Those were new.

Tucker licked his lips and yearned for body heat or a smell or something animal and comforting to tell him Angel was, or had ever been, human.

"Angel?" Tucker asked, his heart thundering in his ears. "What are you?"

Angel frowned but did not move backward. "Today I'm male, late twenties, with longish auburn hair and a broad chin." A small smile flirted with his sensual mouth. "Tomorrow, I might be a petite brunet with large breasts."

"Ghosts don't do that, do they?"

Angel's eyes, the most human things about him, never left Tucker's. "Not usually," he conceded, a faint flush stealing across those once flawless cheeks. "No."

"If you're not a ghost, Angel, what *are* you?"

Angel looked sideways. "I think the Greenaways are calling," he said, and then he disappeared.

"I knew it!" Tucker hollered, putting Angel together with what he knew of ghosts. Ghosts didn't change shape, and they didn't change gender, and they didn't, under any circumstances, sit under your skin and beg you to purge your own poison so they could save your life.

A thing for which Tucker was not sure he'd properly thanked Angel yet.

"Knew what?" Rae called, knocking on the door. "Tucker, are you okay in there? Your bedclothes were getting rank, so I started the laundry. And you were looking a little scrawny, so I started… breakfast?"

Tucker thunked his forehead with his palm.

"Why would I think about how scrawny and peak-ed you were?" Rae was mumbling to herself. "And peaked—who says peaked?"

"Angel," Tucker told her. "I'm sorry. I think he figured he'd put the idea in your head." And then, be-cause he was pretty sure the obnoxious ghost... spirit... whatever was listening, he raised his voice. "I am not scrawny, Angel!"

"You are too!" Angel said crossly, reappearing on top of the toilet.

"What *are* you?" Tucker asked. "And *don't* disa—"

Angel disappeared.

"Goddammit." Tucker pulled on his T-shirt and then his cargo shorts, swearing to himself.

"Tucker, are you okay in there?"

"I'm fine, Rae. I just need to brush my teeth, and then I'll be right out. Are Andy and Josh ready?"

"Yeah. How much stuff are you bringing back?"

Tucker ran his toothbrush under the water and thought. "I don't know. Does Andy have his own fur-niture? Because it might just be clothes and DVDs and stuff. If he wants to use the bed and the couch, that's fine." He thought hard about his humble apart-ment while he brushed his teeth. He'd never brought anybody there—the pickups orchestrated by his gift always ended up somewhere else for some reason, and Tucker had started thinking of this little quirk as a blessing.

It was comfortable. The mattress didn't have lumps, the couch didn't eat people—but then, he didn't have many people over. He'd bought decorations to please himself, and DVDs that he'd loved. His computer held all his music, and he had a modest amount of clothes and the occasional sporting item, like a Frisbee or set of golf clubs, in his closet.

And of course, there were the items on the bookshelf that had belonged to Damien.

Those he'd have to take home.

"Well, we figured he'd take a look at the apartment today, and then if you're sure you want him to take over, he'd move in next week. He registered for school on hope and a whim, but it starts in a month. If he's going to find a job before classes start, he needs to get going."

Tucker spat out the toothpaste and rinsed his mouth, then put the toothbrush back on the holder on the side of the sink. "That's fine. I'd say the pickup truck only," he said. "So maybe me and Josh, and Andy can come with us or drive on his own."

"He'll drive on his own, maybe stay the night," Rae said, still through the door. "Thanks, Tucker. We'll be in the kitchen when you're done."

Tucker looked in the mirror and decided he might need to shave. "Ten minutes," he promised.

Angel appeared over his shoulder as he was in midswipe of his cheek. "Dammit!"

"I'm sorry!" Angel said. "I'm sorry. I just hoped you wouldn't badger me, and look! You're hurt again."

Without thinking, Angel swiped Tucker's cheek with his thumb and held it out accusingly so they could both see the blood.

And then they both froze.

Tucker could still feel the touch on his cheek—masculine, firm, but not rough—and the drop of scarlet clung to the pad of Angel's thumb in a smear.

Tucker closed his eyes, expecting Angel to disappear. When he opened his eyes, Angel was still there.

"I can't go," he said plaintively. "I tried. You're not supposed to know what I am. I can't tell you. I don't really remember. But I know it's secret. And I can't disappear, and you're just going to—"

"Sh...." Tucker suddenly got it. He took the washcloth from the side of the sink and wiped his cheek, and then, carefully, because he was hoping so hard this would work, he took Angel's hand in his own.

It felt as real and as solid as Squishbeans, and they both gasped.

"I won't ask you questions," Tucker promised, Angel's hand pulsing warm against his palm. "But you can't surprise me like that either."

"I'm sorry, Tucker," Angel said softly.

Tucker took the cloth and wiped his thumb off, closing his eyes against the tenderness of Angel's skin, flesh, blood, and bones, clasped in his own.

"It's okay," Tucker said. "I understand rules and supernatural things and...." The thumb was clean, and Angel's flesh slid through Tucker's grasp like Tucker had been cupping air in the palm of his hand. "And things that hurt, things you can't control," he finished, voice throbbing.

Angel locked gazes with him and bit his lip.

"What hurt you?" Angel asked softly.

Tucker looked into his eyes, close, so close to telling him. He felt a tickling on his cheek and held his hand up to catch it. His fingers came away crimson, and he stared at the red smear in bemusement.

"Being human," he said after a moment.

He didn't have to look up to know that Angel had disappeared again. This time Tucker didn't call him back.

BREAKFAST WAS blueberry pancakes, and Tucker, per usual, enjoyed the hell out of them. Then he thanked Rae, helped with the dishes, and he and Josh headed out to hop in the truck while Andy took a small used Toyota that they'd apparently bought with the proceeds from the truck.

Before the door closed behind him, Tucker thrust his face into the house.

"Angel, he called. "Angel! Are you there?" His heart fell because he was driving all the way down to Sacramento, and his parents had been killed in a car wreck, and Damien and... and of all people, Tucker knew you had to say goodbye.

"Here!" Angel said, materializing out of the wall between the kitchen and Tucker's room.

Tucker didn't scream this time, but he *did* hold his hand to his heart. "I'm going to my old place. I'll be back tonight, okay? I left lots of cat food and water for the kitten, so you should be okay while I'm gone." He swallowed. "Right?"

Angel nodded and then pasted a patently false smile on his face. "We will be fine. Have a nice day, okay, Tucker?"

"Sure," Tucker said. "You have a nice day without me."

As he closed the door and went running down the stairs, he could hear Angel's voice, floating weakly after him.

"Sure."

ONCE MORE
INTO THE BREACH

RUTH HAD been gone for three months before Tucker had been able to pick up her thread, and Angel had never felt alone.

Yes, he'd known about the ghosts, but it was more than that.

Angel was by nature a solitary creature. He'd wandered the lower rooms, looking out, getting familiar with the ghosts and the objects inside the house; he'd been comforted to know what came next.

And then Tucker had barreled in and blown all of his plans out of the water.

Tucker left, and Angel could barely tell him goodbye, even for a day.

And Angel was so glad to see he was feeling better than he had been the day before.

Angel had worried so much. He'd worried about Tucker getting attacked; he'd worried about Tucker getting better. It wasn't until Tucker started asking him about the house that he realized he wasn't worried about the mission—the thing Angel was actually *supposed* to be worried about. Angel was anxious about *Tucker*. About whether he was strong enough, about Tucker getting hurt.

About Tucker getting sad, and the secret, scared places inside him that Tucker seemed to mask with sarcasm and activity.

About making Tucker smile, just for Angel.

About maybe not seeing Tucker smile the same way at any other human being.

And then Angel thought about all of the things in this monstrosity of a house, all of the landmines just waiting for Tucker to unleash hell upon himself.

Oh gods.

Why couldn't Angel have worried like this about Ruth?

By all rights, Ruth knew less about her job than Tucker did—and she'd been very innocent.

But Angel had felt a toughness in Ruth, and while Tucker was strong—there was no doubt—Angel saw a vulnerability in him that Angel could barely face. And he certainly couldn't walk away from it.

Tucker *needed* someone. And as much as Angel had distrusted the Greenaways at the beginning, knowing that there was another group of people who had an eye out for Tucker was a big relief. Angel had watched the children and heard their mother, and he was reassured.

Ruth had been alone—and that had been unfortunate. Angel would bear responsibility for that. And regret. But Ruth had been happy alone, in the end.

Angel was starting to see that Tucker had been alone most of his life, and it was killing him now. Every

memory of his past pulled something tight and irrevocable around his heart, making it harder for Angel to
feel good about leaving him in Daisy Place with just
his memories.

Angel even wanted him to take this break.

But that didn't mean it wasn't painful being left
behind.

"What do you suppose he's doing, Squishbeans?"

The kitten purred and dug her claws into Angel's
side, kneading. The first time she'd done this, he'd been
surprised and hurt. Tucker had been sleeping, so inert
his breathing had been suspect, and suddenly Angel
was being punctured with tiny needles.

But he hadn't wanted to wake Tucker, and so he'd
counted to ten, breathing like humans did, and realized
the pain was not nearly equal to the comfort of having
the kitten purr and make tiny kitten biscuits against his
suddenly corporeal skin.

He'd pulled up his shirt after Squishbeans had tod-
dled off to do the same thing in Tucker's hair.

His skin had been perfectly smooth, not even a
spot of broken skin or a tiny bit of blood to tell him
he'd been hurt.

Unlike Tucker.

Angel sat at the window box overlooking the garden.
The ghosts were out there—they were always out there
when the sun hit the lawn—but he did not see them.

Instead he saw Tucker, that first day, lying in bed
looking sleepy and relaxed, the pale skin of his upper
arms almost blue in contrast with the tan of his fore-
arms. There were small freckles, the occasional mole,
sparse dark hair under his arms and across his chest—
but it was the body of a man who had not endured too
much physical pain in his life.

One day, one hunch to investigate a place Angel should have investigated years ago, and his body had been changed irrevocably.

Maybe it matches his heart now.

It wasn't the first time Angel had thought that either.

Vulnerable.

Tucker Henderson, for all his swagger, for all his stubborn insistence he was making the best of the situation, had been hurt on a fundamental level.

Angel closed his eyes against the ghosts on the lawn and remembered that moment, that heady, terrible moment when Tucker's blood, after he'd nicked himself shaving, had made Angel real.

You shouldn't bleed for me, Tucker.

But he wasn't sure Tucker could stop.

Angel opened his eyes and regarded the kitten soberly. "I would like for him not to get hurt again. Not so soon." Ruth had endured some rough things, but not with the pain and frequency Tucker had. No wonder she'd wanted to keep her nephew away from Daisy Place.

The kitten meowed and played with Angel's fingers, pulling one in to lick it.

"There's no salt there, kitty," Angel told her sadly. "You need to wait until Tucker gets back." But Squishbeans kept at it, and Angel wondered what was waiting for him in the Chrysanthemum Room when he returned.

"Should we go see?" he asked.

Squishbeans did that sudden startlement thing that cats did, hissing and spitting and wiggling out of Angel's lap and running away.

Not encouraging.

Angel disappeared, then materialized in the Chrysanthemum Room and looked around. The desk had been pushed to one end, loaded with the objects Tucker was reluctant to touch. That nice Greenaway father had been in here the day before and left a battery-run humidifier running all day. The once-vibrant wallpaper hung in curls down the walls from the ten-foot ceiling, and Angel thought that the least he could do would be to feel along the walls and check for traps.

Heaven help them both if someone had engaged in intercourse while pressed up against the wall.

Angel started to the right of the door, holding his hands in front of him as he ghosted his body around. He was so busy checking for spiritual energy that he almost missed the very real anomaly peeking out from behind where the strips of wallpaper met in the corner of the room. Previously the bedframe had obscured them, but now, loosened by the humidity, Angel could see the yellowed pages of what looked to be a letter wedged in between the layers.

Angel passed immaterial fingers through ragged parchment several times, cursing his limitations, before he remembered that Squishbeans was more than a cat.

"Kitty, kitty, kitty," he sang. "Kitty, kitty, kitty."

Nothing.

Not a damned thing.

Angel sat cross-legged on the floor, staring at what he was certain were the pages of the letter he hoped had been written by Sophie's brother, and cursed his luck that Tucker was not yet home.

HE WAS not sure when Squishbeans wandered in and sat on his lap—it could have been ten minutes later, or it could have been hours later. The shades over the window overlooking the garden were so thick, Angel was pretty sure the house could have gone flying into the stratosphere to have its own adventures and the inhabitants would notice nothing more than an irregular shifting underfoot.

One minute he was hating everything; the next his entire being had blissed out and he was stroking that somnolent furball with moody precision. When Squishbeans reached out with her little claws and began to knead his inner thigh (ouch!), Angel stopped petting and went ahead with his plan.

He had to lean over a *lot* so as not to disturb the kitten, and he had to wheedle and tease and gently extricate the trapped stationery, but eventually it was in his grasp—two pages, written in a brief, masculine hand:

> Sophie—
> I am sorry to hear of your troubles with your husband. Pa should never have let him grace the front door. I hold no grudges against you for divorcing him—I'd divorce him from his senses with my fist had I had a moment alone with the man, or with his father.
> You are welcome to come stay with me and my wife in Auburn. We have a small cottage out back for you and your maid. If you can help Henrietta with her laundering for extra money, we would be much obliged, but your stay is not contingent upon your service.

I am just happy to hear from family, Sophie. I miss Ma and Pa every day. It's rougher out here, and railroad men are often wild and uncouth. I do not mind so much, but Henrietta misses manners and civility. I think a sister would do much to ease that longing.

I shall leave to fetch you two weeks after sending this. I know not why you chose such an inaccessible place as your refuge—the journey there and back shall not be pleasant. I hope there is room at your hostel to give me a few nights' rest.

I look forward to seeing you, Sophie—

James Beaufort

Angel read the letter once, then again and again, leaning his chin on one fist while stroking Squishbeans with his other hand.

"Did you see this?" he asked after a few moments wherein the activity in his whirling mind could probably be heard in the silent house. "They had rescue coming. Do you understand what this means?"

He smiled down at the kitten happily, then gathered up the pages. Very carefully, he stood up with the kitten in one hand and the letter clutched in the other. He took them both to the desk and set the old paper down on the side of the desk with the "happy" objects.

"The green bottle, you think?" he asked, and the kitten hung out, happy in his hand and apparently unmoved by how strange it should be that Angel could pick her up.

Angel smoothed the pages very deliberately and put the green bottle—the object still humming with passion and happiness—on the top.

It wasn't much. Tucker still had to strip wallpaper and sand floors. There was still the glass paperweight and all of the terror it held for the both of them.

But just this once, Angel had been able to provide some safety, a happy moment, for the man who had become the center of Angel's universe. Angel wasn't sure how to put his work on the house back in that place, but until it happened, he would work for Tucker.

SPILLED LIKE WINE

"YOU LET me do all the talking!" Josh said cheerfully as they got out of the truck.

"I'm a fan of listening," Tucker said, which was true, but only a teeny tiny corner of the truth.

He and Josh had enjoyed the trip to Sac—they'd played music loud and shot the shit all the way down, keeping Andy in the rearview so they didn't lose him as they dodged through traffic.

Josh was partial to classic rock, but Tucker could live with that. A lot of Josh's stories dealt with stupid people who couldn't fix their way out of a paperclip trying to deal with complicated engines, but Tucker could deal with that too. Honest folks making an honest living were his favorite kind—but perhaps that came from living so long on his inheritance and feeling like a cosmic whore for most of his adult life.

The apartment itself was one of the converted Victorians down by the legal district. Tucker had slept with a lot of lawyers in the past fifteen years, as well as a not-surprising share of policemen, judges, and nonviolent offenders. For the most part, the criminals had been his favorite—in particular the businesswoman who woke up in the morning and said, "Oh my God! I hurt *all* those people! I *do* deserve jail!"

Yet another story he couldn't tell.

Letting Josh talk—*encouraging* his friend to talk—was one more way to evade what Tucker's life had become.

His apartment was a depressing reminder of that.

They trotted up the narrow stairwell, Andy bringing up the rear, and Tucker let them into the second-floor apartment. "Oh, holy cow," Andy breathed. "This is awesome!"

Tucker looked around and smiled bitterly. "Thank you," he said, leaching the irony from his voice.

He did keep a nice place.

Refinished hardwood floors, bright throw rugs, curiosity shelves with an eclectic mix of tchotchkes. Tucker's apartment had been his haven—but it had also been solitary confinement.

Out on the street was his next one-night stand—or the ghost of someone who didn't know he was dead or a vampire or an elf who would look at him with raised eyebrows and oh-so-chic insouciance.

Tucker's world was not everyone else's world. His home, the movies, the music, the puzzle books and history books and romances—these were the most normal things about him, and he wrapped them around his body like a fur-lined cocoon.

He didn't have to be an empath to know the place emanated a deep and soul-consuming loneliness.

He just hoped Andy's chirpy confidence, his belief in home and the undying love of his family was enough to overcome the chill of Tucker's thirteen-year depression.

"I'll get a box for the knickknacks," Tucker said. "Andy, you can plug your phone into the stereo for music if you want—"

"No!" Josh complained good-naturedly. "He likes that alt-rock crap!"

"Mountain Goats it is." Tucker winked at Josh. "Besides, you get your music in the car. Andy, you may want to make a list of stuff you want to bring—"

"Tucker, who's Damien?" Andy asked, and if Tucker hadn't had a long conversation with Andy's mother and his family the day before, it would have taken him completely by surprise.

"Bring stuffed animals," Tucker said, begging Andy with his eyes to not pursue the matter. "Bring music. Pictures of your family. Ask your mother to give you plants—they'll make the place yours. And…." He thought of all the times he'd wanted a kitten but hadn't known when he'd be home. "A pet. Even if it's just a goldfish. A pet will make it more yours than—"

"Who's Damien?" Andy insisted.

Tucker looked at Josh and shook his head. "There's some boxes down in the truck. I'll go get them."

"I'll get them," Josh said. "You're looking tired. Andy, come with me."

"But Dad—"

"Son, let me tell you something that going to school won't, *once we get outside*!"

"It hurts in here!" Andy burst out, and his dad grabbed his upper arm and hauled him out the door.

Tucker took a deep breath and looked around. It hurt in there.

Tucker needed to get the most haunted objects out.

Damien's baseball mitt and the ball he'd gotten signed by Barry Bonds in their junior year of high school. His collection of baseball hats, hanging behind the couch. A picture of Tucker and his family, and Damien, taken at an amusement park—they'd gone for Tucker's fifteenth birthday.

Tucker and Damien with awkward dates at the junior prom, taken by Tucker's mom. Tucker and Damien graduating from high school, taken by Damien's dad. From college, taken by some poor parent they'd grabbed by the collar.

Damien in a standard-issue bronze urn, in a place of honor on top of the bookshelf in the corner.

By the time Josh and Andy came trundling up the stairs, bickering the whole way, all traces of Tucker's childhood crush and adult heartbreak had been gathered into a pile so Tucker could put them in a box. He didn't need to protect himself with gloves or his T-shirt—he'd been living with that pain for so long it had seeped into his skin like a Damien callus.

"Good," Tucker said brightly, making eye contact with nobody. "You brought them. Here, I'll go get tape."

He started toward the kitchen, where the standard junk was in the standard junk drawer, and then he turned around. "Uh, go ahead and start packing up the clothes in the bedroom," he said. "I'll get this crap."

"Sure, Tucker." Josh said it, but as they were walking by him to the bedroom, Andy was the one who reached out and squeezed his shoulder.

The contact burned, almost as bad as Angel pushing the ghost energy out, but Tucker controlled his gasp. They disappeared into his bedroom. Telling, wasn't it? That he didn't feel as though his privacy was being violated by people in his bedroom, but he couldn't bear to let them touch pictures on the shelves?

He went into the kitchen for plastic grocery bags—which he usually recycled—and pulled out the mitt and the ball to wrap them up.

His hands only shook a little with that one.

He was okay as he wrapped up their baseball trophies from grade school.

His hands started shaking harder when he started with the pictures.

By the time he had the last picture wrapped in plastic and was reaching for the sealed urn, he could hardly breathe.

He'd been living with this—with *all* of this—open and looking him in the face every day. And it hurt so bad. His throat was raw with the screaming he wasn't doing. His chest ached with the sobbing locked inside.

Oh God—had this been his life every day since Damien died?

How could God or the gods or the Goddess or whoever make exorcising ghosts his calling? Could they not see that he couldn't even exorcise his own?

He managed to get the heavy sealed urn in the corner of the biggest box and taped the top closed. *I don't have to unpack this. I can take it back to Daisy Place and find a closet, maybe in one of the disappearing rooms. I can put Damien in the back of one of the closets and leave him, and someday when I'm dead, another promising young man will stumble on it, and Angel will say—*

Oh, Angel!

How was he going to tell Angel that this shrine to a lost friend had become his life?

He didn't even want to think about it.

And then he remembered his scrapbook.

Oh hell. The damning scrapbook. He didn't even wrap up his monument to the times *he* hadn't failed but *something* had. He rooted through the bookshelf, because he didn't want Josh or Andy to see it either, and threw the damned thing on top of the box. He tried to blank his mind against what Angel would say about *that* too.

Grimly determined not to imagine spilling his soul to that perceptive set of green eyes, he schlepped the first box down, then the second. By the time he got back after the second, Josh and Andy had heaps of clothes in garbage bags, ready to go down into the truck too.

There were dishes at Daisy Place, but Tucker brought his comforter, pillow, fuzzy blankets, and some of his linens, as well as his backup toiletry supplies and one of two dressers.

"This one is shorter," he said apologetically. "My computer will fit on it better."

Andy shrugged. "Your system," he said.

They lugged that down next, and then Tucker stood in the middle of the apartment and looked around.

He'd been going to take his recliner, but it matched the couch, and Josh told him he and Rae had a club chair and an ottoman that would fit in Tucker's bedroom.

"It's leather," he said. "Real nice. And this way, we can leave Andy here with a matched set of furniture."

Andy darted a furtive glance at Tucker, and Tucker understood. That way, Tucker wouldn't be sitting in the same throne of self-pity he'd inhabited for the last thirteen years, and Andy would have a chance to clear the grief out of the furniture.

Well, if the kid wanted to cut his teeth in the weird psychic half-world Tucker inhabited, let him.

The scars on Tucker's heart were still bleeding. His psychic scars were now indelibly etched across his skin. If Andy, with his enthusiasm and his desperate need to get laid, could jump into the fight, Tucker was in no condition to stop him.

Tucker could barely take care of himself.

"That's fine," Tucker said, summoning a grateful smile from he knew not where. "Is that it? Are we done?"

"Yeah," Josh said, looking around. "Andy, did you wrap those framed prints in blankets?"

"Yeah," Andy said promptly. "They're snug in the back of the pickup. Tucker, can you think of anything else?"

Tucker looked around, and it hit him.

Whether he'd wanted it to or not, his inheritance from Aunt Ruth had officially changed his life.

"I'll call you if I think of anything," he said. "I'll email the landlord and let him know you're staying here to keep the place for me."

Josh looked at his son uncertainly. "Tucker... I know you didn't ask anything, but you know, we *could* pay a little toward—"

"No," Tucker said, holding his hand up to forestall any argument. "The rent is paid from my parents' trust. I've hardly touched it, really. Mostly it just sits there and accrues interest, and I use that to pay bills." He smiled briefly, hoping the expression reassured Andy. "It'll be worth it to me to know I'll still have a place in the city in case Daisy Place gets swallowed by a hole in the earth, right?"

Andy shuddered. "You say that like it's not a very real possibility. Now let's go eat. Dad, you promised you'd treat."

JOSH TOOK them to Cheesecake Factory and treated them both. Tucker ordered a hamburger and a slice of chocolate-swirl cheesecake and listened to Josh and Andy tease him about his metabolism.

He didn't have the heart to tell them that it was part and parcel of the whole psychic gig—and that it probably meant his lifespan would be cut a little short because of it. His superhigh metabolism was just more proof that nothing came without a price.

HE'D RECOVERED some of his equanimity by the time they got back to Daisy Place. Andy stayed in the city, much as his mom had predicted. Josh was keeping the truck for the day so he could haul Andy's stuff into the city in the morning, provided he spent the night okay.

Tucker hoped with all his heart that most of the sadness would disappear with Tucker and his measly possessions. He wouldn't wish his problems on any-body, much less Andover Greenaway.

About halfway up the hill, Tucker dozed off, arms folded, head resting against the window. Josh pulled up the driveway and ordered him into the house.

"In bed, Tucker—there's nothing here that will need two people. You look like one of the ghosts that's supposed to live here."

Tucker barely remembered to step aside as the grand tide of ghosts ebbed and surged, but after the churning movement in the psychic sphere had eased, they made it inside. He even managed to turn on the lights, both inside and outside, so Josh could come in through the kitchen. Angel was waiting for him at the table, Squishbeans lying in the middle of a place mat in front of him, asleep on her back, paws outstretched to the world.

"Oh, Tucker!" Angel said happily. "You're home! I've made the most excellent—never mind. You're exhausted. My discovery can wait. Let's get you to bed."

Tucker was too tired to even scowl. "Angel, look at you, all human and everything. I like it."

Angel's face fell, his excitement fading away. "Oh, Tucker. I hope you're not counting on me to be human. I am doing my best, but I'm not sure—"

"Don't sweat it," Tucker mumbled, stumbling to his room. He didn't even need to turn the light on. He found the bed on instinct and kicked off his shoes. Then he fell face-first onto the pillow, too weak to be embarrassed that it was barely eight o'clock at night.

"I just don't want you to rely on me for something I can't—"

"I said don't worry," Tucker told him, meaning it. "You're a better human being than I ever was, even if you were never human."

And that's the last thing he remembered saying for a while.

He believed that with all his soul. It's what allowed him to feel safe while Angel was watching him sleep.

HE WOKE up sometime in the night to take off his clothes and use the bathroom. Angel's voice from the bed didn't startle him at all.

"Tucker, you're not sleeping well."

"Just uncomfortable," he mumbled. The mattress hadn't gotten any better since that first night, it was true, but there were so many other things to worry about now.

"You're crying."

Wonderful. "If you're going to be a man, you need to not mention the crying," he replied, voice clogged. "It's not polite."

"So can I mention the crying now?"

Tucker half laughed—in the light from the bathroom, he could see that Angel was now a slim brunet with long straight hair, dusky skin, and smoky green eyes.

"Very sexy," he muttered. "But you don't have to change for me."

"But can I talk about the crying now?" she demanded plaintively.

"No," he said. He turned out the light and crawled back into bed. It was probably his imagination, but he could swear he smelled musky perfume.

"I like musk and lime on men," he muttered. "Lavender on women."

The smell went floral, and Tucker chuckled.

"I'll try not to cry and bother you," he said softly.

"Just tell me why," Angel insisted, her voice tender.

"My life hasn't... hasn't amounted to much, Angel."

"Oh, I doubt that."

Tucker's eyes were closed—he could almost imagine the kiss on the cheek.

"What makes you think I'm worth something?" He needed to know. Sad, perhaps, but true. Angel's opinion had come to mean a lot to him.

"Because of how you talk about using your gift," she said. "Nobody who believed you had to use it and do good things with it as passionately as you do could have lived a worthless life."

"Awesome," he muttered bitterly.

"You are also nice to be around," Angel said, sounding as though this had just occurred to her. "You are… considerate. You like people. You work hard to make sure they're comfortable around you. Maybe it's because I've seen the bad people who come through here—the bad memories linger when the good ones have gone on with their makers. That's not a small thing—being considerate. I think it makes you worthy."

Tucker half laughed. "Thanks, Angel."

"And you try so hard to laugh, even when your heart has been sore for a long time. You don't want anybody in your life to feel your pain. That's… that's hard. You try to find happy things about life, even if it's only a television show, and you like to share. *I* think that's very important."

"Well, it does benefit you," Tucker mumbled, soothed by the sound of her voice.

"It's a gift," Angel admitted. "And I'm grateful. And I'm sorry, because you still sound sad."

"I…." The ache pounded in the pit of his chest, but he stomped it down like he always did. As Angel had said, if he'd learned one thing in the last thirteen years, it was how to function. Eat, sleep, be happy with what you couldn't lose. A nice meal, a pretty day, the particular nice qualities of his hookup du jour—all of those things were in the moment.

Right now, he had a comfortable bed, a kind voice in the night, and the smell of lavender and… he smiled. Mint.

"I'll be fine," he said and then closed his eyes.

He was almost asleep when he heard her whisper, "But you're not. You won't be. Please, Tucker, talk to me."

He wanted to say "Not now," but by then he really was asleep.

THE NEXT morning, he stumbled into the kitchen in his underwear, the better to make coffee. Angel hovered at the far end, where Josh had stacked his boxes and the dresser, her long dark hair twisted into a knot on the top of her head, her jeans and T-shirt fitting her slim body ever so perfectly.

It was like she knew which people turned Tucker on the most and only picked them—right down to the leather daddy, who had been his type once upon a time.

The look on her face tore a little at Tucker's soul.

"Angel, get away from there," he ordered gruffly. "There's no reason for you to—"

"This stuff is haunted," she said stubbornly. "And you haven't told anybody the story. Don't you know by now that you have to tell the story or it becomes a ghost?"

"Yeah, well, I figured that out when I saw my friend's headstone in the goddamned cemetery," Tucker snapped back.

By the surprise on Angel's face, Tucker figured she hadn't realized that.

"I'm sorry," she murmured.

"You're a horrible detective," he said back.

She shrugged, the pain in her green eyes hard to take. "Ruth said as much, many times."

"You'd think if the powers that be were going to send someone to help clean this place out, they would have picked somebody with better skills," Tucker said, and then he grimaced. "That's no slam against you,

Angel. It's only you're not really… adept at all of this, you know? You're brave and clever, but—"

"I'm not usually good at following clues." Angel's disheartenment cut him a little deeper.

"Maybe you were learning too, just like Ruth, just like me." He dug deep and found his most winsome smile. "Think of it as improving, right?"

She smiled a little and then completely brightened. "Actually, Tucker, I wanted to tell you—Squishbeans and I found something last night!"

"Yeah?" Oh, it was good to see those green eyes light up like that.

"Yes. I want very badly for you to see it. It's important. That letter you saw on the table of Bridget and Sophie's room, remember?"

He nodded, bemused, because he did. "Yes?"

"I know who it was from!"

She was bouncing on her toes, smile sparkling, cheeks flushed, and Tucker felt a totally inappropriate shaft of attraction. He smiled back at her, caught up in her enthusiasm, and tried really hard to use this moment to break her away from the pile of objects she was still hovering around.

"That's great. Let me eat breakfast first. Then I can go see after I've showered and changed. How's that?"

Angel's expression hardened. "You're evading the point, Tucker. How are you going to tell me Sophie and Bridget's story when you won't tell your own?"

Crap. "I'm starving. Ham omelet? Maybe some tomatoes? Some spinach? Oh, hey, we've got garlic. Let's throw the whole thing in the pan!"

With cheerful determination, he started raiding the refrigerator, figuring he was feeling adventurous enough to cook eggs in his boxers but not to go through those boxes of emotional eggs.

"Fine," Angel said behind him, sounding resigned. "Eat. You need it. You look pale. But I'm not going up-stairs again until you tell me what your pain is, Tucker. And you need me to set these ghosts free."

Tucker plunked his armload of omelet fixings down on the counter. "Fine," he muttered, pulling a chef's knife from the clean dishes. "I'll go look at the letter anyway. You pout because you're not getting your—"

"*I'm not pouting! This is killing you!*"

Tucker gasped and dropped the knife on the floor. "Goddammit, Angel!"

But she was gone, out of the kitchen entirely, and he didn't have the heart to find her.

BLURRED LETTERS

Angel didn't go far. She hovered on the ceiling, looking down at Tucker as he cracked eggs dispiritedly into a pan and chopped up meat and veggies to go on top of them.

She realized she was frantic.

This place—it was going to kill him. It was going to destroy him, inside and out, and he didn't seem to care or mind or even want to avoid it. And all of that indifference to his own safety seemed to center around that pile of... of... *excrement* he'd brought from his home.

Augh! Tucker! Couldn't you have brought your knitting?

And nothing she could do seemed to help.

He finished the omelet and set the table, then poured himself coffee and settled down heavily to eat. Angel studied his body helplessly, seeing the fading scars from the psychic burns and wishing she'd been able to save him some other way.

He said his friend was in the dimensional grave-yard. What does that mean?

She would never figure it out without him.

Tucker sighed heavily and lifted a bite of food to his mouth, and Angel wafted down from the ceiling and materialized in the chair next to him.

He changed form, back to the auburn-haired warrior he'd chosen the first time he'd seen Tucker pleasure himself and had wanted to give Tucker that same pleasure. He was starting to admit, deep inside, that he understood the significance of this body and why it was becoming his go-to.

God, he wanted to please Tucker. And protect him. And make him safe and warm.

"I'm sorry," Angel said quietly. Tucker didn't even start, which probably meant he knew where Angel had been all along. "I shouldn't use ultimatums. They're wrong. You've done everything I've asked of you. You've done more. You've made more progress and asked more questions than Ruth and I did in fifty years."

"I can do the job," Tucker said tersely, taking a bite of omelet.

"Of course you can." Angel had no doubts. "I'm just worried about the cost to you. And before you say you're fine, you need to know, I'm not like this. I probably could have used your aunt like a pawn for many more years and not worried. But you I'm worried about. So please...." And that was when he ran out of words.

Tucker sighed and took another bite. His usual zeal for food seemed to have deserted him, and Angel mourned that he'd been the cause of that.

"Tell you what," Tucker said after swallowing deliberately. "I need a nap—which is pissing me off by the way. And Josh is probably going to show up around two with the truck. We'll wait until then. I'll shower, shave, try to look and act like a human being, and we'll just leave it for a while. Will that make you happy?"

Angel closed his eyes, so damned grateful he had no words. "Can we watch *Buffy*?" he asked plaintively.

"Yeah, sure."

Tucker cleaned up, showered, and then slept through two episodes of *Buffy*. As promised, Josh Greenaway came knocking around twoish, his wife waiting to take him home.

"Don't you have a job in Auburn anyway?" Tucker teased.

Angel was looking over his shoulder and saw Josh roll his eyes good-naturedly. "Yeah, yeah. This is the weekend, son, and guess how I used it."

"D'oh!" Tucker muttered. "I'm sorry! Didn't mean to suck up all your spare time."

Josh winked and gave a brief salute. "Sir, you just gave my boy a chance to live in the big city. With any luck, he'll get laid and chill out a little about the whole psychic business. That would make my life just peachy, I shit you not. So you suck up my weekends all you want, hear?"

Tucker nodded and waved goodbye, then hung his keys on the hook by the door.

"You ready?" he asked Angel, and Angel's heart fell.

When Tucker had first arrived, Angel would have accused him of taking his duty too lightly, not having the comfort of the undead at heart.

Now Angel knew better.

Tucker would push himself as far and as hard as he needed to in order to escape the sorrow hanging over that pile of objects in the corner of the kitchen like a funeral pall.

"Sure," Angel replied with a game smile. He was not used to lying—he was pretty sure the smile looked sad and sickly, but it was all he had.

So Angel was reluctant already, but he was not prepared for what awaited them when they walked into the room.

"That's the letter?" Tucker asked, his voice cracking in disappointment.

"Yes!" Angel stuttered. "No. I mean, the pages were there but…. Tucker, they didn't look like that when I set them down. *Don't touch that!*"

Tucker snatched his hand back from the seascape paperweight as though it were molten iron.

"What in the hell? How did you even get that on top of them?"

"I *didn't!*" Raw terror bloomed deep in Angel's bowels. He'd worked with ghosts for fifty years, and not once had one of them pulled something like this. He looked at Tucker, letting his panic show. "Tucker, I put the glass bottle on top of the letter. I… I had Squish-beans in my hand, Tucker. I never would have…."

"Shh. It's okay, sweetheart," Tucker said softly, surprising him. "You wouldn't do anything to hurt the kitten. I hear you. But… what happened?"

They both drew near the desk, although reading the letter was obviously not going to happen. Great red stains, like new red wine or fresh blood, completely obscured the pages, soaking through to the top of the desk and spreading in a pool under most of the "good" objects they'd gathered there.

The green bottle lay toppled in the resulting mess, and the paperweight sat, heavy and irrevocable, on top of the bloody letter.

Tucker took a deep breath and moved closer.

"Maybe we should have Josh do it." Angel spoke rashly. "He has no talent, no empathy. Maybe if he cleans up the mess, it won't hurt him!"

Tucker looked over his shoulder and shook his head. "Angel, we can't fob this off on someone else. If we can't fix this, nobody can."

"But what are you going to—"

"The paperweight. Isn't it obvious? There's something buried deep inside it that someone wants us to know."

And without another word, Tucker stepped forward and lifted it off of the desk.

BLOOD

AT FIRST, there was just the cool weight of the glass in his hands.

And then the weight changed.

HE LOOKED down at it, frowning, because it was on a base now—a hard bronze base, thick and heavy, with sharp corners.

His hands were not his own.

These hands were coarse, wide-palmed, perpetually dirty from working with steel, picking up hot bolts before they were cooled, putting oil on a wheel axle before it turned red, warping with the friction. They were dependable hands, the hands of a good man, and they were shaking with anger.

The paperweight rose, his heaving muscles barely straining as he raised it over his head.

"Leave 'er alone, damn you!"

Sophie's screams echoed through the room, and the redheaded girl, Bridget, lay inert in a corner, blood dripping from a wound on her forehead. Oh God, that man! Sophie was terrified of him, was fighting him like a hellion, biting and scratching, and the man didn't look up, just flailed at her clothing, cracking her hard across the face, across the breasts, battering her with his body.

"Leave 'er alone!"

"This hardly concerns you!"

Oh God—it had to stop! It had to stop!

The paperweight crashed down on the back of the attacker's skull, so hard the bronze base flew off into a corner.

The crunch of bone followed, and brains, and a full-grown man fell with a thump, bleeding and convulsing, blood puddling from his hair, from his nose, his body a heap of useless flesh.

TUCKER SCREAMED, thunking the paperweight down on the desk and backing away, shaking.

Blood.

So much blood.

Blood streaming from a wound, through graying black hair.

Blood and brains in a nest of dark blond—God no.

No.

He couldn't remember that.

Couldn't remember a face, one moment beloved, the next moment destroyed.

Couldn't remember the sound of wind chimes in the silence following a gunshot.

Couldn't remember a body thrown into him by the force of the blast, by the momentum of a footstep, just one footstep, putting the skull in the line of fire....

Couldn't remember....

"Damien!"

He took a breath and tried to figure out if the sound came from his mind or his heart or his throat.

His throat was raw. It must have been from his throat.

"Damien! Oh God, Damien!"

"Tucker!"

Tucker dragged in a breath through lungs that burned fiercely, like acid, like rusty wire, like the putrid memory of long-rotted souls.

"Tucker!" Angel screamed. "Tucker, stop. Stop! It's not him."

Tucker shook his head and looked around, the wind-chime garden disappearing, Damien's corpse disappearing, the real world—the empty room, the curling wallpaper, the desktop full of haunted objects—falling into hyperreal focus.

"Not who?" he asked, feeling lost.

"The man you saw die. It wasn't him. It wasn't Damien."

Angel was standing in front of him, hands on his shoulders, and Tucker could feel them. Could *feel* firm human flesh and bone, and see the panic and gold flecks in Angel's green eyes.

"How do you know about Damien?" Tucker asked, trying hard—so hard—to be in the here and now.

"Oh God, Tucker. How could I not know his name?"

Angel was crying. Tucker reached out and brushed his fingertips across a freckled cheek, feeling the softness of skin, the roughness of stubble, the heat of tears.

He brought them to his tongue and tasted.

Salt.

And citrus and lavender.

"Angel, how are you doing this?" he asked, desperate to not *be* in the place with Damien's shattered skull and brains and blood.

"You're bleeding," Angel said through his tears. "Oh, Tucker, your heart is bleeding. It's in the air. It's sinking into the woodwork. Please, Tucker. Tell me your story!"

Tucker scrubbed at his face, his hands coming away wet, and shook his head.

"I'm hurting you," he said thickly. "I'm hurting you. And I've got to get out of here."

And with that he ran blindly down the hallway and out the door, barely remembering his car keys and wallet as he put Daisy Place in his rearview.

The pull under his breastbone started as soon as the truck's tires hit the pavement.

HE ENDED up at the Ore Cart again, finding his way on instinct and hoping for a beer before he was farmed out to cosmic stud.

He was greeted by the Greenaways—Rae, Josh, Tilda, Murphy, and Coral—sitting around the biggest table in the place, splitting two giant burgers between them.

"Come sit down, Tucker," Josh called, smiling and waving.

Tucker had to blink several times to frame a refusal. What was he going to say? "No, I'm going to sit in a corner and drink until a stranger comes along to use me for my magic fuckstick?"

"Come on, Tucker," Coral said. Their ten-year-old girl had thick curly brown hair and Rae's witchy brown eyes. "You have ghosts in your heart."

Tucker gaped at her, and then, just like that, he felt the *pop*.

He was *supposed* to find this family, find this place.

He was *supposed* to sit here and eat pieces of hamburger soaked in ketchup and drink soda.

That was the reason he'd been pulled out of Daisy Place?

You weren't pulled out of Daisy Place.

The voice wasn't Angel's, but it could have been.

This is where I'm supposed to be if I'm not there.

Oh.

Tucker smiled at them weakly and sat down, allowing Coral to make him a sloppy plate of burger and fries and letting Dakota Fisher's old student serve him root beer.

"You're looking sort of shitty," Rae said gently. "Rough day at the ranch?"

Tucker shrugged and looked at Tilda and Murphy, who were arguing over which *Overwatch* character was the best and who had the coolest skins.

"You could say that," he said. His voice sounded scratchy to his own ears.

"Did you leave Angel all alone?" Coral asked plaintively. "He hates it when you do that."

"Angel has the kitten for company," Tucker told her automatically. He was thinking about the taste of Angel's tears on his tongue, and his next breath felt more like a sob.

Coral patted him gently on the back. "It's okay, Tucker. He still likes you more than Squishbeans."

Tucker took a deep breath and tried to pull himself together. He wasn't going to get drunk this time and wake up in a stranger's bed, and the relief of that shook him to the core. He needed to remember how to be human again if he wanted to keep these people in his life.

"Thanks, kiddo. I'll try to make sure that stays true."

"Here." She handed him a french fry. "This will help. It has salt."

"That there," said Josh, "is a kid who has never heard the word 'hypertension' in her life."

Tucker managed a better smile this time. "Let's hope she never will. Thanks, Coral. You're right. Fries make it better."

"Let me order you a milkshake," Coral said wisely. "I can have the extra in the cup, and then we can *both* feel better."

He was in the middle of his second milkshake when the bell over the door rang and a voice he hadn't heard in weeks called out, "Tucker? Tucker, is that you?"

"Miz Fisher!" Jordan called out, waving. "Look-it you!"

Tucker looked over his shoulder and found his Foresthill welcoming committee, Dakota Fisher, standing in the doorway, resplendent in her sheriff's deputy uniform, her blond hair pulled back into a ponytail.

Tucker didn't feel a *pop*—not even a tingle—but he was glad to see her.

She strode up and made herself at home at their little table, and soon the kids were pumping her for information on her transition from schoolteacher to law enforcement, and did she *really* get to fire the gun at her hip?

Tucker finished off his cold fries and let the talk at the table wash over him, and that sense of dislocation, of unreality, vanished.

This here was healing time.

He was a human being, among his fellow human beings, and they were welcoming him into the fold.

THE GREENAWAYS lingered over pie and ice cream, but eventually they had to go. School was starting in a week, and apparently Rae had a list as long as her arm of stuff she needed to accomplish to get everybody to their destination in adequate clothing with enough food.

Tucker remembered his own mother saying much the same thing. Oh, she would have loved to have been a grandmother by proxy to the Greenaway kids.

Tucker and Dakota followed the family out, and Tucker was surprised to see that the sun was almost down. He'd been sitting in the Ore Cart for over two hours, shooting the shit and playing cheeseboxes on his place mat with Coral and Murphy.

His face hurt from smiling.

"So," Dakota said, pausing by her cruiser and leaning on the door. "I'm actually off shift early and not too tired to do something with my life." She raised her eyebrows suggestively. "Any plans?"

Tucker thought about it seriously—about taking a lover who was not part of the cosmic plan. It looked like the gods or whoever were giving him a break now, didn't it? No pickups tonight, right? In fact, *Tucker* was the one who had been picked up by the lovely family, and he'd been made to feel special in their midst.

Maybe, as long as he hunted ghosts and told their stories like a good little empath, that chapter of his life would be over now.

The air whooshed out of his lungs as he realized the truth of that.

That chapter of his life could be over now. Perhaps his strengthening bond with Angel was what started the new one.

Damien.

How could he close out that entire chapter of his life if nobody heard the story? He didn't want to tell that story to Dakota, not even for an enjoyable moment in bed. If the adult years of his life had taught him *anything*, it was that sex was easy. But real emotion, *that* was a currency that was hard to find and even harder to keep.

"I can't," he said softly, touching her cheek with his knuckle so she'd know he took the offer seriously. "I've got some business to finish at home."

Dakota shrugged, obviously hurt but dealing. "Some other time?"

Would there be? He closed his eyes and tasted lavender and mint. And salt. "I wouldn't rule it out," he said with a wink.

She shrugged. "You already have. Later, Tucker. Call me if you need anything—anything not sex. I mean that."

"Thanks."

She climbed into her cruiser and pulled away, and Tucker got into the truck. He didn't need a supernatural pull under his breastbone to know the only place to go was Daisy Place.

The person he needed to talk to was most undoubtedly at home.

HE LAUGHED as he pulled up because Angel's face was pressed against the front window of the house, pale and wraithlike.

Tucker walked in through the kitchen. "Angel, ghosts like you give haunted houses a bad name."

Angel materialized immediately, and Squishbeans came trotting in on his heels, as though they had been waiting together.

"Tucker?" He sounded uncertain, and Tucker managed a brief smile, hoping to calm his nerves.

Maybe calm Tucker's too.

"I'm going to have a beer," Tucker said, pulling one out of the fridge. "I left here feeling like I needed nothing in the world more than a drink. Or six. Or twelve. And I got milkshakes and hamburgers from the Greenaway children, which was fine. But damn, I need a beer."

"Will it make you feel better?" Angel asked, and Tucker cast him a bleak glance.

"It would be nice if something did," he said softly and then plopped down in the kitchen chair.

"Did you eat enough?" Angel made fretful gestures with his hands—even as a man, he had long-fingered, graceful hands. Funny how Tucker had never noticed that before.

"Yup. All the comfort food a man could ask for." Tucker popped the cap and took a swig. He'd ordered imported, and yeah, that was good. "But not beer."

"I was worried," Angel said softly, sitting down across from him.

"I know you were, Angel," Tucker said fondly. "It... you probably don't know or don't care, but it means a lot to me that you were looking out the window for me."

Angel nodded, green eyes disturbingly perceptive. "You are not used to anyone waiting for your return."

"Not since my parents died," Tucker confirmed. He sighed and took another drink. "My power *really* kicked in right after they passed."

"You were a teenager," Angel said sadly. "That's usually the time—"

"Yeah, I know. But this... this was different. My *power* was different. I mean, as a kid, you see ghosts or elves or whatever—but you figure that out. This was.... I was just walking by a McDonald's, you know? And suddenly, I just *had* to have a soda. It was like I'd *die* if I didn't."

"The pull," Angel whispered, leaning his chin on his hand. "You didn't know what it was."

Funny, how Angel talked about it—*the pull*—like it was a thing every empath should know about.

Tucker hadn't.

"Nope. But I walked into that place anyway and ordered some nuggets and a coke. While I was waiting for my order, I had to pee. And damned if the clerk didn't follow me into the bathroom and blow me."

Angel's chin fell off his hand. "I beg your pardon?"

"Sex. In the bathroom. It was my first time. He was cute and all, and I sure did like blowing him back. But a blowjob. In the bathroom. And when it was done, his life had changed. I mean, it worked out great for him—he got to come out, he learned something about himself, he got a blowjob. Go him! But me?" Tucker took another pull of bitterness. "I went back to my parents' house, where the social workers let me stay as long as they visited once a week, and there was not a soul there who cared that I'd just gotten laid in a bath-room. Lucky me."

"Oh, Tucker—"

"The second time, it was a woman in a car. *That* was uncomfortable." His beer was empty. He stood up and grabbed another one. Hell, he wasn't drinking on an empty stomach. He wasn't even *weeping* on an empty stomach. He could polish off a six-pack tonight. Why the hell not?

"Did she have a… a reckoning?" Angel asked as Tucker popped the top off the new bottle.

"Of course she did," Tucker said, feeling expansive. "And so did the next one—a guy. And the next one. I've got a magic wang," he said proudly, belching.

"I've seen it in action," Angel said, the dryness of his voice hitting Tucker like ice. "It's very impressive, Tucker, but what I think was at work in those cases was your soul."

Tucker suddenly had a problem drinking his beer. "You think?" he said, suddenly needing the compliment so damned bad.

"Of course I do!" The softness of Angel's presence brushed over the top of Tucker's knuckles, and he closed his eyes against the sweetness of it. "You—your kindness, your bravery, your humor—those are much more important than your… your cock, Tucker. Even *I* can see that!"

"That's kind," he said, swallowing. "So very kind."

"I'm not a kind being, Tucker. You need to know that."

Tucker wanted to touch him back. "You're kind to me," he said. And then, because the moment demanded it, he added, "Damien was kind too."

He actually heard Angel's indrawn breath. "Are we going to talk about Damien now?"

Tucker cast a baleful look at the piles of boxes. "His baseball mitt is in there. Are you sure you don't want me to just grab it and let our thing do its thing?"

"This isn't about your gift, Tucker." Angel's voice fractured, and he wiped his face—his incorporeal face that was now gleaming with lavender mint tears.

"What's it about? Why do I have to do this?"

"It's about your heart!"

Angel's voice rang in the small kitchen, and Tucker took a deep breath against the anger that threatened the moment.

They'd both know what the anger was masking anyway.

He took another breath, managing to push the fear down his throat, where it rumbled and growled, stalking his stomach with ulcerating claws.

Then Angel put his hands on Tucker's, and faint heat under the coolness of Angel's skin drove the animal of fear even deeper into his cave.

"Am I bleeding again?" he asked dryly. That was the connection, wasn't it? Whenever Angel could touch him corporeally, it was because Tucker was sharing his blood, his humanness, with Angel.

"One of us is. Here." Angel squeezed his hands. "You're safe. Tell me the story, Tucker. I'll see it, like I see Sophie and Bridget. I'll know what happened in your heart, and not just the scary thing that's in your mind."

Tucker closed his eyes against Angel's gaze and nodded. Then he turned his hands over, palm up, and squeezed Angel's fingers.

Angel squeezed back.

"So?"

Damien looked over as they walked and smiled. Tucker loved that smile—it was the one Damien had given him when they'd been playing ball in high school and Damien was pretty sure he was going to get a hit or when Tucker's mother had packed him extra cookies and Tucker offered to share. It was the smile he'd given when Tucker had tripped in junior high and knocked over three desks, and Damien stood to help pick them up.

Damien had offered Tucker a quiet version of the smile the day Tucker's parents had been buried because he knew Tucker would know it was all going to be okay.

"I had a dream," Damien said, that secret, sharing smile twitching against his full lips. "You know. A sex dream."

Tucker grunted. "Damien, I told you. I've got somewhere to go tonight."

Damien nodded seriously. "I know. The pull. You told me. You'll...." He grimaced. "You'll still go. I mean, I'll let you go in a minute. I just thought, you know. Instead of going straight to wherever, we could stop. Have a cookie or something. You know." He bit his lip and his smile went shy. "Talk."

Tucker's whole body flooded with hope.

"Talk?" he asked.

"Yeah." Damien turned into a local bakery, but not before licking his lips. "You know. A treat." Run by a family of tree gnomes (or so Damien claimed), the place was cheerfully yellow, decorated with wind chimes from all corners of the globe. It had a patio that opened onto H Street and into the summer evening.

The pull under Tucker's ribs was getting painful.

"I want to," he said, shuddering against the ache. "But Damie, you gotta understand—it's... I can feel it. Something bad'll happen if I don't."

The disappointment on Damien's face was acute.

"One cookie," Tucker agreed rashly. "What's one cookie?"

Damien's smile amped up, his eyes sparkling. "I really want to kiss you," he said softly. "I feel like I've been waiting my whole life."

Tucker closed his eyes and said a prayer of thanks. "Me too."

Damien bought them two cookies, the sugar kind with the thick layer of frosting, and two cartons of milk. Together they made their way outdoors and sat down underneath the wind chimes.

Tucker bit into a cookie, and sugar, butter, vanilla—all of the good things in life—suffused his senses. He tilted his head back and let them.

The pull hurt—denying it always hurt—but Tucker was outside with his best friend, and Damien might just want him as much as Tucker had yearned for Damien. The wind chimes sang above their heads, and for a moment, the world was a lovely place.

"That's good," he said, opening his eyes and grinning. "But I'm going to get fat."

"No you won't," Damien laughed. "With your life? What you have to do every night? You get to control when you eat cookies or what you have for dinner. I say the gods owe you a break!"

Because Damien knew, didn't he? Tucker had no secrets from Damie—he never had.

Tucker shrugged and took another bite of cookie, and j... right there. He felt it.

He felt the pop. *He looked around frantically. His person. The person he was supposed to meet was* here, *but Tucker didn't see him. He just felt this terrible, corrosive foreboding.*

"Damie, I—"

"Here, you've got frosting on your nose," Damien said, smiling whimsically. *And then he stood up to walk around the table, probably to wipe the frosting off....*

And his body pitched forward, lifeless, because his head... his face... oh God. Damien!

Tucker caught him, blinking against the blood spatter, and the report of the gun reached his ears. As he looked around frantically, the scream lodged in the back of his throat, crammed there by shock, by denial, he saw the shooter.

An average guy—blondish, weak chin, eyes swimming in misery and doubt. Tucker's chest popped again and the killer raised the gun to his chin.

And pulled the trigger.

ANGEL WRAPPED strong arms around Tucker's shoulders and rocked him gently while Tucker howled his grief and rage and guilt onto the kitchen table.

INNOCENT

ANGEL MANAGED to walk him to bed, but he was never sure how. Tucker stumbled, so lost in grief that he was easily led but unaware of where he was going.

They reached the bedroom, and Angel sat him down, helped him with his shoes, fumbled with the button of his cargo shorts, and finally laid him down, where he wept into his pillow while Angel draped over his body and whispered in his ear.

A part of Angel bore the secret shame that, in the midst of Tucker's grieving, Angel enjoyed touching him very much.

Enjoyed his smell—sweaty and boozy, with hamburgers and french fries thrown in.

Enjoyed the way their fingers twined together and the way Tucker's hair felt under Angel's chin as he sobbed.

Most of Angel was lost in heartbreak with him.

What a terrible, terrible gift.

What a painful way to come of age.

Oh, Tucker. All of that, and you were alone?

As if in answer, Tucker's voice, lost and shattered, filled the darkness. "Angel, don't leave me, okay?"

"No," Angel whispered. "I'll stay, even if I have to break the rules of heaven. I promise."

The air seemed to shimmer around them then, but maybe that was only Angel, recognizing that somewhere in the shadow of that promise lay the bones of truth.

Tucker wept some more, but the tears felt cleaner, gentler than they had, and Tucker rolled from his stomach to his side and faced Angel. Angel kept stroking his hair back from his face, and when Tucker leaned into the touch like Squishbeans, searching for more contact, Angel continued to stroke. Down his arm, across his chest, the skin soft over hard muscles. His waist was slender, his stomach concave, and when Tucker made a hissing sound, Angel snatched his hand back.

"It feels good," Tucker said sleepily. "I... I have sex all the time, but nobody touches me like they know me."

Angel yearned to know more of him.

He splayed his hand across Tucker's stomach, stroking the soft skin, the fine hairs below his navel. Tucker sighed, a sex-saturated sound that Angel recognized from his "alone" time after he'd come across the green bottle, and Angel pushed against the shape forming in his boxer shorts.

"Yes," Tucker whispered. "Angel, keep touching...."

Angel wrapped his hand around Tucker's erection, squeezing, shuddering with the raw animal emotion of giving a human body pleasure, and Tucker arched against him.

"Please...."

Tucker hooked his hand around the elastic of his shorts and pulled down, and in the dark, Angel was assailed with the forbidden erotic landscape of Tucker's naked body.

He wanted to lick, touch, nibble, penetrate—all of the aggressive sexuality he'd seen Tucker succumb to. He wanted to *be* that person.

Tucker stretched and hummed as Angel rubbed both palms against his thighs, and Angel pulled back on his own wants. Tucker had been made a puppet to the vagaries of fate for so long. Somebody needed to please him, and tonight, what Tucker's bleeding soul needed was gentleness.

And selflessness.

And a touch that gave him the sweetness that had been missing from his pleasure from the very beginning.

Angel bent his head to Tucker's chest, wondering if he was solid enough to touch, would he be solid enough to—

"Oh damn, *Angel!*"

Tucker's taste blossomed against Angel's tongue, salty and earthy, things Angel had never known. Angel licked again, his hand continuing its amazing journey over Tucker's thighs, along his length, skating the silk of his lower abdomen.

The movement of Tucker's fingers on his own startled him and brought his attention to the frightful ache in his own groin. But Tucker needed, and Angel let him wrap Angel's fist around his cock, and then Angel squeezed and stroked, as he'd watched Tucker do not that long ago.

Tucker let out a soft groan, not tortured but needy, and Angel stroked again and harder. Tucker spurted against his fingers, hot and sticky. Angel wanted to taste it, but he feared it too. Would Tucker's seed make him human forever? Would that break one of those rules of heaven?

Then Tucker tangled his fingers in Angel's hair, urging him back to Tucker's chest.

"Your hair, Angel—it feels amazing. Thank you. Thank you."

Angel kept stroking, his breath coming faster as Tucker broke into pants, his hips thrusting in Angel's hand.

"Angel, I want…. Oh God, I want." Tucker made a move then—reciprocation? Perhaps to explore Angel's masculine human body with his own hands, his mouth. Oh, Tucker's mouth looked sinful and wanton, and Angel found himself craving it all over his newly discovered skin.

But Tucker moved, and his hips arched, and Angel's thumb caught the edge of his cockhead. Tucker let out a gasp and a soft moan, and his entire body tautened in one giant arc of climax.

His cock spat come, graceful and scorching, covering Angel's fist, wrist, and forearm, making him shake with the intimacy of the seed on his skin.

Tucker grasped his hair—not harshly but firmly—and pulled Angel until they were face-to-face. Then Tucker lifted himself off the bed and pushed his lips against Angel's, invading his mouth with an urgent, beery tongue and sweeping Angel into the whirlwind of his first kiss.

Angel fell into it with a violence of need, and Tucker ravished him, still on his back, his body splayed, with spend cooling on his exposed skin.

"Let me," Tucker whispered. "I want to give you everything."

And then Tucker's hand slid through Angel's body, like Angel was mist, or a wish, or a prayer, and Tucker's cry of loss shattered them both.

"Angel!"

"I'm sorry, Tucker," Angel whispered, laying his head on the pillow next to Tucker. He wanted to cry, but he wasn't sure he could shed tears, even ghostly ones. His incorporeal construct ached, though, ached with need, ached with loss, ached with wanting the touch of the man next to him.

"But what happened?"

"I think…." Angel skated his hand over Tucker's chest, not setting it down in case he slid through skin and flesh. "I think it's because, for a moment, you stopped bleeding." When Tucker was hurt, Angel became human enough to touch him.

But Angel had given him sex and comfort, and the bleeding was staunched.

And Angel was incorporeal once again.

Tucker's sound of hurt almost made Angel disappear. He didn't want to face it—didn't want to feel Tucker facing one more goddamned loss.

But he'd promised.

"But I won't leave you," he said again.

"You promised."

"I did."

Tucker let out a breath and pulled up his boxers, then tugged the covers up around his chin.

When he'd settled himself back again, he stared at Angel in the darkness until Angel burst out, "What?"

"Thank you."

"I promised."

"Thank you for that too, but that's not what I meant."

Angel's incorporeal construct heated.

"I would have done so much more," he said wretchedly.

"You stayed for the kiss."

Angel saw back into Tucker's memory, that terrible, wonderful, tainted memory of a kiss that never was.

"Anyone would want to stay for the kiss, Tucker. If there was anything they could do at all to make that happen. I promise."

"Mm."

His eyes were closed. Grief, sex, and grief again. That would exhaust a man.

"I'll stay, Tucker. I swear that I'll stay."

BEING CORPOREAL apparently expended a lot of energy—Angel slept contentedly on the bed until long after Tucker's usual time of rising.

When he came to, Tucker was gone, but Angel could hear him in the kitchen, and morning smells as well as morning light and sounds were coming through the wall.

Angel materialized in the kitchen to find Tucker sitting in front of a half-eaten plate of eggs and toast, looking at the notebook Angel had pulled from his backpack the day they'd visited the cemetery and a bigger, half-filled photo album he'd apparently gotten from the boxes in the corner.

Every so often he'd find something and grunt, then write in the notebook again.

"Tucker?"

Tucker looked over his shoulder and smiled tentatively. Dark circles saddened his eyes, and high patches of red showed up against a waxen complexion.

"You should eat," Angel said.

"I was...." Tucker gestured. "Damien was in the graveyard."

"I remember now." Damien was the ghost who'd come the closest to taking Tucker over. Even if the pile of boxes hadn't screamed his name and Tucker hadn't dropped it occasionally, Angel would have remembered Tucker's anguish at seeing a noxious green spirit body of the man he'd once loved above all others. "Are you okay?"

"I... I resisted the pull twice. Once when I tried to have a girlfriend, and once with...." He pushed his plate away as if he suddenly couldn't stand the thought of food. "But a few times, I couldn't *find* the pop—the person I was supposed to be with that night. I felt the release in my chest, and I just knew I was too late or in the wrong place or... or something had happened."

"That wasn't your fault." Angel's chest tightened, and a shiver raced up his spine. He no longer questioned whether his body was real—too many visceral reactions related to Tucker Henderson assaulted him almost every minute.

"I'm not saying it was," Tucker muttered, looking down at his pad again. "It's just—I started to keep a record book. When it happened, I searched through the newspapers and clipped out, you know, bad weird things. Because a banker shooting a guy in the middle of a cookie shop before offing himself isn't an everyday thing. I figured those other misses would have a… a thing. Something would show up."

Angel swallowed against the fear that Tucker wasn't made for this life—not like Ruth had been. Tucker *was* the sweet boy Ruth had told him about. He was vulnerable. He needed Angel's help, Angel's protection, more than Ruth ever had.

"Why would you do that to yourself?" Angel asked, his voice rough. He sat across from Tucker, realizing that the red-padded kitchen chair had been pulled out for him already, as if Tucker was hoping he'd sit there and was trying to make him comfortable.

Angel's hands shook. He was tired of asking himself how that could be.

Tucker looked up at him, surprised and, Angel was relieved to see, sane. "Just to keep it from happening again, Angel. I wanted to see how I'd missed them— how we hadn't connected."

"So you could stop it from happening again?" This, at least, was proactive. Angel could understand this.

"Yes." Tucker flipped through the scrapbook again. He pulled in a deep breath through his nose and made a notation in his notebook.

"What are you writing?"

Tucker gave a half laugh. "I'm sorry. I'm not communicating well. That day at the graveyard I recognized two of the names."

"Damien's." Angel remembered Damien's ghost, the twisted features of what had once been a laughing—and kind—young man.

"Yes. And the name of my ex-girlfriend's father."

"Who?"

"The first and only relationship I tried to have, Angel. I resisted the pull, and she had to leave town

because her father died of a heart attack and she needed to be with her family. It was... too convenient.
I knew that it was blowback of some sort, I guess. It
was why...." He swallowed and shrugged, studying the
scrapbook in front of him with intent. "And his headstone was out there. I was looking to see if any of my
other misses were."

Angel grunted, trying to put this information together. "Were they?"

"Yeah. See?"

Tucker shoved the scrapbook at Angel and flipped
the pages. "George Alvarez—that was my girlfriend's
father. Gary Kunis—I missed him because I had pneu-
monia. I was in the hospital, and they'd doped me,
right? And I kept begging them to let me go, I guess.
They thought I was delusional." He rubbed his wrists,
and Angel bit his lip.

"They restrained you?"

Tucker shrugged like it hadn't hurt.

Angel wrapped his hands around Tucker's wrists,
their flesh colliding, because Tucker's heart was bleeding again, and it obviously had hurt. No shrugging and
denial could change that. "They restrained you," he re-
peated bleakly.

Tucker shook his head and wiped his eyes, but he
only pulled one hand from Angel's grasp.

"I was trying to get up in a rainstorm," he said, and
Angel pictured him, ill, desperate, fighting restraints to
go out in the rain to answer the pull. He opened his
mouth to cry. Howl. But Tucker shook his head and
kept going. "Then there was this one."

Angel looked at the scrapbook, at an article about
a young woman who had stepped onto the light-rail

tracks at K Street; then he looked at the notebook. "Courtney Julian?"

"I went out that night—I swear I did," Tucker muttered. "I got pulled into a pizza joint, and I sat down, and it was like she was right there, and then she wasn't. She must have walked out the back door or gotten pulled out by a phone call or—"

Angel squeezed his hand. "It wasn't your fault," he whispered.

"I know," Tucker snapped. But still he didn't move his hand. "I know it wasn't my fault. But see? There's three more—Chester Phillips, Todd Harold, Chastity Cardeno—all the names in my scrapbook are names you wrote down from the graveyard. All of them missed me and met their untimely end. And now they're somehow in the invisible supernatural graveyard in the backyard. But that's not the worst part!"

Tucker's anger must have given him some immunity to the pain, because his hand slid from Angel's grasp. For a moment, they both looked mournfully at their hands resting separately on the tabletop, and then Tucker stood up and began to pace in restless circles.

"What's the worst part?" Angel was almost afraid to ask.

"I don't know all of those names in the notebook!" Tucker yelled, running both hands through his hair.

Angel tried to assimilate this. Failed.

"I don't understand."

"I thought… I thought I knew who they all were. I could deal if *I'd* brought them here. But I didn't. I brought six. But there were, how many?"

"Twenty-three," Angel said thoughtfully. "Squish-beans! Here, kitty, kitty, kitty!" Tucker had set up the cat food and water in a corner of the kitchen, and

Squishbeans pulled her gray muzzle out of a can of soft food and licked her whiskers. "C'mon, pussy, I need to touch you."

Out of nowhere, Tucker laughed.

"What?" Angel asked, scooping the kitten up and cuddling her. He glanced up at Tucker and saw that some of the sadness, some of the desperation, had dropped from his shoulders, from his eyes, and he was laughing, the sound wholesome and sweet.

For a moment their eyes met, Tucker's twinkling with joy and Angel's....

Angel had no idea what was in his own eyes, but Tucker suddenly sobered and bit his lip. "Stay right there," he murmured. He took two steps forward and bent his head, the touch of his lips on Angel's as solid and as real as Squishbeans in Angel's arms.

Angel tasted him, allowing his eyes to flutter shut, and savored. Just savored. When Tucker pulled back, Angel was pretty sure his own expression was slack and dreamy.

Tucker cupped his cheek. "I wanted... I want...." He grimaced and turned away. "We're not having sex with the cat in the bed," he said unequivocally. "And we need to find a way to touch in happiness as well as in pain."

Angel gazed at the set of his shoulders and thought, *If I have to break all the rules of heaven.* "Okay, Tucker. It will be like our mysteries."

Tucker turned around slowly, some of his earlier happiness leavening the shadows under his eyes. "Our mysteries?"

"Bridget and Sophie and the others. The grave-yard. Every time we turn around in Daisy Place, we stumble over a clue. I'm sure we'll solve the mystery of…." His face heated. "We'll solve the mystery of us along the way."

Tucker's grooved cheek twitched as he pulled back his mouth in a half smile. "The mystery of us?"

"Yes," Angel said with dignity. "Of us."

"I like that mystery. I think you're right. Solving the mystery of us. It will be something to shoot for." He swallowed and strode back to the table. "Now why did you need the cat?"

Angel smiled at him. "You are so strong," he said, his throat thick and chest aching. "No matter what the mysteries show us, Tucker, you need to remember how strong you are."

Angel watched the flush creep up his pale cheeks and along this throat. "Thanks, Angel. What are you looking at?"

"These other names," Angel said, using the power of Squishbeans to leaf through Tucker's notebook. "I mean, your computer, the internet. Surely you could research these people and see if they're alive, right?"

"Yeah!" Tucker's tired smile gave Angel hope. "That's a great idea—"

"And this name!" Angel felt a thrill through his stomach and up in his chest. "I know this name. *You* know this name!"

Tucker leaned over Angel's shoulder, and for a moment his breath against Angel's face made Angel yearn for all that was human. "Wait. That's Senior. That's Thomas Conklin Senior. Angel, that's the guy who… who…."

"That's who you saw die," Angel said, his mind racing. "So… so six of these are people you brought here. They're your ghosts, Tucker. But this man—he's a man who was killed here. They should all be the same."

"But there were more!" Tucker backed away from the table. "There were lots more than just the twenty-three down on the ground. And what were *my* ghosts doing here anyway?"

"Well, this place does capture energy. Maybe they were... they were on your *mind*. You dragged their energy up here."

"Great. Like I need that on my conscience too!"

"Well, maybe if you let them go from your conscience, they could get off your property!" Angel burst out, frustrated and hurt. "Tucker, you are carrying around too many souls. It's because you're a good man—I know that. And you were given a job." Angel wanted to howl, but he refrained. "A job that would have broken someone without your... your good humor. Your honor. But you have to let go of them. You have to let go of at least *one* of them." There was no doubt as to which one he was talking about.

"I don't know how!" Tucker stood and pounded the wall behind his boxes. "Don't you think... don't you think I wanted to live all these years? But what was I supposed to do? I still had to get up every day and wait... just wait for that thing in my chest to pull me to bed. How was I supposed to go somewhere, do something, *be* anybody, if I got pulled away any time of day or night? And the one person—the *one person*—I could talk to about it, about how much it sucked, about how strange it was that my whole life was spent being the fuckpuppet of the gods, I *killed* him with my one act of rebellion!"

"*You didn't kill him!*"

Squishbeans meowed and leaped from Angel's hands.

"Sorry, pussy," Angel said sadly, and the high tension in the kitchen eased back a touch. "You didn't kill him," he said again. "I don't know why it happened—and you're right. The divine probably had something to do with it. But...." It was Angel's turn to stand and pace, although it felt like was moving through gelatin. Something was pushing against him, as though he had a giant sail on his back, but Angel was too preoccupied to figure out what.

"The divine doesn't do things like that." Angel stopped pacing, tired out by the forces acting to keep him still. "There is not supposed to be anything cruel in the divine. If the fates are screwing with you, Tucker, there's got to be another force at work."

Tucker sank to the table, apparently as tired as Angel. "It would be nice to think the forces of irony weren't just dicking with me," he mumbled, laying his head on his arms.

Angel sat down next to him and stroked his hair back with an incorporeal hand. The strands stirred under the wind of his passage, and Angel was content with that for the moment.

"Even if they are," he said, voice hoarse, "it's not your fault. You need to let him go."

"I loved him, Angel."

"I know."

"Nobody is going to love me like that." He wiped his eyes with the palm of his hand. "Ever again."

"I told you." Angel felt Tucker's scalp under his fingertips and closed his eyes, living in the moment, in the touch. "I'll break all the rules of heaven for you."

A faint smile tinged Tucker's lips. "That's a pretty promise, Angel. What's it mean?"

A shiver built up then, from the pit of Angel's groin to the outer edges of his aura, and he clenched his hand in Tucker's dark curly hair. "I can't tell you now, but I think we'll find out."

Suddenly Angel frowned. "Tucker—what is that thing on your neck?" He recognized it actually. Tucker had looped it over the rearview mirror the day he'd gone out and gotten the truck—the day they'd gotten Squishbeans.

Tucker frowned and straightened in his chair. "It's Rae's pendant. I left it in the truck."

Angel nodded. He could still remember it dangling from the mirror as he and Tucker had driven back in Tucker's body, while Angel was trying to force out the interlopers.

"But you didn't have it on last night," he said.

Tucker sat up and frowned. "No, it's been in the truck." He fingered it softly. "It's not hot. When I first tried it on, it was too hot for me to wear comfortably, but it's not hot now." He smiled faintly. "Maybe you broke the rules of heaven and it can protect me now. What do you think?"

"I don't know why it couldn't have protected you before," Angel sniffed.

"It's a pagan symbol. You know, the same sort of thing you won't acknowledge that exists fifteen miles away?"

"Oh." Angel wrinkled his nose in annoyance. "That." He frowned. "Do you think that's why it was hot before?"

"Because I was"—Tucker frowned—"protected by heaven? I don't *think* so!"

"Well." Angel shifted uncomfortably. "I… I am oddly possessive of you," he said humbly.

Tucker blinked. "It practically leaped into my hand, but you didn't like pagan forces. And now that you've vowed to break some rules...."

Angel didn't like this speculation. It led too uncomfortably to that big blank spot in his brain that didn't know where he'd come from or why he was here. "Okay," he said. "Maybe this *is* altering the rules of heaven. If it keeps you a little safer from the spirits in this place, then I will gladly let it break some more rules. Although I don't know if it counts when I didn't know I was breaking a rule in the first place."

And then, glory of glories, Tucker smiled. "So we're *both* not excited about the rules of heaven. I think that's one more thing that puts us on the same side."

Angel brightened. "That—and we want to see happy endings. Tucker, I know the letter got ruined, but would you like to hear what was written in it?"

Tucker sat up, frowning. "I almost forgot. You got a chance to read it?"

"Yes! Yes, I did. Would you like to know who it was from?"

He slouched, the excitement draining from him like blood. "It was Sophie's brother," he said miserably. "I saw what happened, remember?"

Angel shoved at the table and then jumped when it scooted across the floor with a groan. "I need to figure out when I'm doing that." Then he concentrated on what frustrated him so badly. "We don't know what happened. I mean, yes—Sophie's brother probably killed Thomas Conklin Senior. I can't say I'm sorry about that."

"Me neither."

Tucker was still so pale. Angel closed his eyes and went on. "Well, he deserved to die. But we don't know if Sophie's brother was arrested for the crime. We don't know if Bridget was dead or hurt badly. She could have just been knocked unconscious. And Sophie was still alive. So we saw a moment—a bad moment, I won't argue—but maybe it didn't end as badly as that. Conklin's grave was here, but in dimensional space, not in real space. And James Beaufort's was not. Neither was Bridget's or Sophie's. Now, that's not the only cemetery in this area. There's one out on Church Street in town and one in Auburn, where James said he lived."

"I thought he lived in Sacramento," Tucker mumbled.

"Well, the railroad went through Auburn. I assume he moved." Angel felt vaguely superior and then continued. "But you're missing the point. The girls had safety. James Beaufort wasn't going to condemn them or reject them. He was going to give them a cottage—just like you wanted, Tucker! They would have a cottage behind the house, and chickens and laundry and peace."

The lines of tension in Tucker's forehead and jaw eased. "Do you think they got it?" he asked wonderingly.

Angel let out a breath, his entire body, corporeal or not, easing with Tucker's optimism. "We can find out," he said. "But first, a nap. You need to rest. When you wake up in the afternoon, we'll go looking for them. There are record offices and graveyards, and you have a computer, Tucker. I understand they are quite useful."

Tucker laughed like Angel hoped he would. "Okay," he conceded. "A nap. Because apparently, I can't get through breakfast without one. And then we'll go looking for a happy ending. Then I can rip off that damned wallpaper and resurface the goddamned floor."

Tucker pushed away from the table, and Angel followed him into the bedroom. It would be good to get out. This house had been the center of Angel's world for so many years. He didn't want to do that to Tucker too. It felt bad enough to remember how that claustrophobic view of the universe had become Ruth's world.

"Tucker?"

"Nungh?" Tucker had put jeans on that morning, and now he kicked them off and threw himself across the bed.

"What color are you going to make the walls?"

Tucker smiled, even though his eyes were closed. "Blue," he said dreamily. "Like the sky. When I'm done with my nap, let's get out and see some sky. How's that sound, Angel?"

"Like you read my mind."

But Tucker was already napping, and Angel was taking comfort in his snores.

TUCKER DIDN'T wake up until late afternoon, and he was still groggy and tired. Angel watched as he made himself a sandwich and then urged him to eat out on the back porch.

"You can see the garden," Angel said wistfully. It was the one part of his time with Ruth that he was proud of. He'd cared for the woman, but their relationship had developed into such a fractious push-pull. Angel had babied her gardens as an attempt to say thank you, to show care, to show that he appreciated the life she'd spent in service of the dead.

At the end, he thought she'd understood, but he still wasn't sure if it had been enough.

He wanted Tucker to see the things he'd done, even though nature was already starting to take over, wreaking entropic destruction over the already riotous flower beds.

Tucker sat in the shade of the porch steps and nibbled on his sandwich, his eyes tracking the figures of Daisy Place's ghostly residents. Angel settled next to him, feeling that strange weight on his shoulders again.

"Stop looking at the ghosts," he urged. "Just for a minute. I want you to see the flowers."

Tucker turned to study him for a moment, and Angel knew his face had probably gone flush by now.

"What?"

"Nothing. I'm just waiting for you to turn into a woman again."

"Why? Why would you want me to do that?"

Tucker shrugged. "Because if you do it again, I might figure out why you do it."

Oh, that was embarrassing. Angel did *not* want to go there. But Tucker had been so honest with him that morning.

"Well, at first I wanted to find someone you trusted!" he blurted.

Tucker grimaced. "Except you found someone whose memory hurt so badly, I hated you on sight."

Angel shrugged. "That was a failure on my part."

Tucker snorted. "And then?"

Angel frowned. "Then I was trying to find someone you would trust—so that's this form. And then…." Damn. "Well, I was confused. I was attracted to you, and you seemed to be attracted to me, and that broke the rules. So I tried to find someone you *weren't* attracted to."

Tucker's throaty belly laugh was his reward and almost worth the embarrassment. "Epic. Fail!"

"And then… then I just gave in and tried to find forms you would find appealing."

Tucker's glance went coy, and Angel's heart did a little flutter.

"I find most of your forms appealing, Angel. Last night's form was probably my favorite."

Their activity the night before flooded Angel's memory, and he felt honesty was required here too. "I'm not entirely upset about that," he admitted.

"No," Tucker said softly. "I'm not either. Not in the least."

Angel wanted it again. Wanted to feel Tucker's flesh under his hands, wanted Tucker's hands on his own skin. The sudden, surprising weight of sexual desire flooded him, and he had to fight to remember what they'd been talking about.

"Would you just look at the daisy bed, please? The nasturtiums? The prairie fire and the asters? There are asters all over the damned yard, Tucker—asters! Five different varieties. And big purple morning glories climbing over the fences. This was not easy to achieve!"

Tucker—gratifyingly—turned his attention back toward the garden, which ran riot in the setting sun. Ruth had hired a gardener to set up an automatic watering system as she'd aged, and Angel—with his gift for phone messages and basic electronic intervention—had kept watering the garden during Tucker's absence. He'd managed to find a boy to mow the lawn once a month, but that month was almost over, and the grass was more than ankle deep. But it *was* grass, thick and luxurious bluegrass and not the stingy, deep-rooted Bermuda grass. Angel had worked so hard to keep these things. Ruth had loved them. This garden, in the evenings, in the spring and fall, had provided Ruth's happiest moments, and Angel wanted Tucker to see that he could be kind.

Tucker had needed kindness. Angel was capable—with some prompting—of providing it. He may not have started out that way—he still couldn't remember what had brought him here to Daisy Place, but he remembered his single-minded need to leave it. It was what had driven him, had driven Ruth, at the very beginning. He'd been selfish in a way Tucker could never understand, for all his talk of self-indulgence. But those years with Ruth had taught Angel to care about someone else's needs, no matter how fractious their relationship.

And this week with Tucker had been a master class in how another person's needs could supersede every agenda he'd ever had.

"It's beautiful, Angel," Tucker said softly.

"Yes." Angel couldn't help the pride that resonated in his voice. "Your aunt used to say flowers were the best people she knew." The garden faded, and he saw instead a lonely woman, staving off bitterness, taking great draughts of peace and beauty in her own backyard. "She dealt with some of the worst actual people—you've seen that. So I tried to give her the most beautiful flower people I could."

"Mm." Tucker had set his sandwich plate down and was leaning forward, chin on his hand, elbow balanced on his knees. "You did good, Angel. You're right. The flowers are beautiful. You can keep them up?"

Angel smiled, appreciating that Tucker could see it was no small endeavor.

"If you could pay the boy who mows the lawn in cash, it would be a *whole* lot easier." Angel's head started to actually ache in the human way, and not in the figurative way it had been aching every time he tin-kered with the lawnmower boy's bank account.

Tucker's chuckle warmed his heart. "I don't even want to know."

Angel made vague gestures and then realized his words got fuzzy when talking about electronics. "Let's just say that once I got over my surprise, I wel-comed computers and all that came with them," he said delicately.

Tucker laughed some more, and then he frowned. "But Andy told me he stopped mowing lawns after Ruth died. Why didn't you hire him back?"

Angel grunted. "Because he wanted cash only, Tucker. That didn't work for me."

More laughter, and Angel glowed a little inside. Then Tucker raised his head quickly, like a rabbit sens-ing a hunting cat, and gazed out into the purpling shad-ows of the garden.

"The ghosts are coming in," he whispered.

"We should go." Angel didn't want a reprise of their first night, when Sophie and Bridget had in-troduced Tucker to the harsh world of otherworldly redemption.

"But look." A sweet smile tilted at Tucker's mouth, and Angel checked the direction of his gaze.

The two women, arm in arm, walked toward the stairs. Sophie's spectral face was full of mischief, and Bridget scowled as she tried to resist Sophie's charms.

For a moment, love was bright as a star in the sky, and the lovers possessed more hope than fear.

The tension in Angel's shoulders relaxed in that moment, and he and Tucker both turned their heads and watched as the two ghosts walked up the steps on the other side of Tucker, avoiding the two men out of their time as though by instinct. Angel smiled, a shaft of joy penetrating his heart like sunshine through storm clouds, and for the first time since he'd started this quest, he felt, fully throughout his being, the thing that would be gained by setting the spirits free of this very earthly prison.

He wanted what Tucker wanted. For these human souls to be happy.

He reached to squeeze Tucker's knee, to share the revelation, and his hand slid through. Tucker didn't even shudder, and Angel opened his mouth to tell him, to share, when he saw Tucker's gaze fixed on a point not five feet in front of the stairs.

Angel turned slowly and froze.

The rules of heaven indeed.

I Know You

TUCKER WATCHED the women pass by, feeling the breeze from Sophie's skirt. They didn't see him or Angel, and he was pleased with that.

They deserved privacy, and he'd already intruded so much.

He was aware of Angel's touch—and as he felt the point of sorrow that they seemed to forever be either too much flesh or too much spirit, he turned his head—

And froze.

He recognized this ghost from Sophie's point of view. To her eyes, he'd loomed like the monster he was, but in truth he was a midsized man, even for the turn of the twentieth century. He might have once been handsome, square-jawed with high cheekbones, but his face was lined with more than age and more than greed. Every line, every burst capillary, every bag and pouch of skin was twisted with the work of the twin destroyers: malice and madness.

His nose, bright and bulbous, should have made him a ludicrous figure, and so should his great drooping mustache, but instead both features added to the grotesquerie of his fury.

He was glaring at Tucker with so much hatred Tucker's stomach roiled.

His mouth worked: "I see you!"

Tucker stood, his weariness falling away. "I see you too, fucker. You know what I saw you do?"

The apparition snarled like an animal, and as Tucker watched, it crouched. "You watched me *die*!"

"You were hurting them," Tucker snarled. "I would have killed you myself!"

The ache in his chest, the one that had dogged him all day, exploded, and he crouched, mirroring his opponent. He wasn't sure what he would have done then, enraged by pain, but another shadow stepped forward.

"You wouldn't have. I wouldn't wish it! Let me take it back. It's ridden me these years, every day another twist in my heart!"

Tucker straightened, trying to put this new contender into context. Tall and broad, with hair that might have been blond in his youth, James Beaufort had been a true railroad man in life. His hands were rough and bore the scars of working with hot metal and sharp iron, and his biceps bulged, as did his chest and thighs. He had a mustache too, trimmed into his goatee, and something about his weathered face, some curve of his lip or line by his eyes, suggested that here was a man capable of great tenderness.

Which made the anguish in his eyes that much harder to bear.

"You had to," Tucker told him. He pushed with his feet to make sure the ground was solid beneath them.

The women had strolled right by, not sparing him a glance, but these men, the ones bound by violence, they were squaring with Tucker as though readying for a fight.

"He was hurting her. You came to rescue her, right?"

"She was my baby sister," James pleaded. "And he was... he was...."

Tucker closed his eyes against the memory—Bridget, sprawled against the wall, Sophie on the floor, skirts hiked up over her head.

"Violating her," Tucker whispered. "I understand. You had to."

"She was a whore!"

Tucker and James Beaufort turned toward the cry, and James launched himself at Conklin, ever the protector, even in death.

Whatever metaphysics were at work, James flowed right through the man, and Tucker reached for his pendant automatically, holding it in his palm, hoping for protection, any protection, as the maddened ghost surged forward, ready to dive into Tucker's body and live inside his skin.

The idea of feeling what this monster felt, *being* this monstrous human being, terrified Tucker right down to the pit of his balls.

Whatever he hadn't done with his life, whatever he'd become instead, he was his own person, forged in the crucible of his gift, given the most basic of imperatives: help people, however you can.

This thing rushing at him was the bitter corruption of a man who caused pain because he could.

James rolled across the lawn toward them, bounding to his feet in a way that told Tucker all he needed to know about violence and being a railroad man back when a man's body was his livelihood and fighting wasn't a sin. Tucker squared his feet and held on to his symbol of protection, offered casually by a woman whose family had slid under his skin with their kindness.

"C'mon, Conklin, c'mon. You think you can hurt me? You think *you* can hurt me?"

With a roar, Conklin was upon him, a wiry, enraged hurricane, battering with fists, kicking, biting. Tucker let go of the necklace and fought back.

The connection of his fist with Conklin's jaw rang up Tucker's arm like a bell, and Conklin fell back with a grunt.

"You hit me!" he growled, and Tucker didn't care about metaphysics.

"Felt good," he snarled. "Let's do it again."

They squared off then, opponents in the ring, and James Beaufort bounced on his toes by Tucker's side.

"He's vain," he muttered. "And afraid of pain. Go for his nose."

"I'd rather knee him in the balls," Tucker growled, sick all over again at what Sophie had endured. "C'mon, man!" he shouted. "C'mon. If we're gonna do this, let's do this, ghost to psychic. Let's see who walks away!"

"Tucker, don't!" Angel called, and Tucker turned his head.

Conklin attacked, his first punch getting Tucker in the stomach, the second breaking his nose. He howled in pain and struck back, his muscles, honed in hours of boredom at the gym, finally getting to do something interesting.

He could hardly see through the pain-blossom in his nose, and he was having trouble breathing as well, but each blow filled him, invigorated him, gave him purpose.

"You like causing pain, motherfucker!" He threw a hard right to Conklin's ribs. "I'll give you pain you'd fucking *die* to escape!"

James Beaufort laughed heartily at that, the hysteria in the sound reminding Tucker that he'd lived over a hundred years with the pain of killing this asshole.

"And this one's for Sophie!" Kick. "And this one's for Bridget!" Punch. "And this one's for James!" And he came down hard on Conklin's kneecap.

It worked as well on ghosts as it did on humans, and Thomas Conklin Senior went down, writhing in pain. Tucker pumped his fists and howled, because God, he needed this win. Just once, he needed to come out on top, to finally not be karma's fucking whoring bitch again.

Conklin's screams let off, and his body went still. Tucker stopped crowing long enough to see that the blood he'd drawn was disappearing, the bruises he'd inflicted fading, and whereas Tucker's nose, bleeding and swollen, was not going away, Conklin's dislocated knee was relocating, fixing itself as if it had never been injured.

With a smile and a dry laugh, Tucker's antagonist pushed himself to his feet, and the terrible implications hit Tucker hard.

This would never end.

If Tucker took off the pentacle that apparently made him a part of Conklin's world, he'd be vulnerable to possession.

If he left it on, Conklin could come attack him at any time. This ghost *lived in his house*! Now that Conklin had seen him, and they'd touched, Tucker could never sleep. Never rest. And even if he left Tucker alone, others were vulnerable. Angel. Was Angel open to Conklin's attack? What about... oh God. This fucking sadist. He wouldn't!

Tucker's panic overrode reason. He stared at Conklin, terrified for the one helpless being he knew.

"You monster!" he cried, "You stay away from Squishbeans!"

Conklin looked baffled for a moment, mouthing "Squishbeans" in puzzlement, and Tucker took hope. Maybe the cat was too small a thing for the ghost to bother with. Maybe it had no bonding symbol around its neck. Maybe it was safe.

Tucker relaxed, and Conklin took that moment to charge again.

At that moment, a fluttering darkness passed over them all, and Angel stood in front of Tucker, his back toward their enemy, arms out to pull Tucker close.

Conklin fell back with the sound of a tolling bell, and Angel gazed at him over his shoulder. "*Nobody* hurts him!" he thundered.

Tucker found himself tucked into Angel's embrace, some sort of shield wrapping around them both as Conklin tried one more time to get at him.

Tucker felt this charge ringing in his bones, and he closed his eyes and clutched Angel tighter, his body, neatly muscled, solid as the ground, filling Tucker's arms like the lover he'd never been able to hold.

The supernatural ringing stopped, and night fell.

Angel made a whimper—a hurt sound—and his arms slid away, hanging at his sides. Tucker had buried his face against Angel's neck, but they'd stood chest to chest. Angel brought his hand up to the side of his throat, where Tucker's pendant had been mashed between them, and Tucker gasped.

"Oh, Angel," he whispered, running his fingertips around the pentacle-shaped burn right above Angel's white T-shirt. "How did that—"

"Did he hurt you?" Angel asked, upset. His fingers whispered along Tucker's face, skirting his swollen nose, the cuts on his cheek and chin. "Tucker, why would you let him hurt you?"

Tucker shrugged. "I hurt *you*!" The pentacle had. Angels and pentacles didn't mix—perhaps that's why the pentacle had burned Tucker in the first place. Angel had put his mark on Tucker's heart, even then. The more human Angel had become, the more the pentacle had been compatible with Tucker's skin.

Tucker refused to think of the implications of this. He hovered his finger over the burn at Angel's throat, hurting for his… his lover. Oh God. This man had loved him the night before.

Tucker turned his face up slightly in confusion and supplication.

"I didn't mean to hurt you," he whispered.

And now it was Angel's turn to shrug. "As long as you're not doing any more bleeding for that man's crimes, Tucker, I can live with the pain."

Tucker half laughed and looked around them. The black veil had disappeared, but that didn't stop the purpling night shadows from looking otherworldly. Tucker and Angel didn't belong here at night. They were barely tolerated during the day—they knew that now.

"Inside," Tucker urged, turning toward the door. Angel's hand, tugging at his, stopped him. "What?"

Angel shook his head, looking absurdly shy. "Just…."
He tugged Tucker closer, and Tucker's heart, which had

slowed down a bit since the ghostly attack, sped up now as Angel wrapped his arms around Tucker's shoulders, sliding his hands into Tucker's back pockets.

"The twilight is beautiful," Angel whispered.

Tucker smiled and turned his head into the kiss....

And Angel dematerialized, the kiss landing on Tucker's lips like a cool mist of fog.

With a groan of frustration, Tucker stomped into the house, Angel drooping dispiritedly after him.

HIS NOSE wouldn't stop bleeding, dammit.

But Tucker decided to use that.

"Tucker, why won't you just sit and put some ice on it?" Angel asked plaintively.

"Angel, come here," Tucker said, scraping his finger along the threshold that led from the hallway to his room. "I need to know this doesn't trap you too."

"What are you doing?"

"I have a degree in ancient religions and defunct languages," Tucker muttered. "Seriously. I know school was a long time ago, but I had to wait to get beaten up by a ghost to figure out how this works?" He turned toward Angel and gestured to the blood he'd scraped on the threshold as a protection spell. "Here, see if this bothers you."

Angel frowned and moved his hand over the Enochian symbols that Tucker had drawn using the thick blood pouring down his face.

"No. I can feel the symbol tingle, but I'm fine with it. It bothers me that you're bleeding. It bothers me that I couldn't hold you, but this doesn't bother me much at all."

Tucker smiled at him wearily. "You know, I thought the fact that you could hold me was the plus side of the bleeding. I don't get it myself."

"You were happy," Angel said glumly. "I think the blood means something else when your heart aches."

"Oh, for fuck's sake." Tucker finished off the symbol and looked around the room. "If I pour some salt on the windowsill and put another one of these there, do you think that will do?"

"What exactly are you doing?"

"Thomas Conklin and I just beat the crap out of each other and he's been dead for a hundred or so years. I would really like for him not to come into my room and slit my throat as I sleep!" Tucker's ribs hurt from the ghost's kidney punches, and his nose and head were one giant throb. At least the exhaustion was physical—mostly. Dealing with the dead was a lot harder on his energy levels than fucking the living; he was getting used to feeling like the cat's breakfast.

Angel sat back on his haunches and put his hand in front of his mouth, clearly horrified.

"No," he said. "Tucker, take the necklace off. He'll kill you!"

"The necklace that means protection? I don't think so. Better he beats the hell out of my body than takes it over!" Tucker finished the rune and stalked over to the window, blowing his bleeding nose into his hand to use as a painter's palette.

"Gross," Angel muttered, shrinking back.

"You are telling me." Tucker didn't even want to think about it. But that didn't stop him from dabbing his finger in it and starting to draw. "Do you think I need to do this on the shower walls? Can he come through the walls now and attack me physically? Have all the rules of metaphysics just gone down the fucking crapper in this place?"

"I will watch over you when you bathe," Angel said virtuously.

Tucker sputtered blood all over his shirt with his burst of laughter. "Glad to know that's a hardship for you. I'll keep that in mind."

"I could be naked too, if that would make you more comfortable."

Tucker stopped drawing for a moment and stared at him. Her.

Two green eyes in a triangular face, with lush lips, high cheekbones, and a sweet buttercream complexion, stared back. Angel had a riot of red curly hair piled on top of her head, drooping ringlets around her eyes and down her neck.

Tucker swallowed. Most of it was blood, and he sighed, going back to work on the rune so he could bathe, put his head back with some ice, and stop his damned nose from bleeding any more.

"Either form," he muttered. "Either form would make watching me naked a really bad idea." And then, dammit, he thought about that. "Can you *be* naked in either form?"

Angel appeared to think about it. She was wearing a scoop-necked T-shirt—sort of the feminine version of what Angel always wore—and jeans cut for generous hips and round thighs. Curiously, she pulled the neck of her T-shirt out and then fiddled with her bra.

"My nipples are the color of cinnamon," she proclaimed, and Tucker groaned.

Forcing himself to concentrate, he finished the damned rune and stood, still cupping his hand.

"Is there anyplace else I can draw a rune?" Runes in blood—crude, basic, the oldest protection spell in the book.

Angel stopped looking down her shirt and shook her head. "No, Tucker—the entrances are where you need to worry, and you got those. And besides...." She wrinkled her nose. "I don't think you have to worry about him violating you in your sleep."

Tucker shuddered. "I'm anxious to hear why."

"You wore the pentacle and he saw you. It made him capable of attacking you. Outside the house. But the house has thresholds—human sanctuaries do. Ghosts often stay inside the confines of a house even if it's burned to the ground. They recognize boundaries. They're hungry for rules, since the basic rules of humanity have deserted them. I think he will—consciously or unconsciously—shy away from violating the rules of the world as it's set up inside the mansion."

Mm. "Interesting theory," Tucker muttered as he walked to the bathroom and washed the gunk off his hand. "But he didn't seem all that happy about rules when he was alive."

"I disagree," Angel said thoughtfully. "I think he was actually locked into the rules of his time. Women were believed to be inferior creatures. He subscribed to that rule. His wealth gave him privilege. He believed that too."

Tucker grimaced at his black eyes and swollen nose in the mirror. "I guess, yeah. Even the drug use would make sense. Cocaine was a big thing back then—and not particularly illegal either. Not yet. So yeah, he was a monster. But he locked his monstrousness behind social rules. I guess I get that." He met Angel's eyes in the mirror, marveling at how, in the middle of that lush beauty, those eyes were still perfectly green with luminous gold flecks and still perfectly Angel's. "So we'll hope the old rules of hospitality don't desert him, now that we're supposed to be sleeping under the same roof. Still...."

He grimaced, not sure whether he felt better or worse about asking for help from a beautiful redheaded woman than from a ruggedly handsome auburn-haired man.

Maybe he just didn't like asking for help from a potential lover, period.

"You are going to stay with me when I sleep, right?" he asked.

"Of course," she agreed, those green eyes as wide and as earnest as they had always been. "I... I wish I didn't have to rest as well. When Ruth was here, I'd de-materialize—float in the aether, waiting for Ruth to call me. I did not feel time there. Sometimes she wouldn't call me for weeks."

There was a plaintiveness, a forlornness in her voice, something that made Tucker ache.

"I'm glad you've been there for *me*," Tucker told her, smiling gently so she'd know he meant it. "I don't think I could go a week without hearing your voice—any of your voices—so I'm just as glad you stay with me."

"But I need to rest too. That's when you see me sleeping. I can't stand eternal watch over you, Tucker. I'm not that kind of—"

"Girl?" Tucker supplied sweetly.

"Apparition," Angel said with dignity. "All things wax and wane."

Tucker frowned. "Hunh. Interesting. Strength and weak—" His nose dripped. "Fuck me. I'm tired of blood."

He started to strip, throwing his clothes in the hamper, and then he turned sheepishly toward Angel. "Could you, uh, you know, milady, maybe…?"

The smile that tilted those full lips was whimsical and knowing. "Still the same person."

"Forgive me for long-ingrained sexist mores," Tucker replied stubbornly. "And don't watch my naked ass, okay?"

He heard Angel's low and womanly laugh as he hauled his sweaty, blood-crusted body into the shower. He kept the water cool, and as it sluiced down his body, he tried to imagine that sound as a manly chuckle—and failed.

Whoever—*what*ever—Angel was, the two genders fit her as easily as Tucker's one gender fit him.

Tucker managed a smile, thinking that he was exceedingly lucky that being attracted to all of Angel was not going to be a problem for him.

Following *through* on that attraction? That was going to be a problem for both of them.

TUCKER GOT out of the shower and looked around, realizing that he was alone. "Angel?" he called.

"In the other room, Tucker. Giving you your 'space.'"

That was sweet. "Thanks. Augh!" His nose was still dripping. He wrapped a towel around his waist, then grabbed a clean washrag from the shelf. Holding the washrag up, he bumped the door open. "Uh, Angel?" Again, this was horribly embarrassing to ask. It was one thing when Angel looked like a clueless guy his age, but right now, she was about as intimidating a woman as Tucker had ever known, and he'd had sex with a lot of judges and high-profile attorneys—and one congresswoman. And a congressman for that matter. But none of them had been as stunning as Angel was in this body.

"What do you need?" she asked, stepping into his view like a regular flesh and blood person.

"An escort to the refrigerator," he said sheepishly. "We didn't paint any runes there."

"But it's a modern part of the house. I don't think he'd go there." Angel tapped a long scarlet fingernail against vermillion lips. "And he thinks the kitchen is beneath him."

"Yeah, well, brawling in the garden should have been beneath him. Could you just walk with me and keep an eye out while I get some ice?"

"Of course. Aren't you going to get dressed?"

Tucker dabbed at his nose. "Not when I'm still dripping like a faucet. C'mon, let's go."

It all went smoothly… until he was bent over the freezer, scooping ice into a bag, and his towel dropped.

Angel's throaty laughter drew an allover body flush, though Tucker just kept scooping ice.

"Like what you see?" he asked, his words muffled by his swollen nose.

"Even the skin of your bottom is turning pink!" Angel chortled.

"Wonderful." He refilled the ice cube tray, staying almost defiantly naked. To his horror, his cock started to wake up in the open air, and once he put the tray in the freezer, he grabbed the towel off the floor and hiked it up around his waist again, then tied the knot as securely as possible.

"A shame," Angel said, the wicked enjoyment in her voice as mortifying from a woman as it would have been if he'd been a man.

"I'm flattered," Tucker muttered. "Okay—I need ibuprofen. Did you stock some in the cupboards, or do I need to root through my boxes?"

"Second cupboard to the right of the refrigerator," Angel said softly. "It's left over from your aunt, but it should still be good."

She sounded so contrite, Tucker relented. "It would have been okay, you know. If I'd had to go through the boxes."

"No," she said shortly. "Just... just no. I'm tired of watching you hurt today. I would just as soon you fix your nose and go watch some TV." The perpetual smile at her lips turned wistful. "I wouldn't mind watching *Buffy* too."

"Of course," Tucker conceded gracefully. He grabbed the ibuprofen, washed it down with water, and then snagged a bag of chocolate-covered pretzels from the same cupboard. He held them up and shook the bag. "These are great—thanks!"

"When you were downtown, getting your stuff, I wired the grocery boy extra money if he'd come in and put the groceries away," Angel said modestly. "He didn't try to steal anything at all. I was very impressed."

Tucker chuckled. "You don't trust much of humanity, do you?"

"I helped Ruth for a very long time," she responded. "Very often the dead who won't leave are the ones with the most to regret."

Tucker *hmm*d and grabbed his ice, his pretzels, and the towel around his waist. "Like Sophie's brother. That's interesting."

"Why?"

"It just is," Tucker said thoughtfully. "I think he killed Thomas Conklin—and good for him, because wow. Just *wow*. Conklin was a bad guy. But it left James Beaufort with a mountain of regret. I think it's the regret that haunts the paperweight as much as the violence."

"Oh," Angel said in a very small voice.

Tucker nodded because it was something to chew over as he padded through the kitchen and made the abrupt left into his bedroom. For a moment, he started, but nobody was waiting for him, nobody had broken his runes.

Thank God. Because Tucker would bleed all night if it meant Thomas Conklin's ghost would leave him the hell alone.

ANGEL WATCHED *Buffy* from the bottom corner of the bed, her shapely legs, clad in comfortable jeans, stretched idly in front of her.

Tucker lay on his side and balanced the big ice pack on his nose while trying to sop up the still-trickling blood. Eventually, he fell asleep like that.

For a moment as he was drifting off, he tried to make himself reach out and close his computer, but the screen saver went on, and he felt a soft, sweet presence at his back.

"Stay with me," he mumbled.

"As long as you need me," she returned.

And then she did something to the lights, and he didn't wake up until morning.

ANGEL TALKED him into resting the next day. It wasn't hard to do—his nose still ached, and he'd stayed up until one in the morning just waiting to see if a vengeful ghost was going to break into his room. He slept late and spent most of the day eating junk food while Angel shotgunned season four of *Buffy*.

The next day Margie called them, asking if Tucker could use his truck to haul stock from one of her stores to the next.

Tucker agreed pretty much before he got out of bed, and then she said, "And be sure to bring Angel with you!"

Oh hell. "Margie, I'm not sure what Angel has in mind today. It might just be me."

He hung up and turned in bed to see Angel leaning her head on her hand and looking at him pensively. She was still a stunning redhead, and Tucker felt a bit of sadness that he hadn't been able to run so much as a knuckle down the swell of her breast or hip in the past two days.

"I could always change form," she said regretfully. "I like Margie." She looked down. "It was… a luxury, to be human for another human."

"Yeah, but we're going to be at her stores," Tucker said. On impulse he feathered his fingers through her ringlets, pretending that he could feel the strands. "It would be cruel to let her speak to you when nobody else could see you."

Angel reached up and grabbed his hand—for real.

"I am not sure I ever wished I could be seen before," she mused. She pressed her lips against back of his hand. "But I'm also not sure how ready I am to be…." Her hand slid through his.

"Seen," Tucker supplied. He could have said "human," but that bordered on the things that made Angel disappear. As far as Tucker knew, he was supposed to believe Angel was a ghost of a deceased human. But the more they got to know each other, the more Tucker became convinced that wasn't true.

"Yes." Angel turned onto her stomach, kicking her feet over her bottom again and staring moodily at the headboard. "Seen."

Tucker showered and left—but he remembered to pet the cat and wish Angel goodbye. She went to the door to see him off, and he knew she'd be there waiting for him when he returned.

Margie was in fine form about his nose that day. She bought his story about slipping and falling in the shower to avoid the kitten, but pestered him repeatedly about letting Angel take care of him.

"That young man would do anything for you. You know that, right?"

Tucker couldn't look her in the eyes. "Yeah, Marge. Well, you sure did see through us."

Her delighted laugh bolstered something inside him. *Margie*, at least, believed.

When he returned from his errand, he had to concede to an afternoon nap. One more day of rest before he and Angel started their quest again. He left the wallpaper alone, although he double-checked to make sure he had a putty knife and the other things Josh had stressed for the wallpaper removal when he was ready. But mostly he stayed downstairs, putting away his clothes and moving a bookshelf—clean, per Angel—from the living room to his bedroom so he could find places for some of the stuff in his boxes.

When he was done, the room was a little more his—but he thought it could use some color.

"Drapes, a throw rug, the furniture Josh was going to give me…." Tucker turned a full circle and tried to imagine this room with just a little more effort.

"It's cozy," Angel decided. "And… and alive."

Tucker grinned at her as she swung her legs over the bed. "Good. If I could do that here, I can do it in the Chrysanthemum Room. And I can do that for the rest of the house, right?"

Angel lifted an elegant shoulder, but she looked hopeful. Tucker ate his dinner out on the porch, almost defiantly, although he fingered his pendant often.

The only ghosts who showed had the decency to stay ghosts, for which he was grateful, and he and Angel stared at the lowering shadows while Tucker told terrible jokes that he and Damien had shared in high school.

Maybe it was the fact that Conklin, at least, seemed to have left him alone. Maybe it was that he and Angel had resolved some of the sexual tension between them, and that whatever they were doing—whatever Angel was—they had the same mission and were doing it together.

Maybe it was that Tucker felt like he had friends here, in this town, and roots that he'd never been able to set down before.

And maybe it was that he'd shared all the pain of Damien's passing and could remember some of the joy the two of them had had as kids, inseparable and happy.

Whatever it was, when they went to bed that night, his heart was filled with a surprising amount of quiet mountain peace.

THE NEXT MORNING, though, Tucker couldn't wait another day—in spite of Angel's objections. While eating breakfast, he looked up archives and birth and death records, Squishbeans on his lap.

"I *got* it," he cried. "Angel! Come here."

"I'm right next to you," she said, and if she'd been human, he would have expected her to be rolling her eyes over a cup of cream-and-sugar coffee.

"But look over my shoulder here, at the computer," he said with patience. "I found them. Or at least I found James Beaufort."

"Oh!" She dematerialized from her chair and rematerialized over his shoulder.

"You could have just stood up."

"I was startled," she said with dignity, checking the knot of curls on top of her head and pushing the strands out of her eyes.

Tucker eyed her narrowly. "You don't usually stay in a woman's form for this long."

Those green eyes glinted wickedly. "This one unsettles you. I'm not sure why, but it arouses you more than the others."

"No," Tucker said, swallowing through a dry throat. "That's not true. It unsettles me, yes, but, uh, arouses? No."

Angel's eyes narrowed. "Which form *are* you most attracted to?"

Tucker smiled enigmatically and tried not to contrast the imagined comfort of what could have been Angel's soft breasts pressed against his back with the remembered comfort of Angel's hard chest, strong hands, and citrus-lavender smell. "I'll leave that for you to figure out. But for right now, I've got some death dates here. Let me grab the pen and paper."

"Why? What are we going to do?"

Tucker gnawed his lower lip. "Well, I know we have to touch their objects and see their stories and, through the process, tell them to you. But I'm thinking, what if we make it easy? What if we take their objects to *them*? I've got a Sophie, Henrietta, and James Beaufort all buried at the Manzanita Cemetery in Auburn, as well as Bridget Shanahan."

"Conklin?"

Tucker shook his head. "No, I haven't seen mention of him, but…." He pursed his lips grimly. "I think all *his* energy is captured here, probably in the damned paperweight. And that seems to be what holds James's spirit too."

They both let out hissing noises through their front teeth, and Squishbeans started and took off.

"That would be a horrible fate, Tucker."

"Yeah."

"The madman and the kind man who killed him."

"I know."

"We *have* to release James Beaufort."

"I'm saying, Angel!"

"It's imperative!"

"I *know*. But listen—James didn't die that day. In fact, he and his wife weren't buried until 1945 and 1947. They were…." Aw. Damn. "They were buried with their two sons, who were killed in the war."

"Oh."

Tucker hated that story. "But at least they had some peace before then," he said desperately. "I hope so anyway. And Sophie and Bridget—they were interred the same day in 1952. They lived a good long life, and together even. But something is holding them to this place, Angel. Maybe most of their spirits passed on, but not all. And James Beaufort may be mostly with his wife—"

"But something is keeping that part of him here that we saw out in the garden, and it's attached to the paperweight," Angel finished. "Yes, Tucker, I agree. So maybe if we take the objects to them, their stories will be told?"

Tucker pulled his fingers through his hair. It had dried wet the night before, which meant it was sort of a haphazard mop right now. He'd slept well, so he had a little more energy than he'd been having, but his nose hurt, and his head hurt, and generally, getting the hell out of Daisy Place would do him a world of good at the moment.

"Could it hurt?" he asked, a little desperately.

"I can come, right?"

Tucker shrugged, trying for nonchalance. "I don't see why not. But I warn you—on the way back, I was going to stop by Rae's house." He fingered the pentacle at his neck, with the mysterious garnet at the heart of it. He would need to look at it in the mirror, but right now, at his throat, it felt changed somehow. "I think there's something about this charm that got me beat the hell up but kept me from being possessed."

"I don't mind visiting the Greenaways."

Tucker stared.

Angel was back to being the broad-chested young blue-collar man who had been steadily growing in Tucker's memory as someone important.

"Why?" he asked, frustrated. "Just why?"

"Well, the Greenaways are used to me being male, and to you talking about me as male. So I thought this form would be most appropriate."

"Sure."

"No, really, Tucker." Angel gave him that guileless smile. "Why else would I have changed?"

"To dick with me," Tucker said flatly. "But you know what I *have* noticed?"

Angel shifted his weight from foot to foot. "What?"

"I'll let you know when I feel like it. Now let me go find my gloves. I want to gather the girls' things. Do we still have the boxes from the grocery delivery?"

"Do you think that will be enough?" Their banter—and sexual tension—was forgotten in an instant. "Those objects are pretty powerfully charged, Tucker. They may bleed through."

Tucker would have pinched the bridge of his nose, but it was still pretty sore. "They may," he admitted. "But I don't have anything made of lead. We can bungee cord the boxes to the truck bed, like the stuff I hauled up from Sacramento. Will that work?"

Angel scowled at the boxes holding the remainder of Damien's memories like they were to blame for all their troubles. "Sure," he said sullenly. "Maybe the tragedies can meet and console each other, and you can let Damien go."

"Sure," Tucker said. But not like he meant it.

THEY LEFT the snuff box and the paperweight on top of the desk. Angel confirmed Tucker's suspicion—the paperweight was getting darker inside, a brownish stain spreading like old blood.

"Yeah," Tucker muttered. "I almost want to lay the girls and James to rest so this fucker can't get to them. If we can bring them outside of Daisy Place and give them peace...."

Angel nodded and filled in the rest. "We can concentrate on what to do here. I understand."

It was the age-old concept of getting the children to safety before putting out the fire, and it felt good to know they were in this together. Something about their investigation, about Tucker's handling of the paperweight, seemed to have brought the evil that was

Thomas Conklin closer to the surface. What had once been one shadow of many lingering in the garden had resolved itself into a restless sprit strong enough to kick the crap out of Tucker and malevolent enough to make Tucker remember the ghosts in the graveyard who had wanted so badly to take Tucker's body.

Fortunately, the brush and the bottle felt happy, somehow, in the palm of his hand before he set them in the small box. So did the diamond hairpin and the cameo broach they'd established had been gifts from Sophie to Bridget.

Tucker picked up the soiled sheaf of papers that was James Beaufort's letter with gentleness. Obviously if a part of him was here in Daisy Place, those pages were what was keeping him. Them and the paperweight. But Tucker didn't want that thing anywhere near the little family, dead and buried and still haunting this room.

Tucker put the items into the box and bit his lip. "He was happy to hear from them?" he asked for the umpteenth time.

Angel apparently had no problem following where his mind was going with this. "He was welcoming them with open arms, Tucker. I don't know what Conklin was doing here, but Beaufort had come to take them home."

"That's comforting," he decided. "That's… they were all in the same cemetery. None of them died alone, I don't think." He brightened. "And at least we know Bridget wasn't killed by Conklin." He thought about James Beaufort, pleading for him to take away the stain of killing a man. "Maybe he just needs to know it was worth it."

Tucker finished packing the objects and turned to leave. He looked around the room before he crossed the threshold. "Tomorrow," he said decisively. "Tomorrow we strip the wallpaper. The next day we finish the floors. Then we repaint. This room, at least, will be clean."

"What room will you do next?" Angel asked as he closed the door.

"I don't know. I'll have to look into some of the other rooms, you think? I just sort of hared off and found the first ghost I met. Maybe the next room should be closer to the stairs. Or I could really go for broke and do the living room so we can maybe install a TV and you can watch *Buffy* on a bigger screen."

Angel turned a shining smile his way. "Oh, Tucker. That would be marvelous. I would really love that. Could we?"

Tucker shrugged. "Do you think the ghosts will wander in and out while we're in there?"

"Probably." Angel's shoulders slumped as he started down the stairs, and Tucker considered.

"Well, it would be a good way to size up the next project. I'll think about it."

Angel's spine straightened, and Tucker followed him with a half smile on his face. This having a partner thing was nice. He could deal with having someone—anyone—to talk to about the uncertainties of what he was doing. He knew for damned sure he could have used some help trying to figure out what he was supposed to do when his gift was tugging him in the other direction.

The oppressive heat of July had faded into the more mellow heat of August, and Tucker rolled the windows down for part of the journey. Angel's hair didn't flutter back with the breeze, but Tucker caught him, eyes closed, turning his face to the sunshine on more than one occasion. When they passed the road that led to the fairy hill, he shuddered and frowned.

"What's up?" Tucker asked.

"There's… there are complex things here," Angel muttered. "I'd never thought of this, uh, pagan place as a bastion of good, but good is exactly what I felt coming from it." He made a complicated movement then, a sort of rippling of his back and ass, like a bird settling feathers. "I need to realign my view of the world, that's all."

Tucker laughed. "That's all? That sounds dire."

"I just…." He frowned again. "I don't know where that prejudice came from," he said after a moment. "You're right. It doesn't make sense at all. But I thought all of the things about a fairy hill must be evil—promiscuous sex, rampant desire, terrible indulgence, and blood. But that's not what energy the fairy hill is giving off, and it feels like I was wrong."

"Wow, Angel. That's quite a change."

"Change is not weakness." Angel made that back-ruffling motion again. "It's when we refuse to change in the face of upheaval that we fail."

Tucker thought about it as he drove through the foothills under the August blue sky. "Okay." And the more he thought about it, the more it filled him with joy. "All *right*!" His iPod was playing something that was simultaneously melancholy and thunderous, and he turned that up, immersed in the sudden freedom of a basic truth.

Change was not weakness.

Tucker's life had changed—most assuredly—since he'd gotten the summons to Daisy Place, but answering the change didn't mean he was weak. He may not have been being used for his magic wang anymore, but that didn't mean this thing he was doing—giving peace to the long-since departed—wasn't just as important. Maybe, on some level, it was even *more* important.

Angel wore a half smile as the music pounded, and Tucker grinned. Small moments, Damien had taught him. Small perfect nuggets of time and place. A good hamburger. A sugar cookie. A favorite song.

A moment shared with someone who seemed to understand.

CAN'T FIND MY
WAY HOME

THE FOOTHILLS of the Sierra Nevada languished in the summer. Hot and weighted by dust and sun, even the sky had heft and mass, as blue and as clear as it may have appeared.

If the Manzanita Cemetery in Lincoln had been crushed under the footsteps of time long ago, the sun and the dust had rendered it almost flat to the eye. The marble headstones—usually representing the family patriarch—were all well spaced, and some even cleaned, but most of them bore carved words so faded they may as well have been runes in a language ages ago forgotten. The grass was watered once a week, and a few spare blades of crabgrass clung to a defiant green, but most of it was withered, sere, and too dead to even be called brown.

It was beige. Beige grass.

Angel had never seen anything quite so deceased, and he lived in a haunted mansion with a haunted garden. Even the multidimensional cemetery with the ghosts that wanted to jump Tucker's body looked more alive than this place.

If the zombie apocalypse that seemed so prevalent on Tucker's selection of videos ever occurred, it would be on a ruined landscape like this one.

"Angel, would you stop obsessing over the grass?" Tucker scowled with impatience. "They water as often as they can."

"It's much browner this close to the valley," Angel said mournfully. "I wonder if the cemetery would be less depressing if the grass were greener."

"Probably," Tucker conceded. "But seeing that even the people who mourned these people have passed on, I don't know if they're focusing on morale anymore."

That struck Angel as desperately sad. "Then nobody remembers them?"

Tucker frowned. "I didn't say that. Family stories persist. Look at these three graves—see?"

Angel drew nearer. "'Morgan Peters, beloved husband of Sarah.' So?"

"Now look at the graves on either side."

"'Elizabeth Peters. Beloved wife of Morgan.' Wait—"

"Now the other one," Tucker said with a wicked smile.

"'Sarah Clayborn. Beloved wife of Oren.' Wait—how do those dates…? I mean, how could they all…?"

"And over here," Tucker said, taking a playful leap to the pinnacle stone sitting in the midst of a large family plot.

"'Oren Clayborn, beloved companion of Clancy Matthews, and the children they protected in their home.' Tucker, I am so confused!" Had all these people been married at the same time?

Tucker laughed, and the sound was as giddy as Tucker had been the morning he'd run out of Daisy Place, excited to buy a truck and get a kitten.

"So am I!" he cackled. "But you know what? I bet it's a hell of a story."

His grin was infectious, and Angel caught it.

"We tell stories," he said, feeling a bit of wonder. "You and me. We tell stories."

"We do indeed." Tucker sobered. "Now, it's time to go tell the stories of our friends the Beauforts, you think?" He went on without giving Angel time to respond. "I'm going to guess a big centerpiece headstone, like our buddy Oren here. Something weighty that dominates a family plot. The Beauforts had two sons, so it's going to be big enough for six people. There's not too many of those."

"Will it have the women's names on it?" Angel asked. Most of the centerpiece stones he'd seen so far had been erected by the women for the men.

"Probably not," Tucker said sadly. "It seems like the headstone was for the one who died first, and that was usually the guy."

"Men's bodies are made to burn out more quickly," Angel said. He looked down at his male body. "Maybe it's because of all the testosterone." He isolated it in his mind, could feel the hormone flooding his incorporeal being, attacking hair follicles, sending sex signals to his gonads. "It's almost a toxic hormone."

"You'll have to tell me how estrogen feels sometime," Tucker muttered. "I'm dying for your opinion on that. But now, let's find our...."

He paused, scenting the air almost like Squishbeans did when Tucker was going to feed her bacon. With trancelike slowness, he turned his head and bowed.

And Angel saw them.

Only they were not as they had been at Daisy Place—young and full of fear and the suppressed excitement of whatever was to come.

They were older, but not gnarled and tough like the roots of crabgrass they trod upon. They were gently old—the wrinkles were deep, but not bitter because the women hadn't fought aging. They'd let it have its way with them while they'd gone on with their lives.

Judging from the deep smile lines at the corners of their eyes, the gentle dimples of their mouths, their easy posture, hand in arm, as they strolled among the other ghosts of the cemetery, their own lives had been sweet enough to forgive the years their toll.

Tucker bowed deeply, and although the women were dressed in what appeared to be the favored rumpled sundresses of the forties, the two hearkened immediately back to the days of their youth and curtsied back. They were still regal. The bustle and corset of the turn of the century were gone, and so was the intricacy of the Gibson girl hairstyle. Sophie's white hair was pulled tight in a flyaway knot on the back of her head, and Bridget's shorn, careless curls blew back from her face in the breeze.

But the formality, the shyness of two girls who had fled across the continent to have freedom and love—that was still there, and Tucker responded to it with an innate nobility that Angel had missed at their first meeting.

He'd come to treasure it since.

"Good afternoon, ladies," Tucker said, holding his unwieldy cardboard box to the side. "How are you this fine day?"

The women exchanged glances, and Sophie stepped forward. "We're just fine, young man. What can I do for you? I haven't seen a stranger here in quite some time."

It was Tucker's turn to look at Angel, his eyebrows arched. Angel shrugged one shoulder.

They could see him; they could speak to him. Was it the pentacle at work or just Tucker's basic empathy? Probably Tucker's empathy, Angel thought, remembering the ghosts of the city. Sometimes they'd seen him too.

"I'm not actually taking up residence," Tucker said, biting his lip. "In fact, I'm probably breaking a bunch of rules showing up here at all. But the thing is…." He looked around. "Which one of these is yours, by the way?"

"The one back near the corner," Bridget said, her Irish brogue still a playful lilt on her tongue. "See? A bit of shade there, so it doesn't get too damned hot. A little rain—would it be too much to ask for?"

"We've had quite a drought," Tucker apologized. "Here, may my friend and I escort you ladies to the shade?"

"Of course," Bridget allowed. "Your friend there is looking a little bit more like our type. Are you sure he doesn't belong here?"

"No, no, Bridget. Look at…." Sophie frowned and whispered in her companion's ear.

Bridget raked Angel with eyes that were still Ireland green, even after eighty years in the afterlife. "Oh yes," she said mildly. "I see them now. Well, aren't we honored, then."

"The honor is mine." Angel took his cues from Tucker's garden-party manners. "But let us venture near the shade. Perhaps we'll see your brother there."

Sophie's eyes flickered, and her neck drooped. "James hasn't had an easy time of it, settling in here," she said softly. "So much of him is elsewhere. Bridget and I, we've tried to give him some peace, you know. His wife, Henri, has moved on already to be with their boys. I can't think what he's waiting for." She bit her lip and looked at her mate.

"He's been kind to us," Bridget acknowledged. "In ways I didn't know kin could be kind. Henri and James—they were lovely. And the thing... the thing James did for us...."

For a moment, the women flickered, transported, as it were, to a thicker, richer lawn in the shade of a great hotel.

Angel understood in that moment.

He imagined that back at Daisy Place, they would have seen the two women appear from nowhere and go traipsing by, arm in arm, lively with youth.

"Yes," Tucker said, holding out his arm. "I think we have a pretty good idea of what your brother did for you. And we're so very glad he did. My dear?"

Sophie laughed, becoming more solid in this cemetery, more in tune with this place where she'd gone happily to rest. She took Tucker's arm, with Bridget still firmly attached to her other side, and Angel kept pace a few feet ahead.

"Are you truly?" Bridget asked, all suspicion. "Glad at what he did?"

Angel grunted because he knew that was a falsehood. Tucker wouldn't gain their trust with lies.

"Did you live good lives?" Tucker asked wistfully. "Gentle lives? Did you have chickens?"

"And cats," Sophie said, nodding. "How did you know?"

"Tell me."

Angel caught his breath.

They were going to tell Tucker a story.

"There's not much to tell, really," Bridget said, voice soft. "We... that night we got the letter from James. We knew he was coming, and Sophie was—"

"So happy," Sophie supplied. "We didn't know how he'd greet us, you see? I wanted a divorce. You just didn't do that in those days."

"I am aware." Tucker dimpled at her, and Angel's heart gave a little ping. "You were very brave."

"We wanted to live." Simplicity and courage rang in her voice, and Angel's heart gave a *big* ping. "We wouldn't have if I'd stayed with my husband. No cottage by the river, no chickens, no parade of kittens. We wanted to live, so we came here. And my brother—he missed our family so badly. He'd been violent as a boy, you know. So angry. His school years had been terrible for him. He was much smaller than the other boys. He grew up using his fists more than his chalk. He went west hoping to find a place where he could start over and become known neither for his temper, nor for being a scrawny, put-upon boy."

"He did well?" Tucker prompted, although both Tucker and Angel knew the outcome of this endeavor.

"He did," Sophie said simply. "He made a name for himself, became a foreman. He had a reputation—tough but fair. It was a reputation that followed him the rest of his life on the railroad, even when he stopped laying track."

"Even after…?"

"Oh yes." Both women nodded. "Especially after," Sophie continued. "See, nobody knew about that night." She grimaced, and while Angel was screaming, *That's your opening, use it*, Tucker had apparently already jumped light-years ahead.

They came to the shade, and a low wooden fence offered a sort of bench. A grown man would crush it to slivers, but Tucker and Angel both bowed and the women settled on it, no heavier than a thought.

Tucker sat down on the brittle crabgrass, folding his legs and looking up at Sophie and Bridget like they were his favorite grade school teachers, the gentle ones who read stories and played music.

Angel made himself comfortable next to him, their knees touching, and the two of them leaned their chins on their fists in classic listening pose.

Sophie dimpled at them. "Aren't you sweet. Such lovely young men." She cocked her head slyly. "Are you a couple?"

Angel waited for the negative Tucker had given Margie. He was unprepared for Tucker's nakedly wistful look in his direction. "There's some yearning," he said, turning back to the women, "and a few obstacles as well."

"Oh, isn't that always the way." Bridget's sympathy spoke of experience—and it gave Angel some heart. Of course, these women would know about yearning.

And obstacles.

"Your story gave me hope," Tucker told them. "But we didn't see all of it. And I'm worried about James. He spends too much time at the hotel—and it's not healthy there."

"No." Sophie's hand visibly tightened over Bridget's. "We couldn't feel it back then, of course. It was new and bustling. People thought the place would boom, become a metropolis. Silly thought, of course. You don't build a metropolis in the mountains. You build a sanctuary—or a prison."

They both shuddered.

"Tell us what happened." Tucker reached into the box and pulled out the brush, the pin, the broach, and the letter. "Perhaps…." He looked at the things in his hand. "Perhaps, once the story is all told, these things will just be things again."

"Oh!" Sophie reached out her hand, but Bridget snatched it back.

"Not yet, Sophie luv," she said, lacing their fingers firmly. "The boys need to hear the story."

"Yes. Indeed they do." Sophie turned to Tucker and Angel. "Come, take our hands, boys," she said. "And hold tight to each other. It was a terrible, terrible night, that, and if you weren't holding tight to someone you loved, you could find a part of yourself lost at Daisy Place. Indeed, I believe you're right, and that's where my brother has been all these years."

Tucker put the objects back in the box and stood, reaching for Sophie's hand. Angel did the same for Bridget's, and the touch of her skin, dry and papery, with a few calluses, sent a shiver of longing coursing through him. Not for sex, but for sensation, for a grandmother's hug or a hand held during a walk or a lipstick kiss against his temple. He'd never had these things—would have once said he'd never imagined these things—but they were running like a current under Bridget's skin.

"You had children?" he said, perplexed.

"Henri and James had two boys," Bridget said, squeezing his hand. "And their wives had three apiece. Those children are buried in a different place and grew to live different lives, but their childhoods—those are still in us." She and Sophie smiled fondly at each other, and Tucker breathed deeply through his nose.

Angel turned to him just as he wiped his eyes on his shoulder. "Oh, Tucker...."

He reached out, and Tucker grabbed his hand like a shipwrecked man clung to a spar of wood to stay alive.

The circuit of the dead and the living, and those suspended between, was made complete, and the memory of their last night at Daisy Place rippled through the four of them like shock waves from a bomb.

"SOPHIE! SOPHIE!" Bridget knew her way around a corset, and her first order of business was to rip open the buttons of Sophie's blouse and tug at the knots that held the corset tight. The thing exploded outward, and Sophie pulled in a great gasp of air.

Her eyes fluttered open, and she whispered, "James. James is coming."

The door flew back, rebounding against the wall, and Thomas Conklin burst in.

"Get your hands off her," he snarled. "Trollop, stealing my son's wife and spiriting her to this ungodly place."

Bridget stood and turned, facing Conklin and protecting Sophie with her body. "Ye keep yer bloody fuckin' hands off 'er," she snarled. "Yer not 'er husband, and 'e don' care enough ter chase 'er 'ere."

"Speak English, you filthy peasant." Conklin smiled, chilling in his arrogance, and reached into his pocket for his little snuff tin of courage.

His pupils were already tiny pinpoints of madness.

"Snort some more," Bridget urged, feeling ugly and murderous. "Snort until yer brains run out yer nose. But leave 'er out of it."

Behind her, Sophie struggled to her feet. "You need to leave now," she said. "My brother is coming. He wants us. He's a railroad man, and he won't let you take us back. We won't go back, you hear? You'll have to kill me before I go back to your hateful house and let you use me at your will."

Bridget wanted to weep for pride. Oh, her Sophie girl, so sure of her own weakness. She sounded like a warrior right then. No hands would touch her that she didn't invite, and Bridget was the most blessed of women because Sophie only wanted her.

Conklin moved wicked fast, though, and when Bridget saw he was heading for Sophie like Bridget didn't exist, she charged.

She didn't feel the cruel backhand that sent her crashing across the room, but the wall—that she did feel.

She lay there, dazed, trying to push herself up through the ringing in her ears. Sophie started to scream, but Conklin punched her, and the next sound she made was a mewl of rage and pain.

And that was when Conklin lost himself, blind to all but his drugs and his madness.

The door was open; anyone could have seen. Bridget stared into the hall, praying for salvation, praying for help as Conklin ripped Sophie's skirts from her body and drove himself into her, frothing and gibbering as he fucked.

Sophie sobbed, and Bridget put her hands under her one more time, and that's when he arrived.

Bridget would spend the rest of her life thinking the only man she'd ever admire was James Beaufort.

He strode into the room and froze, but for just a moment. Just long enough to take in the scene.

Just long enough to see the paperweight.

The bronze base of the thing went rocketing across the room when it crashed down on Thomas Conklin's head. He fell to the side and his baseless gibbering stopped.

The only sound left in the room was Sophie's furious sobbing.

Bridget managed to find her feet as James sank to his knees. "Sophie?" And well might he have been confused. As she wriggled out from under the body of her attacker, his sister was a mess, half-clothed, blood dripping from her face, bruises on her chest, her breasts, her thighs.

"James?"

"Oh, baby sister. I'm so sorry—"

And then she fell upon him, weeping.

It was a fine tableau, and one Bridget would revisit many times in her long life—but they could not stay there any more than they could breathe life back into the monster leaking his brains out on the floor.

"We need to get rid of the body," Bridget said, her voice echoing into the room. "We need to hide him and clean up and take him down the stairs tonight and bury him. There's a small graveyard out back—they keep the earth there soft."

"I'm sorry?" James asked, dazed and purposeless in the aftermath of murder.

Sophie struggled to her feet. "She's right, James. We need to get rid of the body."

James studied the blood on his hands. "But... but he was he was forcing himself on you, Sophie. Look at you. You're—"

Sophie nodded and wiped her ruined dress over her bleeding mouth and nose. "Do you think he didn't pay off the management?" she asked bitterly. "Do you see a soul here, James? We were making a ruckus fit to bring down God himself—but Conklin Senior, he's got more money than God, you understand?" She flew to the door and slammed it shut and then returned to her brother's side.

"James." She hugged him tight, and he wrapped arms around her shoulders, clinging to her like she was a glimpse of sanity in a madhouse. She pulled back, though. "James, you must listen to me. We'll leave tonight and bury Conklin in the cemetery. Who knows you're here?"

"Henrietta," he said, sounding puzzled.

"Anyone you work with? Did you talk to anybody when you came to town?"

James shook his head slowly. "Cover yourself, darling."

Sophie grimaced at Bridget and went to grab a bath sheet from the pile crumpled in the corner. She wrapped it around herself.

"Now, James, think. Conklin was coming to find me— we don't know how many people he told or who knows where he is now. But he's not well liked. If he disappears, I'm not sure who will search for him. And nobody knows about you or Henri. I never told Tommy about you."

"Why not?" James asked, frowning.

Sophie shrugged and looked at Bridget sorrowfully. "He wouldn't have been interested, Jimmy. Nobody in Maryland cared who I was." She gave a surprisingly vicious kick at the cooling body at their feet. "This one wanted to use me—wanted to own me. I ran away because I wouldn't be owned. You don't deserve to be tried for this, James, but they'll do you. If we bury him and disappear, nobody will come looking for us. If we tell them we killed Thomas Conklin Senior because he was abusing his property, they'll hang you before you're done speaking."

She looked at Bridget for confirmation, and Bridget had trouble nodding. She was brilliant, Sophie was. Bridget would have followed her into hell—she was just as glad to be following her into a better future than that.

The rest of the night was sort of a cloudy nightmare. They didn't want to use the lovely quilt on the bed, so Bridget snuck downstairs to the linen closet for a clean sheet while Sophie cleaned up and packed. They used Sophie's ruined blouse and skirt to scrub the blood from the floor, and from the walls and the damaged paperweight. They rolled the tattered clothing into a ball and shoved it with Conklin's body into the tight linen wrapping of the sheet.

They were interrupted once by a knock at the door asking if they wanted to attend dinner with their one guest. Bridget answered in discreet tones and said her mistress was overwhelmed with her father-in-law's visit and was resting.

That was their only visitor.

Sophie's face was swollen and bruised—there was no hiding it—but since James had ridden his wagon in and left it down at the stables, nobody would see Sophie up close once they got on the road. All they had to do was bury the body before sunup and make sure their bill was paid.

They left Sophie in the room to finish the cleaning, al-though Bridget knew she had no talent for it. Bridget was left to help James heft the body, long after all the occupants of Daisy Place were safely tucked into their beds.

Bridget never forgot that strange journey in the horse and wagon, under a moon stained the color of Conklin's blood. James muttered to himself about witches and bad luck the whole way there, and Bridget couldn't find the words to reassure him. As they got to know each other in later years, Bridget would realize the enormity of the murder, and how it sat on his shoulders like the dead weight of a corpse. But on this night, she only hoped Sophie's brother could move a bit faster and not break under the strain of their bitter work.

He stayed steadfast, though. Bridget was no stranger to hard work, and they took turns using James's camp spade to dig the grave. The graveyard had seemed alive that night, watching—even breath-ing—in the chilly autumn dark. James would not shut up about how lucky they were to escape the snows that year, and all Bridget could remember thinking was how lucky they'd be to escape the law.

But eventually, about an hour before the skies tinged gray, they finished their grim task and rode back to the house.

"You stay here," Bridget told him. "I'll get Sophie and our bags." They hadn't brought much.

"I can come—"

"No! Because if someone catches us, that will be us alone. Nobody will believe two women killed an old man by themselves. But you—you're sturdy as a tree. They'll know. Just stay here. I'll be back before the sky's more than a minute lighter."

She clutched her skirts up to her ankles and pattered through the great entryway and up the stairs.

Sophie was asleep on the bed, fully clothed, her hat lying next to her. Asleep she looked delicate, ethereal, even with a swollen nose and mouth. She'd packed as well as could be expected, but Bridget had a feeling she'd left more than one thing behind. She saw the lump in the wallpaper, where Sophie had hid James's correspondence, and she tsked.

"Sophie girl—what did you do that for?" With more tenderness than Bridget thought she'd ever possessed, she smoothed the loose tendrils of butter-yellow hair from Sophie's forehead.

Sophie stirred on the bed and smiled sleepily. "Do what?"

"The letter, love. Behind the wallpaper."

Sophie's grin was so proud. "I wanted to hide proof that James was here." She yawned. "I would have burned it, but there's no fire or grate in this room."

No indeed. Daisy Place had a radiator, slow to turn on even in the frost-laden autumn mornings.

"Well, let me hide it just a bit better," Bridget said practically. "We can at least shove the bed a little closer there, and no one will see it."

"No. You wash off your hands, Bridge. You're a mess. I'll tuck them in farther."

Sophie stood and adjusted her clean skirt and smoothed a strand of blond hair back into the bun she would soon hide under her bonnet.

At that moment they heard a rumble and froze. It was the same moan they heard every morning—that of the pipes being used before the boiler had quite heated enough water.

"We'd best just leave," Bridget whispered.

Sophie nodded, and they seized their bags and fled.

They saw not a soul as they tripped down the halls and exited the foyer. As they were leaving, Sophie turned around and stared at the place that had given them sanctuary for the most glorious of autumns.

She gasped and held her hand to her mouth, and Bridget turned back to see what had spooked her.

"Oh God," she muttered.

They both saw it, pressed against the window of the front room. The bulbous nose, the drooping and bushy mustache. The eyes with more than a touch of madness corrupting all that lay behind them.

"Sophie," Bridget whispered, her voice not carrying under the rumble and jouncing of the horse's hooves and the buckboard.

"That's him," Sophie whispered back, her voice taking on a vicious pleasure. "And if that's where he stays, then good for him. May he lord his madness over that house for as long as God lets him."

"I'd prefer God kicked him right in the teeth," Bridget prayed in a fit of fear.

"Well, I'd prefer God not know about anything that transpired tonight," James said glumly.

Both the women startled, and Sophie said clearly, "James, you have nothing to hide from God. Do you understand me?"

James couldn't meet his sister's eyes. "Oh, such brave words. I'll try to believe them, Sophie my dear. For your sake, I shall try."

"HE DID," Sophie said sadly, her voice breaking the spell the memory had woven over the four of them "He tried. I know he tried desperately for Henrietta— he loved the two of us, loved that we kept her company when he traveled." She used the apron tied around her waist to wipe her eyes. "But he would fall into black moods in the autumn, and even after he confessed to Henri what we'd done, he still had trouble forgiving himself. He lived a good life, mostly, but a part of him died in that room that night. That's what happens when a good man murders, even for the best of reasons, you understand?"

Tucker nodded, and Angel squeezed his hand. He gave a bare hint of a smile and turned back to the women.

"Sophie?"

She looked at him expectantly.

"Can you think of anything in that room that might have been James's?" He showed her the rest of what was in the box. "Are any of these things his? A button? The letter opener? The hole punch?"

Sophie shook her head.

"No, my dear. What is it you're looking for?"

Tucker sighed. "I'm looking for a memento. Something solid that will pull his spirit away from Daisy Place and bring it back here where it belongs."

Bridget suddenly popped up, releasing Angel's hand without thought. Angel's other hand slid through Tucker's like mist, and Angel suppressed a sigh.

It had been a lovely interlude, but now it was over.

"Sophie! Sophie!"

Sophie grinned like a girl. "Oh, I know what you're excited about." The two of them began walking slow circles around the pinnacle stone. "Come on, boys," Sophie cried. "It's a treasure hunt for sure!"

Tucker and Angel looked at each other and then began to follow in the women's footsteps.

"What are we looking for?" Tucker asked.

"Oh, it's too wonderful," Sophie exclaimed, clapping. "Tucker, right there, can you feel it?"

Tucker paused then and dropped to his knees in the corner of the family plot. His face lit up, and he began to dig. The crabgrass was horrible—Angel could see that—but Tucker kept going in spite of the cuts the tougher-than-fishing-line roots left in the corners of his knuckles. Soon he had a four-inch by four-inch hole, and he rooted delicately with his fingers.

"Yes!" he cried after what seemed a breathless hour. "Angel, come here. Can you feel the story?"

Angel came toward him, and in his head....

LITTLE JIMMY, James's namesake, whose father had died in the war, had stood there. His coat, a solid red wool, was many sizes too large and worn through in places. But it had belonged to his grandfather, and Poppy Beaufort had sat Jimmy on his knees and played clapping games with him for hours at a time.

Jimmy's mother told him sadly that his poppy was gone to the same place his father had gone, and Jimmy had asked, in all innocence, "Iwo Jima?"

His mother had laughed, sputtering tears, and Jimmy was left in the same confusion as before.

So now, when all the grownups were wearing black on this dreary rainy day, Jimmy was making plans to visit Iwo Jima someday, to see his father and his poppy. Maybe his poppy would recognize him in this old wool coat.

He was holding so tightly to Aunty Bridget and Aunty Sophie's hands that he didn't even notice when the brass button popped off the cuff. Bridget and Sophie didn't worry so much with buttons and cuffs as his mother, so Jimmy kept holding on to them even after he saw it missing, all the time planning to visit a faraway

*place where his father and grandfather would read him
stories and let him come in from the cold.*

TUCKER HELD in his palm the dirt-encrusted
bronze button with a sailing ship impressed across the
front.

The bit of nylon thread that had come loose from
Jimmy's coat still trailed from the post in the back.

"Perfect," Tucker breathed.

"Oh, Bridget, look!" Sophie exclaimed. "My brush
and your pin, and see? The letter from James."

Tucker looked up quickly, and Angel didn't understand the panic in his eyes. This was their job, wasn't
it? To tell the stories of the dead so they could pass
gently into the next world? The women, touching those
objects that held such strong memories, would simply
pass over, but the thought seemed to hurt Tucker in
ways that Angel didn't understand.

"No, ladies, not yet, please—"

Sophie reached into the box and lifted the brush
and the letter with one hand and pressed Bridget's pin
into her hand with the other.

"Oh, boys," Sophie said, fading diaphanously into
the shadows. "Thank you for the lovely summer day.
Send my brother if you can. We miss him."

Bridget's blue eyes remained bright, though the
rest of her was transparent as glass. "And you two don't
put off yer own fine love, if you can help it!" she cau-
tioned, and then....

They were gone. Leaving Tucker on the ground
clutching a brass button, an almost empty box beside
him on the grass.

"No!" The cry was ripped from him, open grief for
women long dead. Angel sank to his knees next to him

and wrapped his arm around Tucker's shoulders, holding him close.

"Tucker. Tucker, you knew this would happen—"

"Oh, Angel, I was going to give them their things. I wanted to tell them goodbye, and I wanted to see them happy in the house by the river. I wanted to tell that story too!"

Of course he would. Angel dropped a kiss in his hair, knowing he couldn't feel a thing but hoping. "It's okay—we've met them. We know that story. They don't need us to tell it to them. Nobody needs absolution or catharsis for two lovers living a long and happy life."

"But…." Tucker wiped his eyes on his shirt and sagged into his spot in the shade. "Angel, I just need to…. God! Don't you just want to know there's a happy ending?"

"Of course I do!" Angel told him, the bitterness welling, blood in an old wound that he couldn't remember sustaining. "But they had their happy ending, and you haven't. I'd rather work to get *you* your ending than see someone who's lived a happy and full life live theirs. That's *their* story, Tucker."

Tucker turned a tear-ridden face toward him. "But it's the only happy ending we're likely to get," he whispered. He was as destroyed as a child, as innocent as Jimmy hoping his father and grandfather were in Iwo Jima. The cynicism, the bitterness—it had washed away under Angel's hands four nights before, and Angel had given him no armor to replace it.

Angel opened his mouth to say something, anything at all, but he could make no promises.

He couldn't even kiss Tucker's tears away.

STAY

Tucker stopped for In-N-Out on the way home, so dispirited he almost forgot and asked Angel what he wanted.

When he realized what he'd almost done, he changed his fries to "animal style" on general principles.

In a life filled with strangers touching his body, he couldn't ever remember needing the touch of one person—casual or intimate—so much in his life.

Angel's tentative voice broke into his savage mastication of a double cheeseburger.

"I just wish I understood the rules."

Tucker swallowed. "Of what?"

"Of us touching. Like, we know it happens when your heart is bleeding—as long as you're not wearing the necklace."

"We know it happens when you're getting all badass and protective," Tucker said, smiling a little.

"Or when you're holding hands with ghosts," Angel said, also smiling.

"That was both of us, Angel."

"Oh yes!" Angel brightened. "I've got it. I think I get it." He frowned. "I'm pretty sure I get it."

"Well, then, would you give it to me?" Tucker finished off his cheeseburger, and silence descended on the cab of the truck.

And the tumblers clicked, unlocking the erotic potential of what Tucker had just said.

"Is that how you like it?" Angel asked, sounding coy. "Do you *want* me to give it to you?"

Tucker gasped. "I *knew* it! I *knew* that's why you picked that form."

Angel disappeared and came back as the redheaded woman. "What form?" he asked guilelessly.

Tucker broke into a cackle of laughter he almost couldn't stop. "Oh my God, Angel. I know your secret!"

The redhead disappeared, replaced by the Angel Tucker was most familiar with. "What secret?" he asked carefully.

Tucker sighed. "Not the big one. I still don't know what you are. I was talking about the...." He couldn't fight the flush, so he gave up and let embarrassment sweep him. "You want to top. You want to... to...."

"To give you pleasure," Angel said humbly. "Yes. I'd like to experience it from you, but...."

"But what?"

"But you have given so much. I just wanted to give you something." After experiencing pleasure at Angel's hands, Tucker could smell the heat washing through him. "And it seemed like a very pleasurable thing for me too."

"Having, uh, gotten it from both ends, as it were, I can vouch for both those things." Instinctively Tucker reached over to squeeze Angel's knee.

And his fingers met the resistance of flesh.

He almost cried. "If there was a place to pull over so we could put our boy parts where our mouths have been, I would so do it."

Angel grabbed his hand. "I would probably enjoy that. But I do not think it's what you really need."

Tucker squeezed back. The warmth, the physical reassurance of having a real person there in the car seeped into his soul, and he could breathe again. Finally he could admit he'd been battling the loneliness—the terrible, life-draining loneliness that had wrapped him in grieving for over a decade—since the women had faded from the graveyard on the hill.

"I'm grateful," he whispered.

"For what?"

"That you're at least here when I'm bleeding."

Angel stroked the back of his hand until he needed it to steer again.

TUCKER PULLED up to the Greenaways' little ranch-style about twenty minutes later, grateful when he saw Rae's minivan in the driveway, with a little Ford truck behind it.

"So the sedan really was for Andy." Tucker had guessed, but apparently the Greenaways' oldest bird had really flown the coop.

"Do you think Josh misses the truck?" Angel asked.

In answer, Josh came running out of the house, barely waiting until Tucker had stopped before patting the beaten quarter panel. Tucker gave Angel's hand one last squeeze before throwing the door open in time to hear Josh say, "Oh, baby! Did you miss me? Don't mind the other truck in the driveway, baby—she's a harlot and means nothing."

Tucker met Angel's amused glance. "Yes," he said. "I think he missed the truck."

"Shh," Josh whispered, draping his body across what must have been a fairly hot hood. "She thinks this is forever."

"Is your sane half in the house?"

Josh grinned at him, but he didn't stop hugging the quarter panel. "Indeed she is. She's working, though, so it better be important."

"It's a little bit important," Tucker said. In his peripheral vision, Angel was nodding like mad.

"You go on in."

They turned, and Josh frowned. "That's weird. When you drove up, I could have sworn there were two of you in there. I was going to ask you to introduce me to your friend, but...."

Tucker stared at him.

Josh stared back. "Please tell me I was seeing things."

"Sure." Tucker nodded. "You were seeing Angel."

"God*dammit.* I do *not* want to get sucked into this. It's fine for Rae and the kids to think that shit's real, but—"

"That shit's real," Tucker said, no bullshit in his voice. "And it could be dangerous. Just have a little respect for it, okay?"

Josh patted the hood mournfully. "I'm probably going to want to hear whatever you and Rae are talking about, aren't I? Dammit, baby, I thought you and me would get some time alone."

Tucker chuckled as he and Angel followed the poor man inside.

Rae was standing by the sink washing her hands when they walked in. She nodded at Tucker and then squinted behind him.

Then she squinted at Tucker again and just that quickly invaded his space. "What did you do to your face?" she demanded. "And what did you do to my work?"

Tucker touched the necklace at his throat and frowned. Glancing at Angel, he pulled the chain over his head and held the circumscribed pentagram in the palm of his hand.

"It's… twisted," he murmured. The points of the star remained firmly soldered to the circle around them, but all stretches of the silver had twisted, warping, creating a three-dimensional sphere, with what had once been a garnet suspended in the middle.

The stone was now black as an onyx, but cut in facets, like a diamond.

"That is very interesting," he said, wondering what it meant. "Angel, any ideas?"

"Well, the pentagram is supposed to represent the five senses," Angel said thoughtfully. "And safety— hiding—because of all the angles, the nooks and crannies it holds. This looks like the epitome of that. The shape is using the nooks and crannies to protect the rare thing inside."

"Is that really a black diamond?" Tucker turned the sphere to try to get a better look at it.

And then it turned red.

Tucker looked to see what Rae thought, but she was looking over his shoulder. "Angel, you are almost visible. Do you know that?"

"Even Josh saw me," Angel said, sounding proud.

"Tucker, what in the hell is going on over there?" With a frustrated grunt, Rae pulled a scrunchy out of her pocket and used it to capture the frothy wealth of graying hair on the top of her head.

"I'm thinking hell is sort of the problem."

"Sit down," Rae gestured. "Both of you. God, Tucker, your nose is truly special, you know that? You sit too, Josh." She turned her head and started to holler. "Coral! Murphy! Tilda! You guys get in here and listen and fetch, okay? Coral, you especially—we're going to need you!"

"Mom! I'm in the middle of *Overwatch*!"

"Coral Catherine, do you ever want to play that game again?"

The grumpy sound of irritated preadolescent was enough to lighten the air in the kitchen, so by the time the kids came in, big-eyed and sober, Tucker managed to not feel like he was including grade-schoolers in on a council of war.

"Oh!" Coral said, hanging over what was probably a vacant chair to her father and mother. "Sorry about your face, Tucker. Hey, Angel. You're looking very solid today."

"I can't see him," Tilda said flatly. "Am I excused?"

"No," her mother told her. "Just 'cause you can't see shit, that doesn't mean it can't hurt you. Tucker, tell us what happened."

Tucker started with discovering the pentagram around his neck and the confrontation with a dangerous ghost in the garden.

"Angel doesn't think Conklin will come in—he thinks it violates all of the rules Conklin valued."

Rae snorted. "Yes, well, you and Angel violate all of the rules *you* value, so I'm with you, Tucker. I wouldn't trust Conklin's ghost, not for a minute."

"What do you think he will do?" Josh asked, frowning. Tucker was relieved that he didn't look doubtful—it was good to have Josh on board.

"I'm not sure." Tucker leaned on his elbows. "If he's corporeal, he could come in and attack me as I slept. I'm worried about that, but not too worried." He smiled briefly. "Me and Angel could take him."

Angel snorted.

"What if he's not corporeal?" Rae asked, equally serious.

"That's the scariest part," Tucker admitted. "When we tangled in the front yard—" He touched his swollen nose gingerly. "—he wasn't running at me to attack me. He was running at me to do what the ghosts at the graveyard tried to do."

Rae and the kids all shuddered, apparently understanding the direness of having another person's soul inside them.

"He wanted to take you over," Rae said, and Tucker nodded. "Why didn't he try before then?"

Tucker tugged at the charm at his throat. "I don't think he saw me without this. So this was like a gift and a curse. It helped me fight that ghost off, but it took away my camouflage as a standard member of the living."

"Hmmm…." She tightened her scrunchy and paced. "Why this guy?"

Tucker and Angel exchanged glances. "He's an asshole?" Tucker said after a moment.

She pinned him with a "mom" gaze. "You will elaborate."

"He was some sort of millionaire back east—one of those captains-of-the-universe types who think they own everyone. He was sexually abusing his daughter-in-law, so she fled out here with her lover to see if her brother would take her in."

"Did he?" Josh asked, apparently captured by the story.

Tucker smiled, remembering Sophie and Bridget and how happy they'd been. "Yes. He was going to take the girls in. He didn't care that she wanted a divorce, in fact. He'd been missing his family, and his wife was lonely when he was gone working. He was…." Tucker shrugged, trying not to wish for the perfect ending. "He was a good guy."

"Girls?" Tilda apparently forgot this was boring and gazed at him like he was the TV.

Tucker winked. "Yeah. Girls. Bridget was Sophie's ladies' maid. They… they were special. They were nice, nice ladies. And they came out here because they wanted to get far away from her father-in-law."

"But he followed?"

"Yeah." Tucker thought about it—thought about the terrifying glimpses he'd had into Thomas Conklin Senior's life. "He thought he owned them. He was furious that they would try to escape. He was an addict and entitled and…." He shuddered. "His heart was as black and as evil as they come."

He had them. The whole Greenaway family was staring at him openmouthed, and he found he didn't want to stop. The fairy-tale words fell from his lips, framing the story in mystery and beauty and terror and ugliness and joy, because that was the way of all the best stories.

"So the girls arrived at Daisy Place, and for a while, it was paradise. They stayed in the gardens and their rooms, mostly, but some days they walked through town and along Church Street, seeing the steep drop of canyon beyond the cemetery and talking about flying under the sun. Sophie sent word to her brother a few weeks after they arrived—"

"Why so late?" Murphy wanted to know, as entranced as his sister.

"It was a honeymoon to them," Tucker said, guessing. He'd known they'd fled in the spring and James had arrived in the fall. He would fill in the gaps as he may. "But also they were afraid, and they wanted to get their courage up. Sophie had traveled across the country uninvited, and she was leaving her husband. She was afraid her brother might not want the disgrace she brought upon her family name."

Coral socked her brother in the arm. "He'd better take her," she said, glaring at Murphy as if he'd rejected *her*.

"Hey!"

"Wait—you said he did!" Tilda burst in excitedly. Then, to her mother, "See. I *was* listening."

"You were indeed." Tucker inclined his head. "Very good. So her brother was coming, and the girls were so excited and nervous. And just as they read the letter, they heard another voice calling from downstairs."

"Oh no!" Josh was leaning his chin on his fists like a girl in a '50s movie. "Conklin?"

"Oh yes," Tucker said. "It was Sophie's father-in-law, and he was furious. He was maddened beyond reason. He burst into the hotel room and stormed forward to attack Sophie. Bridget stepped in, and he backhanded her across the room. She fell, hitting her head, and struggled to get back up. Conklin, enraged, continued his assault, and poor Sophie." Tucker swallowed. He hadn't seen inside Sophie's heart for this rape, but he'd been there for the first one, and he would carry her helplessness, her degradation and pain, for the rest of his life.

"She was in pain," he said softly. "And being abused terribly. And just then, in the middle of all that chaos, her brother walked in."

"I'd *kill* somebody who'd touch my sister!" Murphy growled.

Tucker regarded him sadly. "Of course you would. You're a good brother. And so was James. He seized a glass paperweight, one with a solid base of bronze, and he crashed it down on the back of Conklin's head."

Everybody in the room put their hands to their mouth in horror. Including Angel.

"Oh, he was dead all right," Tucker told them. "But Sophie and Bridget, they were strong and quick-thinking. They knew James could get charged and convicted of murder—Conklin was very powerful, and James was a railroad man, no more, no less. So they rolled the body in a sheet and used Sophie's ripped clothing to sop up the blood and clean the room. Bridget and James took the body into the graveyard in the dark of night, by the light of a waning moon, and buried it. They thought it was on consecrated ground, mind you, and they did not realize that Daisy Place is built upon an abomination. The metal there is made to trap the souls of the dead. Or sometimes, parts of the living."

That was what had happened to James Beaufort, after all.

"So they buried Conklin's body and then went back for Sophie, and the girls ran out of the hotel and left all of the trouble behind them."

"You can't leave that sort of thing behind you," Rae said with the certainty of an adult.

"No, you can't." Tucker closed his eyes and saw Damien. "A part of your soul always stays behind. Every time. And so the girls, Sophie and Bridget, left a part of themselves at Daisy Place. Part of it was the happy part—the part that made love and took walks and enjoyed breakfast with strawberries and days with no fear. But some of what they left behind was that terrible, terrible night, the one that nobody ever spoke of. The one that ended when James drove their buckboard away and they looked behind them and saw, pressed against the glass of the window, the bloated and insane face of Thomas Conklin Senior."

Everybody gasped—as they should have—but it was Josh who asked the question that had truly haunted Tucker.

"But what about James? He couldn't have walked away free and clear either."

"No, he did not," Tucker answered, nodding, the storyteller's spell still upon him. "He left a big chunk of his soul there in Daisy Place, much of it out of doors, on the moonlit ride to and from the hidden grave. He was haunted by what he'd done—haunted even more because it was a secret, one he could barely stand to tell his wife. And he'd had no friends to absolve him of the guilt and the pain of taking another life."

Tucker took a deep breath, finding something resonant and painful in this fact. He felt a squeeze on his shoulder and a kiss on his temple. He closed his eyes and savored Angel's touch for as long as it would last.

"Although James was a good man and died a peaceful death, much of his soul is still on the lawn of Daisy Place, in a constant battle with Conklin as he tries to keep the man's viciousness from harming people, even in death."

A collective sigh went through the family as the story ended.

"Wow," Tilda said softly. "That was cool. Awful, but… you know. Cool."

"But Sophie and Bridget had a good life?" Coral asked.

"Oh yes. They had cats and chickens and nephews and then great-nephews and nieces to play with," Tucker told her. Something in his heart healed as he said it. Angel had been right. Telling the story made it true; he hadn't needed the women to tell him that part. He'd known it in his heart. "They were very happy in the end, and all of the suffering they'd undergone faded in their memory, until, for the most part, they only remembered the joy of falling in love."

And now the family seemed to inhale.

"But that doesn't tell us anything about the bauble at your neck," Rae said, frowning. "Except… it changed. Tucker, how did you get that story?"

"I felt it," Tucker said, feeling like one of the children now. "Angel finds the items in the room with the emotional charge, I touch them, and the story sort of plays for both of us." He looked at Angel for confirmation. "It's how Angel and my aunt helped dispel the trapped spirits in that house for years. I guess ghosts need catharsis and absolution as much as humans do."

Rae nodded but was still troubled. "So you knew much of Conklin's story before he attacked you?"

Tucker thought about it. "Yes. I mean, I had an idea. I was hoping Sophie and Bridget had gotten away, but…." He remembered the terrible night he'd seen from James's point of view. "I had no idea how badly

James felt about it. That changed. I thought it was just a story about madness and violence. What it should be is a story about redemption. Not for Conklin—he was a douchenugget. But James. James was a good man, and part of his spirt is still at the hotel because he was forced to kill a bad one."

"Oh," Rae said, her soft smile of wonder lighting her plain features with a luminous beauty. "That's it. That's what happened. The pendant—its power—it's not broken, it's *changed*. Like you. You changed toward the situation you were watching." Her eyes flickered over his shoulder. "You and Angel changed toward each other. I know you were afraid because the ghosts, the protective symbol—the falling in love with Angel—they all seemed to be *breaking* rules of dealing with the dead. You're not supposed to be concrete to a ghost. You're not supposed to fall in love with one. You're not supposed to wear a pagan symbol to a place of Christian burial. These are the rules as you know them."

Tucker gasped. Some of those rules he'd known internally but had never vocalized.

"But they're not true," he said.

"It's like how I felt about the fairy hill," Angel murmured. "That wasn't true either."

Tucker nodded, and so did Rae.

"You're right," she said. "The rules of dealing with the dead are always fluid. They depend on who and where and why and how we understand their lives. You *were* afraid because it felt like this thing you were doing—dealing with the spirits—was *breaking* rules. But it's not. It's changing the rules. Which means *the rules are still there*. You just need to figure out what they are."

Oh. Tucker swallowed. "What was that thing about Angel?" he said, his voice lost in the babble in his head.

Rae grabbed his hand and held it to her cheek. Augh! He was being mommed again, and he was not so blind as to fail to see how much he craved it. "Tucker, I don't even have to see Angel. I just have to see how you look when he's near."

"I *do* like the way you look at me," Angel said modestly. "In all of my forms. Once the initial surprise is over, the look doesn't change."

Tucker choked back an emotion-fraught laugh. "Your eyes are the same," he said shortly. "If you want to try to make me look at you different, you need to change your eyes." He sighed. "And even then, I'd still know it was you."

Again he sensed a kiss on the temple he couldn't feel—but it was just as well. An actual kiss from Angel right now might destroy him.

"Anyway," Tucker said on a deep breath, trying to recover, "I was wondering about some more charms. I can pay—"

"Don't finish that sentence," Rae barked, and Tucker subsided.

"Okay, well, if you need anything—yardwork, exorcism, sexual epiphany, ghost hunting; those are pretty much my specialties—I can help. But something for my room, so I can sleep, would be nice."

Rae nodded and fingered the pendant again. "I can do that."

"Thanks. Also, can I borrow your sketchbook for a minute?"

"Sure." The book appeared, with a pencil and a pen, and Tucker looked up at the family and smiled weakly. "This is going to be sort of boring," he apologized.

The children just watched, wide-eyed, as though expecting him to pull magic from the plain page. Well, in a way, he was.

He muttered to himself as he sketched, trying hard to pull up the obscure pages of a misspent youth in college behind his eyes. Even then he'd known holding a job would be impossible. He'd tried a few times, things with flexible hours. The time he'd worked in a movie theater had been the best, until he'd gotten busted having sex in the bathroom. Twice. The other times had ended up much the same: the job was great, and he'd enjoyed the employment, until that thing in his chest started up... again.

But he'd gone to school, and he'd learned (and cut a few classes, but since he'd had his share of professors, that had worked too), and one of the things he'd learned had been....

This.

He spelled the words out because this was all about stories, and linked the letters because it would have to be jewelry. He finished in the breathless silence and rubbed his eyes. How long? How many days had it been since he'd not been emotionally exhausted or not worried about his life or his privacy as he slept?

He gave the picture to Rae and grimaced. "It'll take a while. You don't have to get it done in a day. And if it's too much—"

"What's it say?" she asked curiously, tracing the connected runes with her finger. "It looks pretty, but you're right—it's going to take a few weeks if I'm going to do it right. Any particular metal?"

Tucker looked at Angel, who was staring at the picture, mesmerized. "White gold," Angel said softly. "It should be in white gold."

"You know what it says?" Tucker asked, wanting him to be sure.

"I know what it means," Angel told him. "Is that the same?"

Tucker thought about that. "Not always." He looked at Rae. "It says 'touch, blood, and song.'"

"Oh!" Rae brightened like she'd heard this before. "Like the folks on the fairy hill."

"You know about the fairy hill?" His whole life he'd thought his interest and involvement in the arcane had been singular and isolated. Apparently, not in this tiny town.

"It's right down the road. You can't miss it."

Tucker looked at Angel. "See?"

"I admitted it," Angel defended. "I get it now. You can't pretend it's not there."

"You know," Coral said, "every time he talks, he gets a little more real. Is the necklace going to help that?"

"Yeah," Tucker said. "I think it will."

"Why?" Tilda hovered over her mother's shoulder and traced the letters with a finger rough from playing sports and doing chores. Still young, Tucker thought. Young enough not to worry about her nails or care about the dirt in the calluses or worry that her hair was too long and in her face. Young enough to hang her arm around her mother's shoulders.

"Because touch, blood, and song make things real," Tucker said. "It's like I'm asking him to stay."

"I'll stay," Angel told him, and this time Tucker could feel the grasp of his hand. "If I have to break—"

"All the rules of heaven," Tucker finished. Because that was what this was about, wasn't it? Changing the rules of heaven?

Tucker yawned and stood. "I'm sorry. I just disrupted your day and dumped a bunch of work on you. I should leave and let you get to your regularly scheduled lives."

Rae held up a hand to forestall him. "Tilda, is Andover's room cleared out, or is the bed still made?"

"Bed's made," Tilda said promptly. "Everything else is gone." She smiled up at Tucker, and although she didn't have the same level of witchiness that Coral had, the expression in her brown eyes was still very much her mother's. "Go take a nap, Mr. Henderson. Don't worry. With all the runes and shi—stuff mom has here, no ghost in the world's going to try and stop you."

"Thanks," Tucker said, "but—"

"But what? Tucker, that ghost has been dead for a hundred years. What's a few hours of sleep and some dinner going to hurt?"

Tucker smiled and tried one more time not to impose. "I was going to strip the wallpaper and borrow Josh's sander to do the floors."

"I'll bring it over tonight, after dinner," Josh said promptly. "C'mon, Tucker. I thought the goal was to get Angel to be human, not for you to fade away like Angel. You're pale as a—heh, heh, heh—*ghost*." And Josh, being Josh, lapsed into giggles.

His wife rolled her eyes. "Please stay, Tucker. I'd love to have some intelligent conversation over dinner tonight."

All three of the kids protested. "Hey!" "That's not fair!" "Murphy's the stupid one!" "Now that Andy's gone, we're plenty smart!"

Tucker laughed, and his resistance tattered away. "Down the hall?" he asked, a little wobbly on his feet.

"Second door on the left," Rae said. "Don't look under the mattress—we're afraid of what's there."

"Pot? Porn? Alien sex toys? Only Andy knows for sure." Tilda smirked, and Tucker had to laugh.

Rae didn't. "How old are you?" she asked Tilda darkly.

"Seventeen," Tilda returned with a pert smile. "Old enough to know of which I speak."

Rae sighed. "Dammit." Then she glared at Tucker. "Now go lie down, and I'll see if I can get a couple of these things ready for your room. They won't be pretty, but hopefully they'll keep you safe."

"Thanks, Rae." Tucker's gratitude came from the depths of his soul. And so did his yawn. "That nap sounds really, really good."

TUCKER SLEPT for three hours, Angel pressed up against his back in various stages of density the whole time.

He woke up with Angel's hand draped along his chest, and he clasped it, bringing it to his lips.

Angel's frustrated grunt ruffled his hair. "It would be inappropriate to make love in this room," he said, and Tucker laughed a little as Angel pressed his swollen groin against Tucker's back.

"Feeling frisky?" Tucker teased, in that weird fugue state between sleeping and waking.

"Andover Greenaway masturbated a *lot* when he was in this room," Angel told him, wonder in his voice.

Tucker's eyes flew open, and he felt the mutters of his gift, which he'd been too exhausted to receive earlier.

He scrambled off the bed and stood up as though he'd been shot.

"Oh my God. No. Just. Okay. Nap over. Do you think…?"

"Tucker?" Rae peeked inside the door. "Good, you're awake. Dinner's ready—come out and eat."

"Absolutely," Tucker said brightly. "Let me wash up. I'll be right there!"

"I don't know what you have to wash up," Angel grumbled. "It's not like anything happened."

"Drool off my face, dirt off my hands, *teenage sex out of my brain*!" Tucker hissed, and Rae broke into raucous laughter.

"Tucker, I can hear him. You know that, right? And you too. I told you we didn't want to know what was under the bed."

Tucker shuddered. "Do yourself a favor and never look."

"Of course—the bathroom's down the hall."

THEY LEFT Angel a place to sit, although they didn't offer him a plate for obvious reasons. Tucker filled up on spaghetti and garlic bread and salad and, once again, on the table chatter of the Greenaways.

He glanced up and saw Angel, green eyes moving from face to face, soaking up the family's reaction to Coral, who was telling a very involved story about the girl at school she sort of liked last year and who she may or may not want to play with when school started in two weeks because she'd been mean.

When she was done, Rae gave the patented parental "Okay, honey, well, whatever you think is best" while crossing her eyes at Josh, who widened his in return.

"I don't understand," Angel said, eyeing the child suspiciously. "If the little girl was not kind to you, then why would you want to be friends?"

Coral looked at him and smiled. "Angel, your eyes *are* very distinctive. I would know them in any other face."

Angel disappeared, and Coral dug into her spaghetti with grim satisfaction.

"She's terrifying," Tucker said with respect.

"I am frequently terrified by her," Rae agreed. "You look well rested now. Do you still plan to work on the house when you go back?

"Wallpaper and floors," Tucker confirmed. "I think the wallpaper tonight, and if Josh can lend us the floor sander, we'll do the floors tomorrow, and then we'll... uh, *I'll* go shopping for stain for the floors and wallpaper and such the day after."

"I would love to have input," Angel said, appearing again.

Rae shrieked and threw her fork across the table. "*Dammit*, Angel. I may not be able to see you, but I know when you're there! You guys want rules? I'll give you rules. If you're at the goddamned kitchen table, you need to *stay* at the goddamned kitchen table. It's *rude* to just disappear when someone makes you uncomfortable."

Tucker arched an eyebrow at him. "I told you."

"Fine." Angel sulked. "But I still think I should have a say in how the place is decorated. After all, I have to live there just as long as Tucker does."

"Which is how long, exactly?" Josh had the look of a man who was trying to do math in his head.

"Long after Andy is done with school," Tucker told him dryly. "For that matter, probably long after *Coral* is done with school. Hell, probably long after Coral's *children* are done with school. You've got time."

"That's still not forever," Angel said evenly.

Tucker cocked his head. "Well, who says if we move you wouldn't come with me?"

Angel gaped at him, and Tucker took a couple of bites of spaghetti in peace.

"He's being awfully quiet," Rae commented, staring at what was, for her, an empty chair at the table.

"I exploded his little mind," Tucker told her, enjoying the thought, "when I suggested that maybe, after the house is done, he and I could move somewhere else. Let's see how he can use this idea to say something that depresses the hell out of me."

Five, four, three, two, one—

"But Tucker, once we're done with cleansing the house, I'll probably… I mean, I was only supposed to be here long enough to…."

"Stay," Tucker said, looking him in the eyes like the whole family wasn't there. "All the rules of heaven, remember?"

Angel gaped at him some more.

Tucker looked back at Rae. "I don't know what he's so upset about. Given how many ghosts are traipsing through that place, I'll be dead and gone before it's cleared out. He'll have to work with someone else then, and God knows how that'll go."

"Stop," Angel snapped, visibly upset. "Just… stop. We'll deal with change when things change. In the meantime, it's enough that we're both here now."

Tucker smiled, feeling a little reassured. He'd been alone for more than half his life, but no matter what happened with Angel, no matter what Angel *was*, he wouldn't be alone now.

"Agreed," he said.

"So," Josh broke in, apparently oblivious to the relationship currents raging around the table. "What do you know about sanding floors?"

"Not a damned thing." Tucker took another bite of garlic bread. "By all means, enlighten me."

By the time dinner ended, Tucker had a sense of how hard he'd be working the next day.

TUCKER OFFERED to stay to wash up, but Rae told him to help Josh load the sander into the back of the truck instead. Tucker came back inside to say goodbye, but before he could leave, Rae shoved three charms into his hand.

"The chains are my best silver, and the pentagrams are too. The stones inside are pure—I used garnets since that was the one on your necklace, and whatever happened to it, that's where it started. Now you put one of those in your truck and hang one on your doorway and one on your window. They should keep anybody out, even from your bathroom, 'cause that's attached. I'll make you a few more."

Tucker felt bad—he'd used up so much of her time. "Now, Rae, I can deal with—"

"Stop it," she said. "Just stop. What you did for our son was amazing, but this isn't just paying you back. We like you, Tucker. And you obviously need *us*. So just take the gift." She looked over his shoulder and frowned at her husband. "Josh, would you grab the one off my table and put it on—"

"No," Josh said shortly. "The damned ghosts want no part of me. Let Tucker have the last charm."

"I made it for you, you stubborn asshole," Rae returned. "Dammit, Josh, it's for protection. So much shit can go wrong."

He kissed her cheek and winked. "I'm just going to check out the room. Now, Rae, I'll be back in an hour, okay? Tucker's going to need help unloading the sander, and as soon as I get it up the stairs, I'll come home."

He grabbed the keys from the pegboard by the door and headed for his little Ford truck while Rae was still sputtering. "Dammit, Tucker, stay with him and keep him from doing anything stupid!" she called.

"Will do!" Tucker called back, a little worried himself.

He hopped into the truck, Angel materialized through the door, and they both took off.

Broken Glass

ANGEL WASN'T sure how Tucker didn't just fall over from boredom when Josh was talking about sanding floors, but somehow he seemed to find it fascinating. Maybe because he'd spent so much of his life *not* having a job, and having a purpose completely out of his control had made Tucker supremely grateful for tangible proof that he was doing something.

Either way, Josh had dominated the conversation over dinner and dessert, and Angel was quite grateful for the relative quiet in the cab of the truck with Tucker.

"We're not *really* going to pull wallpaper tonight?" Angel complained. He hadn't eaten, of course, but he was more than ready to sit with Tucker and let his meal digest while they watched more popular television.

"Yes," Tucker said, his jaw squaring up. "I just keep thinking that getting the room clear will help, that's all. It's not a pull or a hunch—it's my own twisted logic. I can't even understand it."

"Maybe if Josh helps, you'll have the wallpaper done tonight and you can quit obsessing."

"Your support is appreciated," Tucker said dryly. "I think it's really awesome that we get to sound like we're married and we don't even get any of the bennies."

"We get each other's company." Angel was quite sincere about that. "Ruth and I, we rubbed each other the wrong way from the get-go. I was not... human enough, I don't think. I'm going to be ashamed of that for a long time."

"Well, when we do her room, I'm sure you'll get a chance to apologize," Tucker said.

Angel brightened. "You know, I hadn't thought about that. That's true. Can we do her room next?"

"No."

"Why not?"

Tucker shuddered delicately. "Let me get good at this before I potentially fuck up Ruth's afterlife, okay, Angel? Besides," he said, lowering his voice, "you came to Daisy Place when she was a young woman. I have the feeling there's something important about that timing. I don't.... I'm selfish. She hung out in that mansion for over eighty-five years. It would be great if she could hang out just a little bit longer while you and I figure out how to get you to stay. I've been thinking about it, and I'm afraid that when we confront her, you'll figure out how you got here in the first place, and that might pull you away."

Oh. Naked self-interest had never bothered Angel before, but realizing that his agenda might take him from Tucker sure did bother him now.

"I hadn't considered that," he said. And then he remembered that when Tucker had arrived—hell, for most of Ruth's life—Angel had wanted nothing *but* to clear out the souls so he could leave. Tucker would have figured out that was the ultimate endgame.

He felt a weight in his shoulders, a tightness in his back, as though he were bearing something unsupportable, and his head drooped.

"You're right, Tucker. We should save Ruth's room until you and I have more of a handle on what we're doing. Your powers are very different. Your perceptions are very different. I...." He tried not to look out over the property as they drove alongside it. He knew that the dark cloud of distorted souls and malice would loom to the northeast, where the graveyard stretched into the unmentionable beyond. "I think you and I need to figure out how to clear the graveyard together. I need to be here for that."

Tucker's sigh almost rocked the cab of the truck.

"And of course I want to stay for you."

And the atmosphere lightened again—even the weight on his shoulders.

They pulled into the driveway at Daisy Place with an almost unbearable optimism... considering what followed.

JOSH INSISTED on helping Tucker haul the sander up the stairs while he was there. He also wanted to see if his efforts with the humidifier had made the wallpaper as easy to pull as he hoped. They parked the sander in the hallway across from the bed, where Josh paused.

"Hey now," he said, looking at the bed. "That's a real nice frame. Are you putting that back into the roo—"

"Don't touch that!" Tucker and Angel both cried together.

Josh eyed them dryly and stuck his hand out like a grade-schooler to touch the bed with one finger. Nothing happened, and he rolled his eyes.

Tucker shuddered. "You will *never* know," he said. "You will *never* know how lucky you are to be psychically blind."

Josh laughed and shrugged, but he looked a little wistful as well. "You say that. But you've been surrounded by people your whole life who don't see what you do. I've been surrounded by people who see *way* more than I do, and I gotta tell you, it hurts sometimes."

Angel felt the hurt then, rolling off him, and wondered what to say.

"Well, yeah." Tucker nodded. "But they share it with you, right? And I'm telling you, that brood of yours? Even I'd get creeped out by all that witchiness. They need you. You keep them grounded. People need to eat, and they need a roof over their heads. You make that happen. That's gotta be worth it, right?"

Josh smiled kindly, and although most of the time he just seemed like a big goofy kid, Angel could suddenly see the "dad" in him that Tucker seemed to gravitate to.

"Yeah, it is. But it's nice of you to point that out. So, this room of yours…?"

Tucker swung the door open, and Squishbeans, who had been gamboling at their heels as they walked in, suddenly hissed, spat, and darted away. That didn't bode well—Tucker and Angel ignored the curling wallpaper and the floor. While Josh went to assess the workload, their eyes swung immediately to the desk, and the paperweight on top of it.

It was almost black.

"Oh my God," Tucker muttered. "Angel, that's not good."

"I know it." It wasn't just black—it was *sentiently* black—the crawling, angry black of a trapped and tortured soul.

They both looked at Josh, who was rocking back on his heels and whistling. "So, you just planned on grabbing the paper and ripping it off?"

Tucker looked around. "There's a putty knife in the kitchen," he said. "Two of them, actually. And it's coming off plaster, right? I mean, a lot of it's been hanging from the ceiling since you did the thing with the humidifier."

"Yeah." But Josh didn't sound sure. He was, in fact, eyeing the paper with cool assessment. "But it's dried out since then. This old stuff, it gets really attached to the surface. You're lucky this place is plaster—it's one of the reasons it keeps so cool, which is nice. If it was drywall, you'd have to buy sealant and sandpaper and a thousand other things, but this…. You still might need sandpaper and probably some base paint, because if it sticks you're going to want to paint over the plaster to keep it smooth."

Angel's attention started to wander with the word "plaster." He was, in fact, fixating on the paperweight.

"Tucker, it's getting lighter."

Tucker wasn't looking at the paperweight, and he wasn't looking at Josh either. He was looking at the open door.

"Josh," he said seriously, "we need to leave."

Josh looked around, frowning. "No, I just said we should see if it comes off easy first. There's no guarantee we're gonna need the paint and the sealant."

"No," Tucker said, fumbling in his pocket. "That's not what I meant." He pulled out the three pendants Rae had thrust into his hand as they'd left and held them in front of him as he approached Josh. "Man, put one on. I'm so stupid, I should have had you put one on before you even walked in the house."

"Tucker, calm down! I thought we both talked about how psychically blind I am!"

"Oh shit!"

Angel saw it too.

The dark mass that was Thomas Conklin's soul was rushing toward the one unprotected being in the room. Tucker reached Josh just in time, wrapping his arms around the man and clasping him, the three silver charms dangling down his back right as the mass hit.

Tucker grunted with the impact, and Angel tried to dematerialize so he could appear over the two of them, hovering, to protect them both.

That curious weight on Angel's shoulders became a brick wall, and he fell to his knees.

"Tucker!" Angel cried, confused, frightened, "Hold on! Hold on to him, Tucker!"

Tucker cried out this time as Conklin's psychic weight pushed at the two of them and his feet shifted.

"Tucker, what's happening?" Josh's voice was pitched with genuine fear.

"Hold on!" Tucker called. "Hold on, Josh. As soon as we get one of these things around your neck, you'll be safe!"

"Leave him be!"

Angel saw James Beaufort run through the door, and he forgot about materializing and gathered the strength to run to protect Tucker and Josh from one more new force. "Get Conklin out of here!"

"Who is that?" Josh asked, desperately confused.

Tucker was buffeted back by the enraged raw energy of Thomas Conklin, and Angel jumped in front of them before Beaufort could throw himself into the fray.

"Don't separate them!" Angel cried. "James, they need to stay together or—"

James crashed into him, and he fell backward into Josh and Tucker. Tucker fell against the corner of the desk, howling as he hit it with his back, and slid all the way down, smacking his head last.

He hit the floor, obviously dazed, and his arms loosened, the hand with the charms falling limply to the wood. Josh rolled out of his arms and struggled to his feet even as Angel jumped in front of the two of them again, facing James Beaufort and the coalescing energy that was Thomas Conklin Senior.

"*You* stay out of this!" Conklin snarled at Beaufort, ectoplasmic spittle dancing from his wet lips. "You have done enough, trapping us here in this tiny, twisted hell!"

"Stay away from them! They're innocent!" James Beaufort was desperate—a protector to the core of his soul, and Angel admired him for it. But Conklin's sneer chilled Angel to the marrow of his incorporeal bones.

"The more innocent, the better, don't you think?" He laughed, the sound ringing off the walls of the empty room like the bells of bedlam, and Tucker let out a grunt.

"Angel. Dammit, Angel, the paperweight—"

Angel whirled and stuck out his hands to catch it as it wobbled, and Tucker scrambled up, putting his hands out, disregarding the cost.

It didn't matter.

The mass of the thing tipped, tilted, and finally landed on the round side, then rolled ponderously to the edge of the desk. Angel would have caught it if it hadn't plummeted right through what should have been his flesh. Tucker would have cushioned it with his bare, vulnerable hands, but it landed on his fingertips, bending his wrist back with a sickening crack.

Tucker screamed, and the glass orb hit the floor, shattering, the blackness inside flowing out of the orb and into the air around them.

"What in the hell?" Josh muttered, and Tucker sucked in a gasp of air that sounded like it tortured his very soul.

"Josh!" Tucker scrambled with his good hand for the charms scattered on the floor. "Take one. Take one and put it on. Please, Josh. Please!"

Conklin started laughing, a window-shattering cackle that punctured Angel's ears and eyes like an icepick, right through to his brain.

The oily black smoke released from the paperweight rose to the ceiling, and Conklin's shape disappeared, leaving only the echoes of his laughter as the darkness descended in a rush into Josh Greenaway's open mouth.

DARK MOON

A DEAFENING silence killed the echoes of Conklin's laughter, and Tucker stared at Josh Greenaway.

His friend stared back at him through an oily film, sparks of madness zinging through the windows of his possessed soul.

Josh leaped toward Tucker, hands going for his throat, and Tucker fell back, the bruises along his body and the back of his head catching fire again. He raised his hands to push Josh off, and his wrist gave a vicious throb.

Josh's hard hands were cutting off his air supply, and Tucker's vision darkened, his windpipe crushed under madness and muscles honed with hard work. He lowered his hands to try to break through the grip around his throat, and Josh/Conklin's scream of pain echoed through the room.

The pendant burned hot against Tucker's throat, and the acrid smell of burning flesh sizzled up from

Josh's hands. Conklin let go and jumped up, holding his hands in front of him and shrieking.

"You think you've won? You think I can't get you? Who's going to keep you safe when I release the prisoners! You think a little bit of silver is going to protect you from hundreds of captive souls?"

Josh went thundering out of the room, and Tucker struggled to stand. He put weight on his wrist and yelped, falling back to the floor.

"I'm sorry," James Beaufort sobbed, as Angel knelt by Tucker's side. "I'm sorry. I wanted to keep him far from any of you—"

"Thomas Conklin is not your fault," Tucker rasped. He struggled up on his elbow, and then used his other hand to sit. Angel was mostly solid, kissing his temple, touching his bruised throat with fluttery fingers, keeping his emotions together by a fragile thread. "James— we need you to go stop him."

Below them, they heard the sound of Josh's truck starting up and revving to life. It peeled out of the driveway, followed by knocking sounds that indicated it hadn't backed up and turned into the street, but had instead gone over the brick border that marked the edge of the parking area.

"Fuck!" Tucker gasped. His bad wrist gave again, but Angel caught him this time, grabbing his elbow and helping him stand. "James, you can move fast enough. He's going to the graveyard."

"How do you know?" Angel asked.

"Those have to be the lost souls he was talking about—and that's exactly where he's heading. One meatsuit—that's all he needs to build a bridge between Daisy Place and the adjoining property line. Some spilled human blood to break the spell of the metallurgy and the ghosts are free to get out of Daisy Place and perpetrate havoc. James, you can get to him—get him to drive off course or wreck the truck or something. Angel and I will meet you—he's going to try to take that fucking vehicle cross-country. He may have used Josh's brain to figure out how to start it, but if I know Josh Greenaway, he's going to crash it into a tree when he can. I need you to meet him, harass him, drop shit in his way. Don't hurt Josh any more than you can help it, but *stop Conklin*. Do you hear me?"

James nodded, pain evident on his face, and Tucker took a moment to ease his mind.

"James, do this for us. Help us get rid of that spirit once and for all, and I can give you peace. I swear it. You can join your wife and your sons and your sisters. They miss you."

James Beaufort's face was plain and square, but the desperate hope that lit it from within gave him a plaintive beauty. "My family?" he begged. "Tell me I might rejoin them."

"I promise," Tucker whispered, his throat aching along with most of the rest of his body. He reached down to the floor with his good hand, grabbed the charms, and shoved them back into the pocket of his cargo shorts, where he could grab them when he needed them. He felt the bronze button with the sailing ship in there and took heart from that. "Once we take care of Conklin, any debt you had is completely discharged. Your spirit can rest easy, James, I promise."

James disappeared then, and so did some of Tucker's resolve. He sagged against the now-stable desk and tried to think past the pain.

"I need a bandage," he said. "For my wrist. A sheet—Angel, do you know where the sheets are?"

"Tucker, you're injured," Angel protested. He put his hand behind Tucker's head and pulled it back, wet with blood.

Tucker groaned, trying to see through the spots in his eyes. "Angel, if we don't get a move on, Conklin's going to do some really shitty things to Josh's body. And worse, he's going to let all the ghosts out of the cemetery, and then we'll really be fucked. Let's worry about me later, okay?"

Angel nodded, his face crumpling. "I am so worried *now*," he whispered.

Tucker nodded, raised his good hand to Angel's cheek, and wiped off the tears that gathered there. "I know. I don't think you're built for this, for the violence, for the fear. But you can do it, Angel—I have faith. We can't fall apart now. Just hang in there. We need to see this through."

With that he took a deep breath and wrapped his arm around himself, rooting through his *other* pocket for his cell phone.

The Greenaways were one of his few contacts.

"Rae, I need you. Man, some serious shit went down, and Josh needs your help."

"Josh?" her voice cracked, and Tucker forced his aching body out of the room, past the fucking sander and down the stairs. "What did he do?"

"It wasn't his fault," Tucker told her. "Man, the thing came gunning for us—and then it rammed itself down his throat."

"It *what*?"

"Rae—I need you to grab as much silver wire as you can, and more than that, and take it to the side road, the one facing the cemetery. He's heading there, and I have an idea."

He explained his idea as he got to the kitchen and found a dish towel to rip into pieces and tie around his wrist. He kept explaining as he and Angel got into the truck and backed down the driveway, then pulled around to head away from town and toward the cemetery road.

That was about the point when Rae hung up, presumably because she'd already grabbed the wire, the nails he'd told her to bring, and her kids to come help, then loaded up the minivan, determined to go get her husband out of the fire.

"Do you think that will work?" Angel asked, looking at him nervously.

"Sure," Tucker told him, setting the phone down and letting his wrist rest limply in his lap. "It's got to."

"But how are you going to get him in the trap?"

Tucker kept his eyes on the road.

"I'm going to bait it myself," he said grimly, and then prepared himself for the argument to come.

They were still arguing when they pulled off to the side road and rattled down the dirt track at top speed. The back end of the truck fishtailed, sending the posthole digger Tucker had tucked there clattering from side to side, but Tucker kept going.

He skidded to a halt, the truck spinning half a donut, just as they drew even with the cemetery.

"The cemetery does not actually look worse," Angel assessed coolly—then he lost his composure and went back to bitching at Tucker. "But that doesn't mean this plan of yours is any safer. Dammit, Tucker, what happens if he jumps ship? Do you think you'll have any more protection than Josh did? Do you? Because I'm thinking no! I'm thinking your empathic ability is going to make it worse—that you'll become this horrible,

horrible man, and that the Tucker I know and love is going to be lost and stomped flat by all of that... that crazy meanness!"

"I won't become this horrible man," Tucker said solemnly. But he had to tell the truth. "I *probably* won't become this horrible man. Remember—I've felt ghosts inside me. I felt *you* inside me. You even took over a couple of times. But I was still me. I still knew right from wrong. Josh was caught unawares, that's all. If he'd known what was coming—"

"But he *did*."

"He didn't *believe* it!" Tucker insisted. "Now look. Unless you've got a better plan, I've got some fucking cable to lay, and not the good kind!"

Tucker slid out of the truck then and grabbed the post-hole digger and the two brooms he'd remembered to get from the gardening shed. Wrapping his good arm around them, he made for the clear psychic line that marked the edge of the property, and the gate in the middle of it. The gate was the focus point, the center, because the ghosts still respected the rules of the physical world. But add some of Josh's spilled blood, and that gate would become a portal to the outside world.

It was a good thing he had some Teflon gloves in his pocket as well—and that the graveyard part of the property line was soft and marshy, with the consistency of rotting flesh. He had to dig one-handed, but the hole was still two feet deep by the time Rae's minivan jounced down the road at the same speed Tucker had been driving.

But Rae had kids in the back, and before the engine completely died, the doors opened and the kids scrambled out, Murphy and Coral falling to their knees without ceremony and petting the ground disconsolately.

Rae and Tilda didn't even stop to reprimand them.

"We're here, Tucker. Where do you want me to start?"

Tucker called her over to where he was digging the hole. "Look, as far as I can figure, the foundation for this place can't be much deeper than fifteen feet."

"What makes you say that?"

Tucker pointed to the skyline. "Notice there are no pine trees?"

Rae contained her impatience and scanned the area around Daisy Place. "Oak and willow," she said, surprised. "They don't go down that far."

"Exactly. I need the hole dug and the wire wrapped around the broom handle and thrust into the ground as far as it will go—"

"My job," Tilda said, taking the digger from him and moving a hell of a lot faster than he'd been.

"Both broomsticks," Tucker told her seriously. "And the post-hole digger. If I had a spear, I'd give it to you. Wrap them in wire and shove them in on top of each other. I need metal of some sort down as close to the foundation as I can get it. All of those metals—and the water seeping here—should connect, and the metal down there should ground a lot of the energy that gets released up here."

"What energy?" Rae asked, looking at the eternal graveyard with big eyes. "You're going to drain this huge psychic waste dump with a little bit of jewelry wire?"

Tucker grimaced at the muttering mass of toxic soul discharge. "I wish," he told her grimly. "No. You have those nails?"

Rae nodded, and Coral came trotting up, pale-faced but composed, holding a third of a bucket of

tenpenny nails with all her strength. Tucker nodded in
approval. "Coral? Murphy?" Murphy followed his sister, hauling several spools of jewelry wire that probably
weighed as much as he did, lined up on an old broom
handle. Tucker reached out with his good hand, but Rae
stopped him.

"Put it down," she ordered. "Tucker—" She
reached for his aching wrist.

"Let's get them started," he told her, shaking his
head and then wobbling. Christ, he was not doing well.
"Okay, kids? You know what a pentagon is?"

"A five-sided figure with equilateral sides?" Coral
said promptly.

"Oh my God, fifth grade has gotten harder since I
was in school! Yes—that's exactly it. Do you guys see
this line of property, the part in front of the gate? Where
it goes from normal and dry to—"

"Creepy and haunted?" Murphy supplied. "We
don't have to go over there, do we? The ghosts are
looking at us like fresh meat!"

"Angel will protect you," Tucker said, and he
reached into his pocket and pulled out the three pendants he'd tried to give Josh. "And these will too. Take
one—each of you. Give one to Tilda as soon as I'm
done. We're making a giant pentagon, about six feet
wide in the center. That's as tall as I am, got it?"

They nodded soberly, putting the charms over their
heads.

"After we make the pentagon, we're going to put
nails in the corners of it, and make it a *pentagram*."
He held up one of the necklaces. He figured that if the
pentagrams worked on a small scale for protection,
then they'd work on a big scale as a trap—and not just
because he'd seen it done in a TV show either. "The

hole Tilda is digging is going to connect with the pentagram—it's like any line of electricity. We're going to trap the electricity in the center of the pentagram and then funnel it to the metal foundation under the property."

Rae stared at him for a moment, blinking. "But Tucker, how are we going to get my husband—and the thing inside him—into the center of the pentagram? Teleportation?"

Tucker snorted. "I've got a plan! Here, take one of these to Tilda."

Rae looked at him doubtfully but rushed the necklace to her daughter. Because that was the thing, wasn't it? Protect the innocent.

Tucker wasn't so innocent.

He turned to Coral and Murphy. "Okay, so where Tilda is digging? That needs to be connected to the closest point in the pentagram. See how it's right by the gate? We're going to attach the giant pentagram to that, okay?"

God. Even now, the ghosts from the graveyard were beginning to regard Tilda with interest. He needed to finish what he was doing and seal the spell before they realized there could be a porthole here while he was working.

"So guys, here's the scary bit. Part of the pentagon needs to be on the creepy side and part of the pentagon needs to be on the normal side, *and*," he added, holding up a finger, "the whole thing needs to be in the middle of a circle. Do you know what that means?"

"At least two spikes outside of each straight line," Murphy said promptly. "And the circle needs to intersect the nails of the pentagon."

"Oh my God. Seriously. Eighth grade?"

Murphy nodded soberly.

"My youth was wasted. Don't forget a spike in the center so we can attach the pentagram to the broomsticks. Okay, guys, we need this done like *now*. Your dad's counting on you!"

They didn't even ask him how, they just followed his orders, and Tucker wanted to cry. God, it was just like Damie. Damien had trusted that what Tucker was doing was safe. But Tucker had wanted a family, he'd wanted friends—he'd wanted them so badly he'd put the people he cared about in danger.

He turned to Rae. "You and me on pentagram duty. We need to leave one outer leg of the circle unclosed, you understand?"

Rae nodded. "So the thing in Josh can go into it, but then we'll close it while…. I'm a little fuzzy on this part."

"While Josh tries to kill me," Tucker said calmly. "Now are you ready? They've got the first one, and it's our—fuck!"

He'd bent down to grab the spool of wire, and his wrist gave with a grinding of bones. His vision went black, and he bent over, trying, oh God, trying, to hold it all together.

"Tucker!" Angel looked up from his position, back to the kids, then to the creepy side of the graveyard as the kids placed the spikes.

"Ignore me!" Tucker stood and smiled, trying to get hold of his stomach. "You too," he told Rae. She'd grabbed his bandaged wrist and—"Oh my God!" he groaned. "Rae, I'm going to puke… just…." He turned away and lost his dinner, spaghetti and garlic bread, into the red dirt of the road. He finished, and Tilda thrust a bottle of water into his hand and handed a towel to her mom. Before Tucker could even reprimand her for shirking her duty, she was back to the post-hole digging, and Tucker could almost see again.

"Tucker, hold still," Rae muttered. "Oh my God! Tucker, your neck is bruised. What *happened*?"

"I think I have a concussion too," Tucker told her, because his head was still killing him. "And what happened was…." He closed his eyes and tried to put that sequence of events together. "There appears to have been a struggle," he said at last, trying for dignity. "And we need to hurry." He closed his eyes. "Rae, I'm so sorry. Look at this. Your family is in danger, and your husband"—possessed by a really evil ghost?—"is in danger too. My fault. I should never have—"

"Hush," she said, wiping his mouth. "Now give me your wrist again. I'm going to wrap it a little tighter."

He held it out, trying not to feel pathetic. "I tried to protect him. I know this is bad, but I tried. Angel tried. We didn't want him hurt. You've got to know that."

"I know it," she muttered, ripping the towel into strips with three quick jerks. "I know it. You're a mess. And this idea of yours is insanity."

"I know," Tucker told her, miserable. "But listen. If this goes like I think it might and the ghost—or *any* ghost—gets me? If Angel can't exorcise me, you guys need to put me down, okay? Don't tell him I said that, but it's really important. The ghosts here—some of them are twisted, and some of them are evil, but what they will do if they get hold of my body… Rae, I don't ever want to be responsible for that. It's bad enough what happened to Josh happened on my watch, you understand?"

"This wasn't your fault," she said, wrapping his wrist just a little tighter. "And I need you to not give up yet, because this plan is the only one we've got."

Tucker nodded and swallowed back his nausea. "You don't have a necklace," he said painfully. "I was hoping you would. You need something, but I need mine for Josh."

"Don't worry about me, Tucker. I've got tattoos no middle-aged mother of four should show, you understand?"

Tucker brightened as she cranked down on another bandage. "Yeah, okay. We can do—"

Far off—but not too far off—they heard the distinct sound of a vehicle crunching into an immovable object.

He and Rae met eyes, suddenly on the exact same page. "We gotta get a move on," she said and then bent down and picked up the broomstick full of wire spools herself. She pulled one of the smaller spools off the stick and called out to Tilda before lobbing it as far as it would go. Tilda looked up and nodded, then went back to post-hole digging—she was about four feet down. Pretty soon, it would be all about wrapping broomsticks with wire and shoving them into the wet earth.

Rae had Tucker hold out his good arm and balance the end of the broom handle in the crook of his elbow, supporting it with his good hand.

Then she crouched down on the earth and got to work.

Tucker held the broomstick still and kept a worried eye on Angel, who was staring the gathering ghostly horde in the eyes while the children placed their nails.

"How they doin', Angel?" Tucker called. Angel didn't risk a look over his shoulder to answer back.

"They're getting angry and upset. Tucker, you'd better be right about this!"

"If I was right about shit, would we even be here?" Tucker asked.

"Shut up," Angel said thickly, and Rae jerked a little at the wire.

"I second that," she muttered, because apparently she could hear Angel now. "Keep up with me, Tucker. We're almost done with the first leg of the pentagram."

The kids worked fast, and so did Rae, and Tucker managed not to keel over. At the end of the giant star in the middle of the pentagon, Rae very carefully wrapped a long length of wire around the second-to-last peg and left it there to make a final leg of the shape, ready to seal it, imprisoning whatever spirit wandered in. Then she wrapped a length about the center spike and ran the rest of the spool to Tilda.

"I'm thinking," Tucker said, trying to stay out of Rae's way as she worked.

"Must be rough with a concussion," she muttered. "Shoot."

"Touch, blood, and song," he told her. "That would make these even more secure."

"You want me to bleed and sing?" she asked, laughing.

"The blood we've got!" Tucker told her. He felt another trickle roll down his scalp. "I've had a bleeding head wound since this whole thing started. Let me rub some of these bandages on my head, and you can put them in your pocket. Boom. Blood!"

"That's sick," she said. "But I'll take it, just as soon as you can tell me we're good to go. Now what about the touch?"

"You're doing it," Tucker said decisively. "Now the song just has to be words. It could be 'Get out of my husband, goddammit!' or 'Josh, get back to me, dumbass!' But say something when you close the trap and seal it with my blood, okay? I think it will make it stronger!"

As they spoke, she strung the wire to finish the giant five-pointed star. She finished the first point and looked up. "I assume you want a continuous line for the circle?"

"Yeah. If I could figure out how to do the whole thing without breaking the wire at all, I'd do it."

Rae frowned for a bit, squinting at the nails the children had laid so far, and in spite of the direness of the situation, Tucker had to laugh.

"Figure it out when there's time!" he urged. "C'mon, hon, he's going to be here any second!"

That spurred her on.

Tucker stayed in the middle of the figure as she wound the wire, and later he would wonder how much magic he'd given his impromptu spell of metallurgy and desperation by simply swaying on the earth, bleeding, whispering, "Please let this work, please let this work, please let this work!" If ever there was a time he needed to direct his mind, his will, and his power, this was the one.

Josh Greenaway was a good man, just like James Beaufort. He was innocent, like Sophie and Bridget. Tucker could not let another innocent, decent person, be destroyed by the corruption of one drug-addled aristocrat who wanted to wreak vengeance.

Vengeance.

"Rae. Rae, as soon as you see him, you need to get the girls to go hide in the car."

"Tucker, I'm busy here—"

"If Conklin's running the show, he's…." Tucker shuddered. "He's not your husband, Rae, and he likes to hurt women."

Rae wrapped the wire around the second-to-last peg and unwound enough to finish the final leg. She double-checked the length and then snipped it off with some wire cutters from her pocket. "You told us that. I remember."

"Rae, I am afraid for you," he told her nakedly.

"Tucker, you and me, we're going to have a conversation after my husband gets unpossessed. I think this thing you do with Angel is real noble and all, but it's gonna fuckin' kill you if you are not careful."

She rose from her crouch to start the next stage—the circle. Tucker moved to the middle, turning as she ran the wire, crouched, wrapped it around the next nail, and the next, and the next. He kept his eyes on the property, not sure which direction Josh was going to come running from—if he was going to emerge from the trees, pop out from the dimensional graveyard, or charge down the underbrush at the fence line. Either way, Tucker needed to be ready. The ghosts were staring at the lot of them making a trap in their territory. To Tucker's left, Tilda was wrapping a broomstick in silver wire. One of the ectoplasmic remnants of bad karma and residual memories started to moan as she threw the thing down the hole and then stood on it, shoving it down until her leg disappeared.

She grabbed the post-hole digger and used it to thrust the broomstick in deeper, and the moan intensified to a scream.

Rae looked over her shoulder at the masses of the disembodied dead staring at her and her children and at

Angel and Tucker with the ferociousness of murder in their eyes, and spat.

"Find your way to heaven, you assholes! If you're stuck here, it's 'cause you didn't fuckin' want it bad enough!"

The ghost stopped screaming for a moment, and Rae crouched down to start inscribing the circle. She'd finished the first leg in the stunned silence when an anguished shriek stilled her.

"*Rae! Dammit, run.*"

Tucker saw Josh then, right at the tree line beyond the cemetery, and called out, "Angel! Get the kids to the minivan. Stay with them!"

"Goddammit, Tucker!"

"*Protect the children, dammit!* Murphy, Coral, Tilda—you guys get your asses to the car!"

Tilda was shoving the second broomstick down on top of the first. "Gimme a goddamned minute," she shouted. "Murphy, Coral, listen to him!"

"Listen to *me*!" Rae snapped. "Kids, *now*!"

They had three more legs to the circle left, the nails pushed into the dirt, and Murphy finished the last nail as Coral turned to grab the bucket.

"Leave it!" Rae hollered, clipping off an end of silver wire. "C'mon, Tucker, we've got time to finish this. Josh can't run for shit!" Tucker ran to the center of the pentagram and watched Josh's progress as Rae wired the center nail of the figure and ran the wire down to the hole.

"Shit!" they both said together. The ends that connected the whole works to the hole in the ground hadn't been connected to the post-hole digger.

"You come here and finish the pentagram," Tucker hollered. "I'll get that!"

Her job required more strength and more finesse—but Tucker wasn't proud. Feverishly, he wrapped the loose ends, connecting the points of the pentagram with the angles of the pentagon inside the circle. Five points when Rae finished the one she was working on. Five was a good number, wasn't it? Tucker tried to remember what five represented in numerology, and all he could come up with was the five of wands and how everybody seemed to be running around with their heads up their asses. Whatever.

"The second broomstick is stopping," Tilda said, shoving at it with the post-hole digger. "If you finish what you're doing and give it to me, I should be able to connect it all."

Tucker finished the last wrap and handed it off, then swung around to look at their handiwork. It looked good—a sparkling, house-sized pentacle, actually, surrounded by the toxic phosphorescence of the angry dead.

Beyond the milling ghosts, Josh stumbled, fell to his knees, and for a moment, he struggled. Tucker could see him, pounding the ground in frustration, as Josh Greenaway fought with Thomas Conklin Senior for control of the form they were both currently occupying.

"You fucker, get *out*!" Josh shouted, and Tucker froze. *Oh please oh please oh please….* Then came a terrible scream, ripped from the throat of a desperate man. "*Noooooooo!*"

Josh got to his feet and lurched forward, every movement a tiny war, every muscle fighting itself in a knock-down, drag-out bitch-fight of wills.

Well, Conklin may have won that battle, but it was obvious that Josh was still in the fight.

Nevertheless he was getting closer, and the ghosts, no longer put off by Angel's imposing presence, were beginning to group on the edges of the pentacle. Oddly enough, they respected the unfinished boundary, and Tucker thought they could use that, but he didn't know how.

"Rae, he's getting close."

"One more," Rae panted, yanking at the spool of wire so there'd be enough for the last leg before she snipped it.

The crowd of ghosts had converged, surrounding the shape wrought in the earth, glaring at Rae in the middle of the figure, and at Tucker, who was protected by the aura of the pendant around his neck.

Tilda offered him a hand up—she'd finished her task and only needed to get to safety now. Tucker groaned and lurched to his feet, scanning the phosphorescent crowd.

He saw the face he was looking for—the familiar one, the one that broke his heart. Saw five more, in fact, and gave a faint moan. "Go, Tilda," he said, thinking about how young she was and how letting Conklin have his way would be unthinkable. He turned away from her and stumbled back toward the silverwork. As he walked, he grabbed the pocket full of rags Rae had given him and started mopping at the mess at the back of his head, staining one at a time.

"Tucker, come on!" Rae yanked at the wire from the spool on the ground, and Tucker wandered to the center of the next figure, wiping blood off his head as fast as he could. He shoved the wet rags back in his pocket and grabbed the spools, standing up and giving her some slack to work with.

"Rae, you might not have time—"

"I'll have time," she said grimly. "He's coming from this direction. We are almost done." She began her frantic sprint, and Tucker watched as the ghosts tested the boundaries of the trap.

He'd expected the wire to keep the spirits out of the finished pentagram—but what was happening was even better. The ghosts near the open leg of the figure were pushing their hands against what was going to be the border and stopping, as though thwarted by invisible walls.

"How's that working?" Rae asked after a brief glance up.

"The kids—your witchy kids—must have had a solid idea of what we were making here. They saw it as real. You'll have to tell them how awesome they are when you get into the van with them."

"Tilda!" Rae called.

"Running now!" Tilda called back. She was almost at the minivan. The ghosts had parted for her and didn't seem to begrudge her leaving, thank God. No, they were saving all their venom for Tucker and Rae.

"Send Angel back," Rae called. "And get that thing the hell away from here! Take the kids home—*not* to the mansion, you hear me? Keys in the car!"

"Call me," Tilda shouted, and then she opened the driver's door and hopped in. Angel came sprinting out from the other side, heading toward Tucker and Rae.

"What in the hell!" Tucker demanded. Rae should be in that car! "What are you—"

"I can take care of myself, Tucker. She'll get them to our house. They'll be safe there."

But what if Conklin wins? What if their father takes this vicious spirit to the place he loves most?

He didn't say it. He didn't even want the thought out there.

There was only one thing to do—one thing he could say to do, think to do, make happen.

They had to win.

"Tucker! Tucker, we're here. You can't ignore us. We're here!"

It was the first time their voices coalesced, and Tucker looked up to the familiar ghosts and muttered, "Oh hell."

Damien looked back at him, his eyes filled with rage.

"Tucker!" Rae snapped, yanking at the wire. "Stay with me here." She paused. "Are you passing out on me?"

"Yes and no," Tucker mumbled. His head ached, his wrist was on fire, his words were raspy, spoken through a raw throat, but he would have endured all of that a million times over rather than see the bitter recrimination in Damien's eyes. "I'm sorry," he said to the apparition. "Damie, I didn't mean to. You just... you wanted me, and I'd been waiting so long!"

"Oh God." Rae started running that last goddamned part of the circle, and Tucker turned his body, trying to stay in the now, trying to stay with her, to protect her and the kids, but Damien was—

"Tucker, you killed me! You didn't do your fucking job, man. I wanted a kiss, and you let me get shot!"

"Damien," he mumbled, working not to squeeze his eyes shut. "I... I was so lonely...."

"But you're not now!" Angel appeared, right in his line of vision, and Tucker startled.

"How are you staying in the circle?" he asked muzzily and then focused. "You're floating."

"Yes, Tucker, I do that." The words were Angel's usual tone, but irritation glared from those bright green

eyes. "Tucker, focus. Please. Please! You'll never forgive yourself if you fail."

Tucker nodded, swallowing the bile and the failure. Angel's hands on him, his innocence, his willing-
ness to learn, his tenderness with the kitten, his gentleness with Tucker—all of it washing over Tucker in a
wave of lavender and citrus, and he suddenly wanted
nothing more than to cuddle in that warmth, in that
smell and—oh God.

Tucker could lose Angel in this. They were making a giant pagan symbol, and Angel wasn't great with
those. It had burned Tucker at first too.

"Yeah. Yeah. Careful, Angel. You'll get burned."

"*Augh*!" Angel's scream was enough to snap
Tucker out of his haze completely. "Tucker, focus on
yourself!"

"Angel, I can't see—where's Josh?"

"He's about a hundred yards away," Rae said
calmly, securing the anchor wire and tugging another
length for the final leg. She pulled out her snippers and
clipped. "There's another man there, yelling at him to
get up and then pushing at him to stay down."

"Oh thank God. That's James Beaufort. He should
be on our side."

"That's reassuring, because the rest of these fuckers want to *eat* us. Tucker, what makes you think Josh
can get to the center of this figure? Your ghost friends
seem to think it's off-limits."

"Conklin has a body," Tucker told her grimly. "He
can go anywhere. If he hadn't been trapped inside the
boundaries of the house and yard for a hundred years,
he would have realized he could have been halfway to
Auburn as soon as Josh touched the paperweight."

"So why's he going to try to get you, again?"

"'Cause he hates me," Tucker said. "He may not look like it *now*, but I *did* beat the shit out of him that night he broke my nose." He tracked Josh's painful progress toward the gate, grateful for the time Beaufort's ghost was buying them and knowing it was going to get harder to see him as he got closer to the phosphorescent crowd grouping along the pentagrams. "I exorcised Sophie and Bridget. He didn't have anyone left to bully." Damien screamed his name particularly loudly, and his attention wandered.

"You can't have him," Angel screamed. "He's mine!"

Damien and the ghosts grouped around him laughed openly. Tucker recognized them, recognized them all, the people he'd failed. The people who had died because Tucker hadn't gotten there in time. Tucker had dragged them here. In his unconscious self-loathing, he'd brought them here, and now they were going to try to make sure a good man died.

"Tucker!" Angel's hard slap at his cheek didn't have full impact—but it had *some*. Tucker swallowed and tried hard to focus.

"Angel?"

"Tucker, you're mine. They can't have you. You tell them that."

"I'm yours," he told Angel, a modicum of peace seeping into him. He still felt his injuries, felt his pain, but for a breath, a heartbeat, he had the strength to put things in their box, deal with the important things first.

"Tell them," Angel said, and he was just solid enough for Tucker to feel his hands on Tucker's shoulders and the little shake he was giving. A hug would have been sweeter, but the shaking was real.

Angel was real.

"I'll tell them," Tucker promised, swallowing hard. "Rae, where's Josh?"

"Getting closer. Are you with me?"

"Mostly," he said, forced to honesty. She gave another tug on the wire, and the last spool completely unwound. "Are we going to have enough?"

She ran the wire toward the final spike and grimaced. "We're about a foot short. Oh, gross!"

Tucker had been soaking up the blood from his head pretty steadily, and he pulled the bandages out of his pocket. "It's a head wound," he mumbled. "It won't stop bleeding." He handed her two bandages, and she tied them together and then secured them to the end of the wire. She stretched the line again, making sure not to touch the ends, and then nodded.

"We're good."

He shoved the rest of the bandages into her hand. "Okay—you know the plan?"

"Get him in the middle, close the circuit, push Josh out."

"And hopefully keep Conklin in," Tucker affirmed, some of his purpose creeping back. "After that, we wrap Conklin in the wire and...." This part was iffiest. "Shove him back in the hole?"

Thank God Rae looked like that made sense. "Bind him in silver and blood—I get the concept, Tucker, but why can't you exorcise him?"

Tucker scrubbed his face with his bloody hand. "I'll try," he said. "Angel said we tell their stories. There's usually a core of their soul that remembers who they are. This guy—the drugs, the entitlement—I'm not sure if there was anything inside him that remembers enough to be exorcised."

Rae frowned. "Monsters are usually made. Most serial rapists don't shoot out of the womb all excited about fucking up people's lives."

"Have you seen the state of politics?" Tucker asked her, completely serious, but not as serious as the daggers she glared back at him.

"Well, something probably happened to those douchebags too! I'm saying find out what his damage is. Find out what made him. You'll have him trapped. At the very least, knowing that should make him vulnerable, maybe weak enough to shove in that damned hole!"

Tucker nodded, getting it. "Okay, okay, are we ready?"

Stupid question. They had their pentacle—the legs not traced in wire traced in the unbreakable imaginations of children—blocking the gate from the property. Whether Josh or Conklin was at the helm, if he was going to try to get off of the iron and silver of Daisy Place, he was going to have to go through their trap.

The ghosts couldn't get through it, but Josh could. If they could close the last leg of a pentacle and lock the ghost inside, then push Josh's physical body out....

Hopefully, they'd have a very confused Josh and the thing that had taken him over in two separate spaces.

"It will never work, Tucker. It's like every goddamned plan you've ever had! Do you think you can protect him? Do you think you can protect any of them!"

"You were never mean!" Tucker cried, distracted, in pain. "Don't be mean, Damien. Not now!"

Angel shook him again, each shake getting harder and closer to being mauled by a real man, powerfully built and frantic as hell.

"He's coming," Angel said, his voice choked. "C'mon, Tucker, I know you're… oh God." His hands tightened on Tucker's biceps. "You're weak. You're so weak. But you need to hold on. You will never forgive yourself if you get lost now. Stay with us. When you fade out like that, Rae is in this all by herself!"

Tucker looked at Rae, then closed his eyes against everything but the imperatives.

"Get on the other side," he said. "The dry side. Nobody can get you from there."

Rae nodded and strode through the pentagram field with no qualms while Tucker positioned himself in the center of the pentagram. Both of them ignored the bedlam of clamoring souls on the graveyard side and concentrated on the shambling figure of Josh, who had finally opened the gate with stiff fingers and was hovering, right before the shine of the silver wires.

His face contorting with the effort, Josh opened his mouth to speak. Conklin's voice came out.

"Do you think I'm a child?" he sneered.

"Don't you want me?" Tucker asked, stabbed by real panic. This whole thing depended on Conklin wanting Tucker so badly, he'd disregard common sense—just like he had when he'd attacked Sophie. "I exorcised them, you know. That was me. Doesn't that piss you off?"

"We'll see you *rot*!" Conklin spat. "But I'm not stupid enough to walk into your trap. What are you? A servant? A worker? A *scholar*?" The last word seemed to hold a particular distaste for him. "Do you think I'll risk myself for *you*?"

With a quick, no-nonsense step, Rae was in the trap next to him. Taking off her shirt and unhooking her bra so she could pull it up to her chin.

"Look, Conklin—tits!" She shimmied shamelessly. "See them? Don't they piss you off? I'm a woman, and I have an opinion, and I think you're dogshit, and I've got *tits*!"

Josh took two steps forward, eyes fixated on Rae's chest. Suddenly he shook himself, the concerned husband shouting, "Woman, put those away. They're mine!"

"Then come get them," she shouted. "C'mon, Josh—you, Conklin—first one here gets the first grab!"

The struggle again, and this time it was Conklin. "Insolent woman! I will rip them off of your body."

"Yeah, sure. You're all talk. I bet when you're not riding my husband, you're a limp-dicked disaster who can't get it up!"

Josh/Conklin took another step. "I'll fuck you until you bleed," he snarled.

"Bet your balls are the size of marbles," she snarled back. "And look, asshole, I've got a *tattoo*!"

She turned her back to him and shoved her jeans halfway down, revealing a cheerful constellation of protective tattoos in rainbow colors, all clustered on her right hind cheek.

Tucker snapped out of his wooziness enough to laugh. "Jesus, Rae—covering all bases?"

"Josh always said I needed every god in the book to watch my ass." Her eyes glittered with grim amusement, and Tucker thought it must be a bitch to admit your husband was right when your life depended on it.

"Well, he's a smart man." Very slowly, careful to pick up his feet, Tucker edged sideways, toward the open leg of the trap.

"He is. And he's strong, so if Conklin decides to go for it, he's going to be very—"

"Confused." Tucker knew this thing she was doing was dangerous as hell. Baiting Conklin with her insolent womanhood—that was one thing. But her husband would be driven by protection and desire. Both drives involved body-to-body action. Rae was a strong woman, but she wasn't an athlete. "I hope you know what you're doing."

"I hope you can tackle like a defensive end." She turned her attention back to their target. "Conklin, I think men are stupid, useless fuckers. I think aristocrats should be exterminated and shot. I think your raping, whoring ass should have been reamed with the red-hot mast of a giant sailing ship and your dick cut into tiny pieces and fed to the chickens. How much do you hate me, asshole? You're gonna let some silver wire on the ground stop you? You gonna let me win?"

"Rae," Josh begged, voice clogged with tears. "I can't hold him back any longer."

"Don't hold him back, sweetheart. Just make sure he picks up his goddamned feet!"

Josh may not have understood the supernatural, but he damned sure understood his wife. He nodded at her for a moment, and then he was gone, Conklin's snarl of rage contorting his face as he high-stepped over the wire, leaving the trap intact while he rushed to the center to attack his wife.

It was a near thing.

Tucker reached for the final rag that bound the trap and waited, his heart in his mouth, until Josh's booted foot hit the center of the pentagram. Then he bound up the rag, screaming, "Conklin, you asshat, you're mine now!"

He felt it.

The charge of the completed trap, buzzing the lines etched in silver. But it wasn't enough—not for a ghost strong enough to attack a human, strong enough to possess someone as psychically blind as Josh Greenaway.

Tucker ran through the next part of the trap and grabbed the connecting wire while Rae, her shirt in her hands, her body pale and vulnerable to the predator she'd enraged, backed slowly away from the thing in her husband.

"Tucker?" she asked, and she sounded strong and not afraid, but he knew that cost her.

"Can you keep him busy? Conklin, you pusbag, you're trapped," he screamed, connecting the second wire.

A stronger pulse this time, running through the figures in the dirt.

Conklin lunged for her, and she danced just out of his reaching hands.

"Doing my best here!" she panted. It was a small space—she was dancing right outside of the inner pentagon, as reluctant as Tucker to test the boundaries.

"You fucking *whore*!" Conklin sneered. "You *dare* bait me like I was a common laborer?"

He lunged again, grabbed Rae by the upper arms and shook her.

Rae kneed him in the balls and jumped out of the pentagon again. "Sorry, honey!" she called.

"'Sokay," Josh panted, hands on his knees as he recovered. He'd apparently been given lease on his own pain, if nothing else. "Good one, babe."

Tucker pushed up from his crouch and ran around the back of the figure, bending down to bind the final part of the trap while Conklin was recovering. "Conklin, may your soul grow roots and stay there!" Tucker snarled, and the howl that came from Josh's mouth told him he'd succeeded in doing *something*.

"Rae, stay out of there," he called. "Run get the other circle!"

She did, sprinting around behind the property line as he had, and as Conklin stood again, turning in a frenzy, they both reached for their final blood-coated wire.

"What do I say!" Rae shouted.

"Something just!" Tucker shouted back.

"I hope you feel every assault you ever perpetrated in the pit of your soul!" Rae screamed, her desperation, her fear, screeching through the howl of the dispossessed spirits around them.

Tucker was distracted for a moment, hearing the familiar note of Damien Columbus over them all.

"Tucker!" Angel screamed on the outside of the figure. "Tucker, finish it!"

Tucker closed his eyes. "And when you've suffered for your sins, I hope you find peace!"

He closed the link then, and the energy of Daisy Place, of the old figures of safety and entrapment, of the combined psychic gifts of Tucker and the entire Greenaway family, bolted through the silver tracings on the ground. Conklin felt it, too late, and tried to charge out of the center of his pentacle, only to fall back screaming, cradling his hand, trapped.

"Tucker!" Rae wept. "Tucker, he can't get out!"

"That's not just Josh!" Tucker called back. "That's both of them. We need Josh to concentrate. Move to the inside. You're protected." He stood, dizzy, and stumbled to the outside of the figures, now glowing in blue-white light on the ground. Then he removed his necklace and clenched it tight in his hand. He was going to have such a short window to do this. God, Goddess, whoever was listening, let him do this right.

"Now talk to him," Tucker called when they stood, three in a row, separated by silver, blood, and curses. "Make him remember who he is."

"Josh! Joshua Cambridge Greenaway. You listen to me," Rae screamed. "You know who you are. You know who I am. I need you back, you big stupid moo, do you hear me?"

"He's whimpering like a fool," Conklin replied. "Why would he listen to a whore?"

"Who's the fool?"

The voice was new, and Tucker looked in surprise. "James?"

James Beaufort stood, close enough to the trap for his face to be illumined in silver. "Who's the fool, Conklin? You were killed by a railroad man and buried in an unmarked grave. Nobody came looking for you—do you know that? We waited. We were terrified. Someone should have come looking for you. But your wife was glad to be rid of you. Your son was off getting the pox, which killed him. Nobody came looking. Nobody cared. Your son's wife lived a happy, long lifetime with her lover, with nephews and grandnieces and grandnephews. They were surrounded by children their entire lives, some of whom are alive today and bear their names. Who was the fool, Conklin? Who lived the good life? Who had the power to leave this world and wasn't forced to live and relive their final moment of bloodshed? You were bested by women the minute you raised your hand to them, Conklin, and you've lived in torment ever since!"

Conklin snarled and lunged for James while Josh reached out his hands for his own wife.

Tucker saw the split between them, saw Josh's flesh and blood go one way and Conklin's poisoned spirit go the other.

He lowered his head, squared his shoulders, and charged Josh Greenaway like a football player and a freight train in one. Conklin's agonized scream rent the air as the power of the silver trap peeled his essence from Josh's body like squashing potatoes through a masher to get rid of the skins.

Josh was the skin.

He and Tucker fell to the earth next to Rae with a thud. While Rae ran her hands over her husband's flesh to see if he'd been burned or wounded—besides what she'd inflicted herself—Tucker fumbled with the pendant in his hand and looped it over Josh's neck. And then, oh God, still dizzy, woozy as hell, he stumbled to his feet.

They weren't done.

"Rae, get him out of here. Take the truck—get him home."

Rae scrambled up, offering her husband a hand. Josh looked at her with a pained expression on his already confused face. "Honey, you're naked."

She stared blankly back. "You were just possessed by a serial rapist, and you're worried about my tits?"

"But you're naked," he said, his lower lip wobbling, and for a moment, Tucker felt a smile at the corner of his mouth.

"He's not worried about your modesty, Rae," Tucker said, feeling wise. "He's worried that you're vulnerable. Fasten your bra and put the shirt back on. It'll make him feel like he protected you."

Rae's laugh was mostly tears, and she wiped her face with her palm before wrestling into her bra and shirt. "Better?" she asked her husband. "Now come on. We're still not safe."

She offered her hand again, and he took it and rose, touched her face with trembling fingers. "I'm so sorry, honey. He was… he was in my head, and it was so ugly."

Her smile through her tears was a thing of beauty. "Josh Greenaway, your heart has never been anything but pure. Today's going to fade away, but your love? I will never doubt that. Do you hear me?" Her bra was still unfastened, poufing up the front of her shirt, ignored, and Tucker felt a surge of love and admiration for the two of them that almost brought him to his knees.

Josh nodded, still destroyed, his face showing the marks of the terrible struggle that had occupied his body for so long, even in the long shadows of the setting sun.

"Oh holy fuck," Tucker muttered. "It's almost sunset. You guys, get the fuck out of here."

Rae grabbed Josh's hand and pulled him around the still-glowing silver-blue of the trap. They got to the other side, and Rae stopped. "Tucker, what are you going to do?"

Tucker smiled grimly, his vision going gray for the umpteenth time. He wondered if he was bleeding into his brain, if his ribs were bruised, if the agony in his wrist would somehow cause cardiac arrest.

"I'm going to tell his story," Tucker said. "Angel? Angel, where—"

"Please don't," Angel said, and Tucker looked up. Angel was hovering above Conklin, glaring at him, keeping him pinned in place like a hawk would keep a rabbit, with his gaze alone.

"Don't what?"

"Don't do what you're thinking of." Angel looked away from Conklin, and Tucker saw something so broken inside Angel, so frightened, that he was surprised Angel could still hover there like a ghost. He had to be human, didn't he? Ghosts weren't that afraid for another soul, were they?

Except James Beaufort had been. He'd been worried about his sister.

And Conklin—that level of hatred often sprang from fear.

"Angel?" Tucker said, voice trembling. "You'll call me back, right?"

Angel shook his head and shrugged. "They're all broken—the rules. The ones I used to keep you safe last time. I don't know how to fix them, Tucker. What if I can't?"

Tucker looked into the trap, saw Conklin's ghost pacing like a tortured animal. "Then kill me and wrap me in the wire," he said, thinking at least the pain would be gone. "Conklin's spirit can rot with mine, and the world will never know him again."

"Tucker, *no!*" Angel screamed, and Tucker took three careful steps into the pentagram.

MONSTERS

Angel watched Tucker step inside the pentagram and right into Thomas Conklin's soul.

And then his terror for Tucker, his fear for his injuries, his aching dread for Tucker's battered soul, faded, and in its place was the same thing that had sustained him through all of those years with Ruth.

The story of the dead.

He saw, from his position above, Conklin remember being a child, riding a horse, excited because of the freedom, the power of the great animal, the joy of a successful lesson.

He wielded the whip with precision but not cruelty. This child was entitled but controlled. He was wealthy but not sadistic.

Not yet.

"Did you see, Meeks? Did you see me ride?"

The handsome young groom who took the horse as he approached the stable did not look excited. He nodded and grunted, pushing his blond hair from his blue eyes while saying the appropriate words: "Ya rode well today, young master." But he eyed the child with loathing that twisted his pretty pale features into something awful. Thomas didn't see.

"Thank you, Meeks. Would you like my help with the horse today?" The words sounded schooled, as though the boy was not naturally polite but was trying very hard.

"Naw. Is not fer yer grace to be getting filthy in the stables, is it?"

Young Thomas's face fell. He had no idea what he could have done to irritate this man, but the man was an employee with a grudge. "I would like to help," he said, smiling prettily. He was young, just out of puberty but not yet considered a man, and the look Meeks gave him was... unpleasant.

The unpleasant, covetous look of the groom was the only warning Angel and Tucker got before the memory changed.

Young Thomas was on his hands and knees in the straw and fetid horseshit, and the thing happening to him—the pain being driven through his rectum—was excruciating.

Tucker screamed, his body feeling every tear of flesh, and Angel dropped from his hover, landing in the center of the pentagram to hold Tucker through the pain.

And then they were both lost in Conklin's consciousness, their bodies living through agony, their souls being twisted like the pendant that now hung on Josh Greenaway's neck, heated in the crucible of pain and betrayal and reforged into a different shape.

When the rape was over, Conklin collapsed to the dirty straw, weeping, blood running from his mouth, from his nose, from his backside. He sobbed into the horseshit, confused as to how his belief in human goodness had gone so terribly wrong.

"Get up," Meeks snarled. "Pull up yer pants. Ye think yer precious dad'll care what I just did? It's no more than what he did ter me. Who's the woman now? Who's the mewling whore? Now get out of my stable. Next time just let me brush the fuckin' horse!"

The boy pulled himself up, sniveling. "I don't need to tell my dad what you did to me," he said, the sneer that would line his face permanently beginning in that moment. "I can fire servants same as he can."

"Do it and I'll tell all yer friends ye put out like any whore," Meeks said with a cruel laugh.

For a moment, Thomas's heart shriveled, but then his eyes narrowed. "You could tell them," Conklin said, bending down and picking a hoof pick up out of the straw. "But no one will listen to a one-eyed fucker like you!"

He turned and swung the hoof pick, and while he hadn't been strong enough to fight Meeks off when they'd been wrestling in the straw, he was more than strong enough to drive the thing through Meeks's eye.

Later, when he was describing the incident to his father, he said the groom had gotten impertinent, and they'd scuffled. That he'd defended himself, as was only proper.

His father had looked coldly at Meeks, cowering and holding a towel to the tatters of his eye, and then pulled out a gun and shot him in the head.

Conklin gasped, staring at the twitching corpse of his adversary, and his father put his hand on his son's shoulder.

"Nobody touches us, son. Nobody."

But that wasn't true, was it? Because his father touched him that night.

And again, and again, until Conklin found the first rich woman he could marry and moved far from home.

And had a son.

Angel came back to himself with a thump and squeezed Tucker's hands in panic, the rough towels wrapped around Tucker's wrist and fingers rasping under his palms.

Tucker looked back, brown eyes troubled—but sane.

"I'm sorry," he said, as though speaking to himself. "That was a terrible thing to have happen. That was a terrible way to grow up."

"Nobody feels pity for me!" The words were coming from Tucker's mouth, but the voice was Conklin's. "I take what I need, and I don't need your pity!"

"Oh, but you do," Tucker said softly. He looked at Angel and squeezed his hands back. Then he let go and nodded up with his chin.

Angel shook his head.

Tucker nodded again. "Go," he whispered. Angel lifted up, hovering, about a foot, and Tucker rolled his eyes and backed up just a little. "Thomas Conklin Senior, I can lay you to rest. I can put a name on your coffin and let you find peace."

"You will do what I tell you to do—"

Angel sank to the ground again and seized Tucker's hand.

And saw the struggle inside. It was like watching the men, all but naked, in a wrestling match. But Tucker had Conklin—the grown, fiftyish man in his prime—pinned.

"I will *not*!" Tucker gritted. "You can concede and let me lay you to rest or—"

"Or what?" Conklin sneered.

Tucker's grin was feral, triumphant, the snarl of the warrior who had won the pitched battle.

"You're getting weaker, Thomas. Can you feel it? I can feel it. While we've been toodling down memory lane, your strength has been sucked into the earth of Daisy Place. You're feeding the foundation right now, soldering the gold and the silver and the iron into an unbreakable, alloyed mass. This part of the yard won't be a sponge for souls anymore, you understand? It will be a watershed, where they can escape and fade into dust if they're peaceful. Only the angry souls need stay. Do you feel it? The freedom here? But not for you."

Conklin almost broke free. He thrashed, his elbow catching Tucker in the jaw and then in the eye. Tucker's nose broke—again—with a crunch, and Angel cringed, knowing that if he were to see Tucker from the outside, he'd see the injuries appear as though from nowhere, the blood and the bruising covering him, while Tucker could barely stand.

But that was his body.

His spirit was strong here, and he kept holding, kept his arms locked, until Conklin's struggles weakened.

"What's it going to be?" Tucker asked, his voice muffled by the blood but still sound.

"My hatred will never die," Conklin rasped.

Tucker stood, dropping Conklin's body on the mat.

"Then the heat from your anger will forge this place more tightly together," he said sadly. "You could have had peace. Warmth and sleeping in the sun. You'll have the coldness of iron, the cruelty of silver, the absolute mercilessness of gold. Just remember—it was your choice this time. What happened in the stable, that was wrong, that was against your will. What happened later, with your father—that was worse. But this? You chose this. You chose to inflict that on Sophie. You chose your afterlife."

Tucker met Angel's eyes with his own and winked.

"What you can't change, you need to live with, Conklin. Or die with, if it's your time."

Angel stepped back then and hovered, looking around him at the darkening sky. Rae and Josh were still there, staring anxiously at Tucker, and Angel was so grateful for other humans he could have cried.

"Tucker," he called. "Tucker!"

Tucker's body broke free from the circle, leaving Conklin's fading soul in the center, lying on the ground. The broken boy had become a powerful man, but that power had been a lie. What was left was a shell, the twisting headless snake, the defeated wrestler who couldn't get up.

If Conklin's soul were to bother anybody ever again, it would be as a particularly lowly toxic worm, one that could be crushed underneath a sneaker or driven over by a car—or salted like a slug by a child's laughter.

James Beaufort had been right. Conklin had lost to his abusers the moment he became one, and now he'd lost to his own malice, his pitiful spirit writhing in the dust.

Angel didn't care about him anymore.

Tucker had been facing the dirt road when he stepped into the pentacle, and when he'd stumbled, he'd stumbled backward.

Straight into the crowd of waiting ghosts.

Even Angel recognized Damien, his face pulled back in a rictus of triumph as Tucker delivered himself to his worst nightmare.

"Oh no. No! Tucker!"

Tucker looked at Damien, and the self-possession he'd shown in the face of Conklin's evil disintegrated. His mouth twisted and trembled, and the strength that had held him up through it all crumbled.

"Damie," he cried and sank helplessly to his knees.

The Unsullied
Souls of Men

"DAMIE!"

Oh, everything hurt. Tucker's body was one big throbbing mortal pain. His nose was going to explode through his brain. But he'd do it all again, throw himself in a car and charge a brick wall, if he could escape the fury on Damien's face.

"I'm sorry," he sobbed, at a loss. Rae and Josh were fine. Conklin was vanquished. There was only Tucker and his ghosts, and Tucker had been alone for so long.

"Ouch!" There was something burning in his pocket. He recoiled from the fury of the ghosts surrounding him, closer and closer, and reached into his pocket to see what it was.

James Beaufort's button was cool to his fingers, but he swore he'd have the print of that damned sailing ship tattooed forever on his thigh.

"Dammit," he muttered. "I promised."

"Who'd you promise?"

Tucker looked up, into the ghostly twisted face of the man he'd loved since boyhood.

And Damien Columbus looked back curiously.

Gone were the tatters of flesh remaining after the bullet destroyed his head.

Gone was the recrimination of the vengeful spirits.

In their place was just… Damien.

Happy-go-lucky Damien, whose life had always seemed charmed, and whose smile had gotten Tucker through his worst days.

"I promised someone I'd help him find his way home," Tucker muttered, wiping his bandaged wrist under his eyes, carefully avoiding his nose.

"Well, if you promised them, you need to follow through," Damien said seriously. "I mean, I used to get mad at you, right?"

"You did?" Tucker asked, lost and drifting.

"Yeah. You'd never promise you could meet me, never promise we could do something. You didn't want to disappoint me if you couldn't make it."

"I wanted to make it, so bad," he whispered.

Damien fell to his knees on the dirt in front of Tucker. "I know that now," he said.

"Then why are you, and the others, so angry?" He let out a sigh and slumped into the earth a little more. "You've been scaring the hell out of me, Damie."

Damien's hand went to brush Tucker's hair back from his brow, but Tucker didn't feel it. Didn't even feel the passage of it. It was like Angel's touch had taken the place of the touches he'd longed for from Damien.

"I don't know," Damien said softly. His mouth quirked up a little, and Tucker wished he could move. He'd love to trace that lush mouth. Just once. To say goodbye. "I know I was pissed about being dead," he pondered. "But not at you. Not until we saw you, and it was… it was like those movies about lynch mobs, where you forget who you are and only think about the hate. You were alive, and we hated."

"I don't want you to hate me," Tucker begged, too weak for pride. "I loved you for so long."

Damien's gaze contained the infinite compassion of a thousand angels. "I know, Tucker. I loved you too. I was so afraid. You couldn't promise anything. And then I just loved you so much I had to tell you. I thought we could work it out, promises or not. But I was selfish. You'd told me, and I ignored you—"

"It wasn't your fault." Tucker's throat ached so much he almost didn't get the words out. "It wasn't…. I should have…."

"It wasn't yours either."

Damien framed Tucker's face in both hands, though Tucker couldn't feel it. Would never feel it again. Only Angel's hands—those he could feel. "You need to believe me," Damien said softly. He looked behind him, and as though from mist, the other ghosts—the familiar ones of those Tucker had missed—materialized, as human as they'd been the day their lives had ended.

"I'm sorry," Tucker told them. "I tried—"

"I was depressed for a really long time," said a pretty, pale girl, the razor stripes at her wrists still bleeding. "Yeah, maybe you could have helped, but maybe you couldn't have. Maybe I was just in too much pain. You tried—that means something. A complete stranger tried."

"I got on that train every day," said a middle-aged man in a suit. "I went to a job I hated. I could have turned my life around without you. It's not your fault I slipped on the tracks that day and hit my head."

Tucker couldn't argue; he couldn't even stand. He could only sit there and listen, mute and weeping, as the people he'd hated himself for, one by one, came forward and told him that it wasn't his fault.

He'd wanted to help.

He'd tried.

He was only one man.

He could hardly breathe for the tears by the time they were through.

"See?" Damien told him. "Forgive yourself, Tucker. We forgive you."

"Will you be at peace?" Tucker asked. "Can you leave now that we've fused the foundation?"

They looked at each other, frowning like sleepers from a collective dream.

"Yes," Damien said slowly, a man testing the boundaries of his world with his mind. "But... but we're tied to you. We're conscious because you know us." Damien shook his head. "Tucker, we're in a bubble here. Can you feel it? As soon as we're gone, as soon as we find freedom and peace, the rest of the spirits here are going to converge on you. We can't protect you, and we can't hold this forever."

Tucker remembered Angel, afraid of letting go. He must be panicking. He'd broken so many rules of heaven already. Maybe Tucker could break one or two of his own.

"Just long enough for a kiss," Tucker begged. "That's all I wanted that day. All we never got."

"We would have been glorious," Damien whispered. Close, so close. Tucker couldn't smell him, couldn't feel his breath.

"I would have loved you until time ended," Tucker told him.

"Maybe we'll have each other then."

Tucker closed his eyes and felt it, the whisper of their lips together, their first last kiss goodbye.

He opened his eyes, and Damien was backing away. "Get up, Tucker. We can hold them off for a little while, but you need to make a break for it. Please, baby, live to fight another day, okay?"

Tucker planted his good hand on the ground and pushed up. The brightness of the bubble they'd inhabited was growing dim, dark as the night beyond, and he turned grimly toward the dirt road. The trap was fading, Conklin's spirit on its last dregs, but Tucker wouldn't risk breaking that, not when it was so close to done. Instead he turned toward the end of the trap, ready to run away from the graveyard and hopefully make it to the property line.

"Tucker!"

Tucker turned as the spirits lost their coherence, drifted backward, drifted away.

"Damie!"

"Love you, man!"

"You too!"

And then, all together, they turned toward the still-hostile gathering beyond and created a wall.

Tucker ran for freedom—ran for Angel, for his safety, for his acceptance, for his exasperation and kindness and his warmth and his worry—except he couldn't run.

He could barely see. The bubble disappeared, and his body threatened to fail, and he stumbled, pushing himself up, then looking behind him.

The press of angry souls was right there, close enough he could see features—old, young, male, female, 1910, 1940, 2001.... Tucker turned away and thought of Angel, thought of the chance he might have with Angel that he'd never had with Damien, and pushed his body one more aching step, and another, and another, and he could hear them, feel them, the iciness of their clammy spirits teasing along his skin.

"Angel!" he cried, thinking this couldn't be the end. Even Damien got one last kiss. "Angel! Where are—"

There was a dark fluttering sound and a great wind.

Angel's arms closed around Tucker's shoulders, and then they were safe, wrapped in the softest cocoon imaginable, and Tucker was sobbing in Angel's arms.

"Shh, Tucker. I'm sorry. I couldn't see you. I was there the whole time, but I just needed to see you."

And maybe he'd needed Tucker to see *him* too. "Angel, oh my God. It's been the worst fucking day."

Angel's laugh fractured, and Tucker could smell lavender and citrus, soaking through his hair. "I was so afraid for you," Angel whispered. "But you were stronger than all of it."

"I had to be." Tucker clung to him tightly, for once not asking questions. Outside their safe cocoon, a storm raged. Hundreds of angry souls were thundering around them. But in here, wherever here was, there were only the two of them, and they were touching.

"I had to be," Tucker said again, leaning his sore head against Angel's chest. "I wanted to see you again so damned bad."

Angel's featherlight kiss brushed his hair. "I wouldn't want to exist in any world without you in it, Tucker. You need to stay."

"Sure," Tucker said, so comfortable, so pain-free in the circle of Angel's arms. "I'll stay as long as I can."

He closed his eyes and saved the rest of his energy for clinging, and the storm weathered itself out.

He barely managed to open his eyes when he heard his name called from outside the cocoon.

"Tucker? Angel? Oh my God, *Angel*!"

Tucker looked into Angel's green eyes and smiled. "Sounds like Rae is okay," he said happily. The cocoon unwrapped from around the two of them, and Tucker turned from Angel's chest to see Josh and Rae, eyes enormous, walking over the blackened, twisted wire of the used-up trap.

"Tucker, are you okay?"

The pains all returned with a vengeance, and Tucker would have fallen to his knees, but Angel's arms were tight around his chest. Tucker looked up into his face and smiled, even as Angel reached underneath him and cradled Tucker's body against him like a child's.

Oh. He knew what that cocoon was now. Tentatively, he reached up past Angel's shoulder and stroked the feathers over the smooth muscle that must have always been a part of his Angel.

"Angel," he said in wonder. "Look at that. You have *wings*!"

"Oh Jesus," Josh said. "*That's* Angel. Now I see him, and he's not even a ghost."

Tucker lost his hold on consciousness and slid into darkness, as safe and as comforted as he'd been since he was a teenager, when his mother was cooking breakfast for him and his father was downstairs and his best friend in the world was coming over to see a baseball game.

PROMISES OF RECOVERY

NOBODY COULD tell him how he'd arrived at the hospital.

"I don't know," the night nurse said for the thousandth time. "One minute this room was empty, the next minute you were bleeding in it. We didn't see anything, don't know anything. Do you have any idea how you *received* all of those injuries, sir?"

They'd had to tell him he had a concussion three times.

He managed to remember the broken nose, broken wrist, cracked ribs, bruised trachea, and blood loss from the head wound that wouldn't quit.

"I have no idea," he said blandly. "One minute I was working in my house, the next minute I was here. It's a mystery."

The nurse—in her late fifties and not particularly sympathetic—rolled her eyes. "The mystery is why anyone would want to save you. Now we're pumping you full of sedatives, so would you go to sleep?"

Short answer: no.

He sat there in the darkness, letting the painkillers wash over him, grateful for them. But he couldn't sleep.

"Angel?" he whispered tentatively.

Angel was immediately there, sitting on his bed. Tucker tried to see his wings, but they flickered in and out of his peripheral vision. "Yes, Tucker. Are you okay?"

Tucker giggled to himself, very stoned. "Apparently I'm beat the hell up. But they say I'll live." He found the wings were clearest when he just looked at Angel's face and didn't try to see deeper. Perhaps when he forgot about the wings, they would materialize for real.

It was possible: Angel's hand on his was as real as anybody's hand he'd ever held. "I was very worried."

Tucker squeezed his hand. "Me too. Angel, you're going to stay with me, right?"

"Why wouldn't I? I was going to before."

"Because, Angel, you're not a ghost."

Angel's feigned innocence was priceless. "I'm not? Oh no! What on earth could I be?"

Tucker laughed anyway. "A pain in my ass!"

"Not yet, but maybe someday," Angel promised.

"Oh my God, you're making a dirty joke. I really am dead."

And then suddenly things were serious again. "Not dead, Tucker. You're here. I'm here. We're together." He paused, as though looking for more information. "That's important."

Tucker's eyes closed, and finally the medication kicked in. "It's the best thing in my life."

"I will not argue."

"Angel, could you lie behind me?" He was scared and tired and needy.

"I was afraid you'd never ask."

Angel's breath kept time with his own, and he fell peacefully asleep.

DAKOTA ARRIVED the next day, in her khakis with a little notebook in her pocket. She was surprised to see Tucker, looking like hell, in a hospital bed.

Angel disappeared at his back the minute she walked in. She squinted.

"Was there just a…?"

Tucker shook his head subtly, meeting her eyes. "If you can't see him, he wasn't there," he told her. He watched her eyes widen and knew somehow that she knew.

She put her notebook away and pulled up a chair. "Am I going to get a story from you?" she asked cautiously. "The nurses say you just woke up here."

Tucker shrugged. "That's mostly the truth."

"Would I get a better story if I called Josh and Rae?"

Oh hell. "I really hope you don't," he said honestly. "I mean… they're nice folks. They certainly didn't do this." Well, technically, Josh had—but technicalities were often the furthest thing from the truth.

Dakota sighed and stretched her feet out. "Does this have anything to do with that… that weird cloud over the graveyard clearing out? People have been seeing their dead grandparents *all day*. I had to answer six calls before this. They weren't doing anything—just smiling and waving as far as I can tell—but coming across dead grandparents isn't a usual thing in my job. I know. I asked."

"Were they happy to see their dead grandparents?" It was an important question. The release valve may have seemed like a good idea, but if someone's awful child-molesting grandfather was on the loose, Tucker might be back in the hospital again very soon.

Or the graveyard. Also a possibility.

"So far, yes. In fact we've had two newly discovered wills and one grandma who held her hand over her granddaughter's belly and said, 'Name her after me.' The girl still lived at home—gee, weren't her parents surprised."

Tucker laughed and then gasped. He couldn't laugh *that* much yet. It still hurt.

"So," Dakota asked gently. "That you?"

"I had no idea she was pregnant, and I swear I'm not the father." Tucker kept a straight face, but Dakota laughed.

"No. I think you're probably taken by the invisible man behind you."

And Tucker's composure broke. He laughed until the nurse popped her head in and threatened to sedate him, and Dakota stood to leave.

"I'll file you under dead grandmother," she said dryly. Then she sobered. "But Tucker?"

"Yeah?"

"Next time you're… having a dead grandmother moment, you can call me, okay? Whatever went down with you—and it looks bad—I would have believed you. I would have come."

Tucker swallowed. A friend. A true platonic friend. It was a gift. "Not many people would have," he said, blinking hard.

"Yeah, well, not many people scream 'I'm gonna change my career' during sex either. And you didn't even bat an eyelash. In fact you looked relieved. I get the feeling you've done that for a lot of people. Is your, uh, invisible guy going to be okay with that?"

Crap. "So far that gift seems to be laying low," Tucker said, hoping. "Maybe, uh, dead grandmothers are my calling now."

She got close enough to cup his cheek. "I'm not sure which one I'd wish for you more. Dead grandmothers seem awfully hard on the body, but I'm not sure how good that other thing was for you either."

Oh, if not for Angel, she would have been a lovely companion.

"I'll take the dead grannies," he said. "If nothing else, I seem to be getting a vacation out of it."

"Sure." She kissed his forehead and left.

Angel's heat seeped again into his back. "I might not like her," he said darkly.

"She knows I'm taken." Tucker closed his eyes, exhausted by the visit but glad she'd come.

"Does she still want you?"

"No."

"Then I like her very much."

"You are very jealous," Tucker mumbled. "I really hope my other talent *is* laying low. I don't see how that would work with you like this."

Angel grunted. "That's not a rule you can break." He took a deep, cleansing breath. "Dammit."

"No fucking people into epiphany right now. No fucking period. Just hold me, Angel. We'll start there."

Angel nuzzled the back of his neck, and he smiled.

A WEEK later, Josh Greenaway came and got him and brought him back to Daisy Place. While he'd been gone, the Greenaways had brought in an area rug and some bright drapes for his bedroom, as well as the club chair and the ottoman they'd talked about that day in Tucker's apartment. They'd also set up an actual television on a dresser at the foot of his bed and had even—at Angel's insistence, Rae said—replaced the mattress and pillow.

Tucker looked at Squishbeans, curled in the center of his pillow, and thought they may even have fed his cat.

Tucker ran his fingers over the worn leather of the club chair, touched. "Not to be ungrateful, Josh, but, uh, why?"

"For saving me," Josh said.

Tucker shook his head. "I'm the one who put you in danger."

Josh shrugged. "I'm the one who put me in danger. I live with four psychics—well, five if you count Tilda. Wait—four, because Andy's not living at home anymore. It doesn't matter. My wife's as witchy as they come, and I should have listened to her, and to you. I shouldn't have gone in unprotected. Anyway, it wasn't your fault, but you sure did go above and beyond to fix it." Josh gave him an awkward hug, which Tucker returned gingerly. He hadn't even felt the ribs break at the time, but boy, had he felt them for the last few days.

"You all have been really nice to me," Tucker said, embarrassed.

"Consider us your family, Tucker," Josh said. Then he pulled back and grinned. "Besides—you've already seen my wife's tits. If you weren't family, I'd have to kill you."

Tucker blushed and laughed. "I've seen her tattoo as well. I really must be family."

Josh grimaced and then made Tucker take his pain-killers and go to bed.

Angel appeared this time too.

It took some doing, but Tucker managed to shove and shimmy until he could step out of his sweats and wriggle out of his T-shirt. There were no guarantees he and Angel could touch on any given day, but he wanted access to as much skin as possible. When he was done, he lay carefully on his side, facing the inside of the bed, where Angel stretched out, staring at him with the intensity he'd shown during Tucker's stay in the hospital.

Here, in the familiar surroundings of their one safe room, it disturbed Tucker in ways that hurt.

"I'm not going to die just yet," he said with a smile.

Angel's brow—usually clear like a child's—knit sternly. "That's not funny."

"And if I did, we'd still probably see each other. I mean, it's a *haunted* house!"

"No." Angel's lower lip trembled. "We wouldn't. I don't talk to the ghosts here, Tucker. I can only see them with your help. Who's going to help me talk to *you*?"

Oh.

Tucker felt it then—the pull. Tight under his broken ribs, as real as it had always been. But it wasn't leading him to the road, to a stranger, to an epiphany he could never share.

It was leading him right here, to a realization he was a part of. To a place in his heart, a wisdom that *must* be shared or it would do neither of them any good.

"Nobody," he said, reaching out and smoothing his fingertips down the side of Angel's freckled face. Stubble. He felt stubble under the soft skin of his fingers. "One life. We get one life. And no guarantees."

He saw it then—the shudder through Angel's body that surprised him. A sob.

"That is of no comfort." He shuddered again.

"You want comfort?" Tucker flattened his palm and ran it down Angel's chest, which remained reassuringly hard under his hand. "I'll give you comfort. Souls find peace—together. Like Sophie and Bridget. That's comfort."

"But what if I don't—"

The pull intensified, and Tucker experienced a profound gratitude that, in this moment of his homecoming and Angel's bleeding, they could touch.

"Do you think you're the only one?" he said, risking a kiss. Angel's mouth opened under his, and he tasted human heat and human need. And the faintest bit of mint.

"The only one what?" Angel whispered.

"The only one who would break the rules of heaven?"

Angel shuddered again, and Tucker pulled at Angel's thigh until he lifted it and slung it over Tucker's hips. Angel's erection pushed against his abdomen, as real as Angel's chest under his palms. The denim of his faded jeans rasped the tender skin of Tucker's thighs.

"What rules?"

Tucker kissed down his neck and nibbled on his collarbone over the white T-shirt Angel habitually wore. "If I close my eyes, will you take off your clothes?"

"Why would you need to…? Oh."

Tucker smiled, eyes closed, as the T-shirt and jeans melted again and he had access to Angel's tiny nipples. Tucker lowered his head, and Angel arched his back, and ah… his skin had the faintest tang of salt and citrus.

Even Angel sweat in bed.

Tucker suckled his nipple, enjoying Angel's whimpers, the arching of his naked body against Tucker's, the smoothness of their bodies, skin to skin.

"Tucker," Angel gasped. He blatantly groped Tucker under his boxers, and Tucker knew what he would find.

"You're not even—"

"I'm drugged, Angel," Tucker breathed. "Painkillers. It'll take a while. Now move so I can lick your other side."

Angel whimpered and rolled so Tucker could torment his other nipple. Angel cried out softly and tightened his fingers in Tucker's hair. The tang of pain—the good kind, the urgent kind—helped Tucker's erection along, and in a moment, they were cock to cock, separated by Tucker's boxers.

"Keep moving," Tucker whispered. "While I can still taste you."

Angel didn't argue, scooting up the bed until his erection fell, long and fat, even with Tucker's mouth.

Straight, pale as marble, hard, uncut, and without veins—Tucker filed this hidden part of Angel away for the moments they slid through each other like water. He stroked it, memorizing the hardness, and licked the head, savoring the texture.

Angel's noises became urgent, and Tucker licked him again.

Moisture welled at the tip, clear, tinged faintly purple. Tucker licked and smiled. He should have known.

"Tucker," Angel pleaded. "Please. I don't understand... it's...."

"Hold on." Tucker licked him again, and Angel whimpered.

"Please."

Tucker took his straight, perfect member all the way down his throat, then pulled back, using skills honed in a thousand encounters to send human desire burning through angelic veins.

Angel's flailing hand glanced off Tucker's shoulder, and Tucker winced, then pulled back. "Hold on to the bedframe, sweetheart, and trust me."

"Tucker," Angel sighed, and Tucker took him all the way down again. And again. Slow and hard, not teasing, not this time.

Angel's hips caught on before Angel's brain, and he started arching and retreating, a slow fuck of Tucker's mouth that roared arousal through Tucker's veins like wildfire.

Tucker wanted. He'd thought he remembered the joy of wanting when Angel's hand had been stroking *him*, but this was harder, more painful, more necessary. Tucker *needed* to taste Angel's pleasure. Angel could disappear at any moment, and Tucker needed the taste of his come, proof in his body that he had a lover, one who knew him, one who would do anything to protect him from pain.

Angel cried out again, and Tucker swallowed, playing with smooth and hairless testicles with his outside hand, the one without the cast. His other hand was busy stroking Angel's stomach, his thighs, anything—desperate to feel the bare ripple of skin and muscles where thought and will used to hold sole domain.

"Tucker!"

A massive climax shook Angel's body, and even as Tucker swallowed the come of a more-than-human man down his throat, he felt hair tickle his hands, the coarse silky pubic strands that protected testicles and led a merry path from a man's navel.

Angel's first climax—and it had changed him, physically, forever.

Angel's orgasm swept him again, the tremble in his muscles becoming massive and spastic, and Tucker fought the pain in his wrist, his ribs, his head, to hold on, stay right there, take all Angel had to give.

At the last moment, he bucked away, sobbing, wanting more of Angel's seed down his throat but pulled back by his own orgasm, a shadow of Angel's but enough to make him jerk his sore body, enough to make him cry.

The front of his underwear grew hot and wet, then cold, as his spend cooled.

He listened in fierce satisfaction as Angel's panting breath rocked the bed.

Angel's gentle hands on his face soothed some of his pain, and he smiled, eyes closed.

"Proud of yourself?" Angel asked, but he sounded too satisfied to be smug.

"You taste like lavender and lime," Tucker said, laughing in the dark. "And a little like mint."

"That's not what humans usually taste like?"

Those hands kept up their tentative exploration of his face.

"No," Tucker murmured. Oh man. The cold of Daisy Place chilled his skin. He wanted this moment to last for—

Angel moved away to grab a blanket from the foot of the bed and pull it up around Tucker's shoulders.

"My shorts," Tucker mumbled, already falling asleep. "I should wash up."

"I'll be back."

And then Angel's hands, tender and personal, wielded a warm washcloth and helped him into a clean pair of boxers.

Tucker grunted thanks and curled more deeply under the covers.

Angel's hands on his cheeks were all the reassurance he could ask for.

"How do you feel?" Angel asked, finding Tucker's stubble as Tucker had found his.

"Sore," Tucker admitted. "That was awesome, but—"

"Too early," Angel whispered. "I'm sor—"

"Don't be." Tucker opened his eyes. Fine lines had appeared at the corners of Angel's mouth and green eyes. He was even more beautiful than Tucker remembered when he'd first closed his eyes and hoped Angel would stay.

"Don't be sorry?" The hope in his voice was hard to bear.

"No. Be grateful. It was glorious having you in my mouth, Angel. I got to make love to you. A thousand lovers or more, and I've never gotten to choose a single one. And I touched you and sucked your cock and loved you. I didn't know mortals were even allowed such beauty."

Angel's faint smile actually glowed. "Poetry." He pushed Tucker's tangled hair back from his brow. "My human lover speaks poetry."

"My angel lover comes in different flavors," Tucker said crudely, just to watch Angel's eyes open in surprise.

Tucker smiled, happy, as his eyes fluttered closed. Angel's flesh dematerialized sometime after he fell asleep, but even when Angel's breath stopped fanning his face and his hand on Tucker's cheek faded, Tucker knew he was still there.

TUCKER NEEDED him to be there—especially during the next week.

Angel kept the nightmares away.

And the nightmares were plentiful and painful.

Not even Angel could banish them completely. All he could do was be there when Tucker woke up, incoherent, in pain.

The kitten was good at curling up in front of him during these episodes, which was sweet but not enough.

They were one more souvenir of a life that was not going to stop throwing them curveballs just because one almost took Tucker out of the game.

After a week of being at home, Tucker and Angel sat on the porch in the early shadows of the late August evening under a canopy of invisible—and yet shady—wings. Squishbeans purred in Angel's lap until suddenly she hissed and stalked away. Tucker looked up and saw a familiar transparent form gazing at him soulfully from the lawn.

"Wait right there!" he told it and then hurried inside. "Angel! Angel! Where's my shorts from the day—"

Angel pulled them out of the drawer, laundered and repaired. He must have stitched them himself.

Tucker looked at him and smiled fondly. Whatever they were now, whatever they would become, being this sewn into each other's pockets made Tucker as happy as he'd ever been since childhood. He wanted it to last.

"Thank you, Angel," he said sincerely. Careful of his cast and the bandages still around his rib cage, he went rooting through the pockets of the shorts. "Yes!"

He grinned in triumph and then leaned forward to kiss Angel on the lips.

It was their first kiss—their first sexual moment, in fact—since Tucker fell asleep after making love. Tucker had been in a lot of pain the next day, and the next. The pain had been worth it, but Tucker had missed the physical contact. Even reaching for it, hoping for it, had become a memory.

Angel's mouth opened now, and he gave a groan of such loneliness, Tucker had to answer him. Their mouths fused, Angel's taste, lavender and citrus, permeating Tucker's senses, flooding his heart, his stomach, his groin.

Only the feel of the little metal object in the palm of his hand could pull him back. "Tonight," he said hopefully.

Angel frowned, obviously still upset that Tucker had been hurt the last time. "When you can breathe without bandages." He looked disapproving and stern, but Tucker didn't have time for this argument. Not now.

The last light of the sun had almost faded by the time Tucker got back to the front lawn.

"Here," he said, holding out his palm. "James? Your grandson wore this to your funeral."

James Beaufort came stepping forward, nothing but patience and kindness in his eyes.

"I remember," he said, smiling softly. "Little scamp did love his poppy, didn't he?"

"He did," Tucker said. "And so did Sophie and Bridget. I know it's been hard, living—or being dead, I guess—with what you did. But what you did made Sophie and Bridget possible. You were a good man. When you touch the button, I need you to see how your loved ones saw you. You've paid for your violence enough."

James Beaufort reached out and took the button from Tucker's palm.

As he faded from sight, he smiled brilliantly, at peace in the end as he'd always deserved to be.

Tucker sighed.

"What's wrong?" Angel said, draping an arm over his shoulder and steering him back inside. It was late

August, and the heat didn't always carry through until the evening now. Angel had been pulling out sweatshirts for Tucker these last mornings and bemoaning the fact that he had no scarves and gloves for the fall.

"We know where Conklin's grave is now." Right where Josh had crashed his truck. Conklin had been cogent enough to steer Josh there but hadn't realized what he was leaving behind as he'd gone searching for havoc to wreak and vengeance to take.

"Yes. Conklin could have had peace. You offered it to him enough, Tucker. It was more than generous. There was too much hatred in him to take it."

Tucker grimaced. "But we... we changed the topography. We made a release valve. We've already set free a whole cadre of dead grandmothers. What else do you think we'll let loose into the world?"

Angel shrugged. "I've been watching it, you know."

"Really?" It shouldn't have surprised him. He'd been sleeping a lot in the last week. Angel probably got bored.

"Yes. I've learned my lesson, Tucker. I can't afford to only look to the house—or to my person." He kissed Tucker's temple gently. "And you *are* my person."

Tucker smiled just a little. It had been so long since he'd been anybody's. He couldn't deny it felt good.

"So what did you see?"

Angel gave a thoughtful sigh. "So far, only the peaceful have taken the pathway you offered." Angel frowned. "In fact, I think the people who do are probably the ones who could find peace anyway. Perhaps that's why the graveyard became so backed up. Because this place was made to trap all the spirits, not just the ones in pain. So maybe…."

He looked away.

"What?"

Angel sighed. "Maybe the graveyard got so bad because the spirits Ruth and I were freeing couldn't find their way out. They could find their way out of the house, but not off the grounds. Maybe that's why *your* ghosts were added to the masses. They calmed down, became friendly, as soon as you gave them a way out. You may have saved us from a terrible, terrible explosion of psychic energy, Tucker. We shall have to see."

Tucker grabbed Angel's hand. "That's we, though, right?" After so many years of being alone, he now had a family who called him every morning, and a partner—a lover, possibly—who he saw and touched and even kissed every day.

He found he needed the companionship, as though he'd been dying of thirst and now his cells were struggling to replenish the water.

Except it wasn't water. It was love. And he needed it. It was love that watered his soul.

"Of course." Angel squeezed his hand and kissed his temple. "I told you, Tucker."

"I know." It was a serious vow, and Tucker would hold fast to Angel's hand, no matter what the consequences. "You'd break all the rules of heaven to stay with me."

"And so I have," Angel said soberly.

"And so shall I."

Together, they walked back into Daisy Place, as ready as they could be for what the house would throw at them next.

AMY LANE lives in a crumbling crapmansion with a couple of growing children, a passel of furbabies, and a bemused spouse. She's been a finalist in the RITAs™ twice, has won honorable mention for an Indiefab, and has a couple of Rainbow Awards to her name. She also has too damned much yarn, a penchant for action-adventure movies, and a need to know that somewhere in all the pain is a story of Wuv, Twu Wuv, which she continues to believe in to this day! She writes fantasy, urban fantasy, and gay romance—and if you accidentally make eye contact, she'll bore you to tears with why those three genres go together. She'll also tell you that sacrifices, large and small, are worth the urge to write.

Website: www.greenshill.com
Blog: www.writerslane.blogspot.com
Email: amylane@greenshill.com
Facebook: www.facebook.com/amy.lane.167
Twitter: @amymaclane

Vulnerable

The First Book of the Little Goddess series

AMY LANE

Little Goddess: Book One

Working graveyards in a gas station seems a small price for Cory to pay to get her degree and get the hell out of her tiny town. She's terrified of disappearing into the aimless masses of the lost and the young who haunt her neck of the woods. Until the night she actually stops looking at her books and looks up. What awaits her is a world she has only read about—one filled with fantastical creatures that she's sure she could never be.

And then Adrian walks in, bearing a wealth of pain, an agonizing secret, and a hundred and fifty years with a lover he's afraid she won't understand. In one breathless kiss, her entire understanding of her own worth and destiny is turned completely upside down. When her newfound world explodes into violence and Adrian's lover—and prince—walks into the picture, she's forced to explore feelings and abilities she's never dreamed of. The first thing she discovers is that love doesn't fit into nice neat little boxes. The second thing is that risking your life is nothing compared to facing who you really are—and who you'll kill to protect.

www.dsppublications.com

Wounded Volume One

The Second Book of the Little Goddess series

AMY LANE

Little Goddess: Book Two, Volume 1

Cory fled the foothills to deal with the pain of losing Adrian, and Green watched her go. Separately, they could easily grieve themselves to death, but when an old enemy of Green's brings them back together, they can no longer hide from their grief—or their love for each other.

But Cory's grieving has cut her off from the emotional stability that's the source of her power, and Green's worry for her has left them both weak. Cory's strength comes from love, and she finds that when she's in the presence of Adrian's best friend, Bracken, she feels stronger still.

But defeating their enemy is by no means a sure thing. As the attacks against Cory and her lovers keep coming, it becomes clear that their love might not be enough if they can't heal each other—and themselves—from the wounds that almost killed them all.

www.dsppublications.com

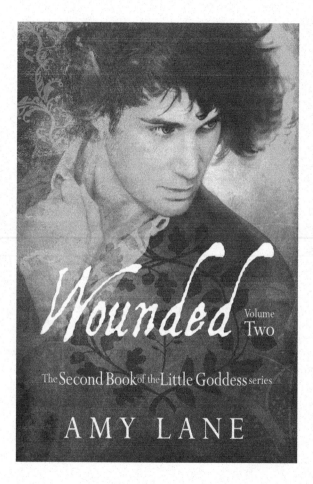

Wounded Volume Two

The Second Book of the Little Goddess series

AMY LANE

Little Goddess: Book Two, Volume 2

Green and Bracken's beloved survived their enemy's worst—with help from unexpected vampiric help.

But survival is a long way from recovery, and even further from safety. Green's people want badly to return to the Sierra Foothills, but they're not going with their tails between their legs. Before they go home, they have to make sure they're free from attack—and that they administer a healthy dose of revenge as well.

As Cory negotiates a fragile peace between her new and unexpected lovers, Green negotiates the unexpected power that comes from being a beloved leader of the paranormal population. Together, they might heal their own wounds and lead their people to an unprecedented place at the top of the supernatural food chain—a place that will allow them to return home a better, stronger whole.

www.dsppublications.com

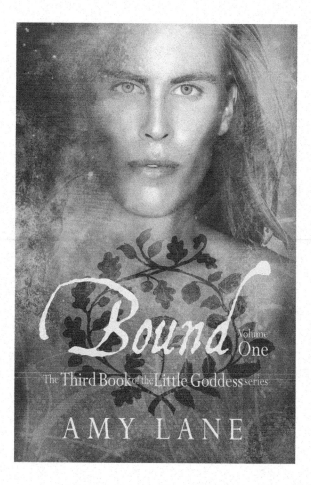

Bound Volume One

The Third Book of the Little Goddess series

AMY LANE

Little Goddess: Book Three, Volume 1

Humans have the option of separation, divorce, and heartbreak. For Corinne Carol-Anne Kirkpatrick, sorceress and queen of the vampires, the choices are limited to love or death. Now that she is back at Green's Hill and assuming her duties as leader, her life is, at best, complicated. Bracken and Nicky are competing for her affections, Green is away taking care of his people, and a new supernatural enemy is threatening the sanctity of all she has come to love. Throw in a family reunion gone bad, a supernatural psychiatrist, and a killer physics class, and Cory's life isn't just complex, it's psychotic.

Cory needs to get her act and her identity together, and soon, because the enemy she and her lovers are facing is a nightmare that doesn't just kill people, it unmakes them. If she doesn't figure out who she is and what her place is on Green's Hill, it's not just her life on the line. She knows from hard experience that the only thing worse than facing death is facing the death of someone she loves.

Loving people is easy—living with them is what takes the real work, and it's even harder if you're bound.

www.dsppublications.com

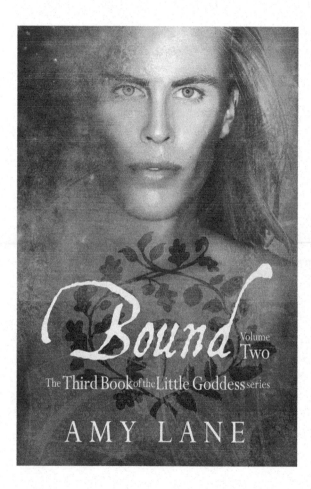

Bound Volume Two

The Third Book of the Little Goddess series

AMY LANE

Little Goddess: Book Three, Volume 2

Cory's newly bound family is starting to find its footing, which is a good thing because danger after danger threatens, and Green can't be there nearly as often as he's needed. As Cory learns to face the challenges of ruling the hill alone, she's also juggling a ménage relationship with three lovers—with mixed results.

But with each new challenge, one lesson becomes crystal clear: she can't be queen without each of the men who look to her, and the people she loves aren't safe unless she takes on that queendom with all of the intelligence and courage in her formidable heart.

But sometimes even intelligence, courage, and steadily increasing magic aren't enough to do the job, and suddenly the role of Cory's lovers becomes more crucial than ever. Nobody is strong enough to succeed in every task, and Cory finds that the most painful lesson she and her lovers can learn is not just how to deal with failure. Cory needs to learn that one woman is only so powerful, and she needs to choose wisely who sits outside her circle of family, and who is bound eternally in her heart.

www.dsppublications.com